The Island Retreat

Cathy Kelly is a bestselling Irish author known for her stories about real women's lives – the messy relationships, the love, the loss and everything in between. She has written twenty-two novels, selling millions of copies globally. In addition to her writing, she is a UNICEF ambassador and lives and writes from her home in Bray, County Wicklow, Ireland, surrounded by her family, two dogs and a cat.

Also by Cathy Kelly

Woman to Woman
She's the One
Never Too Late
Someone Like You
What She Wants
Just Between Us
Best of Friends
Always and Forever
Past Secrets
Lessons in Heartbreak
Once in a Lifetime
Homecoming
The House on Willow Street
The Honey Queen
It Started with Paris
Between Sisters
Secrets of a Happy Marriage
The Year That Changed Everything
The Family Gift
Other Women
The Wedding Party
Sisterhood

Cathy Kelly

The Island Retreat

HarperCollins*Publishers*

HarperCollins*Publishers* Ltd
1 London Bridge Street
London SE1 9GF

www.harpercollins.co.uk

HarperCollins*Publishers*
Macken House, 39/40 Mayor Street Upper
Dublin 1, D01 C9W8, Ireland

First published by HarperCollins*Publishers* 2026

1

Copyright © Cathy Kelly 2026

Cathy Kelly asserts the moral right to be identified as the author of this work

A catalogue record for this book is available from the British Library

ISBN: 978-0-00-854500-0 (HB)
ISBN: 978-0-00-854501-7 (TPB)
ISBN: 978-0-00-879828-4 (ANZ)

This novel is entirely a work of fiction. The names, characters and incidents portrayed in it are the work of the author's imagination. Any resemblance to actual persons, living or dead, events or localities is entirely coincidental.

Set in Sabon LT Pro by HarperCollins*Publishers* India

Printed and bound in the UK using 100%
Renewable Electricity at CPI Group (UK) Ltd

All rights reserved. No part of this publication may be reproduced, stored in a retrieval system, or transmitted, in any form or by any means, electronic, mechanical, photocopying, recording or otherwise, without the prior written permission of the publishers.

Without limiting the exclusive rights of any author, contributor or the publisher of this publication, any unauthorised use of this publication to train generative artificial intelligence (AI) technologies is expressly prohibited. HarperCollins also exercise their rights under Article 4(3) of the Digital Single Market Directive 2019/790 and expressly reserve this publication from the text and data mining exception.

For Lucy, Francis, Dave and Mum, with love.

Chapter One

Shading her eyes against the glorious Greek sunset, Rose Talisman stands beside the sapphire-coloured infinity pool at Villa Artemis and takes a moment to admire the beauty of the great honey-stoned house she's been renovating for four years with the people closest to her in the world, her sister, Adriana, and brother-in-law, Christos.

It's taken time, money and much cajoling of expert builders, but it's perfect now: Villa Artemis, hewn into the cliff face above the village of Xanthe and gazing down over the Ionian Sea.

Rose loves her new home in Corfu.

There are no late-night police sirens, no Los Angeles city smog, no randomers accosting her in the street saying 'OMG, *it's you! My family are all totally nuts – can you help?*'

Here, nobody knows who she is. She's not afternoon television's favourite therapy guru anymore, star of *The Talisman Effect*.

There are no more '*Do you want to know what the paternity test tells us?*' moments.

No more family mediations done at high speed with people who really needed four years of intensive therapy instead of one hour-long show trying to speedily knit together broken families.

Rose Talisman has left that crazy life behind.

The late September air is redolent with the scent of lavender and aromatic bay laurels. Rose, who once couldn't tell one plant from another, has added night-scented stock, nicotiana plants, rosemary and oleander to the terraced gardens.

Cicadas murmur rhythmically in the background and a soaring bird of prey rides the thermals, empress of all she surveys.

The beautiful island of Corfu has healed Rose and she never ceases to be grateful to it.

It's a land of myth and legend. *Nobody* can come here and be unchanged.

Corfu has set her free.

The woman who once moved only when her personal trainer put her through her paces on the Pilates reformer now loves walking the herb-filled hills, clambering over jagged limestone rocks and swimming in the sea.

Her overachieving brain calms down to the gentle rhythm of waves undulating against the white beach below.

She's about to test if the island, and the house, can do the same for other people.

Tomorrow she starts her first retreat on the island, a retreat that has promised to start the healing process for six people who are willing to try Rose Talisman's newest therapy venture.

She's promised a life-changing week where the six guests can begin to look inside themselves, often for the first time, and start the long, slow journey to healing themselves. It's a huge risk for her, Adriana and Christos. They all have so much to lose.

Stepping into the limelight again is risky. Despite her fame, Rose has managed to skilfully hide her past. Almost nobody knows the real Rose and she hopes it will stay that way.

The sun is nearly gone now, just the misty hint of dusk rising up with the darkened sky, hinting that the gods and goddesses so beloved of the ancient Greeks are ready to roam across the sky again.

Tomorrow is the first day of therapy.

The first day of turning Villa Artemis into a retreat for therapy and healing.

Mentally, Rose scans the list of her patients.

There were thousands of people who wanted to be first on the Villa Artemis retreat but Rose, Adriana and Christos had narrowed it down to the final six.

Tomorrow at half nine it all kicks off.

Rose can't wait.

Chapter Two

Dianne Wilkins growls under her breath at the woman in front of her on the airport travelator.

If only she could growl loudly.

That would clear the travelator, for sure.

'Excuse me,' she says loudly, and the woman ahead looks back, startled, and finally hauls in the suitcase which has been blocking the way.

Dianne is not a laid-back traveller. She's an enraged one.

People walk too slowly in front of her in airports, stop in the middle of busy walkways and just dawdle.

In Singapore airport, they lean lazily against the side of the travelator and let their huge suitcases block the other lane so that nobody can get past.

Inevitably, they huff loudly if Dianne mutters 'Excuse me' to make them move their ruddy bags.

Dianne barrels past traveller after traveller, notching up more steps on her Fitbit and burning off some of her inner fire.

She wonders why this anger was never available to her before. Or why women weren't told about getting angry.

Because it turns out, anger is fabulous.

On the outside, Dianne looks like an ordinary sixty-something lady with curled frosted-blonde hair. She's wearing a beige comfortable tee, an indigo padded gilet and actual mom jeans as well as a nice lippie. People probably can tell she plays tennis at a mildly competitive standard.

In short, she looks like a nice, cake-baking granny until anyone really looks into her eyes.

Her eyes tell the real story.

That she's an enraged woman with dagger-sharp senses, screaming *Hurry the hell up! I will stab you with my blood donor gift pencil if you don't get the hell out of my way!*

On the fourth Singapore airport travelator, Dianne yet again refrains from doing this.

I deserve something, *possibly a medal for self-restraint*, she thinks, but then, getting angry at inappropriate moments is why she's doing this long-haul journey in the first place.

Since January, she's been on a warning from her three kids after a road rage incident culminated in The Intervention.

The Intervention is why she's just come off an eight-hour flight from Melbourne. She's heading on to a connecting flight to Athens, before she gets another flight to Corfu. Three flights! Of course she's angry.

She *should* be home waiting for Ellie's baby to be born, but no: she's being held up by stupid tourists with huge bags dropped all over the place, and if she doesn't control herself, someone's going to die.

'The coppers could have charged you with road rage!' Toby, her youngest, said in shock when it all began to come out in the open.

He had a pal in the police who'd told him that it was sheer fluke that Dianne wasn't being charged over the screaming row with the Tesla driver.

'That moron took my parking spot,' snarled Dianne. 'I only kicked his tyres. I could have done worse.'

'Mum?' said Lauren, her eldest, holding out her hands in supplication like she was about to catch a beach ball or hold a church service. 'The police called it a serious incident. You screamed at him for ten minutes and *wouldn't let him leave the car park*. What's wrong with you?'

'Nothing's wrong with me!' Dianne had shrieked back, which had turned out to be a mistake too because Ellie, middle daughter, had weighed in.

'You never used to shout?' whispered Ellie, sounding heartbroken and then bursting into tears. 'I love you but you haven't been the same since Dad died.'

Lauren, who ran an architect's practice with a chromium hand in a chromium glove, was less emotional. She listed Dianne's transgressions briskly.

'You've fought with all your neighbours. If a kid's ball comes into your garden, you apparently puncture it and then throw it out, which is dreadful. Now the police are involved because of your road rage. You need help.

'So,' Lauren continues, 'I can only find one anger-management live-in programme and it's full, but there's this place in Greece, run by that woman who was on American TV with her therapy show. She can fix anyone. Rose Talisman: remember her? *The Talisman Effect*. She's been off TV for years because of some disaster on her show, but still. She was good.

'It's a week-long stay in Corfu. Late September. It's expensive but frankly, it's either this island retreat or we'll have to get you put into a psych ward.'

'Psych ward?' hissed Dianne furiously. 'I'm not mad,' she'd added in a deliberately calmer tone.

'Yet here you are, behaving as if you're a complete psycho,' Lauren snapped back.

Lauren had been the queen of debating at school. She hadn't lost it.

Dianne wishes she could explain about the anger thing but she can't. They won't get it.

'If you can't do something about your behaviour, we're taking ourselves out of your life. You have to go to the island or accept the consequences,' Lauren had said.

Dianne is going to the island.

She'll pretend to join in.

Dianne can pretend at Olympic level.

She doesn't want to change.

Why would she?

India knows exactly what she wants her wedding to be like.

For starters, she's chosen the dress: well, she has a top three.

Number one is an ivory column dress in heavy silk satin that shimmies down her long legs and makes her look a little bit Grace Kelly. Her wedding flowers consist of a calla lily arrangement, and her copper hair will be in a slightly distressed bun at the nape of her neck.

The number two is a different vibe altogether: an antique lace garment with a demure heart-shaped neckline and teeny cap sleeves that somebody's great-grandmother made. In India's mind, it's a dress which is riddled with memories of great love. Everyone who's worn it has had a Great Love which has never failed. Made in some tiny village in the middle of nowhere where the ladies hand-made lace for decades, centuries even. She can just imagine this on Instagram.

The Great Love bit is what's important.

An Italian great-grandmother dress could do, she thinks as she sits in the back of the taxi on its way from Corfu airport to Villa Artemis.

She loves Italian fashion and her closet wish list is Gucci, Prada, Versace – stuff she buys after much rummaging at vintage stores and car boot sales. Making a unique outfit out of vintage buys is her idea of absolute heaven.

Maybe Albania not Italy. An Albanian antique/vintage garment is just that bit more unique.

India's a bit hazy on geography and honestly cannot point to Albania on a map, but she'll ask one of her stepmother's people to look into finding this fantasy gem. Georgie, her stepmother, has an amazing team. Georgie's an interior designer and does houses for rich people, mainly Russian and Chinese billionaires, in London.

There is nothing Georgie's people cannot source: Mesopotamian doors made of ancient wood with iron ornaments; Warhols that nobody's ever seen before; museum-quality fragments of Napoleon's uniform set inside an ebony box frame with a painting light to hang over the frame. Nothing is off limits.

Georgie sounded surprised that India's heading to Corfu for a therapy retreat, but she never criticises.

'You make your own choices, darling,' is all she said.

It's dark now in Corfu and, as the taxi winds its way along the coast to the Villa Artemis and her Brand New Adventure, India's busy scrawling notes in her metallic-pink fake-crocodile-skin notebook with her initials in gold lettering on the front. She prints out pictures she likes on her portable baby printer. She sticks them on with stickers of daisies.

She's found her third dress choice – Daphne's dress in *Bridgerton*.

If that isn't the stuff of fairy tale, India doesn't know what is.

India isn't built like the petite Daphne: instead, she's tall and has ultra-long legs like her mum, Sonja, who was a famous model. Sonja left India when she was a baby to run off with a successful guitarist who played with one of the world's biggest bands.

Even though India basically grew up without her mother, she's inherited her best features: her legs, general skinniness, snaky copper hair which falls to below her angular shoulder blades, and sky-blue eyes.

There's only one teeny problem about her wedding plans: India and her last boyfriend, Chad, split up a month ago, which means it is handy she had booked the retreat.

A wedding dress is somewhat surplus to requirements.

But she'll need one soon, she just *knows* it. She knows she has a big heart, and there's got to be someone out there who'll love her the same way, surely?

'Rose can fix me!' she had said cheerfully to Georgie and her father.

'You don't need to be fixed, pumpkin,' said her dad, reaching out and twirling a bit of her long coppery hair wistfully. 'You're perfect.'

'We can always improve ourselves, Dad,' India said seriously. 'Since going to Pune in India, my Iyengar yoga has been epic. You should see my downward dog. I was doing it wrong for years. Shocking, right? It's all about getting expert help, Dad.'

When India was a teenager, she spent a lot of time skipping school and watching daytime TV. Her favourite show was *The Talisman Effect*.

Nobody was judged no matter what they'd done.

People were urged to do their best but also told to realise that nobody's perfect.

India loved this. She often felt like a klutz because she wasn't brilliant at stuff like her dad, who'd left school at fifteen and built a car rental company from nothing, or beautiful enough to be a model like her mum, or clever enough to do up giant houses for rich people like Georgie.

Her dad and stepmum both work hard for a living. Meanwhile, India's been living on money her mum set aside for India from her modelling career – and the money's running out.

India needs to know what to do next. How to earn a living after abortive attempts to be an influencer and a stylist. How to – she feels silly even thinking this – but how to *be*.

India's convinced that Rose Talisman alone can help her with these things.

Also, and India is almost embarrassed to have to mention this, perhaps Rose could explain why India finds a lovely man, thinks he's the one, and then it fizzles out in weeks.

Like, why?

India's thirty-four now.

Men of thirty-four all want twenty-four-year-old girlfriends. India's ageing out.

And thirty-four is standing at the side of a very big cliff in fertility years. Like, a really big cliff.

At least she'd had Chad, until his sister got pregnant and Chad – perfect on paper – told everyone that his sister was ruining her life and *Why bring a baby into the world, man?*

India, lost in imagining soft baby feet curled up in her palms, a downy head nestled in the crook of her elbow, had let out a tiny moan of loss.

Clearly, that was the end of Chad. India knows she's soft as butter but even she couldn't stay with him.

The final shock was when Lizzie, one of her two best friends from forever, gave birth to Lily-Blossom, a fairy child with Lizzie's dark hair, dark eyes and a dimple.

Going into Lizzie's apartment to meet the baby for the first time, India felt a vast gaping abyss open up inside her at the thought of never having her own Lily-Blossom.

The pain was like carving a giant blade-sweep across her abdomen. It burned and ached but was startlingly invisible to the rest of the world.

Lizzie had a job as a Pilates teacher, a partner and now a baby.

India was manless, and her most recent job was as a sales assistant in a very posh shop where the owner was a friend of Georgie's.

India's honesty does her no favours when people try stuff on.

Saying 'Don't you have six Lululemon jackets already?' gets you fired.

The taxi slows down and takes a sharp right up a steep drive to a beautiful stone building that glitters with lights in the dusk.

India hops out of the taxi.

'Attack each day with enthusiasm,' is what Georgie always advises.

India has taken this motto to heart, no matter how weirdly anxious she is.

Nobody can ever call me a quitter, she thinks stoically.

She tightens the belt on her travelling cardigan, a very elderly cashmere jacket she has endlessly washed to get the charity shop smell out of.

This is going to be fun, she tells herself. It has to be.

Chapter Three

This is not going to be fun, thinks Keera, as she stands in the huge queue at Corfu airport passport control and decides that if hell is a place, it's here.

The line is five people wide and has no end in sight. Fractious children are crying, there's a low rumble of discontent from the queues and if the airport air-con is on, it's at its lowest setting.

Keera's head is sweating from the sheer weight of her long blonde hair, currently tied up into a pony with a baseball cap on top. A marl-grey sweatshirt hides the tattoos on her right arm – there's one that says 'Keera 'n' Cat for ever' and another one with a full-colour Irish tricolour flag rippling over a full-colour American flag.

If anything symbolises the moment when drinking and drugging got the better of her, it's the flags.

They took six hours to ink in a tattoo parlour in the Tenderloin where there was a sign that said clients could not get inked if they were tripping.

'Not tripping!' Keera had said triumphantly, weaving

through the ink shop into one of the big leather-and-chrome tattoo chairs and sinking into it.

'It's your arm, baby,' shrugged a guy with a handlebar moustache. 'But we don't do discounts or compensate for people's dumb choices.'

'I never make dumb choices,' Keera had declared, sitting on the chair, laying her arm out and displaying the picture of the flags. That was a lie for sure.

She had a water bottle full of tequila with a bit of orange juice in it for extra Vit C and by the time her flags were done, she was entirely numb pain-wise.

She'd relived the experience six months ago in rehab.

'What were you feeling when you said that?' asked Sasha, the toughest counsellor in Little Rock's Haven Clinic.

'I was feeling on top of the world,' Keera said. 'I always felt on top of the world when I was early on in the drinking or drugging experience.'

'And later?'

'Later I felt either sexy—'

Someone in the group sniggered and Sasha shot them a filthy look.

'—or really sad.'

'What did you do when you felt really sad?' Sasha asked.

'Drink more and do more coke, have something to take me down when I got too high, a little kiddie coke to straighten me out.'

After six weeks in Little Rock, Keera now knows that this is not the correct answer to future clean and sober living.

Six weeks in rehab has battered her into shape.

When she feels really sad now, she has to live with it, and *it hurts. So much.* Living without substances means she has to feel everything.

To distract from these thoughts, Keera thinks about getting her tattoos lasered off as she stands in the Corfu airport passport queue.

Some things make people very recognisable.

The hair and the tats were the trappings of the old Keera, the one who was on gossip magazine covers when she was 'dating' fashionable guys. Her mom, Dr Bobbi, had come up with the boyfriends for times when Keera needed a photogenic date.

The 'dates' were generally shy or awkward and both parties knew it was a business relationship.

'COOL DJ OR UPCOMING ACTOR SEEN WITH SINGER KEERA'.

'IS IT LOVE?' the supermarket tabloids would ask in giant letters.

It was never love, and Keera is astonished that any website even gave these dates the barest of credence.

It was just business.

But not any more.

That version of Keera is gone.

The new one wears boyfriend jeans, loose T-shirts and sweats that cover her body up because she's obviously not as thin as she was when she was doing coke, smoking way too much and basically living on straight tequila.

It transpires that no food plus a diet of pills, margaritas and thirty cigarettes a day is an excellent if precarious way to stay incredibly thin.

Keera mourns the loss of her concave stomach but likes that nobody recognises her any more.

The last thing she wants is to be snapped with somebody's iPhone and displayed all over social media.

'MYSTERY OF FIREBIRD SINGER KEERA'S DISAPPEARANCE SOLVED!'

'Firebird' is her most famous song, the one that shot her from Disney-Channel-cute-star fame to one-name-only singer fame.

Keera's amazed that her time in rehab hasn't emerged onto social media – but then, her mother would have been the person to leak it.

Dr Bobbi, her mom and Keera's manager, didn't agree with rehab at all.

'You don't need it! So you drink a little, and doing coke is not a good look, but nobody has shots of you using! You just have to stop the cocaine,' Dr Bobbi warned. 'You're the girl next door, Keera! That's your brand. Rehab would destroy that.'

Thanks, Mom.

Keera knows that her girl-next-door image would have been destroyed for sure if anyone had heard her addiction diaries in Haven Clinic.

Even a guy named Sketch (addicted to crack) had opened his slitty eyes long enough to look at her when she told them all the worst thing. Telling people about your drinking and using was a big part of Haven Clinic.

Sketch had looked her up and down when he heard Keera's drugging confession with everyone else in the group.

'I would,' he'd hissed, because he didn't have much of a voice left thanks to years spent smoking crack.

'Not helpful, Sketch,' admonished Lexi, Keera's favourite counsellor.

But the words had lingered in the air.

Keera still cringes when she thinks of Sketch.

His deadened shark gaze and hissing voice should be enough to keep her clean and sober for life, she thinks. Because when she was drinking and using, she could have easily ended up with Sketch.

Drink and drugs totally skewed her judgement. She shudders.

It's four months since she left rehab.

Stopping using was one thing.

Keera needs the retreat to work out how to fix the rest of her life. But some of it just seems too complicated.

Plus, she's now broke. The Keera bandwagon was an expensive show and she and her mom spent far too much early on.

This trip to Corfu is her last expense before going back to the real world.

But just what is the real world and what is her place in it?

It's ten at night when Dan steps out onto the balcony of his room in Villa Artemis and lights up. He's tried stopping smoking so many times and, as a man of science, he knows how ruinous cigarettes are to his health. At least he's now down to a few a day, which is better than twenty.

He wonders if Rose Talisman can help him stop smoking, but that's a side quest, really.

'Sort your head out, Dan,' his sister, Vicky, had told him when she showed him the Instagram post about Rose's new venture. 'Nobody has to know you've gone to a therapy retreat if you really think it's weird. Keep it private, sure. But Julia's left you. You've got to deal with that, or who knows what'll happen. Julia's a complicated woman. I don't want to wake up one morning to find that she's dead and everyone says it's your fault. It'll destroy the rest of your life thinking of the part you played in it. So you need help.'

Dan's cigarette has gone out as he's been staring blankly out at the view.

He relights it and inhales deeply, blowing smoke out

towards the inky sea. Adriana, the woman who'd checked him in earlier and who's one of the house's proprietors, has told him that there will be some time off for people to swim and possibly sail but not much.

'Rose has a pretty full schedule for you all,' Adriana said, dark head bent over the weathered oak table where she welcomed them to the villa.

What exactly will we be doing? Dan wants to ask, but he can't.

He's booked this and has arrived without allowing himself to even *think* what's involved in a week-long retreat. Does he have to stare deep into his soul?

Does he have to confess everything he's ever done wrong in his life?

Dan is a neuroscientist: he has no idea how this sort of delving into the mind works.

He likes facts.

The current facts are stark, however: his beloved Julia is no longer his girlfriend. She wants a break from their relationship so she can 'figure out what to do, babes'.

That conversation nearly broke Dan.

He adores Julia more than life itself. He sees them together for ever and cannot bear to think that anything he says or does could harm her.

And yet, here he is, forced into a therapy retreat.

There's a fresh notebook with 'from Rose' written on a label ready for him to 'journal' through the week. Dan hates that sort of thing.

All questionnaires and holding hands to feel each other's pain?

Answer twenty questions and we'll tell you what sort of person you are? Which is obvious bullshit. How is there a scientific method in asking people who they are and relying on their answers? People lie. Over a thousand miles away from his small, spartan Bristol home, with his bike – he loves his bike – and his gaming chair – which he also loves – Dan aches at the thought of Vicky's words.

His sister is not the swearing kind of person. She's gentle, thoughtful.

But she was insistent that he get help. Him, not Julia.

This rankles. Why the hell does *he* need help?

He resents the whole concept bitterly.

Plus, Vicky never told him that Rose's one-time-big TV show had been cancelled over a scandal, which he found out from googling in the airport.

He resents not knowing that too.

In fact, he resents every single thing about being here in Xanthe.

His cigarette has gone out again. Annoyed, he drops it into the saucer he's using as an ashtray and lights up another one. He does not need fixing. He'll make that plain first off and maybe he can leave early?

Dan has two decent pens with him. He takes one now and flicks open to the first page of Rose's notebook. It's too small for him. He likes A4 pads and hardback laboratory notebooks. He has tiny handwriting that's always easy to read because no scientist wants a lab notebook with indecipherable writing.

He has no idea what to write.

I'm here and isn't that enough?

His phone is on the desk beside him.

He is tired and irritable, tired of being blamed.

He writes *Piss off* in the notebook, which gives him a frisson of being a teenager again, always the good, quiet one, always doing what he was told. Until Julia came along, of course.

THE ISLAND RETREAT

He fills in a whole page writing *Piss off* in a giant scrawl, then scribbles over it, partly in irritation, partly in shame.

Rose Talisman has him here on the damn island retreat – what more is he expected to do? Carve his own heart out of his chest and leave it on the big olive-wood table outside? *Fat chance, Rose.*

Chapter Four

Rose stands in her bedroom, which is above the sun-filled terrace in the private part of the villa, psyching herself up for her first day of therapy work in five years. She's doing this with some ultra-strong Loumidis coffee with a cube of brown sugar courtesy of Christos.

The Fear is upon her and, despite herself, self-doubt ripples through her.

All the clever therapy phrases she wrote in her wildly successful book have dried up in her head. The royalties have dried up too, which is why she, Adriana and Christos have to make both this retreat and the Villa Artemis work. They ploughed all their money into it: Adriana and Christos remortgaged their now-rented-out home on the other side of Xanthe. Rose has no more income.

If this fails, Rose doesn't want to think about the financial peril they will be in. Not to mention the fact that if she can't run this retreat successfully, then her reputation as a therapist will be destroyed beyond repair.

Of course she's feeling The Fear.

Amusingly, *Stop being afraid of fear* was one of her

therapy commandments for a happy life: written on the backdrop of the studio where she filmed *The Talisman Effect*. How's that for ironic?

Create healthy boundaries, was another vital message on the backdrop.

Personally, Rose would have this lesson drummed into students at school.

She thinks of the sheer number of people she worked with either in her original private practice or on *The Talisman Effect* who had not a single boundary in place.

No boundaries was the car crash of therapy.

Find a person who desperately wanted to please other people without having a clue what *they* wanted or didn't want, and the car crashed right off the road.

It took time but it *always* crashed.

You can do this was another favourite phrase of Rose's – she told people to write it on Post-its and stick them on mirrors in their homes. Viewers loved that one.

Trite pop-psychology, screamed her detractors.

Rose had learned to more or less ignore the haters.

Despite its simplicity, the Post-it made people aware of the critical inner voice in their heads: the voice that told them they were useless, stupid, fat, whatever. Becoming aware that the inner voice was just that – a voice and not reality – made a huge difference.

But on the cusp of piecing her career back together, of facing actual patients for the first time in five years, all her TV therapy mottos seem insanely simple.

You can do it even though you crashed and burned out of your successful TV career five years ago!

Rose knows she'd need a very big Post-it to write that.

Breathing, she decides: that's what she needs to do now to quell her last-minute nerves.

Pranayama breath can solve anything.

The six guests waiting will know how her career ended. Breathe in and hold.

That they still want to be here on the island with her shows that they believe she's a good therapist.

They trust her. That matters hugely to her.

Rose knows she looks way different from back in her TV days: she has no wardrobe of Spanx and figure-hugging trouser suits, no chestnut hair blown out and sprayed into place.

Now she wears Birkenstocks and flowing dresses she buys in Xanthe. Her skin glows with health, and her hair is a long, healthy coil of sheeny silver that she wears in a soft plait or loosely around her shoulders.

Theo wouldn't recognise this vibrant, earthy woman. Rose ended up hiding who she truly was from him.

Ironically, darling Theo was the only man she'd ever lowered her guard for. He adored her and yet she hid a huge part of herself from him, she reflects sadly.

'Loving someone honestly for who they are and not trying to change them is one of the purest and most mature definitions of love,' Rose said once in an interview when she was still in Los Angeles, still a ratings magnet in the afternoon TV slots.

She and Theo were together and she loved him heart and soul, but he didn't know everything about her.

Six years in, it was hard to say: 'You know the story about where I grew up? Well, I lied . . .'

Rose sighs. No point in dwelling on the past and thinking of how she'd messed things up with Theo and with her career.

The past is always full of lessons and once you've learned them, you have to move on – she's told many people that.

Personally, she's really tired of learning lessons. She feels as if she's learned damned near everything.

Rose finishes off Christos' murderously strong coffee and then downs a glass of water.

It's a hot day for late September and Rose does not plan to miss a moment of the week because she's suffering from heat stroke.

With Theo still in her thoughts, she can't help but think of the caveat of her week-long programme here in Xanthe: *Nobody gets healed in a week. But – this is not just a week-long programme.*

It's the start of something.

This week will be her chance to see if she still has what it takes.

Chapter Five

'Are you ready, darling?'

Bernard loves Grazia's accent.

They've been married for twenty-five years and he still loves the way she says 'darling' so that it comes out as 'darlink'.

She's lived in Britain for longer than she ever lived in Tbilisi, but Tbilisi is inside her in every way. For Christmas she makes Georgian khachapuri, cheese-filled bread, and the classic plum cake, drizzled with rum. Last Christmas, she made forty for all her friends. Forty small cakes! Bernard had just smiled but he thought she was mad.

Why not *buy* the cakes? Bernard believes that money can sort everything out. It's one of life's most obvious truths and those who say he's wrong haven't lived the sort of life he has. From the slums of post-war Liverpool to running a huge company that's made him very wealthy, Bernard finds that money always helps.

'Yes, I'm ready,' he says, scanning around to make sure he has got everything. Handkerchief, sunglasses and his two phones which he is keeping in his shorts pocket no matter what the literature told them about 'no mobile devices' in the sessions.

He needs to be in touch with work.

Does this Rose person not know who he is?

Grazia is taking a small bottle of orange juice out of the minibar. He knows it's in case his blood sugar gets low.

Old age has been creeping up on Bernard slowly and he hates it. Would fight it if he could but age is a stealthy adversary and never gets straight into the ring.

It lightly touches many things at once so it's hard to fight ageing in the aggressive way he fights people in business.

Once, he was agile, lithe, loved playing squash and flattening the hell out of younger guys. The sheer buzz of that made him feel like a hero. But smashing people with humiliating defeats on the squash court was a million years ago.

Now his knees are creaky as hell and he gets up from chairs with painful slowness, saying 'Oomph'.

The skin on his arms has become covered with age spots, so that almost overnight, Bernard's once-strong forearms are now dotted and paper thin.

Now he has to be careful of blood sugar and needs a scan to check his bone density because of his childhood lack of calcium.

His accent is no longer reminiscent of a poverty-stricken childhood in Liverpool but his bones still are.

Grazia buys him multi-vitamins, and watches to make sure he takes his cholesterol medication.

He can't help it: he resents it all.

'Shall we go?' Grazia's at the suite door, tall and poised in an outfit covered in colourful psychedelic swirls which she says is vintage.

Bernard always feels that vintage is second-hand, and

he had enough of that as a kid. No thank you, he likes new clothes. Expensive, made-to-measure clothes. But if it makes her happy.

He's here for Grazia. For now, at least.

His wife swings back to him with her little handbag rattling on her arm.

'We'll be late, Bernard!'

He shrugs. 'We're paying them enough. No matter if we're late.'

'If we're late,' his wife says, 'we get thrown out of the programme.'

Normally, this is a red rag to a bull. Nobody throws Sir Bernard out of anything, but he sees the tautness of Grazia's normally full upper lip, the slight whitening underneath her nose.

He will do this for her.

For one day, anyway.

After that, he'll have to see. Nobody gets to tell him he can't be late, certainly not some charlatan of a therapist who's been in hiding for five years.

Bernard has researched Rose Talisman: he knows exactly what she did and what she's been up to since. He's ready for her if she annoys him. Bernard has spent his life making more and more money so that nobody ever gets to tell him what to do or reprove him for anything.

He will decimate Rose Talisman if she attempts to do so.

For now, Bernard will go along with this to make Grazia happy. But if Rose steps out of line, Bernard will flatten her.

In the private quarters of the house, as the guests file out to the breakfast that has been lovingly prepared and laid out, Adriana and Christos are having a rare five-minute sit-down in the shade of their terrace and drinking iced tea.

Christos is trialling a new breakfast smoothie: made of watermelon, mint and pomegranate juice. He has a small glass of it for Adriana because she has amazing taste, despite not being born into a family of restauranteurs.

'I think it needs more mint...' ponders Christos, sipping it again.

He's left the door into the kitchen open so he can hear if Beata, the hotel's waitress-cum-housekeeping-stalwart, needs any help.

Most of Villa Artemis' small staff are related to Christos in some way. Without them, he, Adriana and Rose would not be able to run the place. His cousin is the villa's yoga guru, Beata's two daughters run the tiny spa, his nephew takes care of gardening. His second cousins, the amazing Sia sisters, make the natural candles, soaps and aromatic oils that are used all over the hotel.

His yaya, or grandmother, is the boss of the local sewing ladies: she has designed the villa's cushions, and the pretty tote bags available in the tiny shop are made by her and her friends.

'I hope Rose will be all right,' frets Adriana, not even seeing the glass of pink perfection her husband is holding out to her. 'This is such a high-pressure way to go back to work. I worry that we pushed her into it.'

'Nonsense,' says Christos.

He's a big bear of a man who never ceases to feel lucky he found his tiny, beloved wife. Adriana is as dark-haired and dark-eyed as any Greek woman but has creamy pale skin like her sister, Rose.

'Rose is a therapist at heart,' Christos reassures her.

'Sure, she enjoyed renovating the house, choosing colours, lamps, candles.'

Adriana grins at him.

She loved choosing candles and lamps too. Pure linen throws for the beds, shell-shaped light sconces around the hallways, embroidered pillowcases, crystal vases ready to be filled with flowers.

It was like being in charge of a luxury doll's house, naming rooms after goddesses, picking plants to go beside the new infinity pool, helping design the cool, airy dining room which they'd created by knocking three of the original rooms together.

Adriana feels her body tighten with stress at the thought of all the money they have spent turning Villa Artemis into a luxurious jewel of a destination.

Christos has finished his smoothie. 'What Rose loves most is fixing people. She's good at it too.'

Adriana zones back in.

'But this will be her first time since . . .' she pauses.

'Yeah,' agrees her husband. 'She's so confident, so ready. She can do this.'

Adriana murmurs a quiet prayer. She's not exactly religious but, sometimes, she finds comfort in the quiet of a cool church or the ritual of a prayer.

'Let this be the right thing,' she says.

'It will be.' Christos sounds convinced. 'I've got some photos of the terrace for when we launch the next therapy week. I was thinking November?'

'This one needs to work first,' says Adriana.

Christos shrugs. He does good shrugs – huge shoulders raising, large arms that like to hold his beloved wife splaying out. 'What can go wrong?' he says cheerfully.

Chapter Six

Keera steps onto the terrace, an expanse of beautiful stone with a wooden pergola and a long wooden table under it, set with cushioned chairs.

The scent of pink bougainvillea drifts lazily in the air and, when she walks to the edge of the terrace, Keera can see down to a different level where there's a gleaming infinity pool that looks almost too perfect to be true.

In the distance is Xanthe, a village of blue-roofed houses, whitewashed terraces and abundant greenery. Below is the sea: a blue so shimmering it seems unreal in its perfection, only a few small dots of boats sprinkled on the horizon.

Keera can understand why Rose Talisman is having a retreat here.

Even Keera, whose personal natural setting is a low-level hum of anxiety, is feeling a little calmer in this blissfully peaceful place.

She picks a chair with fat cushions embroidered with traditional Greek whitework and puts her stuff on the table.

A buffet breakfast of juices, coffee, fruit, rolls, yogurt and honey is laid out to one side but Keera's too nervous to eat.

Please let this not be as hard as rehab, she thinks.

Rehab was hell – she'd thought she'd be OK coming off all the stuff she took because it wasn't as if she was on opioids.

Boy, had she been wrong.

Shivering at the memory of detoxing off the pills, cocaine, uppers, downers and tequila she'd been happily consuming all her life, she gazes around at the stunning view of turquoise sea below the hotel.

Despite the calmness of Xanthe and the beauty surrounding her, she feels nervous at what the morning will bring.

All this ripping into your inner self is incredibly hard.

Four months ago, when Keera came out of Haven Clinic, she felt as shaky as a newborn foal.

'The good news is that you've got your feelings back,' Lexi, one of the counsellors and a one-time heroin addict, had reminded Keera in her final session before she left. 'The bad news is that you've got your feelings back.'

Since rehab, Keera hasn't written a song or contacted a producer about her album. She's out of contract with her record company and they haven't been in touch. It's like she's disappeared off the face of the earth.

She's changed her look for Greece. She doesn't want to be recognised on the island. Hence the blonde hair.

She feels relief at disconnecting from her stressy world but it's also scary. Who is she if she's not a singer/actress? Who is she without the drugs blurring the world and making it liveable? What does her future look like?

A tall man walks onto the terrace.

He looks as if he runs marathons, but seems very tightly wound.

Keera's good at figuring people out. She knows she's an empath. She must be, right?

She can feel the mood of any room she goes in, has been

able to since she was a small child. It's her superpower but it's a difficult one to have as it makes her nervous.

In a room with shouting, Keera's stomach swoops into a tight knot. That's why drugs and booze helped so much.

This tall man does not give off angry energy, though. He feels safe to be around.

Keera watches him surreptitiously, pretending to be arranging her notebook and pens on the polished table.

He's sad and confused, she decides.

Maybe this might be OK. If the people on the island retreat are also messed up, Keera can cope. If they're all uber sorted out, then she's not going to enjoy it.

Behind him is another woman, not much older than Keera: very pretty with huge blue eyes, a smile on her face and wearing a floaty amber chiffon dress that looks as though it came from a 1930s film. She has long, slender legs that end in narrow elegant feet, which Keera would love instead of her solid feet with the ginormous big toes.

Her eyes are beautifully made-up with inky black lashes, and a fat silken peony in a combination of pinks holds her stunning hair back. It's the same glossy red of the fox-fur jacket Keera's mother picked up second-hand and insisted on wearing all last year.

'It's dead already,' Dr Bobbi pointed out whenever Keera objected to the coat on animal rights grounds.

Keera bites her bottom lip. She has to get her mother out of her head. If only removing people's reproving voices was as easy as uninstalling computer programs.

Delete Mama voice: 1 minute.
Install Rehab Life Tools: 2 minutes.
Perhaps Rose has a mantra for that.

*

Rose watches the guests arrive on the terrace from her vantage point in her bedroom. A tall man with olive skin, unruly dark hair and a high-boned face that speaks of Eastern-European ancestry is now standing at the breakfast buffet in front of the fruit, seemingly unable to decide between the slices of watermelon or the figs sitting beside blue pottery bowls of local yogurt swirled with honey.

He's in old denims with leather sandals on long feet and wears a ragged-looking band T-shirt that should have been thrown out with the clothes recycling years ago. A man unused to taking care of himself, perhaps?

He certainly appears uncomfortable, out of his comfort zone.

The scientist.

Dr Dan Talbot from Bristol, who has been at the forefront of some breakthrough in genetic research only for it to falter at one of the last hurdles, or so it had said in her quick research of him.

Rose pictures Dan in a lab coat, staring at mice, wondering, was this batch going to cure disease?

Did they use mice? Would someone at his level of research be at the mice stage?

She had no idea.

It's not that Rose's life has been without science, but her involvement has been more at the cutting-edge connection between neuroscience and therapy. She used to talk on the show about how therapy works with the brain to help hardwire recovery.

Listen to yourself, Rose: you're sounding a bit like your old self.

The trickle of self-belief begins to swell in Rose.

She was always good at this. For a while, she lost confidence, that's all.

Next, Rose watches the arrival of a tall, slim red-head with an exquisitely cut bias frock dancing around skinny ankles. India.

A beautiful boho girl with a history of lots of jobs and a very happy Instagram feed full of fun holidays, pictures of vintage clothes finds and quotes on happiness – according to Adriana.

India smiles at the other two, folds herself into a chair and sets up lovely pens and a big notebook in front of her.

Beside her is Keera, the American singer, clad in jeans and definitely the youngest of the group. Keera also has lovely pens.

Rose, who has to keep her stationery habit under control, grins to herself and flicks a glance at her watch.

Five to ten now. The last three are skating on thin ice time-wise.

In her former life, in private practice, Rose had strict rules about lateness.

It was part of her therapist's training to enforce the sense that the participation was a contract. The keen-to-be-healed were entering into a contract with her, therefore lateness – unless accompanied by phone footage of a bona fide disaster – meant you got turned away.

Maybe the business magnate, Sir Bernard, if you don't mind, thinks that rules are for the little people.

What fun to have to take his money and send him home unfixed, Rose thinks with glee. Time spent with wealthy narcissists – and a lot of the ultra-rich are narcissists – means she's extra fierce with the aggressively rich clients.

You pay, you commit. If you don't turn up, you forfeit your fee.

But at the last minute, three people arrive together in a rush.

First, a tall, statuesque woman with a sleek chestnut high pony, wearing a one-sleeved pink-patterned Pucci jumpsuit, strides in.

She's tanned, early fifties perhaps, and wears a gold coiled snake bangle on one wrist, a piece of heavy metal that speaks of serious money spent in the beautiful jewellery shops in Corfu Town.

Rose, who loves jewellery, drools a bit.

She's definitely Bernard's wife, Grazia: a former model, Adriana has told Rose.

The elegant Grazia gives off no sense of herself at all. She's not nervous, not proud, merely calm. Eerily calm, perhaps.

Rose can't get a read on her at all.

Beside the glacial Grazia is Dianne Wilkins.

If Grazia is precisely what Rose imagines as the wife of a very, very wealthy and status-conscious man, Dianne is nothing like the woman Rose has been expecting.

Her adult children have pushed her to be here, her daughter Lauren saying, 'Her anger is corrosive. Dad died suddenly and, of course, that was hugely difficult, but she was never angry before he died. She's said to me: *We all die.* That's it.

'She's obviously affected by grief but she's going to end up in prison for driving into a random stranger in a road rage incident if she doesn't get help. She has lovely neighbours and, since Dad died, she's fallen out with them all. She doesn't want to go on the course but it's an ultimatum.'

Dianne had been the first person Rose had picked for

the retreat. She'd felt kinship with this angry, obviously lost woman and yet, in the flesh, Dianne appears the opposite of a person teetering on the edge.

She's small but very athletic, sports the healthy glow of someone who's spectacularly fit and wears a pink polo shirt with white shorts, neat socks and trainers. All she needs is a tennis racquet and she'll be another sixty-something tennis lady, the one you want on your team and your fundraising committee because she's a dynamo.

As a mask, it's a spectacular one constructed of a neutral gaze, alongside age-appropriate make-up including bright lippie and perfect silvery-blonde hair in a neat to-the-shoulder cut that she probably fixes with hairspray and Velcro rollers every morning.

Rose is still staring at Dianne when she gets the weirdest sensation that the Melbourne lady knows she's being watched from inside the hotel. For a second, fear flashes across her face.

Interesting.

Making up the final member of the class, definitely shorter than his model-wife which makes Rose grin, and with the skin of a man who has spent far too much of his life in the sun, is Sir Bernard.

He's now white-haired, liver-spotted and wrinkled like an old lizard. Just like the crocodile he resembles, he looks as if he hides in the shallows of the river and waits till the bodies of his old enemies float past.

He's no longer quite the handsome silvery fox from his Internet publicity photos.

Older now, his eyes are hooded and he appears to be a great man for smiling without engaging the eyes. He's doing it now, smiling at the others and shaking hands, as if he's running the retreat and they're all his guests.

Enough already, Rose thinks, spurred into action.
This is not your show, Bernard: it's mine.

She grabs her things and silently opens the door onto the terrace.

'Welcome to Villa Artemis,' she says.

Chapter Seven

'Welcome to Villa Artemis.' Rose's voice was once world-famous; she has the husky cadences of a rock singer alongside an accent that hints at French ancestry.

Her voice, one interviewer wrote, *'can pierce into your soul and make you give up your inner secrets within minutes. Every journalist has fallen under her trap and I did too, I confess.'*

This power of the voice is very handy when you're in Rose's business.

She's made millions from this voice and her particular gift.

Rose can read people like a page in a book.

It's not psychic ability, it's something else. Something spectacular. This was why she stayed on *The Talisman Effect* for longer than she should have. Because her gift meant she could see people's particular problems easily.

She loved helping people to the extent that by the end, it was almost an addiction.

Now nobody speaks as Rose crosses the terrace and stands in front of them, having put on her magnificence like a cloak so that she's become Rose Talisman, the almost mystic healer in a dress of shimmering purple which no longer looks like something she pulled from the rails in Mama Sophia's.

She knows she looks a lot different from the Rose they've all seen on television but no matter. The version of Rose Talisman they're getting on the island retreat is far wiser.

Her eyes, a spectacular, glittering blue the same colour as the Ionian Sea, seem to reach into each of the six people's souls.

'Welcome to the rest of your life.

'In a week, you'll all feel different, I promise you,' she says now, staring at the group in front of her: twenty-something Keera wearing what has to be a wig; scientist Dan with his slightly tortured face and falling-apart T-shirt; India, who looks as if she's on a thrilling adventure but Rose feels there's more to her than that; Dianne, smiling that cold, fake smile as if she's on the podium at a charity committee; model-like Grazia who has subtle signs of having a *lot* of injectables now that Rose can see her properly; and crocodile Bernard, also smiling like a man about to lie to a company that he won't break it up tomorrow, when in fact, that's precisely his plan.

Rose feels a surge of excitement.

She has missed this: fixing people, starting them on their journey without wasting years.

Helping people is her life's mission. In all her years of work, she's never promised a cure. Just a way to start the process.

'This week is the start of discovering yourselves,' she says. 'The start,' she reiterates. 'Healing yourself is a lifelong process. My aim is to empower you all to understand yourselves, to see what trouble or negativity is holding you back individually. There's no magic here, no miracle ingredient except what you put into this process and your willingness to work with me.' The people on the terrace listen, rapt.

'Understanding why we behave in certain ways is the key to changing that,' Rose goes on.

She can feel the rising heat of the Corfu sun as another glorious day on the island slowly surges into life.

In the distance, she can hear music from the holiday cottages in the village on the road up to Villa Artemis, and the wild giggles of small children playing near a swimming pool.

Up here beyond the village, generally little can be heard but the rhythmic singing of cicadas and a faint noise of crockery from the depths of the villa's kitchen.

Christos will be working on something delicious: this week he's planning to do a tsipoura or bream covered with salt and baked one night. It's a Spanish technique so, to balance things out, he's also planning some Greek lamb and the classic vegetarian spanakopita.

Dismissing the thought of food, she focuses on her guests. 'I don't promise miracles because that's just quackery. I can promise only that I'll help you on your journey to understanding yourselves and how you came to be here.'

Rose takes a breath.

'When you leave, you'll have a road map to happiness but it will be up to you to continue the work.'

This is where Rose looks meaningfully at her subjects.

Keera lets out a tiny muffled squeak and India's eyes are huge.

Good, thinks Rose.

The *road map to happiness* motto always strikes a chord.

Scientist Dan looks as if he will only believe if he's shown five peer-reviewed papers on the process.

Wait till you see me work, Dan, thinks Rose, feeling her old power surge back.

Dianne is no longer smiling like she's ready for tennis: a haunted look flashes fleetingly across her face, replacing the frozen mask with one of pure grief.

Also good. Rage and grief: an interesting combination to work on.

Only Grazia keeps the smile nailed to her face, but Rose thinks that's the effect of a lot of Botox and syringes of fillers so that any original movement of her actual face is hidden under all the careful cosmetic workings. Grazia could be howling with inner pain and her face would show the faintly surprised look of the heavily enhanced.

Her husband is doing his best with his trademark grin, but it's faltering and his upper face has telltale signs of stress. No Botox there.

'This is a safe space,' Rose continues. 'Your space. If you lie, I will know and you will certainly know. I need truthfulness if I am to help you. So . . .'

Rose pauses. She loves a good pause.

'. . . Let's begin. What trouble brought you all here?'

Chapter Eight

Rose's words float off into a hint of sea air and are gone.

'What trouble brought you all here?'

India stares at Rose and a rush of unaccustomed anxiety floods her. This is not what she'd expected.

For a start, Rose is almost unrecognisable from the sharp-suited, glamorous and charismatic woman off the TV. The flowing silvery-grey hair is very cool, though. Her eyes and the voice are the same: kind yet probing.

She will see inside you, India suddenly thinks in alarm. *What have you done?*

A week in a glorious luxury villa in Corfu with a world-famous healer had sounded utterly marvellous.

The Talisman Effect had been twenty-something India's favourite show.

Plus the pictures of Villa Artemis on Instagram had been blissful: all sunlight flooding a hotel made of cool white walls, with flowing white muslin curtains, exotic plants growing against stone walls and a magnificent expanse of sea from every window.

As for the healing, India had imagined much yoga, sitting

on beaches discussing how they needed to be mindful and possibly a bit of manifestation thrown in.

She wants yoga, swimming, things to stimulate the vagus nerve: that sort of thing. With a hint of Tarot or perhaps a night of psilocybin thrown in.

How had she been so stupid? Rose's show had always been about learning from the past and using those lessons to move forward. No Tarot, no drugs, no yoga.

Shit, shit, shit.

'If everyone can introduce themselves, that would be great,' Rose is saying.

Please let it be gentle, thinks India, desperately trying to manifest a retreat she'd like: bright-green and ghastly purple juices that taste like roadkill; massages with oil from millions of squashed rose petals, a recipe first used on Cleopatra.

All ending up with a hint of advice from Rose; maybe during a walk on the beach, Rose would tell India what she's doing wrong. Nothing intense at all, just a lovely conversation and then India could go back to the yoga and think about how she'd change her life as per Rose's plan. Instead, Rose looks serious, fancy serious with raisins in it.

'You'll have a road map to happiness but it will be up to you to continue the work,' she had said.

She hasn't mentioned yoga or anything that hints of a shamanic idyll in the evening sun.

No, she's talked about work.

Working on themselves.

Deep inside India, something is shrieking '*No!*'

'I'm Keera,' says the blonde girl with the baseball hat.

'What would you like to gain from the retreat?' Rose asks.

India quails at this question even though it's not directed at her. She's next in line.

Wondering why she can't find the perfect man is not going to be an acceptable reason for why she's there. Talking about wanting a baby would be, but India can't go there. Not with anyone. She hasn't told her father, Georgie, anyone—

Keera's hesitating.

'I did rehab a few months ago and I need to sort some stuff out in my head,' she says. 'I thought a group would be good. I like the group therapy concept.'

'Thank you,' says Rose, smiling.

It's India's turn. She suddenly realises that there's something familiar about Keera but she can't figure out what it is.

'I'm . . . er, India, and I wanted something relaxing with yoga and . . .'

She half-waits for the laugh. She always makes people laugh. But nobody laughs here. Shit.

'. . . I thought juices, massage, maybe. To de-stress. I'm not unhappy . . . well, I broke up with my boyfriend a while ago.'

Rose is nodding and India thinks that maybe she's doing OK.

'I loved your show when I was younger, Rose,' she adds lamely.

'Me too,' chimes in Keera, and she and India look at each other properly.

'It's you,' says India, suddenly realising.

Keera nods and smiles.

OK, thinks India, feeling braver. *If someone cool like Keera's here, then it's got to be good.*

'There's a lot of stuff I'd like to sort out but I don't know if this is the right place for it,' India finishes in a rush.

Is this mad? Or very, very wise?

Rose smiles at her, a very warm, understanding smile. India smiles back and forbids herself to nibble a cuticle.

They move on.

'I'm Dan,' says the tall man stiffly. 'I'm not sure why I'm here,' he adds.

India and Keera exchange glances.

Trouble ahead, India thinks.

'I'm Dianne,' says the older woman with the frosted curly hair, speaking out of turn. 'I'm only here because my kids made me.' She flashes Rose a sardonic smile.

Again, Keera and India share a glance but Rose just smiles beatifically at Dianne.

'Thank you, Dianne.'

'I am Bernard Hennessy,' says the oldest person there, announcing his name as if they should all know who he is. '*Sir* Bernard, actually,' he adds with a very fake laugh. 'I'm here for my lovely wife, Grazia,' he adds.

India thinks that Rose has just clenched her teeth but she can't be sure. If she was his wife, she'd tell him this sort of behaviour was not cool.

'I am Grazia and we are here for each other,' says his wife in her heavily accented English.

Whatever could be their issue, wonders India.

Chapter Nine

'Welcome,' says Rose, now that the introductions have been made. She walks to a chair and sits down.

Nobody speaks.

'Collect your thoughts for a moment,' she says, to calm the nervous ones. 'The plan for the week is for each one of you to tell your story and then, as a group, we look at how to move on from the past, how to solve problems. Not every story will resonate with each of you but that doesn't mean you can't take advantage of the lessons from that story.'

Her seat is almost a throne: a curved wooden chair with a footstool, deep with blue and white cushions and in the very coolest spot on the terrace, hidden from the sun and with the sea at her back.

The merest hint of a sea breeze floats up every now and then and Rose can feel it.

Keera and India have moved their chairs so they're sitting beside each other, each with fresh notebooks and pens ready.

She watches Dan, who is sitting between the rest of the group and the two younger women. He's already sunk his coffee and has an old A4 lined pad in front of him with a selection of random pencils. He's left-handed, and his wrist is curved around a pencil now, possibly dating the page like any good scientist.

She looks across to Grazia and Sir Bernard, who have made a little area for themselves away from the big olive-wood table. Grazia has put a very expensive handbag on the small side table.

A Lady Dior, tan leather, lots of glittering gold bits dangling off it. Adorable. Perfect for Greece in the summer for the millionaire class. Screams 'Money!'

Rose prefers the hand-quilted and embroidered little bags sold in the hotel's lobby shop, made by Christos' yaya and her friends in a riot of hand-dyed colours: amber, turquoise, indigo, fern green, blossom pink.

'I want everyone to close their eyes and think about their breath for a moment. Breathing's very important and it's amazing how many of us breathe shallowly, especially if we have some trauma in our life.'

Nobody looks convinced.

'We'll be doing this simple breathing technique every day. Hold the breath for a count of four, then breathe out through your mouth for a count of six. Let's do that again. Slowly, purposefully, feeling the breath fill your lungs.'

Rose leads the group in ten minutes of breathing, then, when they're suitably off-guard, she pounces.

'Now, Dan,' says Rose, 'tell us about yourself.'

There's a startled silence. Everyone was getting into the breathing, and now this?

'Dan, why are you here? What's the trouble that's brought you to this crossroads in your life? Because, trust me, people only ever attempt such desperate measures when there is big trouble.'

She smiles at Dan who has a bunny-in-headlights look on his handsome face.

He has decent shoulders, Rose notices: good looking in a smouldering Byronic hero sort of way. Not a clue that he's good looking either, which is nice. Nobody probably told him when he was younger.

'It's hard to be the first,' Rose says cosily, 'but could you start?'

Dan's shoulders come down and he raises his chin.

There is silence.

Will he bottle it or ask if someone else can go first?

Keera looks at the ground; India stares into space. Sir Bernard looks like he hates silence and is bouncing with energy to fill it, when Dan suddenly speaks.

'I'm not really sure why I'm here,' he repeats.

Rose fixes him with a stern look. *Really?*

Her stern looks can stop traffic and Dan instantly wavers under her gaze.

'I mean, I do and I don't know,' he self-corrects.

He has a soft deep voice with no trace of an accent anywhere but crisp vowel sounds.

'The problem's not actually me – it's my girlfriend. Ex-girlfriend. We've been together for many years but we're on a break. She . . . she tried to kill herself.'

As he speaks, there is a collective inhalation of breath.

Rose, on the other hand, breathes out.

Dan has taken the first step.

Every eye is locked on Dan now but he's looking at Rose.

You're sorry you're here but you'll continue, she thinks.

Unless they walk out, the guests have no other option than to talk.

'This is very personal stuff, I've never told other people

before . . .' Dan says, his body language saying he's wracked with discomfort.

'What happens in group, stays in group, Dan,' Rose says. 'Nobody's going to be broadcasting what you're saying. Everyone who's here has signed agreements to that effect. This is a safe space to share your pain.'

He nods. Appears to be trying to prepare himself for a great ordeal.

'It's the second time she's tried to kill herself. Julia . . .' He pauses. 'That's her name . . . The first time probably was a mistake,' he explains, 'although her cousin says we can't know that. Then, Julia was partying heavily and there were drugs around . . .' He gives a little weary smile but nobody's smiling back.

'But this last time was serious. My sister wanted me to come here,' Dan goes on. 'I didn't want to come. I've done everything for Julia. Everything. Why am *I* here?'

Nobody says a thing.

'Attempted suicide is incredibly traumatic not just for the person involved but for the people close to them. It's life-changing. Realising that someone you love thinks suicide is an option makes a person question everything about their relationship,' says Rose.

She needs to go slowly.

'Let's take a step back from Julia's actions for a moment, Dan. We're here for you. You've said you do everything for Julia. Tell us what you do for her?' she asks him.

Dan shrugs as if he does so much, it's impossible to explain.

'Everything,' he repeats. 'She relies on me. Used to say she couldn't live without me, but we're not together any more . . .'

Nobody says anything and Dan looks off into the distance.

'She wanted a break, you see,' he continues. 'But I love

her. I'm the person who picks up all the pieces. That's what you do when you love someone, isn't it?'

Rose nods.

'Can you tell me about this suicide attempt?'

She looks at Dan with huge sympathy and, this time, he stares straight at her.

'Why do I have to go first?' he asks mulishly, as if this thought has just occurred to him.

'Because I asked you,' says Rose gently, deciding that honey does get more results than vinegar. 'I know that as a scientist, you're used to presenting to an audience.'

Dan says nothing.

The silence on the terrace is broken by the singing of birds and the sound of cicadas sawing their tiny legs together.

Rose keeps her smile and continues: 'You're all here for a reason, and hiding from it is totally understandable, particularly when it's as painful as your story, Dan. But you've made it all the way here. If you give yourself to this programme, who knows what you'll get from it. Dan, you say you don't think that you need to be here. Why is that?' she asks.

'Because it's not my fault!' he replies.

Rose leans forward, nodding. 'Go on,' she urges.

She can see the battle rage across Dan's face. Then he gives in.

'I don't know why Julia tried to commit suicide, I really don't. Julia said it was a mistake, she felt very sad and alone and she acted impulsively. She'd been at a festival the night before, she was feeling low . . .'

He pauses.

Rose needs to keep him talking.

'Go on,' she urges gently.

'My sister, Vicky, says Julia's manipulating me.'

There are gasps on the terrace.

'Which is a horrible thing to say,' Dan says quickly. 'It's almost as if she doesn't understand Julia. I mean, who says something like that? But we're here for this, aren't we? The not-being-polite thing. The telling-it-like-it-is.'

He's no longer adopting the stiff, *I-don't-want-to-be-here* vibe and looks at Rose for confirmation that this rather sad speech is acceptable.

Rose nods her non-committal therapist's nod and says: 'I think it's impossible to say what another person really means when they try to take their own life, and to call it manipulative shows a lack of empathy—'

'I know,' Dan interrupts. 'I'm on Julia's side. Vicky doesn't understand Julia like I do. She's wonderful but complex—'

He stops speaking as if he's revealed too much and stares down at his long-fingered hands.

Pianist's fingers, Rose thinks.

'Keep going,' she urges. 'Julia's very complex—'

He nods.

'I hate talking like this about her: it sounds so one-sided. You're not going to see how amazing she is. It's like you'll only see that one dimension, that Julia tried to take her own life.'

Dan has self-corrected, Rose realises.

Julia no longer tried to kill herself. She tried to take her own life.

He's worried about saying the wrong thing.

'I can tell you that the first time was totally a mistake, not a suicide attempt at all. She was partying and she was with people who were drinking a lot of hard alcohol and had to have her stomach pumped. She was in hospital for a week. It was terrible. Then the last time was four months ago.'

Now his face is twisted with guilt.

'Julia . . .' He pauses as if saying her name makes him wince with remembered pain. '. . . cut her wrists. She'd had a weekend with friends and there were definitely some drugs knocking around, which would absolutely affect her, bring her mood down. But no matter how much I know about brain chemistry, it's still shocking to have someone you love do this. I can't bear to think that she was so sad, so alone, and I still don't know if it was a mistake or if . . .' He pauses again. 'If she meant it.'

Rose is nodding, silently urging him on.

'She's actually doing quite well now. She didn't cut deep enough on either side so she didn't need surgery to repair her wrists. Her psychiatrist said something about "parasuicide" which made it sound not as bad but it was absolutely terrifying. I thought I'd lost her.'

The terrace is silent.

'We'd talked about moving in together and that's off now. Julia says we need time apart, which is heartbreaking. So we're not together, which is not my idea. Then my sister said I should come here and Julia got angry when I told her about this retreat.'

He sounds bewildered and hurt, Rose thinks.

'Why do you think that is?' she asks.

Dan blinks long eyelashes.

'She says *I* don't need to process my feelings – she does, and what do I know . . .? She's angry with me and that's . . .' He actually winces now. '. . . incredibly painful. I hate hurting her because I love her so much,' he adds dismally.

'OK,' says Rose slowly. 'Let's unpack this. Your sister told you to get help by coming here?'

Dan nods.

'You don't really understand why.'

Again, Dan nods. 'Vicky made me book this shortly after Julia got out of the psychiatric hospital. She lives with her cousin, Miriam. They're very close. Julia point blank refused to spend longer in the hospital than the mandatory period. Miriam was going to be away, so I suggested that she move in with me and she said no because her psychiatrist advised against it.'

Rose wonders why the psychiatrist advised this but that's for another day.

Let him get the bones of the story out so he can think about it. Telling your truth to other people is more than the sum of its parts.

'The thing is, I'm terrified my sister is right.'

He finally looks up and, now, he no longer has his calm, disinterested mask on. Now he's maskless and honest.

'I'm terrified that it is my fault, you see. That I drove her to it. But I don't know why. I wish I did. I want to fix whatever it is that I'm doing wrong so Julia's happy.'

The group inhales en masse and Dan stares pleadingly at Rose.

I want you to tell me I didn't drive her to it, those eyes say.

That's not how therapy works, Rose thinks.

Chapter Ten

'Did you make her do it?'

It's Dianne who speaks, her small face taut with anger. 'Did you? Men like you can drive a woman to anything,' she hisses.

Dan looks appalled.

'No—' he begins.

Dianne's out of her seat, rage quivering in every part of her.

'Thank you, Dianne,' says Rose. She rises from her chair too, but she's commanding, firm, utterly in control. 'Let me continue for now.'

Dianne's mouth tightens. She does not sit back in her chair, though: she's bolt upright, tensed for action. If Dianne had a spear in her hand, Rose imagines her stabbing Dan, so great is her fury.

'Dianne.'

Rose moves to Dianne and puts a hand on Dianne's arm.

Dianne jerks at the touch.

'Please, it's going to be all right. I promise,' Rose says softly.

'You can't promise,' says Dianne, and her eyes are opaque with pain.

'I can,' says Rose.

Keera and India are on the edge of their seats now, each ready to step in.

'Please,' Rose says to Dianne, still touching the other woman's arm. 'I can help you, you know,' she says very softly.

'Nobody can,' says Dianne in a whisper, wrenching her arm away, but she sits.

Rose manages to gain enough self-control to sit back in her throne-like seat and turn her attention to Dan.

This is a pivotal moment for him. She has to keep her focus on him or she'll lose him.

'You've been together for a long time?' asks Rose.

'Since we were teenagers,' Dan replies.

'Then it does seem odd that you haven't ever moved in with each other,' she goes on. 'Is there a reason for that?'

'Her cousin, Miriam, owns a lovely house in Bath. They're very close.'

Dan has a quick, well-rehearsed answer.

'What about the rest of her family?'

'They're not close. Apart from Miriam, that is.'

OK, thinks Rose. *Lack of family support for poor Julia. Another piece of the puzzle.*

She tries a different tack.

'You say that you've always been there for Julia, Dan. What would happen if you weren't there? What would she do?'

'I don't know,' he says, sounding confused at this change of direction.

Rose continues: 'Julia would have to choose whether to survive or not. You say she needs you but in this scenario, you are not around. What would she do then?'

'Like I said, I don't know.' Dan's face is now puzzled.

'Let's imagine another scenario,' she suggests. 'Let's imagine you get back together, after this break, but then Julia decides to leave you.'

Dan inhales audibly.

'She packs her stuff and goes to another country, starts a new life, maybe even meets someone new. What would you do then?'

The questions have to be relentless.

'Can you stop her going? What if you try to stop her going but she still leaves?'

The other five are staring at Dan, apart from Dianne, who still has the opaque look in her eyes. She's staring off beyond the infinity pool, not seeing the blissful ocean.

'That wouldn't happen,' says Dan fiercely. 'She needs me.'

Rose cheers inwardly. Dan has reached the important point.

'What way does she need you?'

'Every way,' he says, confused. 'She calls me first thing every morning and tells me what her day's going to be like. I sort out her bills, do her taxes. She's funny about accountants.' He smiles. 'I get her car serviced, fix things around the house for her and Miriam. We have dinner once a week.'

Rose interrupts.

'This sounds like a very one-sided relationship, one in which your needs are not being met. You're afraid of Julia leaving you and you do everything to prevent that. Essentially, you sacrifice yourself to make sure Julia's needs are met, don't you think?'

He's shaking his head.

Rose changes tack, throws in the final important point:

'I want you to think about something, Dan: we can't control other people. Julia is an independent person; she's not your child to be taken care of. She makes her own choices and your choices are based wholly around what she does.

'Your fear of her leaving you is entirely rooted in how you feel about yourself. Do you feel that Julia saved you from something?'

Daniel is the second tallest boy in lower sixth in St Anselm's. The tallest is Willem, who's half Dutch, home of the tallest people in the world.

Willem and Daniel tie for top marks in all the science subjects in their year. Willem is also doing Dutch in European Languages, which he admits is a bit of a fudge, but hey – it's an easy A-level for him.

'Why do you not take French as an extra subject?' Willem asks him. 'Think how good that will look on your CV. All the sciences and French.'

Daniel's stepfather is French but he so rarely speaks to Daniel that there's no way they could manage the conversation to precede actual French lessons.

'Don't want to,' he says to Willem.

He doesn't bother to explain that his actual father lives in Switzerland, with a Belgian girlfriend. Willem doesn't ask anything else about the French thing – he's a very easy friend. Willem's family also move around the world a lot, so he's used to the life Daniel leads: where endlessly ex-pat families, new half-siblings and lots of step-everythings translate into a person becoming very self-sufficient.

'What do you think of the new girls?' Willem asks Daniel.

They're walking across the square to the magnificently appointed science wing, which is certainly one of the reasons why St Anselm's is one of the top-rated public schools in the UK.

The school famously takes a cohort of girl students for A-levels, meaning an influx of girls into lower sixth in a way that focuses the minds of the male students in both the upper and lower sixths. The school is also excellent at preparing students for the Oxbridge exams.

'Haven't noticed the new girls,' Daniel jokes.

Willem laughs and gently punches his friend in the arm.

'Liar. That tall blonde one likes you. The one with the legs, the lips and the Essex-girl accent. You should ask her out.'

'Rubbish, Willem, none of them are looking at me,' says Daniel, which isn't entirely true.

He knows exactly which girl Willem means. Julia.

He's heard her name being called, the way popular people are always being called.

'Julia, look over here, Julia, Julia . . .'

She's their age, almost as tall and has spectacular long legs. She doesn't attempt to hide them in her first weekend outfit of appallingly sexy black leggings worn with a long grey and pink striped cardigan and knee-high suede boots. Pupils can wear non-uniform clothes on Saturdays and Sundays.

The boys wear sweatshirts and chinos. Few boys notice what their male friends are wearing. But at least ninety per cent of St Anselm's boys notice the girls' clothes: hip-hugging jeans, swinging skirts, sweaters that cling to narrow waists and pert breasts.

Daniel has stared at Julia surreptitiously many times: her face is oval and her eyes are widely spaced like a fawn's, only fawns don't use eyeliner and mascara to emphasise eyes the violet blue of a precious gem.

The colour of tanzanite, Daniel thinks. He loves geology.

On Monday, Julia turns up in biology class with her grey uniform skirt turned up to mini-skirt level, a lesson in ingenuity given that it has many pleats.

Looking carefully, Daniel thinks she might have stapled the hem.

'You're a distraction, Miss Chance,' announces Mr Carter, who is known for preferring girl students in the blue-stocking dress of eighty years ago. In other words: glasses, an earnest manner and a traditional uniform that would not shock his mother. 'Kindly leave and come back to us when you are wearing garments in a manner fitting this laboratory.'

Julia smiles minxily, says nothing and collects her things.

The entire biology class is watching her, hips swaying as she leaves the classroom.

One eye, flicked up with painted-on liner and half hidden by strands of silky pale-gold hair, winks at Daniel as she leaves.

'Sir?' Daniel stands up.

This is code for heading to the lavatory.

Mr Carter nods and goes back to his slides about cell structure.

Daniel slides his books from his desk and into his rucksack, leaves the room and heads right, following Julia.

He breaks into a half-run and catches up with her.

'You OK?' he asks, which is probably the most he's ever spoken to any girl since reaching puberty.

'Sweet Dan, coming to get me,' she says, her face breaking into that exquisite smile.

Her full lips are pink and faintly glittery as if she's found lipstick the fairies make.

Her eyes – Daniel has never understood how the

Romantic poets could fall into women's eyes till now but, suddenly, he gets it.

He's part of her, melded to her: she has power over him with her mystery and her beauty.

'I'm going onto the roof to smoke,' she says, and his eyes can't move from those pillowy lips. 'Want to come?'

'Yes,' he says instantly. She wants to spend time with him!

Daniel doesn't smoke but sits in the September sun on a piece of flat roof on top of the girls' rooms. It's hard to know which is more forbidden.

Leaving a class for no good reason, being above the girls' rooms – strictly out of bounds for any male student, being with someone who's smoking long dark-coloured skinny cigarettes which give off a strange, almost cinnamon scent amid the tang of nicotine. Julia lies back on the roof, letting the sun heat her body, school bag discarded and her sheet of blonde hair splayed out around her.

'C'mere,' she says, patting the roof beside her. 'I don't bite.'

She talks differently to most of the students in the school. This difference is fascinating to Dan. He'd never have had the nerve to stalk out of Carter's class.

She pats the roof again.

'I'm sure you don't bite,' he replies, startled at his own savoir faire in this situation. He shoves away his rucksack which contains the essay he has to hand in at physics class inside it. Physics is next but there is no way Daniel is going to make it.

Not now. Not when he can be doing this.

'I've been watching you,' Julia says, offering him her cigarette.

Daniel shakes his head and watches her face, studying it. Willem has said that Julia likes him, but Willem was joking, surely? She's even more beautiful when she's lying down, like a Renaissance painting of a girl lounging on a couch, a knowing look in her violet blue eyes.

'How can I kiss you if you're not smoking too? I won't taste nice, will I?' Julia says with a hint of petulance, a smile still dancing over her lips.

Daniel's transfixed by her lips. Pillowy, sheeny with a full lower lip. Her lips look as if they'll taste of strawberries.

Can he kiss her? Does she want that?

He's never kissed anyone, never thought that anyone would want to kiss him.

He's one of the serious science boys at school, never on the top teams, likes running but the team sports leave him cold. Plus, he wants to hold on to his brain cells and not have them bashed out on the rugby field.

Jarvis in his year is six months younger, hopeless at lessons but captain of one of the A rugby teams. Jarvis has had girlfriends since second year, has a sister at Wycombe Abbey and has cut a swathe through the girls in her year. Daniel's sister, Vicky, is much younger than he is, currently abroad with his mother and stepfather, and her friends are other sweet nine-year-olds.

'Would you like to kiss me?' Julia asks.

Smart scientist boys don't get girls like this, thinks Daniel, but he ignores all the old messages in his head.

There's new data in and it's good.

He takes her cigarette, takes a drag and, somehow, manages not to cough.

'Are we even now?' he asks, wondering what part of his brain is managing these James Bond-type answers.

'Even,' murmurs Julia.

Daniel leans down, puts a very gentle hand behind Julia's beautiful head and presses his lips to hers.

Instantly, her small tongue snakes its way into his mouth and it's the most erotic thing Daniel has ever felt.

His insides swoop with excitement.

He loves this girl, this exquisite creature.

He lies down beside her, cradling her head in both hands now so she won't get hurt on the rough cement of the roof, and kisses her as though both their lives depend upon it. She is a precious princess and he must take care of her.

Right now is the most glorious moment of his life. He wants to say he loves her but how can he, this quickly? Yet she *sees* him, sees exactly who Daniel is, he can tell. And she still wants him, wants to kiss him.

Daniel hopes they can go on kissing for ever, hopes she'll be with him for ever. Nothing in his life has ever felt like this before. They're destined for each other.

Chapter Eleven

'Romantic,' sighs India, turning automatically to Keera, 'and yet I can see Rose's point. Dan is totally wound up in taking care of Julia. Rose didn't say co-dependent but it's hanging there, right?'

Keera watches Dan striding off in the direction of the steps down to the terrace below.

'Apart from that, it's like a storybook romance,' India goes on, 'meeting at school and staying together.'

Rose has left the terrace after commanding that the group cook and serve dinner this evening. Before that, the afternoon session will be at three.

But Bernard is grizzling about having to do anything as menial as cooking.

'I don't cook,' he's storming now, 'I get things cooked for me!'

'Darlink, it will be fine, I will do it,' Grazia's replying, which makes India and Keera look at each other and begin to laugh.

Relief at getting through the first bit makes them giggly.

'Rose isn't going to like that,' India says. 'I can't see Bernard getting out of cooking.'

There's only the four of them left on the terrace – Dianne practically ran back into the hotel.

'I can't cook,' says Keera, shrugging. 'I can reheat pizza, that's, like, it.'

'I can make pasta pesto if I have enough basil, but you need a lot of it. I can do hummus too and a veggie bol,' India says, grinning. 'That's pretty much it. Go to the beach with me?' she asks, standing up and stretching her back with her arms in the air. 'There's bound to be a sea breeze down there.'

She arches her spine just enough to feel her achy lower back loosen up.

'I'd love to go to the beach,' Keera agrees. 'I'll just dump my stuff back.'

'Me too. I need a hat and more sun cream,' India says, looking at her faintly golden skin.

'I need sun cream too,' says Keera. 'Or I'll be red as a lobster.'

Ten minutes later, they're both staring at the prettily hand-drawn map of the villa and its environs, and walking down the small, dusty road that leads to the beach.

'It is not like Palaiokastritsa down the coast,' Christos explained when he gave them the map. 'There are pebbles as well as sand. You need good sandals. The water is very clean if you want to swim. Do not stray too far off the beach, ladies. People get lost around here. They walk, forget water and sunhats, and overheat. Promise you will stay on the path?'

They promised.

'This morning was pretty intense,' says India when they've walked past the low curved stone wall that signifies the entrance to another villa, and then followed the car-free curve of the road. The road's bordered to the right by a field containing goats who watch them with interest, strange yellow eyes narrowed.

India trails her hand along the lavender bushes edging the goats' field.

'Yeah, it was intense,' says Keera. 'I've done rehab so it's not unfamiliar territory.'

'You look too young for rehab.'

'You're never too young,' jokes Keera lightly.

'This might sound silly, but I'm beginning to feel like a bit of an interloper,' India says awkwardly. 'You've obvs got rehab stuff. Dan has his girlfriend attempting suicide. Bernard and Grazia must have something that's a very big deal because there are two of them here. I've no idea what Dianne's thing is – and me: I've got nothing much to talk about compared to that.'

'Don't believe you,' says Keera easily. 'We've all got stuff.'

'Not big stuff, though,' India protests. 'My stuff's all ordinary.'

'I bet it's not. Why did you come?'

India grimaces. 'It really sounds lame. I've been so blessed all my life, I have lovely parents – not that they're together. I adore my stepmother . . . None of this is enough for me to be here. I loved *The Talisman Effect* when I was young. Rose is so cool, isn't she? She looks totally different than from on TV, though. I like the hippie vibe – it suits her. The long silvery hair, cool.'

'Very cool,' agrees Keera.

'I love that she can listen to you and ask the right questions,' India goes on. 'I guess I thought she could sort my life out.'

'You see?' Keera says. 'You do have stuff. What needs sorting out?'

'Normal stuff . . .' India says hopelessly. 'Nothing big. I have this problem with guys – I meet them, we hook up and just when I think it's for ever, they leave. I haven't dated anyone longer than six weeks in, like, two years. I wonder if there's something wrong with me.'

'That's stuff,' Keera points out.

'I suppose.' India's silent.

'I've realised that I don't want to leave it too late to have a child.'

Saying it is a rush. The words are out there.

She's half-waiting for Keera to say: *How can you look after a child, you don't know what you want to do with the rest of your life, never mind take care of a baby?*

She rushes in to correct herself: 'I mean, it's OK if you don't and I'm not making the point that all women should have children because, obviously, it's a deeply personal thing—'

'It's OK,' says Keera. 'Your wanting a child doesn't upset me. You do you and I'll do me. I don't see me wanting kids because I'm not sure I want to pass these genes on.'

She grimaces.

'I've got to say that I'm not in a maternal phase right now – but who knows. Thing is: you *do* want a baby.'

'Yes.' India sighs a huge heartfelt sigh. 'If you did rehab, why are you here? Sorry if that's too personal,' India adds.

'It's life and family stuff,' Keera says quickly. India gets the impression that she doesn't want to scare her off.

They walk on in silence.

As they reach the craggy path down to the beach, the vast, shimmering Ionian Sea is splayed out in front of them: infinite, mysterious.

In the distance, there's a sea haze floating over the blue.

Beneath the gentle waves, there's an unknowable kingdom filled with coral, seaweeds, mysterious fish, big and small.

Both women gaze at it.

The sea has been here for millennia, seeing problems, worries, women's tears falling onto this beach.

And then suddenly, those same women are gone, and the next generation and the next come along. The thought of it was making the two women standing on the shore feel their insignificance beside this huge part of their planet. That their current worries were puny things in the huge scheme of the ancient and modern worlds.

'It's so beautiful,' sighs India, taking off her sandals and delicately walking across the flat rocks that lead to the sand and pebbles lining what Christos had called the Kri Kri beach.

'It means a type of wild goat,' he had said. 'We don't have this goat any more in Corfu, only in Crete and the smaller islands. They are very beautiful but wild, very wild.'

India loves the feeling of the sand and the pebbles on her feet. She feels connected to the earth.

She's a part of the universe here – not simply a cog in a wheel, a lonely cog. Everyone has someone: her father has Georgie, her mother has Magnús, her rockstar boyfriend.

India has nobody.

Nobody actually cares where she is right now, and that hurts. She is fundamentally alone.

Tears fill her eyes, which she knows is a ludicrous reaction. She has so much! She's here on a glorious beach just below a glorious retreat, and she's crying!

Sobbing.

Keera puts an arm around India and squeezes.

'Thank you,' mutters India.

She wipes her cheeks with her arm but the tears keep flowing.

Blast Rose and her opening people up.

India doesn't want to be opened up. It hurts.

She's not even on the rack on the terrace and, already, she feels split open.

'I thought this was supposed to help,' she says to Keera, indistinctly now because of the tears.

'It will, honestly,' says Keera. 'I did it in rehab and it helped so much.'

'Why are you here now if rehab worked so well?' India asks.

'Rehab deals with addiction and once you get out and you're clean and sober, you realise all the other stuff that's wrong in your life. *That's* what I need to sort,' Keera says wryly.

They've reached the start of the beach proper and there's a walkway through the rocks to the pebbled beach below.

Still holding on to the crying India with one arm, Keera guides them over the pebbles to a part of the beach where someone's made a giant circle of pebbles on the sand.

'Thought it wasn't supposed to be a classic sandy beach,' sniffs India, because this side is just that.

'Christos was probably just warning us that there's pebbly bits too in case we sue him for breach of contract,' says Keera, laughing. 'The contrast is cool,' she adds. Then she laughs. 'It's the two sides of therapy seen as a beach: sandy stretches but also lots of big rocks to climb over.'

They both laugh and India rubs her eyes with her hand again, the tears finally drying up.

'I'm a mess,' she says and collapses cross-legged onto the warm sand.

'You're a work in progress,' Keera says, shrugging, sitting down on the sand too and pulling her knees up so that her hands are clasped around them.

India's gazing blankly out at the sea.

'I've been reading this saying online,' she says to Keera. '*The heart wants what the heart wants,* and I think, is that true? Or is it a stupid saying?'

'You seem to have a lot on your mind,' says Keera kindly, 'and the whole *The heart wants* . . . stuff . . . I can honestly say that's total garbage,' she adds.

'Really?' asks India, appalled.

'Yeah. The heart is a totally impractical organ and has the emotional intelligence of a banana.'

India laughs at this.

Keera continues: 'The badly hurt part of us, call it Trauma Central: *that* wants what it wants, which is usually some hurtful scenario to replicate our past.'

India's mouth is an oval.

'Trauma Central feels comfortable when our lives are shitshows or when we recreate past relationships with drugs or alcohol or guys,' Keera goes on. 'So the intelligent bits of us are dialled down to almost nothing while Trauma Central makes all these senseless decisions. *That*,' she finishes emphatically, 'is what the whole *The heart wants* . . . schtick is about. Good on Instagram but not in life.'

India sighs gloomily. 'It did sound too good to be true,' she says. 'You won't say anything?' asks India, feeling stupid, which she so often feels.

'What's said on location, stays on location, right?' replies Keera.

'Thank you,' India says gratefully. 'Do you think Rose gives out prizes at the end?'

'We're going to be happier and understand ourselves better,' Keera says. 'That's the prize. She can be fairly brutal, though. I'd forgotten that. I didn't expect it to be so hardcore so early.'

'I know, right?' agreed India. 'Poor Dan. All that stuff about him doing everything for Julia in case she leaves him.'

'That's very on point in rehab world, I can tell you,' Keera says with a hint of gloom. 'On family day in rehab, it can be carnage.' She shudders at the memory. The *pain* in the room. Her mother hadn't come. Very Bobbi.

India nods slowly.

'There's a lot of self-discovery,' Keera continues. 'If you can't be honest with yourself, you might as well not bother being there.'

'What were you in for?' says India. She'd never normally ask twice but, now, it feels OK. She feels as if she and Keera have a bond.

'Coke, prescription drugs and alcohol. Mainly the drugs. Xanax to lower anxiety during the day, lorazepam at night, Ritalin and dexies to bring me up. Sleeping tablets because I couldn't sleep . . . all washed down with a cocktail or six. Coke, too. I loved coke. I'd be lying if I said it was easy. I have to feel my feelings now and that sucks,' Keera says. '*Really* sucks.'

She strings out the word *Really*.

'If I'm anxious, I have to stay anxious until it passes. No tablets, not even a tiny glass of wine. It's tough.'

'That sounds like hell,' says India, 'but the right thing if you needed it. My mother's partner is in a band and he had a problem with drugs. Not any more, though.'

Now Magnús meditates and does Iron Man competitions. On the beach with her mum, he looked like a medical school's illustration of the body's main muscle groups with his tanned skin stretched painfully tightly over them all.

'Not wishing to embarrass, but you are the singer from the kids' channel, right? That's a wig?'

Keera nods and puts a hand up to adjust it.

'I should have dyed my hair instead. Wigs are very hot.'

'You've black hair, right? We could dye it,' says India helpfully. 'That's something I'm really good at. I bet we could get some quality hair dye around here. So many Greek women have black hair, so I bet the bleach is stupendously strong. With hair as black as yours, it needs to be strong.'

Keera peers around the beach to make doubly sure they're the only ones there. Evidently everyone else in this part of Xanthe is sitting by a pool or having lunch.

She pulls her blonde hair back in one swift move and India gasps.

Keera's perfectly shaped head is shaved down to the skin, only a bare millimetre of dark stubble covers her skull.

'Whoa,' says India. 'It looks fabulous, have to say it.'

Keera shrieks with laughter.

'I love it too!' she says, rubbing her almost-bald head.

'Can I feel?'

Keera bends her head and India touches the exquisite skull with its covering of soft fuzz.

'It's gorgeous!'

'Feels freeing,' Keera shrugs. 'I buzz cut it every few days. Of course, I know my mom will hate it!'

She instantly wishes she hadn't said that. She can't talk about her mother yet. Not even with India, who feels like a kindred spirit.

But India says nothing about Keera's mom. Instead, she says: 'Maybe worrying about other people is the problem. If your mom hates your hair, well, it's not *her* hair, is it?'

Keera giggles.

'I worry what people think,' India confides. 'All the people in my family are successful except me – I want to make them proud of me but I don't know how. Possibly, I shouldn't even try.'

'What do you do?' asks Keera.

India grimaces. 'I've sold clothes in posh boutiques, tried being an influencer, worked for an events management company – mainly jobs I got into because of my stepmum's connections. Georgie, she's so lovely. More like a mum to me than my real mum,' India says, and feels a jolt.

She's never thought of that before. But Georgie has the lightest touch and helps India in so many ways. Her mother lives a different life and left India with her father because floating around the world going to rock concerts wasn't the ideal life for a ten-year-old.

'OK, so you're on the island to figure out what to do with your life, right?'

'Not just jobs but a career, something I love,' India puts in.

'And to figure out if you can have a child on your own . . .'

'Yes!' cheers India delightedly. 'I could, couldn't I? I mean, who says I need a man? I am bad with men. I fall in love *so* easily.'

India shudders thinking of how she'd see a guy for two, maybe three weeks and start planning a future. Was that her truth . . .?

'We all worry about what people think, India. Plus, you're not killing people or taking meth,' says Keera, 'so I wouldn't call falling in love too easily a huge problem. Rose can figure it out, I'm sure. Give you a prospective boyfriend checklist and if they're dreadful on paper, you don't go out with them.'

India laughs delightedly.

'You can watch out for red flags, yellow flags or green

flags,' Keera says. 'Red means avoid at all costs, yellow means watch out and green is "Yay!"'

'I have definitely gone out with some yellow flag guys,' says India. 'A few self-absorbed idiots.'

'Dan and his girlfriend's relationship sounds like a yellow flag racing towards red,' Keera says. 'I wonder what the other three are in for?'

'For Grazia, I'd say being married to Bernard's the main issue,' India jokes.

'She looks as if she's locked down all emotion.'

'Bernard's tricky. Telling us he's a *sir*? What's that about?'

'No idea what his problem is, apart from getting old and there's no cure for that,' Keera says. 'Dianne holds her cards close to her chest, as my mom would say,' she adds.

'She's sort of frozen,' India says thoughtfully, 'but furious at the same time? Scary too when she got angry with Dan. She clearly doesn't think there's anything wrong with her.'

Keera snorts.

'Everyone has something wrong with them. Everyone.'

'Do you think Rose can fix us?' asks India wistfully. 'I'd love to feel I know what I'm doing in life.'

Keera shrugs. 'Don't know. Rose's book was amazing and she has all these fans who say she's changed their lives. It's just . . .'

'A bit high speed?' says India. 'That's what worries me too. Rose is going in deep – what if it's the sort of programme that rips you apart in a week and then doesn't put you back together?'

Keera shivers.

'Rose is legit,' she says. 'She was brilliant on the TV.'

'Yeah,' agrees India. 'She wouldn't do that to us.'

They're silent for a while.

'Maybe after this, we'll be ready to live in nature,' Keera says suddenly, grinning. 'We could live in a commune in the middle of nowhere with a shaman and some sheep. We could make our own soft cheese and wear only clothes we've made from their wool.'

'Can we have alpacas? I like alpacas,' says India.

'We'd have to have dogs,' says Keera. 'And those big cats that look like baby lions – Maine Coons. I bet they're very cuddly. Or the ones with no fur at all. Naked cats. Sphinxes. Someone could make them little sweaters. Not us, obviously. I can't knit. Can you?'

'No!' says India, laughing.

They both stare out at the shimmering Ionian Sea.

'No matter what Rose does, it's got to help,' Keera says. 'I do like her. She's got something really kind about her. She wouldn't hurt us. But she looks so different now than she looked on TV.'

'Right,' agrees India. 'She was very lady CEO on *The Talisman Effect* but now she's sort of hippie-ish. It's cool though, right?'

'She can totally carry it off,' Keera says. 'Suits her better, to be honest. I like the floaty clothes and the hair . . .'

'Yeah, the hair!' says India. 'Silver really suits her. She looks beautiful but I would never have recognised her if I hadn't heard her voice.'

'Wouldn't it be lovely if we could lock ourselves in a room with Rose and get the high-speed fixing done on us first and then we can sunbathe the rest of the week while the rest of them get sorted.'

'I like that plan!'

They look at each other and laugh again.

*

My mother loved him. Adored him. When I brought him home that first time, it was as if I'd found a prince among men.

'I'm so delighted to meet you,' he said, practically bowing to her. He took her hand and kissed it and my mother adored that.

Who the hell kisses hands? Nobody, that's who.

Except for people like him, people who instinctively know which buttons to press. Even with my mother who was the supreme button-pusher.

'It's so lovely to meet you. Finally,' my mother said in her phone voice, which was a bit pretend-posh to make our family seem better than it was. The dig about her finally meeting him was very her. Always a dig. A little bit of poison on the knife.

'I can see where your daughter gets her good looks,' he said, beaming at her.

She was beaming right back. Preening. Glad she'd worn lipstick and her frosted eyeshadow. She'd put in her overnight hair rollers too. A lot of work for a man.

'Oh stop,' she said, and she actually patted his arm with the hand that wasn't holding her half-smoked cigarette.

My mother was not a toucher.

Affection was weaponised in our house.

Smiles and, sometimes, hugs in public. No real affection.

I should have let them have each other. Not that it would have lasted. Two raging narcissists.

Of course, I didn't know what they were then.

I was naive.

THE ISLAND RETREAT

There were four-year-olds out there with more awareness than I had.

I thought I was seeing my new man being happy to meet my mother, and I thought she was glad I had found someone to love me. I was so wrong.

Chapter Twelve

Dianne pulls off her trainers as soon as she gets back to her room. She wants to find her thongs so her feet can breathe.

She wants a cold shower and she's not, absolutely not, going to write anything in the stupid notebook Rose left in each of the rooms.

'Write down why you are here,' Rose had said. 'You don't need to share this journal with anyone but journaling can be a very powerful tool in helping you understand who you are and why you get stuck in certain situations. If you write truthfully, you will see themes reappear.'

Rose had paused then and looked at them all, as if working out who would do their notebook homework and who wouldn't.

Dianne had looked at skinny little India almost leaping out of her chair with the enthusiasm to say: *I'll do it!*

Poor kid. *She has no idea*, Dianne thought, *no idea at all.*

'You don't have to write anything,' Rose had gone on, looking at them all, and in particular Dianne.

She knows I won't do it, Dianne had thought with satisfaction.

'But if you don't, you are cheating yourself out of a hugely important part of the therapy journey. Self-reflection.'

Self-reflection, my backside, Dianne had wanted to say.

She's impressed with Rose, in spite of her initial feelings.

Rose looks totally different from the woman with the US TV show. More natural, not the curated version with manicured nails and power suits.

But not wearing a suit hasn't dimmed her personality, Dianne thinks.

If anything, Rose in real life is more powerful than the besuited woman with the perfect hair.

Dianne picks up the notebook. It's small, handmade, she thinks, and it's coloured yellow, the colour of the sunflowers she used to grow in the garden.

Thinking of her garden at home makes the breath leave her body as if she's been punched in the solar plexus.

Holding the notebook, she goes onto the balcony, sits on one of the wooden loungers and stares out at the breathtaking view.

The oddest thing has happened since she's been on Corfu.

She'd felt some of the anger leave her when she got into the taxi at the airport and drove through the island, through great forests and swathes of olive trees, with tantalising views of the sea backlit by an apricot evening sky.

Despite herself, she'd felt an unusual sense of peace.

Dianne thinks that feeling calm is risky.

Anything can happen when you're calm, happy, relaxed.

She wants rage firing through her veins, making her ready. Because she needs to be ready.

Dianne can't explain to anyone, least of all a former TV guru, how she feels when the rage is searing through her.

It gives her power.

Of course, Rose hasn't a clue what Dianne's life has been like and Dianne's not going to tell her, either.

You can prise my story out of my cold, dead hands.

Her knees hurt as she gets up from the balcony seat and goes inside.

Lately, her body's been aching more than usual. Her knees, her hands, something weird in her lower back. Not that she'll go to the doctor about it.

Dianne has steered clear of doctors for a long time.

She pours herself a glass of water from the bottle in the fridge, feeling the heft of the rustic blue glass in her hand.

'Cheers, Dianne,' she says aloud.

Once, she'd have loved this place.

When she was in her early twenties, she'd have been so thrilled to be here, delighting in the skin and shower products in the bathroom, scented variously with rose, bergamot, geranium and juniper. She can almost see her young self, when she had long dark hair, slender hips and a smile, dancing into the room, opening every drawer, examining every piece of thoughtful luxury, saying: 'Isn't this amazing!'

But who was she talking to in this imaginary moment?

Not her mother, not her one-time best girlfriend Larissa, who'd moved to the Northern Territories with work. Not Lauren or Ellie, her beautiful daughters. Or her sweet son, Toby, who was adored by everyone.

She loved them so much, tried to protect them.

Had tried.

Dianne feels her breath slide into shallowness.

Just like that, the rage is back. Fierce, dangerous.

Excellent.

Rage is the way forward.

It's her friend.

She takes her water onto the balcony and picks up the little notebook again.

A pretty thing.

Sweet. But not for her.

Dianne picks it up and throws it as far off the balcony as her arm can manage.

She can't see where it lands. Probably in the garden. Maybe in the pool? Who knows? She doesn't care. Her secrets are her own.

Chapter Thirteen

Rose has spent the past fifteen minutes lying on her bed fanning herself with a magazine. She's still running on cortisol and the crazy nervous energy that comes from running a successful group session.

Villa Artemis has air-conditioning but, right now, she's fanning herself. If she wasn't off grid, she might see a doctor and get her hormones tested. She's fifty-three, surely somewhere in the warzone that is the peri- or menopausal crisis?

Right now she craves cool and a bar of dark chocolate, in that order.

When she hears the distant noise of dishes rattling, she knows it's time to get up.

Rose pats her face with a hand towel in the bathroom and glugs down a huge glass of bottled water.

Adriana had warned her to drink lots when she first moved here five years ago.

'I'm used to the heat here in September but for tourists, it's still too hot. The only answer is to drink lots of water. Heat stroke is for people from colder places who don't behave appropriately in Greece.'

Rose leaves her room and steps down the marble back stairs to the kitchen, which is built into the mountain and thus is blissfully cool, despite both Christos and Adriana doing things involving the oven.

Lunch today is simple mezes: juicy Kalamata olives; a crisp Greek salad in a turquoise porcelain bowl; tomatoes the size of cooking apples glistening on matching turquoise plates and drizzled with olive oil; bowls of hummus, taramasalata and tzatziki sitting in handmade bowls with homemade pitta bread warm beside them.

Beata is not around – she's worked the morning shift and this evening Christos and Adriana will be on call.

Christos is having second thoughts about Rose's plan for the group to cook dinner tonight. Rose insists that it will shake the group up a bit and encourage them to talk to each other.

'I don't want anyone in my kitchen,' Christos is saying mulishly to Adriana.

He doesn't understand this part of Rose's therapy.

Adriana, small and dark, tiny beside her economy-sized husband, hugs him comfortingly.

'It's part of Rose's system,' she says, patient as ever. 'We talked it all through.'

'I'm not comfortable with it,' he says. 'They won't clean up properly. We will have ants!'

Christos has a constant battle with Greek insect life.

Ants are enemy number one: once they get in, they take over. With opposable thumbs, ants could rule the world.

'The group will clean up.' Rose is firm. 'I need them talking to each other, doing simple things.'

'Huh,' snorts Christos. 'Cleaning this kitchen is not simple. It's vital. Besides, I do not see any natural cooks among them. That Grazia woman has servants, I can tell.

The Australian woman knows work, her hands show that. But Grazia! If her husband died, I bet she would cut him up and cook him. Husband fritters.'

'Dis-gusting,' says Adriana, laughing.

'You've nearly put me off lunch,' says Rose, grimacing, but she takes up a plate and fills it just the same. 'Don't diss the guests, Christos. They're all in crisis. I'll monitor them tonight. The place will be spotless, I promise.'

'Sorry,' says Christos humbly. 'I didn't mean to be rude about the people – they are here for our help.'

'It's OK,' Rose says gently. 'We're all adjusting to this. It's our first try at a retreat. We all grizzle a bit and we all have things we're concerned about. Your kitchen is important to you. No harm done, Christos.'

She takes the plate back to her room and sits at the table where all her notes about the group are laid out.

India and Keera have paired up: that's excellent.

Rose feels that Keera is missing out on normal friendships. Rose has the sense that, despite Keera's seemingly starry existence, her personal life is bare.

Rose cannot put a word on the feeling she gets about people's inner lives: it's ephemeral but always crystal clear.

Someone once called it magical.

Someone she loved.

Theo.

Rose closes her eyes and vehemently wishes she didn't keep going back to thinking about Theo.

How often has she told people that there's no going back, only healing the past and going forward?

But the call of the past is insistent.

She allows herself a moment of quiet and reaches into the pocket of her flowing dress to take out the small piece of turquoise Theo once gave her.

It's a piece from the Sleeping Beauty mines in Arizona, old and glowing.

She carries it everywhere with her, holding its smooth curved shape until it grows warm from her palm. It's like holding onto a little bit of Theo.

'Miss you,' she breathes, every one of her senses remembering.

Soft kisses on her neck. The safety of being with him. Warmth, acceptance, his laugh, his shaggy dark mane of hair tickling her skin. How he swept her off her feet when the snow was deep and she got stuck on the way back to the cabin when they stayed in Lake Tahoe.

'My boots!' she'd cried, laughing as he crashed through the snow and he adjusted her body against his, angling to get the cabin door open.

'I'll get them,' he said, once he'd put her safely on the floor.

The cabin was so warm, had a real fire with crackling logs. It was an escape from real life, a glorious bolthole. Theo was so kind to her, nurtured her in a way she'd never experienced before. The kindness was startling in its newness—

Rose lets go of the turquoise as if it has burned her and it falls back into her pocket. She returns to her files, wiping her eyes.

There's no point wallowing in what might have been. If she was advising herself, she'd allow a little wallowing but Rose Talisman does not allow *herself* to sink into any form of self-pity. The past is the past.

Shit happens. Pain heals. Yadda yadda.

It's over.

Work will heal her.

Rose stares with blurry eyes at her notes about the group.

When she'd had a private practice a long time ago, she was often amazed that patients thought she had her life totally sorted.

As if being the one sitting straight in the therapist's chair meant that you had a perfect life.

But therapists have to have therapists too – someone to talk to when drama shakes their lives. Hers was Vida, a woman so wise that Rose was convinced that Vida could have no issues in her personal life.

'Always with the jokes!' Vida said in amusement the first time Rose said this to her.

People's lives are always works in progress.

'Focus,' Rose tells herself now. 'If work is going to heal you, you have to actually do it.'

Chapter Fourteen

India's first back on the terrace after lunch, holding a small cup of Greek coffee which contains what tastes like a metric tonne of caffeine from Mount Double Espresso itself.

The day is almost too sweltering for a hot drink but India's aware that such intense concentration from the morning and the walk to the beach in full sun has tired her out.

It was gorgeous to walk with Keera. India feels as if she's found a friend, and their conversation made India feel as if she has a right to be here.

Rose can help her, and India will take any help with open arms.

She's swapped her pretty swirling chiffon dress for a pink spaghetti-strapped cotton dress she packed as an emergency outfit. The cotton dress is much cooler and the only item of clothing in her two suitcases that's suitable for the Greek heat.

She'll have to shop, which is no bother. India loves to shop. She manages her love of clothes by selling on things she's grown tired of and looking in vintage shops for bargains.

'You've got an eye, India,' Georgie says, but India's sure her stepmother's just being nice to her.

In the distance, India can see Rose talking to the couple who run the villa.

Rose's dress is flowy and relaxed: a bit psychedelic for India's taste, but Rose can pull it off.

Rose is tall too, tall and regal as hell with that long, curling silvery-grey hair, the tanned skin, and those eyes, like a wild sea creature's blue irises with her pupils outlined in a darker blue, like lapis.

Please Rose, don't pick on me. Not yet, India thinks as she finds her chair and sets up her pretty notebook in front of her.

Maybe she can put Rose off for today.

Give herself some leeway before it's her turn to be autopsied.

Where is everyone else? India finishes her coffee and watches a white cat slowly descend the stone steps from the raised lavender garden, its feline body undulating.

Even though India reaches down and calls it, the cat does not come to her and she sighs and relaxes back in her chair again.

She'd love a cat. She'd love—

Oh, what does it matter? She can't have *any* of the things she really craves.

She's just an idiot who can't *do* life.

She feels like crying again. She cried so much on the beach that her eyes are still puffy. It's like simply being here has broken some wall inside her and let all her feelings come out.

Doodling a bit on her pretty notebook, she's well aware that simple stuff like pretty notebooks make her happy.

Also, neat clear pencil cases for her handbag where coloured pens can sit brightly, all organised.

And make-up. She loves make-up and beauty products. Would spend vast sums of money on them if she allowed herself to.

Does that make her shallow?

Should she only be happy when there's world peace?

India never thought she was shallow before.

To banish these annoying thoughts, she lies back in her chair and lets the heat wash over her, the sound of crickets making their strangely rhythmic noise, and she drifts into dreams.

Dan wakes India up by taking the chair beside her again.

'Hi,' he says.

'Shi— Sorry.'

India rapidly sits up in her chair, entirely discomfited. Was she asleep? Those damn crickets or cicadas or whatever made her sleepy with twinging their little legs. Their constant drone is much better at curing insomnia than counting sheep.

The heat makes her sleepy too.

The sun's high in the sky, glittering off the azure pool, bouncing into her face.

'I must have dozed off,' she mutters to Dan.

She realises that everyone else in the group is trailing in.

Sir Bernard is a bit red-faced and has obviously been sunbathing. Grazia is the same caramel colour as ever.

To India's astonishment, Grazia smiles at her.

India lets her fingers flutter a *Hello*.

She feels guilty for bitching about the older woman now. Who the hell is she to make random judgements of other people? A woman too. So much for being loyal to the sisterhood.

Sweat breaks out on India's face.

'You OK?' asks Dan, passing both a glass and a blue ceramic jar of water to her.

'Yes. No – I don't know,' she whispers back.

Rose has arrived.

The group has loosened up, Rose sees.

India was half asleep in the sun.

Dan was comfortable enough to wake her up, which says he noticed that she patted his arm during his painful storytelling.

'Everyone ready?' she calls.

Keera's adjusting her baseball hat and settling herself in on the other side of India.

Sir Bernard and Grazia are settled comfortably in their chairs, while Dianne slips into the empty chair beside Grazia. Dianne wears a sort of half-smiling mask that's polite and nothing more.

What is *Dianne's secret?* thinks Rose.

She's bottling something up and Rose thinks that when Dianne finally gets to tell her story, it will rage out of her like a tornado.

'I trust you all had a lovely lunch and a walk on the beach,' she says to the group.

Everyone nods and Grazia surprises her by saying: 'It is a pretty beach. We have travelled a lot but I have never been here before.'

Rose smiles. She loves people being relaxed enough to talk without being asked questions.

'Corfu is very beautiful,' she agrees, 'and one of the marvellous things about having our sessions here is that being somewhere totally different allows us to escape our real lives. It's a version of lying on the couch in traditional analytical therapy where you're staring up at the ceiling with your therapist sitting out of sight. Being in a different location works in the same way. You're here with your fellow . . .'

She pauses. What can she call them?

'Seekers of Truth,' suggests Keera suddenly and everyone laughs.

Rose beams at her.

'Brilliant name,' says Rose. 'Now, before this session, I want us all to breathe deeply the way we did this morning. I want you to get in touch with your bodies, settle yourselves. Think about how you feel.'

A few eyes open widely.

Feeling?

'Breathe in slowly. Become aware of how deeply you're breathing: if your breath comes from your chest or your belly . . .'

Rose watches them all.

Dianne seems grimly determined not to feel anything.

India's possibly afraid to close her eyes in case she nods off again.

Dan is doing his best. His chest is rising and falling with deep breathing.

Grazia's trying it too but her husband has merely closed his eyes, his hands crossed on his stomach, and he looks as if he's dozing off.

Keera's glossy blonde head is bent as if she can't hold the weight of her head up.

Nobody speaks. Rose doesn't expect them to.

After ten minutes, she leads them back to open-eyed readiness.

'This afternoon we're going to move on.'

'I hope you're recovering from this morning, Dan?'

She looks at him questioningly and wonders if he is

actually sitting less stiffly in his chair. As if some tiny weight has been lifted perhaps?

'I'm . . .' Dan flounders a bit. 'I can't find the words,' he admits. 'You've given me a lot to think about,' he says.

He pauses as if he's been planning what to say. 'I want to clear up any confusion about myself and Julia. She's a wonderful person, I want everyone to know that.'

He looks around at them all earnestly.

'In case it sounds as if our relationship is over, the bottom line is that we love each other: we've been together for over twenty years. We're just taking a break at the moment.'

Keera's eyebrows lift.

'Rose, I think you're wrong about Julia,' Dan goes on. 'Although she says we're over now, I don't think she wants us to be apart, or to actually leave me, for good.'

Time to nip that one in the bud.

'I didn't say she would,' Rose points out, 'just that she could. Julia can choose not to get back with you. We can't bind people to us. The problem occurs when the relationship becomes one-sided, when one person is co-dependent on the other. Where one person walks on eggshells to avoid hurting the other.'

Dianne snorts loudly.

'You want to add something, Dianne?' asks Rose.

Dianne's eyes narrow. 'You're smothering your girlfriend, Dan,' she says abruptly, her Melbourne accent strong. '*You do everything for her.* What if something happens to you and she's left there, all alone, not able to do anything because you refused to let her be an ordinary person with needs? Or . . .'

Dianne looks very fierce now.

'What if she wants to escape but you won't let her go? What if you're caging her like a wild animal?'

'No!' says Dan. 'You've got it all wrong. She needs me, I'm the person she turns to when she needs help—'

'So you're her all-powerful man, are you?' Dianne demands. 'Poor, bewildered Julia's own personal god. Not that I believe in God,' she adds as an aside to Rose. 'I want to know why God is never there when you call for him. I don't believe in that manifesting rubbish, either. Psychic ordering. Huh.' She snorts again.

India, who loves psychic ordering, looks appalled.

'Why do people get a new car or a new job thanks to psychic ordering and people in poor countries still get nothing but war and famine? Answer me that?'

She's shouting now and Rose, who has let this conversation run on, is pleased that Dianne's cracking open.

'Do you feel God has let you down?' she asks Dianne gently.

'Don't believe in him,' Dianne snaps. 'It's all fake. No point waiting for God. It's up to everyone to fix themselves. All this religion nonsense is to make people feel happy about themselves when they're really horrible people: they go to church, sing along to the hymns, and let me tell you this . . .'

She stands up, feet apart in an angry stance. 'That's all for show,' she hisses. 'Stupid people worrying about how many angels can dance on the head of a pin. Real people can suffer and nobody cares! Worse, the people closest to them don't care. It's all for the audience. But *you* know that, Rose,' she snaps nastily.

Dianne pushes past her chair and storms off.

Rose lets her go.

'She's wrong about me and Julia.' Dan is ashen now. 'I don't control Julia: I couldn't. She's—' He halts, obviously at a loss for words. 'She's a force of nature – I love her so much. We need time apart because she's been so stressed . . .'

Rose lets him catch his breath.

'Dan, I know this will be difficult but can you tell me what happened the last time Julia tried to commit suicide?' Rose asks gently.

'Obviously, I wasn't there when she did it,' Dan says brokenly. 'That rips me apart. That she needed me and I wasn't there for her.'

Rose simply nods.

'She phoned me, told me what she'd done, that she was on her own and then hung up. I clicked onto automatic pilot and I called for an ambulance.'

He starts to cry, tears making their way down his lean face. 'Her cousin Miriam was away, so nobody else would have found Julia in time, nobody else knew what she'd done. Just me. On the phone, she said I'd driven her to it.'

The story is blurted out as if he wants to be sentenced to a hundred lashes for telling it.

Nobody on the sun-filled terrace moves although Rose can see India's hand reach out as if she's flattening a desire to pat Dan's sinewy arm.

Finally, India makes a decision and, for a brief moment, she pats Dan's arm comfortingly, then whips her hand back.

The women in the group look deeply sad at seeing Dan so distraught.

Bernard's expression doesn't change, Rose notes. Interesting.

'Did you go to the hospital to see her?' she asks Dan.

He nods.

'She needed me, she'd rung me to tell me what she'd done. They wouldn't let me in at first but I said I was her fiancé.' Dan looks at the rest of the people as if ashamed of this lie. 'I'd asked her to marry me years before so it was almost true, wasn't it?'

'How do you feel about that day now, months later?' Rose asks.

'All I can think of is the blood. That I should have done more for her, that I could have stopped her doing it,' he says.

He's staring into space, his entire being has time travelled to a hospital casualty department.

Rose keeps silent. She feels such pity for the unknown Julia and for Dan too.

Finally, he closes his eyes. He's still crying.

'She was on a trolley in a cubicle, wearing a white dress, a smock thing, not like she usually wears, she likes clinging things, silvery and gold clothes – sorry. That's irrelevant. There was blood. *Her blood*. Everywhere.'

Dan's voice catches at the memory.

'She's always so – I don't know – *glowing*? In the hospital, she looked as if she was already dead.'

Both India and Keera look horrified.

Dan opens his eyes now. He looks around at them all earnestly.

'Julia's really beautiful. She's always the most beautiful woman in any room. A doctor was examining her wrist to see if she needed surgery. I wanted him gone so I could tell her it was my fault, that I'd help her, fix her, that we were destined to be together.'

India reaches out and pats his arm again.

'Why do you think it was your fault?' Rose asks these questions in a low, hypnotic tone so as not to break the spell.

Dan's eyes are distraught.

'Because she said so. I hadn't been there for her when she needed me. If I'd been there, she'd have never done it.'

Keera rushes into the silence.

'Nobody can make anybody else want to kill themselves,' she protests. 'People choose what they want to do, even something like suicide. Trust me, I know that. It wasn't your fault, Dan.'

Keera's eyes are welling up.

'Julia is her own person, Dan. Sometimes people are so broken that they don't want to exist any more but can anyone else stop them?'

Dan blinks at this information.

'You don't understand,' he says impatiently. 'Julia loves life, she's so vibrant.'

'If you think it was your fault, what do you think you can do to make sure Julia never tries this again?' asks Rose.

'I could be there . . .' he says, trailing off.

'Twenty-four-seven?' asks Rose. 'In co-dependent relationships, one person can be very focused on people-pleasing. That person is terrified of being criticised or rejected, so they try harder and harder to avoid conflict. They enable the other person's behaviour, make excuses for them.'

Dan looks deeply uncomfortable.

'They worry that if they don't take care of their person, something bad will happen.'

Keera gets Dan some water and he drinks it.

'Why did she break off the engagement?' asks India. 'I mean, sorry for interrupting, but if she wants to be with you, she'd be with you, right?'

Keera chimes in: 'I had a friend who overdosed once. By mistake, I think, because she was in emotional pain and she was doing a lot of drugs at the time. It wasn't intentional. She survived and she didn't blame anyone else. Nobody pushed that combo of stuff down her throat. Nobody could have stopped her.'

Keera shrugs at Rose. 'Sorry – does that sound cruel?'

Rose shakes her head.

'She sounds unstable to me, this girl,' adds Grazia, shrugging her elegant shoulders and opening the Dior handbag to extract a gold cigarette case. 'She wants to blame other people for her problems. This you cannot do.'

Dan is drinking his water not speaking or looking at anyone.

Grazia proceeds to pull out the cigarette case and a lighter that is studded with diamonds.

'No smoking,' Rose says cheerfully.

Grazia narrows her eyes. 'Pah,' she says, shrugging her slim shoulders. 'We are outside.'

'I don't care,' says Rose, still cheerful. 'The guidelines say no smoking in any of the sessions.'

Grazia can chew nicotine gum or wear patches if she wants to. *Read the small print, folks.*

'But—' says Sir Bernard, possibly trained to speak up if Grazia's whims are queried.

'If you wish to smoke, please leave and go to the smoking terrace, behind the pool.' Rose keeps the ultra-calm in her voice before she delivers the punchline. 'But if you leave, you can't come back in till the next break.'

Most rehab places understand that addicts need something to do: chain smoking, chewing gum, eating endless sweets. But this is not rehab. Rose hates cigarette smoke and anything that takes away from the laser-like focus on why they are all here.

Grazia stuffs the cigarette case back into her bag with vigour. She gives Rose a fierce glare, but Rose has been glared at by experts.

She smiles back in a sunny way.

Don't take me on, honey, her eyes say, blue eyes flashing fire. *You will regret it . . .*

'Dan, can you see any of your behaviour in my description of the co-dependent relationship?' she asks.

Dan's lost for words.

His hands come up automatically to run through his dark, swept-back hair. Rose can imagine him in a lab when something goes wrong, hands in hair as he thinks his way out of the problem.

He really is good looking. Doubtless there are women who look longingly at him, but Dan is the faithful type: would only ever have one woman on his radar.

'How could you have helped Julia?' Rose prods.

'I'm not sure,' he says.

Rose has to keep going. She needs Dan to answer how he could have stopped Julia's suicide attempt.

'Perhaps you could have married her?'

Rose throws this out there as a red herring because Dan has already told her this is off the table.

'No, you see, she doesn't want to be tied down,' he says.

India snorts.

India sees more than people would guess, Rose thinks. From India's application, Rose guesses the young woman has been dismissed as sweet and dippy her whole life. But there's much more to her than that. What's holding her back?

'What do you think Julia wants, what will make her happy?' Rose says to Dan. They have to move on.

Again, Dan looks lost.

Rose goes in for the final needle-sharp question.

'Let's reframe it, Dan. Let's look at you in this big picture. You look after Julia and always have. But what does Julia do to make *you* happy? Does she worry about you the way you worry about her? Does the care flow both ways or not?'

'That's not how it works—' says Dan frantically.

Rose gazes candidly at Dan's earnest face with its dried tears.

'How it has worked between you in the past is no longer working. I want you to think about this, Dan – if you feel responsible for everything Julia does and if you do anything to keep the peace in your relationship, then that's a co-dependent relationship.

'You feel guilt and shame when Julia's not happy. You don't confront her about behaviour you're uncomfortable with because you're afraid of rejection. But Julia is not your project, she's not yours to fix. You can't change her. What you can change is your own behaviours. You deserve love and care too. But,' Rose pauses to let it sink in, 'you're not getting it, Dan.'

'She does love me—' he protests.

'Maybe that's not enough any more,' Rose says relentlessly. 'Julia does what she is driven to do and you feel the need to continue taking care of her irrespective of the effect this has on you. When someone you love tries to commit suicide, that takes up all the air in the room.'

Dan nods warily.

'If Julia's mental health is the prism through which you look at your relationship, then you are a carer and not a partner.

'My final point is one for you to think about, Dan, and for everyone else too: is it within our power to change other people?'

Rose knows that people will fight to the death to challenge that point.

People genuinely want to believe that they *can* change

others, that they can make their loved ones see the error of their ways. It's a hard lesson to learn that they're wrong.

Dan is watching her, still wary. Keera's shaking her head sadly, India's gazing at Rose, while Bernard and Grazia appear to be gathering their things to leave at the mention of the word 'final'. Grazia already has her cigarettes out. Dianne is now looking at the lavender bushes behind the terrace, looking for all the world as if she is not part of the group.

'Or do we have to accept that we can't change other people and that we can only change our behaviour to them? What they do is out of our control.

'I'm going to leave you with that thought.'

Rose rises from her seat and, with a whirl of her flowing dress, is gone.

Chapter Fifteen

Dan is sitting under a sunshade by the infinity pool, a water and a peach beside him, when India joins him.

She sits on the lounger opposite him with her Diet Coke.

'Are you doing OK?' she asks tentatively. 'I'm not prying – it's just, that was hard. Going first too. And I'm so sorry about Julia. Talking about it must be difficult.'

'Thanks,' he says. He looks white-faced with stress. 'I'm not used to this sort of thing.'

'Me neither,' she says, 'but it's going to help us, right?'

Dan's wearing sunglasses, so she can't see his eyes. She's not sure if he's agreeing with her or if he thinks she's an interfering idiot, but he finally nods.

'I guess so,' he says grudgingly, 'although it doesn't feel like it right now. It's like Rose is saying this is all my fault and that's why my sister wanted me to come here. Who made you come?'

'Oh, nobody,' says India lightly. 'I came for myself, although I stupidly thought it was going to be more yoga and healing ceremonies than hard questions on the terrace,' she adds ruefully.

Unexpectedly, Dan laughs and India feels a warm fuzzy feeling inside.

'I was hoping for Ayurvedic massage and possibly something to bring me inner peace,' she continues.

'It did not say that on the tin,' Dan points out.

'Yeah,' says India in mock amazement. '*Now* I find out . . .'

This time, they laugh together.

India finds that she likes making Dan laugh.

'I used to love *The Talisman Effect* when I was young,' says India. 'Did you watch it?'

He probably didn't, she thinks.

'Never heard of it until Sunday night,' Dan replies.

'Oh.' India's surprised. 'It was huge. The earlier seasons were better, really, because then it got very speedy and they used to have two groups of people on each show – you know, fix two families?'

Dan shakes his head. 'My sister made me come here. I'd never heard of Rose. There was some tragedy – someone got shot?'

India nods slowly. 'Poor Rose. A guy came on screaming saying that she'd told his girlfriend to break up with him. He had a gun – no idea how he got *that* past security but he did. He wanted to shoot someone because he said Rose had ruined his life. The show just ended after that.'

'He didn't shoot anyone?'

'Nope. Fired but just aimed wildly, I think. I'm not really sure what happened after that but it destroyed Rose's career. That's why this is special,' says India, a hand moving out to encompass the pool and the terrace area behind them. 'This is the first therapy thing she's done for five years. So we're really lucky.'

Dan laughs again.

'Lucky? You're a riot, India. I am so not feeling lucky,' he says good-humouredly.

In reply, India touches him affectionately on the arm.

'Let's see how we feel at the end of the week.'

Chapter Sixteen

Christos stares at Sir Bernard and wonders if he's heard correctly.

'You want a boat to explore around the coast tomorrow?' Christos repeats.

They're in the reception area and Christos has just come back from Xanthe after having a coffee with his cousin, Alexei.

Alexei's doing some yoga sessions for the group during the week and Christos has been explaining that Alexei has to somehow disguise his formidable attractiveness.

Women have been falling instantly in love with Alexei since he hit sixteen, women of all shapes and ages. Married or single, they all see something vulnerable and sexy in Alexei, something they want.

'No flirting, Alexei, I beg you, these women are special guests. Plus, Rose will kill you stone dead.'

Alexei had shaken his mane of chestnut hair and his full bottom lip had definitely been pushed forward in a pout.

'I understand, why do you need to tell me?' he said crossly.

Despite this, Alexei had clearly understood his cousin's point of view.

But right now, Christos doesn't think he understands Sir Bernard's position.

'Tomorrow you will be on the retreat, all day, I believe,' he says slowly to Bernard.

The man is tanned, short with a large belly and has a giant gold watch on one wrist as if to emphasise how wealthy he is.

Christos hates giant gold watches. He feels they prove nothing except as a signal to the happy pickpockets in Athens's busy tourist spots, who love fat gold timepieces and track their owners faithfully.

'I know, but tomorrow I'm having a break,' Bernard insists. 'I want to go out on a boat.'

'But you've paid for the retreat,' says Christos, dumbfounded.

'I pay for lots of things,' says Bernard imperiously, 'but I decide where I spend my time.'

If he thinks this is going to impress Christos, he is wrong.

'The retreat is important,' says Christos, wondering if this is another man Rose will have to threaten to kill.

People do things for Rose that they wouldn't do for other people.

For example, the builders worked so hard on the site when they were renovating. If ever there was a day when the sense of mañana overcame the various craftsmen at Villa Artemis, Rose went up to talk to them.

People went back to work very quickly on those days.

She definitely has a gift.

'I am not sure I can do this for you without running it by Ms Talisman,' Christos says to Bernard, delaying.

'Running what by Ms Talisman?' says Rose, appearing cool and immaculate after a brief lie-down in her room with the air-con on full blast.

Bernard isn't even the slightest bit dismayed by her appearance.

Bernard does exactly what he wants. He feels he's earned the right.

'I was telling this good man that I wanted to hire a boat and crew to see the island tomorrow,' Bernard begins. 'I used to have an Oyster 825 myself,' he goes on. 'Lovely sloop, twenty-six metres long, full crew obviously, and she was—'

'Grazia is going to be here tomorrow on the terrace,' says Rose, steel in every syllable. 'She'd be upset if you weren't. But, you might not want to be here when she talks . . .' Rose pauses and stares meaningfully into Bernard's eyes. 'Then that is up to you, Bernard,' she says coolly.

She leaves.

Bernard's tanned face has flushed, Christos notes.

'Maybe find out about the boat anyway, so I can plan for another day,' Bernard says and scurries off in the direction of his suite.

Rose, thinks Christos, is a rare treasure of a woman.

Under the verandah on the terrace, the sea breeze is cooling them all. For the last part of the afternoon, Rose changes her style. She can see that the guests are exhausted from the heat and from expectation.

'India,' she says gently, 'let's start with you.'

She can see India quail under her gaze.

If it's possible for a tall person to shrink into their chair, then India shrinks, one hand anxiously playing with a purple sparkly pen with what looks like a tiny plastic Hello Kitty on top of it.

'India, can you tell us what trouble brought you here?'

Silence falls.

The cicadas are making their rhythmic song and only a goat can be heard bleating in a field nearby.

'Er . . .' India flounders. She has so much to say but doesn't want to say it now.

How stupid would it sound? I feel like a kid living in an adult world. I've never had a proper career. I've had more boyfriends than hot dinners.

She'd had too much wine the evening she'd applied for the island retreat, blindly wrote off in the hope that Rose Talisman, heroine of her twenties, could fix her. Her heart had been somehow broken by the idea of never having a relationship where she could have her own little Lily-Blossom.

'I know it's difficult,' Rose coaxes gently, her legs curled under her, 'but it will help to release the story that's inside you.'

'It's more than difficult,' says India, looking up but not at Rose: instead she stares into the distance as if looking for something in the beautiful craggy mountains beside them, searching for something amid the thickets of rosemary and the olive trees.

'We're here to shine a light on whatever is hurting deep inside us,' Rose goes on.

Lily-Blossom comes into India's mind again. Little fat hands and rounded little arms as soft and plump as a white peach. Lily-Blossom with the cloud of dark hair that smells of baby.

'It feels intrusive, India, but this is a group therapy and you will find that sharing your pain helps. It's difficult, really difficult to unburden in front of a group but,' Rose's eyes flicker towards Dan, 'it's the start to healing.'

Everyone shifts uncomfortably in their chairs at all this talk of shining a light on their pain.

Rose knows that they all want their pain magically sucked out.

'I can't go next,' says India suddenly, her hands held up to her mouth as if she's physically preventing herself from speaking. 'Can someone else take a turn—I'm really sorry. I do want to heal but this is all so new and I thought we'd be doing yoga, sitting in a circle on the beach, something holistic—'

It's Keera who rescues her.

'I'll do it.'

India shudders with relief.

Keera looks questioningly at Rose. 'If that's OK?'

'Of course,' says Rose, with a nod.

'What trouble brought me here?' says Keera, sighing. 'OK, I can do trouble.'

Chapter Seventeen

Keera thinks she might be an empath. *That's* what she is, it makes so much sense.

She's always tried to work out why she's different – and not just because she's famous – but this could be it.

She's an empath. She has all the traits: she connects with other people, feels their pain, can always read the room, jumps at loud noises. These are common empath traits, right?

Her mother, or Dr Bobbi as everyone calls her because Mom is a chiropractor by training and chiropractors get called Dr, is definitely not an empath. She's more of a force of nature, Keera thinks with a smile, but is this a category?

She has written this new discovery down in her journal.

Me: empath.
Mom: force of nature, poss?

The journal is a new thing: in an NBC green room in Chicago, she met a woman who had just written a memoir and who started journaling.

'This has saved me from myself,' she told Keera as they sat on too-low couches – the couches were always designed for really short people so that people got stuck in them – and the woman drank honeyed tea to save her voice from doing so many back-to-back shows.

'I was lost. Trying to be someone I wasn't. I started journaling and this came out of it. Of course, Rose Talisman started me off. Do you know her? She's been off the scene for a while but she was amazing. One of her things is to start people journaling and then she picks the journal delicately into pieces and examines all the clues. Sort of Sherlock Holmes but with your heart.'

That sounded a bit radical but, since then, Keera's been journaling and she's ordered Rose Talisman's book.

Making Lemonade: What to Do When Life's Lemons Appear.

It hasn't arrived yet but the current tour takes them all over the place and it's hard for the mail to catch up. Now they're in Australia, so who knows when her precious book will arrive.

Her current journal entry is about identifying people in her world. If she can't designate Mom as a force of nature, and nobody's talking about this online, then what is she?

She keeps the journal with her all the time and has tied it up with lots of mysterious knots in the ribbons around it, in case anyone finds it and tries to read it.

When you're famous like Keera, lots of people want a piece of you and her diary would be a fabulous piece of saleable merchandise. Despite her years of climbing the fame ladder, she still can't understand what happens to people's sense of personal morality in that they want to steal absolutely anything that belongs to a famous person.

She's personally had a hairbrush taken, her special suede Converse high-tops with the furry stuff inside that she loved on the tour bus, and once, memorably, a piece of paper on which she'd blotted her lip gloss in a bar bathroom and had thrown into the trash.

That had been two teenage girls who'd giggled as they reached into the trash and pulled the tissue paper out, then run out of the women's room. Keera had been sixteen at the time and a minor star on a kids' TV show.

Not Lady Gaga or anything. People are cray-cray.

Keera doesn't go into public washrooms any more unless she has another person for security, although she hasn't had a big hit since 'Firebird', so there's less of a chance of random fans haunting her.

She keeps her personal belongings in a soft leather rucksack she picked up in Four Corners on her twenty-state tour when she *was* a big name. Straddling Utah, Colorado, Arizona and New Mexico, Four Corners is an important site full of facts about the tribes of First Nation people who'd once been the only residents before the colonists drove them out. There had been no time to see anything on the tour, as per usual, but Keera had made the tour bus stop at one First Nation shop and bought her rucksack with its yellow colour and grey-and-red triangle design.

She now keeps it close, not least because it contains her precious journal.

Journaling makes her look at things differently.

She notices that her mom is never aware of the feelings in any room she walks into. Instead, Dr Bobbi spices the whole room up, the way she's doing now, striding into a slightly hidden area of the hotel in Brisbane where the team are congregated. The team is much smaller than it used to be. Keera no longer travels with her own musicians.

It's often just her on her electric guitar, a few local session musicians and backing singers hired by the tour manager.

'Where are my favourite people?' asks Dr Bobbi loudly. 'Are we full of energy and bursting to go, folks?'

The team – Team Keera on paper but actually Team Bobbi because everyone knows that Bobbi runs every part of Keera's career – have found a quiet corner where they're waiting to get picked up by the people carrier to take them to the TV station.

It's just eight a.m., everyone is clutching big takeaways of coffee in this, the land of coffee, and Keera's trademark long black hair is its usual unruly mess before Taniqua gets her hands on it.

Keera had started off in showbiz age nine as the kooky kid with the long black hair and, nearly twenty years later, she still has it.

'You can never cut your hair,' Dr Bobbi reminds her at least once a week and Keera nods agreement because nodding agreement is what wise people do in the presence of her mom.

But this, like so many other things about her life, is weirdly beginning to annoy her.

Really Mom? Don't cut my hair because it's one of my trademarks. I'd have never figured that one out. Duh. Cos twenty-seven-year-olds don't have a brain, right?

Dr Bobbi thinks she knows absolutely everything and, once upon a time, her omnipotence had been a fact of life. She'd been Keera's secret weapon but what worked for a nine-year-old who liked singing and posing in front of the mirror with her hairbrush as a microphone was working way less now.

Keera is sort of tired of other people saying they know more than she does.

She's keeping these feelings to herself, though.

Disagreeing with management – her mom – would cause arguments and, above all, Keera hates arguments.

Because it's a whistle-stop tour of small venues, every day counts.

Today, she has a jam-packed schedule and it's making her feel tired at the thought of it all.

She'd overdone it last night on the cocktails. Mom had seen her drinking wine at the mind-numbingly boring dinner with the local record company people and the show promoter. Keera had merely pretended to go to bed with the rest of them at half ten. Instead, she'd found a snug corner in the hotel bar, and pulled her *Namaste Bitches* baseball hat low on her head with her hair coiled up under it in disguise. A gorgeous bartender had mixed up a thing called a Starward espresso martini for her and he said this drink was 'red hot'.

Either he didn't recognise her or he was being cool, which was definitely a thing in Australia. They allowed famous people, or even once-famous people, to exist and did not wish to grab a piece of her. It was a relief.

With her drink, Keera had curled up in her hidden corner, her fake-glass tortoiseshell glasses on and her hair hidden under the cap. Nobody noticed her and she played happily with her phone, being normal. *Numbing out*, an inner voice told herself.

But everyone numbed out, didn't they?

Six of the Starward espresso martinis did not induce sleep, as it happened.

The bar had remained blissfully quiet till two in the morning when Keera had carefully made her way to bed.

That's when the espresso part of the martinis had done their stuff. It took two lorazepam and some of her mom's nuclear-grade sleeping pills to help her sleep and she only got four hours of rest.

The sleeping pills would make Godzilla sleep, and now she's still dozy from them, her every move lethargic and heavy.

Keera has not eaten breakfast, has swallowed a handful of helpful pills – uppers and a kiddie coke or Ritalin – with some water and is shuddering at the thought of the day ahead of her.

She is so tired. Tired and weary, wishing she could stay in bed, just today, just for one day. Scroll her phone, watch some old much-loved shows on her laptop, just mentally check out.

Instead, she's due to tape a pre-record for Channel Seven at ten a.m., before a quarter of the print interviews she would have had two years ago. Luckily, Taniqua, hair and make-up artist, is totally clued in on why there's no point in coaxing Keera into having her skin officially prepped for TV make-up just yet.

Taniqua is an empath too.

The force of energy that's Keera's mom makes Taniqua jump, much the way Keera jumps.

Taniqua is thirty-two, has amazing bone structure and an afro she often wears tightly back from her face. They've been working together for six years, are as close as anything, and at the sound of Dr Bobbi's voice, their eyes meet.

She's up, get ready to rush! Have we covered everything up all right?

Keera knows her mother has meds that would help with the hangover but she doesn't want to ask. Bobbi does not approve of Keera drinking in bars. She can do it, but not Keera. Nobody is allowed to see girl-next-door Keera drinking. Pills, however, are fine, according to Dr Bobbi.

Sleeping pills, benzos to calm her, beta blockers before a big TV show and some dexies to give her energy, never too many because it makes her heart rate race if she's exhausted.

She worries sometimes but Mom says everyone does it.

'People don't get addicted to pills if the doctor orders them,' Mom says. 'You can't pick up pills in every grocery store in the country, honey, so it's OK. It's not as if it's Cat Valium, right?' she says, using the slang for ketamine.

But Keera likes cocaine too, which her mother doesn't know. Keera's very careful about it because she knows that Snow is a speedy way of getting rid of money and that if her mother cottons on to her use, Keera will be in big trouble.

The sound of Dr Bobbi's arrival in the lobby makes Luka, the stylist, who's been surfing an Instagram high on their phone, and Barb, who's nominally Keera's assistant and who'd been WhatsApp-ing her girlfriend, both get to their feet instantly.

Luka's wearing heels, cream floaty trousers and a see-through crochet top which works wonderfully with their blonde shag hairdo, elaborate eye make-up and androgynous look. Barb wears all black, no matter how hot it is, has inch-long black nails and a pale-blonde Eton crop that shows off an exquisitely shaped head. Barb is Slovakian and has a slightly scary energy to her. Even Dr Bobbi treads carefully around Barb.

Dr Bobbi likes that the team are diverse and talks about it non-stop to show how *with it* she is.

'We have the full run of skin and rainbow colours here,' she says cheerfully to everyone, even when Keera hisses 'Mom!' at her, in case anybody hears and gets upset.

Mom says that she doesn't have a racist or prejudiced bone in her body but why then does she need to remind people that Taniqua is Black or that Luka is non-binary?

Why aren't they allowed to *be* rather than represent certain *types* of people? Gen X just doesn't understand Gen Z.

With Dr Bobbi's arrival, the team spring to life and hustle their way to the door of the hotel where they slip through with almost no interest at all. A few hardy fans of Keera's are clustered outside the hotel's imposing gates but they can see nothing through the darkened windows of the black Mercedes minivan that Charlie, their driver, calls a 'people mover'.

He and Keera had been chatting when they'd driven from Sydney to Brisbane.

Now he drives confidently through the city and Keera looks at it wistfully as they pass.

She rarely sees any part of any place she visits.

The hotel, her room, the gym if she has time. She sees bars, though. Her mother knows endless people who own bars.

It's being Irish, Dr Bobbi explains.

Dr Bobbi grew up in Donegal in Ireland, smack bang in a place she called 'the arse end of nowhere', a constant refrain which means that Keera's grandmother, who's in her late seventies, barely speaks to Dr Bobbi any more. Keera hasn't seen her grandmother since she was a little girl.

'Someday we'll go there,' Dr Bobbi says, which is her way of saying 'when hell freezes over'.

When Keera was touring small venues on her tour bus, they stopped at lots of little taverns along the way to bestow a little bit of celebrity twinkle on them. The pubs were almost always Irish bars.

'Honey, everyone that made good in Ireland had some link to a pub,' Dr Bobbi would say while she drank with the owners and got Keera to pose for a photo with them and many of their friends.

'I know them from way back,' was another of her mother's favourite lines and meant that many oddballs arrived into the green room or her dressing room in cities around the world, smiling at Keera as if they knew her.

'Jesus, would you ever smile and say hello, for my sake,' her mother would mutter when Keera wondered how to behave with these strangers who were happily eating the free green-room food and being stopped from taking photos of any other famous people there by said famous people's entourages.

The actual famous people never complained.

As Keera knew, they all understood that any complaint got them labelled 'difficult' or full of themselves. This was more fatal than a meltdown on TV.

So Keera and the other singers and actors just smiled at the oddballs and pretended they were delighted that some idiot was watching them with his mouth open as he drank free gin/vodka/whatever was on offer.

'Let Taniqua fix your hair before we go in,' instructs Dr Bobbi now, as Charlie says: 'We're here, ladies and gentlemen,' as the minivan arrives at the studio.

Dr Bobbi has been on the phone for the entire trip, flipping through messages and emails, flicking them into delete with ultra-long, coffin-tipped gel nails. This week's colour is Undead Red, a deep plum, a name which made her shriek with delight when she saw it.

'Undead Red and me are perfect! I'm channelling the Morticia look!'

Dr Bobbi's hair, the same pale mouse as Keera's natural colour, is shoulder-length, dead straight and now coloured inky black.

She'd dyed it that colour when she'd first arrived in Los

Angeles from Ireland back in the Triassic Period before Keera was born.

Dr Bobbi's personal fight for stardom as a singer/actor had given her the tools to make her daughter succeed where she hadn't.

The night before Keera's first audition for a commercial, when she'd been nine years old, Dr Bobbi had looked at her daughter's glowing little face with its freckles.

Keera had huge eyes the colour of smoky-green quartz, a hypnotic colour that could make her look infinitely sad or wonderfully inquiring or anything else that Bobbi told her to look when reading a line for a part.

To Bobbi's critical gaze, Keera's nondescript mousey plaits took away from the glittering eyes that stood out even in her adorable little pixie face with its snub nose and pointed chin.

Everything she'd done for Keera – and this Keera had written down in her journal because it all seemed pivotal – had been for this moment. Keera's very name had been Americanised so that the Irish 'Ciara' had been translated into the far more easy-to-say 'Keera'.

The legend was born that Dr Bobbi had found a 'wash-in' black colour because she didn't want to hurt her precious daughter's little head and had applied it.

Nine-year-old Keera had felt the adult dye sting her delicate scalp but by the time it was growing out, Keera was on her way.

The next day, newly black-haired Keera got the job. Got the television sitcom role, got the chocolate advertisement, the tween lip gloss deal, got the career.

The story about using gentle wash-in dye was the stuff of the Keera-and-her-mom legend: fantasy as fact in the career-building world.

She was a child star and child stars were not like ordinary kids. If they needed nose jobs, they got them. Needing professional hair dye when they were nine? No problemo.

'Gimme a look at you.' In the back of the minivan, Dr Bobbi now scans her daughter with a laser eye. Keera puts her head sideways and adopts the cute expression that had won her so many fans on her second sitcom, *The Keera and Cat Party House*.

It had been fun making the series at first, Keera thinks suddenly, remembering. She'd been thirteen when it started, sixteen when it ended and, by then, it was just her.

Cat had been a wonderful friend, her first and closest best friend: very quirky, e-boy-ish, almost, with her blue sparkly eyeliner habit, genuine fondness for boy's trousers, button-down shirts, and her nerdy but expertly cut short haircut.

They'd been so close and had so much fun.

Nothing was fun any more.

Was it normal to be twenty-seven and feel burned out?

Keera gets out of the minivan and says thanks to Charlie, but her head is swirling.

What had happened to Cat? She'd left LA when she was written out of the series. Keera had meant to stay in touch and they'd messaged all the time, but then Cat had sort of disappeared from view. She'd stopped returning messages.

'She's probably busy and you remind her of how badly her career worked out,' Mom had said at the time. 'Who has time for friendship when you've got a career? And never forget, jealousy is a real thing in this business.'

Cat would never be jealous, Keera thinks.

Mom was rarely wrong but perhaps she had been in this case?

She and Cat had sworn to be friends for ever. Cat had never had her head turned by the Hollywood machine, never stopped being the funny girl from New Mexico who loved showbiz but loved her family more.

'We have to keep our feet on the ground, Keera,' she used to say, when they were just thirteen, sneaking into each other's hotel rooms during filming weeks. 'One day, the show will tank, the money will stop and we'll be off the radar. Gotta face it. It'll be OK, I think. My pops says nobody can do this for ever, right?'

Cat had been the nearest thing to a sister Keera had ever had. It was years since she'd tried to talk to her.

The thought makes Keera ashamed.

Just because Mom believes people will try to use Keera, doesn't mean that everyone is a user.

Her mom's narrative doesn't have to be hers. It makes her think of all the normal things she's lost out on because of her career. Like ordinary friendships.

It's a lightbulb moment – the blog she's reading for her journal work talks about lightbulb moments.

The lightbulb moment has another angle: Mom isn't always right.

They reach the studio front door and Keera knows it's time to turn on her magic.

Dr Theatre, as an actress once said to her.

'You hit the stage and *Dr Theatre* appears inside you magically.'

'You look fabulous, honey,' says her mom, patting her cheek affectionately. 'Stay off the snacks if they offer them, OK?'

Keera looks at her mother. Sometimes things feel really good and then Mom says something to smash her self-esteem into pieces. At these moments, Keera hates her.

Chapter Eighteen

Everyone on the terrace is quiet as Keera finishes her story.

Rose says nothing for a while.

She's helped many famous people in her time and Keera's tale is not unusual. Her mother sounds tricky and Rose doesn't want to pin a label on her too soon. People are complex after all. But Rose has seen momagers in action before.

They can't understand when their child doesn't want to be a piece of merchandise any more.

Rose wonders what sort of mother Dr Bobbi is: a dynamic force of nature or someone who wants to use her daughter for her own gains?

Time will tell.

'Is there anyone in your life other than your mother whom you feel you can trust?' Rose asks suddenly. 'What you've told us says that you have friends in the business but that they work for you or with you. If they get too close, like Taniqua or your friend Cat, they affect the family dynamic, perhaps?'

Rose lets the statement drift off into the air.

It's a comment designed to probe.

Keera looks thoughtful, like a student in class concentrating on a knotty problem.

'I'm thinking of who I trust and, for sure, Taniqua's top of the list but . . .'

She pauses: the thoughtful student is back.

'. . . there's also Connie, she's a marketing lady from Xochi, my record label,' she says. 'It's not spelled like it sounds: Xochiquetzal is the most important Aztec goddess, you say it Show-chee-set-zal.'

'I know,' says Dan, leaning forward, 'she's a fertility goddess, the most—'

Rose cuts him off at the pass with a gentle raising of her hand to show that Keera has the floor right now.

'Connie and I spent a lot of time together two years ago when Mom had pneumonia and I had a three-week tour in Canada.'

'I love Canada,' says Grazia approvingly. 'Nice people.'

Again, Rose raises her hand but Grazia's interruption is over.

'Connie lives in LA and she's married but no kids. Has two dogs: one's a French Bulldog and the other's a kind of mixed breed. Mom said they called them "butcher's dogs" when she was a kid. She's not a fan of dogs!'

Keera smiles.

Nobody else does.

Rose waits.

'I love animals: dogs, cats, hamsters. I follow a lot of animal accounts on Insta and TikTok. We couldn't get a dog when I was younger because we were travelling around so much. Dogs tie you down,' Keera adds sadly. 'You've got to give a lot of normal stuff up to be a performer.' She looks at the group as if for confirmation that this is true. 'It means that Mom and I are a strong unit: me and her against the world. We're like sisters. Obviously we argue but, like, who doesn't, right?'

And there it is.

A mother who presents herself as her daughter's closest friend, her sister. Rose thinks this scenario can be possible if the daughter is an adult, if said mother has actually been the parent until their child has grown up. Then, the early parenting is done.

But a best-friend spiel when the kid is just a kid: not healthy.

'So your mother is your best friend,' says Rose idly. 'Is that unusual?'

Keera's face is confused.

'She does so much for me,' she says.

'I'm sure she does,' Rose remarks, 'but you need friends too. Do you have any friends who are not connected to you via work? Say if you and your mother are not getting on, who do you talk to?'

This time, Keera's face goes curiously blank.

'I had my friend, Cat, but we lost touch . . .' she offers.

'Nobody else?' Rose asks.

Keera says nothing.

Rose knows that she's pushed Keera as far as she can go.

Keera has told her story but she needs time to think about telling it to everyone else: that's the magic.

Time to move on, Rose thinks.

She gets up and hands Keera some juice from Christos' little fridge on the edge of the terrace. 'You need to hydrate and a little juice might help. Thank you for your story, Keera,' she says.

Keera blinks up at her, almost dazed by what she's just said.

'See you all in the kitchen at half six,' Rose says.

And she's gone.

*

I don't know when it changed. Probably when I was expecting the baby. Pregnancy is when some men show the world how fertile they are. A woman with a big belly is like a totem pole of virility.

Look at me, I'm a true man.

My mother had been so happy when my brother's wife was pregnant but then, he was her golden child. I was . . . I'm not sure now what I was.

The internet is full of pop psychology pages telling you who plays which role in the family. In my family, there weren't many of us, so it's tricky to figure out where we fitted into the toxic family plan. But we were toxic. I know that now.

So my mother wasn't pleased at the pregnancy, which is a long story. But my husband – we'd married by then – was happy.

Not happy when I was tired and had to lie down.

Not happy when the people next door saw me struggling with bags of shopping.

'Here, let me take that,' said the man next door. He'd been cutting his grass and he'd seen me.

I knew I was in trouble when I unlocked the door and Mr Next Door came in with the bulging grocery bags.

My husband was sitting in an armchair watching sport. He'd watch two flies walking up the wall if he could bet on it.

He barely turned around until Mr Next Door said: 'Mate, you can't have your missus dragging in all this stuff in her condition. She's about to pop.'

Oh, I knew I was in trouble, then.

'Let me take it!' he said, leaping to his feet. 'I tell

her not to go by herself but she sneaks off,' he said cheerily, rescuing the bags off Mr Next Door.

'Women: they're all the same,' laughed Mr Next Door, pleased there was a reason for this.

People don't want to see.

They're happy with a reason for slightly odd behaviour. Considering what the reality might be – that's too shocking. Nobody wants to go there.

He swiftly put the bags on the counter and told me to get my feet off the floor.

'It's a lovely day, sit in the garden. I'll bring you a cuppa, love,' he said.

I sat in the garden even though I didn't want to. I wanted to go to bed, to lie down and rest my belly. But I was scared to do that.

Mr Next Door was still there. I was guaranteed safety by his presence.

'You need to rest,' said Mr Next Door, poking his head outside when my husband brought me tea. There was no sugar in it, of course.

I took sugar. He knew that. Not that he brought me tea normally. I was the cook, the cleaner, the housemaid, the maker of tea. But not adding sugar was a little reminder that I was in trouble.

Mr Next Door had a beer in his hand. He looked happy, grass-cutting forgotten. Seeing his heavily pregnant neighbour staggering in with the shopping had been a misunderstanding. All was right with the world.

The two men drank a few beers and watched the sport. I sat in my deck chair and, eventually, went upstairs to lie down. The baby was a kicker, full of energy.

I was lying there, hungry and wondering if it was safe to go back downstairs, when he came in.

'He's gone,' he snarled. Mr Next Door. 'Why did you do that?' he hissed.

'I didn't want to bother you,' I said in my fawning voice.

I was a wonderful fawner. You don't choose your trauma response: it just appears.

I never tried freezing or running away.

No. I fawned.

'You've had a hard week at work, you need a break. It's all OK, though, isn't it?'

'No,' he said in a voice colder than the North Pole.

He turned and left then, his whole body stiff with rage.

He ignored me for the next three weeks.

That doesn't sound like much – he could have hit me, after all. But he didn't do hitting. The silent treatment was a very powerful weapon.

Imagine living in a small house and trying to exist when one of the people in the house refuses to speak to the other for three whole weeks. When their rage taints the atmosphere, their coldness can freeze a person.

Being silent is like saying 'You no longer exist for me.'

I'd been hardwired to try to make it better.

I tried everything: cooked better meals, smiled, touched his arm, found shows on the TV he liked to see. Nothing worked.

He'd brush off my arm as if I was carrying poison.

He chose to punish me, and only he would decide when that was over.

My waters broke three Saturdays later. I'd been worried because the baby hadn't been kicking for the past two days but I hadn't wanted to make a fuss. I've never forgiven myself for that.

He was out when the contractions started. I didn't

know where because he'd simply gone. I waited nearly three hours for him to return, feeling the contractions deepening.

I was terrified. I didn't want to give birth on my kitchen floor but I knew that if I went for help with him gone, he'd never forgive me. It would be a great public rebuke: he had left his pregnant wife alone.

What mattered was not that I was alone, but that people would know *this.*

That was the crux of everything: how it looked *to other people.*

Nothing else mattered, not me in pain or the fact that I needed an ambulance now.

The fear of giving birth, the knife-point of labour plunged into my lower back: all immaterial.

I rang Mrs Next Door then and said that he would be so upset, he'd feared going out even for a moment in case I went into labour.

This was the mantra. Not the pain or the dreadful fear over the baby not having moved. But how upset my beloved husband would be.

'He'll be so upset, you've no idea,' *I said again and again.*

I almost believed it myself.

'Where's he gone?' *she asked. This was before mobile phones.*

'He's gone to get groceries and buy me flowers,' *I lied.*

I'm not a liar but I can be. Have been often.

'You poor dear,' *she cooed,* 'we'll find him. He'll never forgive himself if he misses the birth of his baby.'

I knew that if he missed the birth of his baby, the person he'd never forgive would be me.

Chapter Nineteen

India and Keera inspect the kitchen. It's smaller than they'd expected but it shines cleanly at them, a tiny palace of stainless steel.

'What are all these gizmos?' India says, gazing at a serried rack of hanging utensils of every shape and size. 'And this? What is this?'

She stands beside a big square machine which sits beside several industrial-looking hand blenders.

'Sous vide machine,' says Keera, then sees India looking at her in astonishment. 'I had to spend half an hour in a hotel kitchen once because I was the support act at a charity event and there was a delay. I couldn't eat anything because I was about to perform – I was wearing a dress I'd been sewn into.'

She grins as India's eyebrows lift.

'Yeah, sounds extreme but at least if you're sewn in, you're less likely to have a costume malfunction. Although nipple covers help with that. So the chefs showed me around the kitchen. Sous vide cooks meat, fish, that kind of thing, in vacuum-packed bags, I think that's it – not entirely sure *how* it works but that's the idea.'

'You've had such an interesting life!'

India feels such enormous pity for Keera and how much she cried on the terrace that afternoon that she wants to find the lightness in her new friend's life.

'Being sewn into your clothes, nipple covers. You've had some fun times – in between the tricky ones, that is!'

She finds a tin opener mounted on the wall and marvels at how huge it is.

'Is this for enormous cans of tomatoes?'

'Probably. Show business is not that exciting when it's all you've ever known, honestly,' says Keera. 'There are lots of downsides to the industry that don't get talked about enough. I know an actress who put duct tape on her boobs for filming because they had nudity co-ordinators, et cetera, but she didn't trust the director not to film her tits if they appeared. Total sleazoid.'

'Me Too stuff?' asks India anxiously.

Keera nods.

'Women actors are treated differently just because they're women. Don't get me started. Much of the casual sexism never gets talked about because you're famous and make money, so you're not supposed to be upset by shit like that. It's like – *You signed up for this life, honey.*'

'Yeuch,' India says. 'Nobody signs up for that. You weren't actually Me Too-ed, were you?'

'Nope. My mom was with me all the time. People were scared of her, which was handy, I guess,' Keera says and smiles.

'People were scared of her because they knew she'd go mental if anyone touched me,' she goes on. 'She's kind of tough. Mama lioness.'

'She's your manager?'

Keera lets out a breath.

'Yeah. I should have said that earlier. Nobody was getting twenty per cent off us while she had breath in her body.'

They both laugh.

'Sounds like the sort of thing my dad would say,' India offers. 'He's in the rental car business, though.'

'My mom used to be a performer, a cabaret singer, that's how I got into this business. I remember her doing shows when I was little.' Keera clears her throat, her voice becoming a little croaky. 'She had this guest slot in Phoenix once for a whole year. It was the best year, actually. I was a kid, seven, maybe, and I loved Phoenix. We lived in this lovely little motel with a kids' playground out the back and a pool that was clean, which was a rarity, I can tell you, compared to some of the places we lived.'

India can see Keera's eyes getting misty as she remembers the past.

'Life on the road is hard but Mom wanted to make it big, so we had to travel. I thought Motel Six was my address for a long time. They're low-budget motels and when you passed from state to state, if you hit the information offices, you got coupons for motels and food. A good motel coupon was like Christmas had come early. I don't talk about this when I'm interviewed,' she says wryly. 'My mom likes the "my daughter just fell into stardom" version.'

'I feel so ashamed of my puny problems,' says India. 'I never had anything like that. My parents both had money. Mum from her modelling and Dad because he built his business. Georgie, she's my stepmum, has a brilliant business too. Very not a wicked stepmother,' she adds, smiling.

'That sounds really nice,' says Keera, 'but you can still have problems even when it all looks fabulous. Sadness and anxiety don't care if you've cash in the bank.

'Right, we are cooking dinner. Where are Dianne and Grazia? I bet they can cook.'

'I bet Bernard can't,' says India, laughing.

Bernard lies on a sunlounger in front of the infinity pool with a vast tumbler of good scotch whisky and ice beside him on a small table. The notebook Rose gave him is also on the table, along with some factor-20 SPF.

He has written nothing in his notebook.

His phones sit on top of it.

Nobody needs him right now. He's not cooking dinner, whatever Rose says. He's had two work calls and ripped the heads off a few people. They deserved it.

He talked briefly to his son, Stephen, and agreed that Stephen's newest business idea is a good one and funding will be sorted out within the week. It's a terrible idea but Bernard would never say that.

He's just pushed more money into his daughter Viola's handbag business even though she has none of his business acumen and won't listen to any advice. Still, he's their dad. His job is to give them everything he was never given. They're happy.

All is well in his world.

He closes his eyes against the luscious heat of the September sun.

If Rose asks what he's put in his notebook, he'll lie. This is Grazia's thing. He's here for her. Doesn't mean he has to do anything, does it? No therapy-guru quack will make Bernard do anything he doesn't want to.

But he thinks of Rose's face when he was trying to book the boat for a day out.

She looked as if she knew something about him. Something very hidden.

Grazia cannot have told her, can she?

Bernard feels a ripple of fear but he knows how to handle it. Bernard is very proud of his ability to handle anything life throws at him.

Rose knows she should be celebrating a successful day on the terrace but instead, she and Adriana are sitting in Adriana's pretty family room, listening to an anxious voice note on Adriana's phone.

It's from Mercedes, the wildly cool twenty-something Corfu woman who has been in charge of all the social media for Villa Artemis and Rose's retreat.

She's been amazing, understands algorithms and how to make Instagram posts pop.

She thinks email and Facebook are for old people, likes TikTok and is dying to see what's coming next.

Mercedes would rather burn her new Louis Vuitton multi pochette with pink flaps than move out of Athens and back to Corfu because she says it's full of people Adriana and Christos' age. With this in mind, she treats Christos, Adriana and Rose like sweet but bewildered people from a different century, one without electricity.

But today, Mercedes is worried, which is why Rose is not sitting on the private bamboo-surrounded terrace, drinking an iced tea and congratulating herself on how well the first day is going.

Mercedes sounds uncharacteristically unsure of herself: 'I saw the message on Instagram a few minutes ago. I don't want to bother you with every weirdo or random hate-watcher but . . .' Mercedes pauses. 'This message *is* a bit weird. I've sent you the screenshot. It's oddly personal, Rose: as if the poster is saying Rose is not your real name. I know, insane, right? I thought I should warn you, thought maybe you had people in America who could make sure there's no problem. I don't know if you had a stalker or whatevs but we can just block this person.'

Rose closes her eyes and tries to calm herself with breathing.

She has no people in the US any more. Her agent's the only one who ever occasionally contacts her to see how she is. Rose feels guilty when this happens. She can't go back there, despite all the work her agent could line up in a moment.

Her special private-banking expert at her US bank has no interest in her any more now that pretty much all her money has gone into renovating and setting up Villa Artemis. Thankfully, she has never had a stalker.

'Let's look at the screenshot,' she says to Adriana.

Adriana shows her the picture of the message sent by Mercedes.

I know all about you, bitch. All your pretending. You might think you got away with it but you didn't. I have never forgotten, 'Rose'. I was waiting for someone to out you but you must have paid them off. But I know who you really are and where you're from and I'm going to do it. Payback time.

Rose feels a combination of anger and fear ripple through her.

Adriana's face is bleached white.

Rose holds out her arms and Adriana falls into them. They stay, hugging, for a few silent moments.

'We need to know who it is for certain,' Rose says finally. 'I won't have someone come and blackmail us like this . . .'

'It could be like Mercedes said,' Adriana says hopefully. 'Just a weirdo?'

'Or it could be someone with the power to mess up everything we've spent years trying to hide,' says Rose, sighing.

Why can't the past ever go away?

The day, which was going so well, feels darker now.

'Perhaps it's better to have it all out in the open?' Adriana suggests hesitantly.

'No!' Rose is adamant. 'Nobody is going to bully us, not after all we've been through. No way.'

She thinks carefully, flipping on the analytic part of her brain. Who could help?

Then it comes to her: 'I know a guy who used to do a lot of online investigating; he might not even be in the business any more.' She shrugs. 'Five years is a long time and internet security is probably totally different now, but if it's possible to find out who this person is, he'll work it out. I'll message him. Give him all the details. I'll use the office computer.'

She doesn't want to email on her own laptop, doesn't want to let this darkness slither in because, for her, social media can be an evil that permeates everything it touches.

Rose had always found it hard to process the avalanche of social media comments on the show. They ranged from messages of wild approval to ones where anonymous people suggested ways in which she might be tortured and killed.

It's why she has almost no online presence any more, why Mercedes runs the retreat and Villa Artemis's accounts.

Rose sends the email then turns to Adriana.

'Tell her to alert us if any more messages come in,' she says. 'Don't block them. We need to watch this carefully in case it escalates.'

'Yeah,' says Adriana, staring at her phone. 'Mercedes is saying that perhaps if we can get some of the guests to post good reviews on their social media it would be helpful. If Keera could say something, it would be amazing. She's got so many followers—'

Rose shakes her head. 'I can't ask her to do that,' she says firmly. 'It's unethical. I'm her therapist and I can't profit off her just because she's famous.'

Adriana looks abashed. 'I know, sorry,' she says.

'We'll have a place on the webpage where they can leave comments afterwards but that's entirely up to them,' Rose says. 'Now, let's forget this. We are not going to let some random idiot get us down. Agreed?'

Adriana manages a shaky smile. 'Agreed. It's just—'

'I know,' Rose says. 'Scary. The unknown.' She dons her therapist's face. 'We will come through this.'

As she speaks, Rose realises how happy she'd been before this threat. What an idyll her home on Corfu has been.

The past five years have flown by, once they'd had the idea for Villa Artemis, and the idea had blossomed into something, they had worked night and day to make it a reality.

'I hate that this can destroy everything,' Adriana says. 'You've lost so much already, Rose.'

'I'm OK,' Rose says, which is a definite fib.

'If you still had Theo in your life, it would be easier,' Adriana adds.

Rose shakes her head. This is an old argument from Adriana.

'Far too much time has elapsed,' she says, which is what she always says to her sister. 'Even if I got in touch with him, Theo will have moved on. He's probably married. He left first, Adriana. He left before the show imploded.'

'But you don't know if he's married, do you?'

'I'm happy here on the island,' Rose says, which is totally true.

'Corfu has worked her magic on you,' Adriana smiles. 'It worked for me and now for you.'

'Maybe I'll find another man like Christos,' Rose jokes.

Adriana laughs delightedly. 'There is no other man like him. The gods had the mould destroyed, he is perfect. Theo sounded perfect,' she adds.

Rose suddenly feels as if she might cry. What is wrong with her?

'He was perfect and I screwed it up because I never managed to tell him the truth. That ship has sailed,' she adds firmly. 'I can't go back there. I wasn't honest with Theo. I couldn't tell him the truth at first and then later . . . later, it was too late.'

'If you told him now, he'd understand,' Adriana says. 'You lied because you had to, not because you were trying to deceive him.'

Rose loves Adriana's hopefulness but Theo is a part of her history now, not a part of her future.

'I doubt that he'd forgive the lie. Either way, let's forget about Theo,' she says now. 'We've got a week to put Villa Artemis on the map. Nobody's going to mess with us!'

She hugs Adriana again, a fierce hug as if everything is all right and they're an unstoppable force together.

Rose has to sort out this threat on Instagram. It's a serious threat.

Calling her 'Rose'.

That was a mistake, Rose thinks grimly. Everyone thinks they know who Rose Talisman is: that she's a calm, serene woman who heals people. All of which is true. But she's also a fighter.

Nobody from the past is going to ruin their future. Not if Rose can help it.

Chapter Twenty

Dianne watches the woman send a high kick into her opponent's abdomen, can hear the roar of the crowd. The kicked woman falls to the mat for a moment, then recovers and is up, fighting again, determination in every move.

Yes!

Dianne loves watching women's kickboxing on YouTube.

If only her kids could see her now, she thinks wryly.

They'd have her committed instead of opting to send her to a Greek retreat.

But watching powerful, muscled women fighting calms Dianne down. These women own their power and she loves it.

Ironic since she can't even do basic stretches any more. Walking is her only exercise.

But if only she'd started doing something like kickboxing when she was in her twenties . . .

Imagine who she'd have been then. Fierce, determined, brave.

She'd have set up her own business, been somebody, run her life *her* way.

Then again, the twenty-something version of her wouldn't have known where to start with getting kickboxing lessons, never mind setting up a business. But she thinks about what might have been.

The world is there for modern women, despite the misogynists, and it might have been there for her too, if only she'd known then what she knows now.

If only are the saddest words in the universe, she thinks.

Dianne looks at the time. Five p.m. Finally.

She's been waiting to listen to Ellie's message and then send one in return when Ellie is asleep thanks to the time difference. Waiting to hear her darling's voice has been hell but she wants to do it when Ellie can't see the blue tick, can't know her mother's waiting to leave a message.

Dianne now needs to be totally alone. Not in the villa, where she feels people can hear her, but away from them all.

She asked Adriana about where she might find privacy and Adriana told her about the little viewing point behind the villa.

They call it 'the acropolis', Adriana says.

'It's Greek for a citadel, really, and our acropolis is not that. But it's high up, very private behind the villa. It's a little terrace half-way up the cliff. When you're up there, only the birds can hear you.'

Dianne doubts the birds will be interested in her conversation.

The sun is moving slowly down the early evening sky. Adriana has told her that this blissful September warmth is a relief after the sweltering summer.

Dianne climbs up the beautifully laid stone steps that seem part of the cliff face.

She holds carefully on to the wooden railing on the outer edge of the steps.

When she reaches the top, she stops and pants a little. She's fit but it's quite a climb.

Dianne peers over the edge which has a curved stone balcony and fragrant oleander and lavender bushes planted neatly around. It's been set up as a little retreat where people can sit and stare at the sea, or meditate, as Rose has suggested.

She figures that the acropolis is some forty metres above the Villa Artemis complex. An eyrie in the sky.

Or a jumping-off place if a person doesn't care about living any more. Dianne is still in the hazy area where she does not know what she actually wants.

Today has been a strange day, she reflects. Dianne had thought everyone would be there for anger issues like herself but they weren't.

She distrusts Bernard: there's something sleazy about him, and Dianne has a good eye for sleaze.

Neither is she sure about Dan.

She's wary of Grazia, who looked at her with almost understanding eyes, which Dianne found most deeply irritating. What can a woman like Grazia understand about Dianne's life?

She likes Keera and India and, in spite of herself, even likes Rose.

She envies Rose because, despite whatever happened to her on the TV show, Rose appears to have her life sorted out. She reeks of happiness and contentment.

Dianne usually can't bear people like that.

Rose will not get information out of her, Dianne vows. She'll go home and tell the kids she's been to Corfu and has done the anger management gig.

Which will be the literal truth.

Sitting on the wooden bench with the hotel beneath her

and the vast expanse of the beautiful sea below her, Dianne takes her mobile phone out of her pocket.

Her fingers shake as she presses the button to listen.

'Hi Mum, glad it's a lovely place but no, I think Lauren would go mental if you came home. I'm fine, the baby's fine and Tate's being so good to me.'

Tate is Ellie's boyfriend and Dianne has sworn that if he hurts her Ellie, she'll bury him in a shallow grave so well hidden that even Google won't be able to find him.

'The kicking is insane! I think the baby's a little footballer even if it is a girl! Get fixed, Mum, I love you, please remember that, bye.'

Dianne plays it one more time and lets the tears fall unchecked down her face.

Ellie said she loved her mother.

Dianne's heart is swollen with relief because she thought she'd lost Ellie. Yet Ellie said 'I love you'.

As for 'Get fixed', that's another story.

Dianne thinks that after all these years, she is unfixable.

She's pretty sure that even Rose, whose show Dianne watched many years ago, cannot possibly fix her.

But thinking of the baby, her 'little footballer', she wishes she could change.

Recover some of who she was a long time ago. Have a new life.

Is it even possible? She doesn't know.

Closing the door to her bedroom at ten that night, Rose immediately lights up a bergamot, lime and cinnamon bark Sia sisters candle. She throws open the French doors to her balcony and the muslin curtains ripple in the whisper of the breeze from the sea. Christos has left a tiny carafe of good wine in her room, and she pours a small glass.

First day over, she thinks with relief as she drinks.

When she was on TV, the first day of any show was always the worst. She had to hype herself up to become Rose Talisman, the therapy guru.

The mystery Instagram message-sender has implied that Rose isn't her real name, and they are correct, which makes Rose fear them.

Apart from Adriana and Christos, *nobody* knows her real name. She was baptised Rosemarie but it was her second name, not her first. Talisman is the surname she chose all those years ago.

It has such a good ring to it: part mystery, part magic.

Not even Theo knows it isn't her real name, which makes Rose shudder deep inside at how much she's betrayed him by omission.

Adriana thinks it's easy to go back and ask for forgiveness, but for someone like Theo, whose very bone marrow is invested in truth, learning about Rose's lies would destroy his opinion of her.

Ironically, Rose had been determined to tell him about her real life, as opposed to her fantasy legend, before he'd left.

Her own therapist, Vida, had urged her to do it.

Vida could analyse with rapier-like intensity.

'Your greatest fear is that he'll never forgive the lies you've told him, not that he'll find your background difficult to accept.'

'It's very boring that you're always right,' Rose had said gloomily.

She hasn't talked to Vida for a long time.

Rose knows that she ought to contact Vida again now that Rose is accepting clients.

First topic would be the sense of fear that accompanied the message Mercedes found on Instagram.

Rose shivers. She'd been brave earlier with Adriana but she fears the Instagram messager.

She can only think of one person it can be and she really hopes it isn't him. He could destroy everything.

Rose finishes her wine and pours some more.

She turns to her notes; work has always calmed her.

Tonight has been good for her six clients.

Keera had been a bit subdued at first over dinner but Dan and India had got talking quite animatedly, and soon Keera was joining in. Dan had spent an internship summer in Boston, it turned out, and India's father had once rented a house on Martha's Vineyard.

There was no discussing their therapy. Instead, as if by mutual consent, the guests talked and chatted about other parts of their lives.

Even Grazia had come out of her eerily calm shell. Bernard was ebullient as if making up for trying to skip the next day. He was very keen on a wildly expensive bottle of the hotel's wine and instead of letting him pour a fourth glass, which Rose herself knew was a recipe for disaster, Grazia gently said: 'Perhaps you have had enough, yes?'

Grazia is truly nothing like the iron-hearted second or third wife Rose had suspected she was.

Sir Bernard had tried to talk to Dianne, telling her about the businesses he owns in Australia.

'Love Melbourne, of course,' he'd said, closing his eyes as if imagining it in his brain. 'I love the buzz of Sydney, though.'

'It is a passionate place,' said Grazia, 'a vibrant place.'

But Dianne did not bite.

'Interesting,' she'd said blankly, looking at Bernard as if she could imagine putting his head in a blender.

Rose blinked as she looked at Dianne.

Blender . . . Surely not. But she'd felt the violent urge coming off Dianne as if it was written in big letters in the air.

Shut your mouth, or I'll blend you to a pulp, Bernard.

Rose wonders if she imagined it.

Dianne didn't drink all evening. She was curiously still, like a person very aware of her physical self.

'How are you feeling, Dianne?' Rose had ventured, and Dianne had smiled quickly and begun to speak:

'My daughter sent me a message, which is lovely . . .'

Then she'd clammed up. As if the smallest amount of sharing was a mistake and she had to seal her mouth shut rather than speak of it.

Grazia had turned out to be excellent in the kitchen – totally different from what Christos had imagined.

'I would eat your dolmades any day,' he'd said, bowing to her and kissing her hand. 'Where did you learn to cook?'

'In Georgia,' she'd said simply. 'My grandmother taught me. Not my mother – she was not the mothering type.'

Rose highlighted that remark in her mental notebook in case she needed it.

Dianne had carried the dirty plates into the kitchen and then vanished, which made Rose irritated, because she should have rinsed them and loaded them into the industrial dishwasher.

If they'd been in a proper rehab place, Dianne would have been washing the floor, cleaning the toilets or doing whatever her day's chores were.

Still, she feels sorry for Dianne and whatever massive burden she carries. Anger is a symptom not the cause.

Everyone else is talking and Dianne is maintaining her little iceberg act.

It gets lonely on icebergs.

Finally, her notes finished, Rose undresses tiredly, taking the little piece of turquoise out of her pocket and putting it on the table.

The pain of holding it burns her and yet it's the only link she has with him any more. Theo is gone.

There's no point thinking about what she could have done better, which was just about everything.

But today has awakened the past for her, which is not what she'd planned.

For a woman who makes her living telling other people how to heal the pain of the past, she feels as if she's spectacularly bad at managing this in her own life.

This was to be a spectacular return to business and a way to build Villa Artemis up.

She's been negligent in not expecting it to throw up so many thoughts about her work in the past.

How she'd lost control of the runaway train that was her TV show. How she'd lost Theo.

The Instagram message has frightened her.

Despite her best efforts to keep her mind on the dynamics of the retreat, Rose keeps thinking about the way she and Theo would have been able to discuss how best to get through to the different people at Villa Artemis.

Accept the pain of sadness and loss, but know it's further away than ever. Remember, your inner critic is rarely your friend.

It's one of her favourite sayings, one she likes to leave people with when their sessions are over.

'Remember it yourself,' she thought, channelling her therapist, Vida. 'You're here to work not wallow.'

She has her notes all ready for the next day.

Who knows what will be revealed as the week goes on.

Rose had talked about it again at dinner.

'The notebooks are private but, tonight, I want each of you to write down the answers to two questions. They're just for your benefit, ideas to think about.

'"What do I want most in the world?" and "What do I fear most in the world?"

'Write the headings down and then any words that come to mind. Peace, health, a better job, to get on with your sister, your uncle, your boss – whatever you feel. Dan and Keera, perhaps you might write about how it felt to open up today.'

Rose wonders now who'll do it and who won't.

People get so crushed by the baggage they carry from the past and by living up to other people's expectations that they neglect to think about what *they* want.

This exercise will help with that.

She reminded them about the thought for the day, too: *You can't change other people.*

She hopes it's beginning to sink in.

Before she goes to sleep, she writes down her fears about the anonymous messenger in her journal. She firmly believes in writing fears and gratitude down in a journal. But tonight, writing doesn't heal her the way it usually does.

The guests on the island retreat would be shocked to learn the real truth about Rose, who has built her reputation on being a clear-sighted, truthful woman. They think that a TV-show disaster is the worst thing in her past.

It isn't.

Chapter Twenty-One

In their luxury suite, the biggest bedroom in Villa Artemis, Bernard sits on the edge of the bed and watches Grazia taking off her make-up.

No matter how tired she is, she goes through the ritual. Then she will do her before-bed stretches. These things keep his wife strong.

Her mother, a tricky woman who had been jealous of her beautiful daughter, had advised Grazia:

'Do not waste time on diets. You may have no food one day. Put cream on your face, any cream is better than no cream. Never try to be someone you are not.'

Grazia never does that, Bernard knows.

She is a remarkable woman.

Given their money, Bernard knows Grazia could have changed every part of herself. But she hasn't. She's had some fillers, as she calls them, and Botox, but no surgery, which is so common now that it surprises Bernard.

His forty-year-old personal assistant has had a full facelift. She looks younger but different somehow.

Grazia goes to fitness classes and has a personal trainer come to the house when they're in France and has another she works with in the New York apartment. Women trainers. Bernard isn't stupid.

He knows his wife is a beautiful woman and younger too.

It's hard getting older, Bernard thinks bitterly.

Sometimes he just longs to sit in a chair all day and read. That isn't an option, obviously.

When Bernard was young, which seems like a million years ago, people like him did not sit in chairs and read.

Instead, they worked for other people until their bodies were broken and they retired to live in poverty.

Learning to read had been an accomplishment for many of his peers. His father had never thought much of reading and had been handy with a belt.

Bernard has not built the company he runs today by sitting down and relaxing.

Neither has he run it by being a softie, even though he knows Grazia hates that he is hard now. It's the aura of power – it becomes a cloak he wears all the time.

His children know how much he loves them: they might have forgotten this but they know, deep down—

'Shall we work on the notebooks that Rose gave us?' asks Grazia.

'Of course, darling,' he says. 'You do it. I might early in the morning, I'll see if I have the energy.'

This is a lie. But then, in marriages, people lie.

He thinks of Rose's questions he's supposed to answer; he doesn't like Rose.

She sees everything and Bernard hates that, hates the sense of being looked through and found wanting.

But her questions are interesting: what lies does he tell himself?

That Grazia doesn't mind his secret.

Because she does mind. He knows it.

He also knows what he is most afraid of.

All sensible people know that, don't they?

But he can't change who he is. Only weak people change.

Grazia takes up one of her husband's pens, not one of his ink ones which he's very particular about. She takes a ballpoint one, still a Montblanc. It's expensive, like all the things Bernard likes.

He still thinks money is a gloss that covers everything.

Grazia's handwriting is fluid and elegant. The writing of a woman who learned how to write beautifully, the way she learned to do so many things beautifully.

Culture learned after being raised in the harshness of Soviet Georgia.

Bernard has no idea how much Grazia has learned after leaving the country of her birth. Neither has he any idea how many of the old ways stay with her: she does not say what she thinks easily.

She swallows down the words.

That he does not know this after so many years together makes her very sad.

When I think of what I must say, I wish there was no need for me to be on your retreat. I wish so many things but, Rose, I do not trust in writing things down. Old ways, it is true, but written evidence is never wise. I learned that from my own country. I grew up in the USSR in a time when people who wrote things down sometimes regretted it.

I understand that this is thinking from the past but the past clings, does it not?

I like it here in your hotel. It is beautiful and clever. I like the fabrics in the room, the embroidery on napkins and pillowcases. This reminds me that my grandmother made lace in the old country. She sewed it onto handkerchiefs. We had little money but our handkerchiefs were decorated by lace. I never learned how to do it.

Such lace was bourgeois. My mother told me we must not make lace or embroider. Adornment was frowned upon.

My mother hid the lace handkerchiefs and they are gone now. Wiped out by the memory of men in power.

It is always men in power who make women and children afraid, is it not?

That makes me sad and yet, how to change it?

Dan sits on his small bedroom terrace, smoking and staring at the pad on which he's made many tiny notes. His handwriting is very small and he can get hundreds of words on a page. Unlike Julia, who writes in a big, flowing script. She's very artistic with beautiful, lyrical writing. His Julia, born in a small flat in Camden, moved five times with her parents, attended seven schools and, finally, ended up in St Anselm's because her uncle, Charlie Chance, had got lucky in the import/export business.

Charlie drives a Rolls-Royce, has a gold curb bracelet like a cow chain and is devoted to his little niece. He'd have sent his own Miriam to St Anselm's too, only she said it was too posh and she wasn't clever enough.

'Julia's OK because she's smart. Not me, Dad. I'd like to go to a finishing school, though.'

Miriam went to one in Switzerland and came home with

a bit of French, a flair for skiing and the ability to adopt a cut-glass accent when she wants to.

She and Julia are thick as thieves.

But Julia runs with a wild pack, the wilder rich people from St Anselm's, a couple from the shiny contemporary flats near Tower Bridge.

Dan is never capable of keeping up with these friends with their wild nights out, drug taking, determination to live fast, die young and leave a good-looking corpse.

What lie does he tell himself most? he wonders.

That Julia will one day settle down and be different, stop going out every night, stop the party scene.

That *he* will be enough for her, as he is.

That the arguments will stop.

Writing down what he lies about is no use.

Everyone in his life seems to see him as the baddie: Vicky and Julia's cousin, Miriam, they both think he's to blame for the way Julia is.

Vicky says: 'Anyone normal would tell her they can't hang around while she takes drugs and parties to excess. You're propping all that crazy behaviour up. She'll never stop if you keep mopping up the pieces, Dan.'

It's not his job to stop Julia: it's his job to look after her. She's a wounded bird and he adores her. What's so wrong about taking care of her?

Even here in therapy, Rose has pushed him about it.

He's supposed to imagine if Julia left him for good, permanently.

What a ridiculous idea. They'll always be pulled back together, even if they are apart for now. This separation is just a break . . .

Winded, he drops the pen.

His cigarette has gone out from lack of smoking.

If Julia left the way Rose suggests she could, he wouldn't be responsible for her any more.

Imagine what that would be like – freeing, like jumping off Glastonbury Tor and allowing the wind to make his body sail up into the sky. The freedom of never worrying how she is, walking on eggshells in case he upsets her, which always results in her going on a bender with her friends . . .

He crumples back on earth with a mental bang.

He will never let that happen.

Julia saved him from the crippling loneliness of his teenage years and early twenties.

It had been a time when Dan felt both supremely clever and hideously shy, unable to exist in the world because he'd been born without any shell.

His Julia had been there: beautiful, fun, one of the exciting people, always.

She went to every party, was top of the list of fabulous people and, holding her hand, Dan was there too. In return for loving her, she gave him acceptance into the world.

She's beautiful, breathtaking, and he doesn't deserve her. He can't lose her.

He feels such guilt about today's sharing about her. It was a cry for help and he'd made it about him.

What a fool he is.

But then Rose's other statements crash fleetingly into his conscious mind: it sounds like a co-dependent relationship, and *you can't change other people.*

Julia's always trying to change him.

India fiddles with the pen and her notebook. Purple writing, she decides, and puts away the pink pen – too girly – and takes up her purple one.

She draws a couple of flowers on the page.

The word that comes to mind is 'naive'.

She'd gone wedding dress shopping when she was going out with Felippe, who was the one before Chad.

India had secretly visited two bridal boutiques on her own, just to see what would suit her, even though she knew it was too soon.

She and Felippe were only dating a month.

She'd told her friend, Lizzie, about the wedding dress trips.

'You can't choose this early,' Lizzie had said on the phone, her voice shocked.

Lizzie was heavily pregnant at the time. The reality of the pregnancy had not yet filtered through to India's brain. It was all part of the fun of Lizzie being married. But the separateness of Lizzie having a baby, being an absolute grown-up – that hadn't registered properly.

India and Cleo had been Lizzie's bridesmaids. Lizzie was a pocket-rocket brunette, and Cleo's mother was from Singapore so Cleo had perfect skin, almond eyes like glowing dark jewels and straight silken hair. Together, they were India's best friends.

Cleo had gone to Maastricht to study for her master's, so India relied on Lizzie for the best friend thing.

'I know Felippe and I are only together a few weeks but I couldn't resist it,' India had said dreamily about her wedding shop experience. 'I've always thought that you can't go into a bridal shop unless you are actually engaged – that a sign pings on over your head if you chance going in otherwise! Isn't that a mad thought? But I pretended I was. Oh Lizzie, I tried on one that was totally Cinderella princess. Tiny waist and a huge skirt that moved with you. You'd love it.'

'You do you, hon,' Lizzie had said, but she hadn't sounded invested in the wedding dress idea.

Now, India wonders what sort of an idiot she'd sounded like. She feels like phoning up Lizzie to apologise for being such a dense friend – but Lizzie has a baby and India has no idea what's a good time ever to call her.

In the end, she types in a message on her phone:

I was being really stupid when I told you about trying on wedding dresses, Lizzie – she writes.

Then she realises that Lizzie has a new baby and that she won't care over something silly her friend had done months ago. How self-absorbed has she become? India thinks with frustration.

She deletes the first message then types again: Missing you out here in Corfu. How is Lily-Blossom? I think about her all the time. I hope she's sleeping, love India.

That's better.

India feels that she can't write anything in the notebook now apart from a few bullet points.

- *Wedding dress fantasy – really stupid?*
- *Daydreaming about relationships.*
- *Perfect boyfriends.*

She can't do any more. There's too much swirling in her head.

She'll think about it tomorrow.

Chapter Twenty-Two

Dan is wandering frantically in a hospital. Sweating, panicked.

There are no signs on the walls and he's looking for the emergency room.

He can hear an ambulance siren, but he just can't figure out where to go. His heart is pumping and he's sweating with fear. All the time, doctors and nurses are shouting to one another while the siren wails in the background.

Dan can feel the sweat all over his body and he's exhausted. It's like his legs are leaden, getting heavier and heavier. Each step is like dragging an enormous weight behind him, but he has to find her. Julia.

He can save her.

Then suddenly, he's in a room with lots of doctors wearing blue scrubs in front of him. He knows he has to get past them, has to see who or what is on the bed.

'Julia!' he cries out. 'I'm here!'

The crowds part magically and he's staring down at Julia's body. It's not like she's on a hospital bed – instead she's lying in a six-foot-long pit in the ground.

Her eyes are closed, her face remains beautifully pale and still, and she's surrounded by gallons of red blood.

'*No!*' he screams over and over, trying to get into the pit with her. But he can't.

People hold him back, their hands slick with her blood.

'Why couldn't you wait?' he screams and his voice is hoarse. 'Why did you do this—?'

Then he comes out of the nightmare as suddenly as he went into it.

There's no blood-covered Julia, no pit.

He's had a nightmare.

In reality, he's in his room in Villa Artemis, with its white walls and the soft turquoise armchair beside the double doors to the balcony, which he left open. The muslin curtains move gently in the half-dawn of Tuesday morning.

He's utterly shaken. He doesn't want to go back to sleep in case he falls into that dream again.

He grabs the hated notebook and writes in it:

Tonight I had a nightmare about Julia in hospital. I'm running to find her but I can't. Up and down all these corridors.

When I find her, it's too late. She's covered in blood. She's dead. In a pit and everyone's covered in her blood. I feel such anguish, like I'm responsible. Because I'm too late to find her.

Then the realisation hits him.

He was angry with Julia in the dream.

Furious.

How dare she risk her precious life. How dare she make the people who love her suffer.

And yet . . .

Dan knows there's a deep grief in Julia that he can never

reach. How can he be angry with her when she's trying to cope with such pain?

Will she ever be able to let go of the pain?

Will he ever be free of it?

Winded at this thought, Dan lies back on the bed.

He probes inside his head, searching for the unaccustomed anger the way he'd reach for a sore tooth with his tongue.

He's never angry with Julia in real life. He idolises her.

But idolatry is not love.

Chapter Twenty-Three

'Hi Keera, it's your momma here. I'm in Vegas and, guess what, I'm too old for the shows! Me! Too old? I am so fricking annoyed. I came to see my pal Ernesto, you know the guy who told me for years he could get me a gig out here, no problemo.

'Turns out he was lying!

'All the jobs go to bands of young dudes doing Eagles covers or girls who can't sing but can rock a pastie, if you know what I mean. What's some twenty-one-year-old Barbie going to know about heartbreak? Jack shit, that's what they know.

'I'm only here because I need the money. We are broke, in case you don't know, Keera! I can't believe you used the money in that last account to go to this "retreat". You got fixed already, for chrissake. How many more fixes do you need?

'I'm staying at Maggie Flatbush's house. I'm in with the lizard. Gecko. Whatever. It has a triplex and a cubic zirconia necklace. I'm on a blow-up mattress on the floor. Lizards have it better than me!

'I've been thinking – I hate that rehab schtick but it could be merchandisable. You hear me? So phone me, Keera. We need to get you on the talk-shows telling everyone about your pain or whatever. Then an album. Then the money's rolling back in again!

'Phone me.

'ASAP.'

Keera listens to the voice message and then deletes it.

She doesn't want to give herself the opportunity of listening to it again.

Once is enough.

She cannot think about her mother now. There's too much whirling around in her head. Bobbi in real life is insistent enough; Keera's only hope is to banish her voice for now.

Chapter Twenty-Four

Tuesday dawns and it's another glorious sunny day in Corfu. Rose bounces out of her soft bed and hops in the shower.

Today is going to be a fantastic day, she thinks, soaping herself with the villa's handmade olive-oil-and-wild-lavender soap.

She is not going to think about the Instagram menace – why worry when it could be just another crazy person who made it sound as if they knew Rose's secret. Nobody knew.

Today, she's going to be positive!

The group are not all open to therapy, that's a challenge. Bernard and Dianne are hold-outs.

When Rose worked in California, one of the advantages was that an awful lot of the population had engaged in some sort of therapy or another. Whereas the group on the island retreat are a mix of people who have, with the exception of Keera, eschewed analysis.

Never mind, Rose thinks cheerfully. She's got this.

At breakfast, she goes into the kitchen to pick up the egg-white omelette that Christos has made her.

It's not on the menu and he makes them just for Rose. She will eat her breakfast away from the group because she's pretty sure that if this high-protein, low-fat omelette *was* on the menu, both Keera and India would order it non-stop.

Rose does not want to give them the chance.

She sits in the small garden behind the private part of the buildings. It's a sprawling site and Rose and the architect wanted to build in lots of little hidey-hole places where people could find peace. Like the acropolis up high behind the terrace, or the little terrace surrounded by lavender under the infinity pool.

Rose knows that she has put on far more weight than is good for her knees, but she is still fit from all her walking over the island.

She likes that she is not tormented by her own body.

It's a wonderful thing. She feels physically capable of so much.

No matter what happens in the next few years, she vows that she is not going to put on a single pair of controlling underwear.

No Spanx or Skims, no more squashing her intestines into cramped conditions like Victorian ladies wearing corsets that made them faint.

As she gets her things after breakfast to start the second day of the retreat, Rose reflects that she's really enjoying working with this first group. The whole point of the island retreat is that it's gentle.

It's not offering instant solutions, which was what Rose had been backed into doing on *The Talisman Effect* by the end. No wonder it had all exploded into chaos.

Here, Rose is not promising to fix them – she is helping them see their problems and giving them the tools to continue working on them. It's a more realistic way of working. She loves it.

And Corfu.

Rose doesn't think she'll ever leave the island. Between the climate, the beauty of the island and the glorious generosity and fun of the people, Corfu is a paradise.

Keera looks at what she's written in her notebook.

It's not much. Just random thoughts as they occur to her.

Want a new life.
   Friends.
   I have no friends.

And then the shadow of her mother appears.

Dr Bobbi . . .? What the hell can she be thinking about merchandising Keera's rehab?

Keera doesn't want to even think about this.

Her mother never stops, does she?

Then one more idea occurs to her: such a huge idea that Keera's stunned to find herself writing it down.

I don't want to perform any more.

That would certainly break her mother's heart. Dr Bobbi has put her whole life into Keera's career so how can Keera tear that bandage off without ripping her mother to shreds?

Even at a low ebb in Las Vegas, Bobbi's first thought is about how they can get Keera's career back on track.

Keera scratches out the last point in her notebook, almost making a hole in the page.

If she can't perform, what does she do? And how to make a living out of it?

Touring is where the actual money is made now: as her mother knows, merchandising is where the cash is.

Keera closes the notebook. Figuring this stuff out is too much for her right now.

Perhaps by the end of the retreat she'll know what to do.

At ten to ten on Tuesday morning, with an eye on the time, Rose takes her coffee into the airy cream-and-blue dining room with its walls covered with exquisite watercolours of Corfu's beaches and cultural sites.

Delicately delineated and painted beautifully, there's the Monastery of Paleokastritsa, the Temple of Artemis, the Old Fortress and Mouse Island.

'Rose,' Adriana greets her with a hug.

She is the only person in there; it's used more for cooler days and some of the evening meals. 'Did you sleep? After the Instagram thing?'

'Yes,' says Rose. 'We are not worrying about that, OK? I've been thinking that there's no way it was anyone who knows what happened. Why would they wait so long to threaten me?'

'You think?' asks Adriana.

'Absolutely,' says Rose firmly.

Through the dining room's big windows, the sisters watch India and Keera arrive on the terrace together, both flushed from what has obviously been an early morning walk on the beach. Keera's in flowy trousers and another white shirt but India looks spectacular. She's wearing a scarf plaited into her fabulous hair, all colours of gold and honey. Her dress today is pure 1940s, white, nipped in at the waist and with blue piped around the collar, and cap sleeves.

Rose thinks that India's quite the artist but doesn't appear aware that this is a skill.

Dianne follows – she's another one who's clearly been getting her steps in: there's a faint breeze today and Dianne's hair is a little bit windswept.

She looks less frozen today, Rose thinks.

Bernard's sitting at a table on his own while Dan has stopped on his way out to chat to the older man.

He's not there long before Grazia appears from the pool area, a miasma of just-smoked cigarette about her.

Rose walks out to them and examines her notes.

Day Two. She needs more of the guests to tell their stories today so everyone can relax somewhat.

That will give her a roadmap for messages for the day.

A little bit of discussion about who filled in their notebooks, perhaps. Time for the group to walk on the beach or sit on the terrace and think, too. Rose found that people needed time to reflect before the lessons of her type of therapy rooted in their brains.

India has arranged her notebook, coloured pens and tiny Post-its on the table in front of her. She likes organisation. Then she turns to surreptitiously study Grazia and Bernard as they settle down at the table on the terrace for Tuesday morning's session.

Grazia catches her eye again and gives a little smile.

India beams back.

Yesterday, she'd thought that Grazia was some sort of automaton who didn't feel things, but here's Grazia being smiley and lovely.

Stop judging people on how they look, India tells herself.

She writes the thought down in her notebook.

'You can't change anyone' is written down with lots of flowers sketched around it. India is conscious that she knew this on some level and yet, seeing this tenet reflected in Dan's life makes it seem more real.

Dan wants to be with Julia for ever, she doesn't appear to want that and there's absolutely nothing he can do to change that.

When Rose sits down, India catches her eye as if to say, *It's OK, I can go next*, but Rose shakes her head imperceptibly and smiles.

'Later,' she says softly.

India's relief is enormous.

Rose starts them off with five minutes of deep breathing, this time asking them to get in touch with their bodies as they breathe.

'I want you to feel what effects yesterday had on you. The mind–body connection is very strong. We need to ground ourselves before we start looking inwards again.

'Secondly I want to say that this week and this sort of therapy is very difficult, so congratulations for how much ground we've covered already. I know many of you are reconsidering why you're here but, I promise, it will help, even if you don't feel that right now.'

Rose looks at them all in turn.

'When I started training as a psychologist a long time ago, there were many parts of the world where therapy was considered strange, definitely woo-woo.'

She steals a glance at Dan who has the grace to blush.

He was the one who described the island retreat as woo-woo, but Rose is not holding that against him.

'For younger people, the idea of stepping inside, looking into your inner thought processes and trying to heal, is a more normal concept than for older people. My generation was possibly the first to seriously think that therapy was good. But for those of us who are older,' and Rose graciously nods to Dianne, Bernard and Grazia as she says this, 'looking back at our lives and the decisions and traumas that have made us is altogether harder. So well done Grazia and Bernard for being here. And Dianne . . .'

Suddenly Rose's gaze is upon Dianne. 'It's hard to speak, I understand, but opening up is possibly the only way you can move on. You need to process the pain of the past or you'll keep getting stuck in it. Unprocessed, the pain of the past will be like wading though quicksand again and again. The only way to be free is to face the pain, walk towards it, take away its power.'

Rose almost can't believe it but she thinks she sees the soft gleam of tears in the corners of Dianne's eyes. Can she be mistaken? So far Dianne has shown absolutely no emotion, apart from quite obvious temper with Dan yesterday.

Is some of this reaching her?

'Looking vaguely into your life, your choices and how you live is fine as a concept,' Rose goes on. 'Doing it is another thing entirely.' She glances around the group.

India grins involuntarily. Rose is totally right.

Applying for an island retreat to restart your life seems like a marvellous idea when you have had three glasses of wine and is terrifying when you actually have to do it.

She personally feels as if she's on a rollercoaster but there's no getting off.

Rose turns back to Dianne. 'How do you get on with your children, Dianne?' she asks.

Dianne shoots her a poisonous look and both Grazia and Bernard, who notice it, are startled.

'Fine,' snaps Dianne.

'They made you come here, isn't that right?'

'Kids know nothing,' Dianne replies harshly. 'They grow up and then think you're an old person who knows nothing. How dare they!'

'So you're angry with them?' Rose asks gently.

There's a tiny chink in Dianne's armour; Rose feels herself slipping in.

Dianne's nostrils flare with anger.

'I am here because they wanted me to come but I should be at home,' she says icily. 'My daughter's expecting a baby; it's due soon. Why the hell am I here on this bloody island when I should be with her?'

'Why do you think you're here?' Rose asks.

'Because I got angry with a stupid man and his stupid car. That's all. I'm not mad.'

The terrace is quiet apart from the distant noise of the sea and the buzzing of insects in the warm morning air.

'Nobody here is mad,' Rose says easily.

'*He* bloody well is!' shoots back Dianne, pointing at Dan. 'He's a controlling bastard. It's written all over him. Only *he* can look after his girlfriend, she's nothing without him. That's what controlling people say.'

'How dare you!' explodes Dan, getting to his feet. 'I have never tried to control her in my life! I've never thought Julia's nothing without me. I adore her and you know nothing—'

'I know more than you think!' yells Dianne, also standing.

'Please sit down,' says Rose in a calm yet very stern voice.

Dianne flushes but sits.

Dan follows suit, his hands balled up into fists.

'We're not here to attack other people, Dianne,' says Rose.

'Do you want to throw me off the retreat?' says Dianne, a hint of hope on her face.

'No, nobody gets thrown off yet,' says Rose, sounding steely. 'You have to stay.'

She pauses for a moment, lets a silence settle, then turns deliberately.

'Bernard? You have a son and a daughter, I think?' Rose asks, smoothly changing tack.

'Yes!' Bernard answers eagerly.

It appears that he's dying to talk, which Rose finds remarkable. Bernard has looked as if he's barely tolerating things up to now. Plus he wanted to go out on a boat today. But for some reason, he's turned into Mr Chatty.

'Stephen's the eldest, very clever chap, not one but two degrees in business. Smarter than me, no doubt about it. Decent too. Lovely wife and a very nice house in Wiltshire, I have to tell you. Three grandkids, all marvellous, marvellous . . .' His voice trails off a little.

Rose feels she might have heard enough about Bernard's son.

'Your daughter?' she says gently.

The look on Grazia's face tells Rose that *this* could be where some of the problem lies. Possibly not the only problem but one of them.

'Girls are trickier,' says Bernard blandly. 'Viola's a marvellous girl. On her second husband, of course, but young people these days have to marry the wrong person before they figure out who the right one is!'

He says this with gusto, as if it's a phrase he trots out a lot: *Stephen is marvellous and Viola's a lovely young thing with one marriage behind her but it's all lovely. Nothing to see here!*

'The new one's Ivor, a charming boy. The first chap she married wasn't the best and it took a while to extract her from him . . .'

He sneaks a glance at Grazia who gives him a look filled with reassurance.

It's a lovely performance, Rose thinks.

'But Ivor's an excellent chap. I'm very lucky,' Bernard goes on earnestly.

Rose has the sense that this is a well-used and carefully crafted line he uses whenever anyone wants to do a profile of him for a business newspaper.

His children are marvellous, everything's tickety-boo and he, personally, has been very lucky.

Blah, blah, blah.

'Interesting,' Rose comments gravely. 'The way you explain it, it sounds as if your life is perfect. And yet you are here . . .'

She lets a nice pause elapse and Bernard glares at her.

Rose thinks his determination to speak has been a lovely little gift.

Dan, India and Keera are now staring at him. Even Dianne has switched her attention to Bernard and is giving him the stink eye.

Rose worked in a rehab clinic when she first began practising and she'd realised that the group therapy was almost magical.

In group therapy, everyone was invested in each other's recovery and they learned from each other.

Of course, patients often liked to focus a laser gaze on each other.

They'd glare at each other, eyes narrowed, and say: 'You're lying' or 'Denial much?'

Bernard is definitely covering up.

Rose would bet anything on it.

She turns her attention to Grazia.

'Do you share these children together or are they your stepchildren?'

Grazia's nervous tic pings into action and her hand reaches automatically towards her beautiful Dior handbag as if looking for her cigarettes.

'No,' she says in her customary blunt way. 'I am the wicked stepmother.'

Nobody laughs.

'Not really wicked, I'm guessing,' says Rose thoughtfully. 'The wicked stepmother trope came about because so many women died in childbirth that stepmothers were common.'

Everyone looks interested. Dianne is nodding in agreement. Somebody knows their feminist history.

'The process of naming stepmothers as wicked allowed the vision of the perfect *real* mother to remain untouched. Like in *Animal Farm* – four legs good, two legs bad. Real mama is good. Stepmama is bad.

'Let's face it,' Rose finishes, 'did you ever hear about a non-wicked fairy-tale stepmother?'

India laughs out loud.

She's thought about wicked stepmothers too, it seems. But Rose doesn't think India's problem is with hers.

'It pitted women against women, too, which was a neat patriarchal trick,' interjects Dianne abruptly.

'I never thought of it that way,' says India, interested.

Grazia smiles back at Rose with a very chilly smile.

'Sometimes people believe fairy stories,' she says.

'Do your stepchildren believe that about you?' Rose inquires. 'Blended families can be tricky.'

Grazia shrugs at this open-ended question. This time,

she grabs the Dior handbag, pulls it onto her lap and opens it, long fingers stretching inside.

'You want to smoke?' Rose says quietly.

'Yes. It is good for stress.'

'I'll tell you what,' Rose says. 'Let's have a little break, you can have your cigarette and, when we're back, we'll talk about your stepchildren in a short session before lunch.'

Grazia beams at her.

'I like this plan.'

In the kitchen, Christos is working on prep for tonight's barbecue on the beach with Alzina, his sous-chef.

He has already been down to the quay in Xanthe to buy fish and he's now examining plump aubergines with gleaming skin.

Alzina's cousin, Lydia, is busy helping Adriana with the hotel's beautiful white towels. Together, they've cleaned most of the rooms, and the industrial washing machine that Adriana loves is working overtime.

'How's it going?' asks Adriana, pausing briefly.

'Excellent,' Rose replies.

'That rich guest wiped up some red wine with the hand towels,' Lydia complains to Rose. 'They will never be properly white again.'

'Bernard?' asks Rose.

'The old one who watches me walk past,' Lydia says with revulsion. 'I hate the way he looks at me.' She's in her early twenties, working for a year after college and saving to pay for her master's.

'He looks at every woman,' agrees Adriana. 'Like he's awarding marks out of ten. He's certainly demanding.'

'Should I say something?' queries Rose.

Adriana shakes her head. Working alongside Christos in some of the top hotels in Europe has given her much experience of hotel life.

'No. I'll handle their room in future. He knows I'm a manager. He won't try anything with me.'

'Does he need to know that I'm your husband?' says Christos, looming over her.

The three women laugh.

'Absolutely,' says Rose, grinning.

Dianne has wandered off to the edge of the infinity pool and is staring at her mobile phone. Still nothing. No more messages from Ellie.

She can understand Lauren not talking to her: Lauren has a very black-and-white world view. She simply wants her mother to be the way she used to be.

Until that happens, she's removing herself from the conversation.

But Ellie was Dianne's little fairy girl who'd followed her mother around like a little puppy, one finger in her mouth and the other clutching Dianne's skirt.

When Dianne thinks back to when her three children were very young, it breaks through the barriers she's erected.

She feels the tears flood up from the tight, painful place in her chest.

Bloody Rose and her talking about painful stuff.

Can't she see that Dianne has had enough of pain?

There's a blue-and-white painted love seat to the right of the pool: it sits under a huge palm tree with two planters full of lavender beside it.

Dianne wipes away her tears with one hand, then sits down heavily and contemplates the sea.

It's so beautiful here but she wants to be at home, holding Ellie's hand before she goes into the labour suite. Dianne would love to be her daughter's birthing partner but she hasn't been asked.

Lots of mothers stay with their daughters when they give birth. Not all men are able to cope, Dianne knows. She'd manage, even if it meant watching her beloved Ellie in pain.

But she's ruled herself out of the job of birthing partner with her behaviour.

She feels the damned tears swell up again and she bends over, her mouth in a silent scream, the emotional pain too much to bear.

What hurts the most is that none of it is her fault. But she's the one being punished.

Back on the terrace, Rose turns to Bernard. She thinks of Lydia's remarks about him.

Working with people she dislikes is never easy. But needs must. She has plenty of experience of dealing with powerful men in LA who look at young women like prey.

'What age were the children, Bernard, when you married Grazia?' Rose asks crisply.

'Maria died when they were in their teens,' he says, another response from the newspaper-interview archives, Rose thinks acidly.

'Stephen and Viola were very young, thirteen and fifteen. Maria's was a sudden, unexpected death and we were all bereft. Brain haemorrhage. There one minute and gone the next. Tragic. None of us ever got to say goodbye. Tragic,' he repeats.

He holds his hands up as if holding up an empty vessel.

'We were alone, the three of us. Not a family but just three people. Maria made us a family. When she died, I was running the business so I wasn't around a lot and I couldn't stop working. We got by with help: Stephen and Viola had a housekeeper to drive them around because by then I had money, and of course I was able to send both of them to public schools.'

Rose would like to shake Bernard by the shoulders now, although her expression does not show it.

From the way Bernard speaks, there's simply no sense of his grieving over the death of his first wife. It's as if he merely replaced her with more staff. Telling everyone that the children went to public school is just another way of showing off his wealth.

She decides to give him a few minutes more to tell everyone his rehearsed story.

'They had amazing educations – they'd both tell you that themselves,' Bernard adds earnestly. 'I'm a grammar-school boy myself, hauled myself up by my bootstraps.'

It's his turn to beam around at the group.

Rose notes another line from his cheery business biography.

'When they left school, they could walk into any university in the world. Stephen chose Exeter, which was where my first wife Maria was from, and Viola . . .'

There's another pause.

'The academic world was not for Viola,' says Bernard, gaining confidence again and giving it a positive spin. 'Clever girl, very clever girl, but she wasn't happy burying herself in books. Went to Edinburgh, had a lot of fun but got into a bit of trouble.'

He looks down at his wrinkled hands.

'I felt I should marry again to give them a mother figure.'
Dianne snorts.
Rose ignores this.

'There was my lovely Grazia,' Bernard says. 'She came to the business long after Maria died.'

'I was his executive assistant,' says Grazia, now holding an unlit cigarette in her hand. She's rolling it between her fingers as if waiting eagerly for the moment she'll be able to light it.

'I speak three languages,' says Grazia, grimly giving her CV. 'I have a master's in business from Charles University in Prague – one of the oldest universities in Europe. I paid my bills my whole life and yet Stephen and Viola think I am a gold digger.'

Her eyes flash fire.

Rose wonders how she ever thought Grazia's face was unemotional.

'They never wanted me,' says Grazia sadly. 'We are married a long time and still I am an outsider.'

Grazia snaps her mouth shut as if she's already said too much.

She's still rolling the cigarette around in her fingers now as if she can't wait to smoke it.

'So, is that why you're here, Bernard?' Rose asks. 'You want to fix things between Grazia and your children?'

Under his tan, Bernard looks old and slightly pale.

He doesn't like Grazia talking about the less-happy facts of their life.

'Once I relished a battle. It always was a battle in the early days in business and I loved it. But I'm getting older.'

Grazia makes a movement as if she's going to touch her husband in consolation but reconsiders it. Her hand returns to her handbag.

'I have grandchildren I rarely have in my home because Stephen doesn't get on with Grazia, so that means going to visit them alone.'

'Your home, Bernard?' says Rose. 'Not "our" home?'

'You understand!' says Grazia fiercely. 'It is always his home, his everything. His children. I am just a second wife, I do not count.'

'That bad?' Rose asks.

'Yes, that bad,' says Grazia. 'Worse, Bernard says he loves me but he never tries to get his children to accept me. He cannot issue ultimatums to them. I must suffer because they are in charge of his life.'

Suddenly Dianne interrupts.

'Kids don't always understand. Even when they're grown up. They think they know more than you, comprehend more than you and yet they know *nothing*.'

The group turns as one to look at Dianne.

'Children never understand their parents' lives. No matter how bloody old they are.'

Rose does not want to jeopardise Dianne's involvement.

'Why don't you think they understand?' she asks mildly.

Dianne grins and it's not a polite grin – more of a grimace.

'They like to believe the fairy tale about life but it's the Disney one they think is real. When it's really the Brothers Grimm.'

'They wrote some fascinating fairy tales,' jumps in Keera. 'I had to read a couple of them for a film script once. Didn't get the part but it was interesting, you know, very dark stuff.'

She shivers deliciously.

'Yeah, they're dark,' says Dianne. 'Like the real world. But kids don't want to know about the real world. They prefer the fantasy.'

No delicious shivering there, Rose notes.

'They're cautionary tales made up to tell people how to live. How to watch out for danger. We've made fairy stories into lovely tales for children but, really, they're warnings about how to be safe in a bloody terrifying world,' Dianne says. 'You don't see they're warnings until it's too late.'

She stops abruptly, then asks: 'Are we on our break?'

Rose decides to call it. This has been an interesting session.

'Yes,' she says.

Grazia's cigarette is lit almost before she's completely out of her chair and she's sucking the nicotine into her lungs as if it's pure oxygen.

'But there's one final thought I want to leave you with for the moment,' Rose says, her voice as clear as any bell.

Everyone's half out of their chairs, keen to move on, but Rose's words stop them.

'We sometimes accept behaviour at the start of a relationship even though it hurts us. And perhaps that actual behaviour becomes less important and sometimes it becomes more important with time.'

She stares at Grazia as she says it.

'When we decide that we can no longer live with ourselves because something is affecting us so much, then we act – if our actions do not change things, if the other party still treats us with contempt or belittles our feelings, then the relationship is in serious trouble.'

Rose pauses and looks Bernard in the eye.

'There are many things a good relationship can withstand, but contempt is not one of them. When one partner chooses contempt, the other may never recover from it. Contempt is a fatal wound, you see.

'The session is over now. It would be useful for you all to make some notes on this.'

Then she sweeps off the terrace.

Grazia's long legs carry her quickly into their suite and Bernard follows her.

But for once, she doesn't wait for him. She lets the door slam in his face so that he has to fumble for his room card to get in.

His wife is at the minibar, reaching for some ice-cold lemonade.

'What are you going to talk about next?' he asks, his voice anxious.

Grazia cracks the lid off the bottle of lemonade, takes a deep draught and turns to her husband.

'Why?' she asks with an edge. 'Are you worried?'

'No, it's just that some things are private. I don't hold with this sort of therapy stuff, Grazia, you know I don't. This Rose has no idea what our marriage is like. She knows nothing, she's merely prodding us. I love you but—'

She interrupts him.

'I love you *but*,' she snaps. 'That's what husbands always say. I am your wife, you could have made it clear to Viola and Stephen that I mattered. You chose not to do that.'

'I couldn't—' he began.

'You could. You chose not to. You let them insult me and then pretend it never happened. That is not love, Bernard. That was ignoring my feelings, not explaining to your children that I was a good person and that rudeness to me would not be tolerated. I always came second, after them, always. Rose is right – it is contempt.'

'Don't be ridiculous, Grazia,' he says, and she turns away.

She has heard this so many times. She has had enough.

Bernard thought he'd placate her merely by coming to this retreat.

But it's a hollow victory if he chooses not to listen to what she says.

'It is a big deal. It upsets me,' she says angrily. 'I never understood the words for it before but I do now: contempt. You treated me with contempt and allowed Viola and Stephen to do the same.'

'Grazia, they lost their mother so young, you must understand that,' Bernard says in lofty tones.

'I understand,' she snaps. 'What I don't understand is how you don't tell them how hurtful I find their behaviour.'

'Please,' he says wearily, 'they do appreciate you, but I'm their father and there's a special bond there.'

Grazia has heard all this before.

She knows that Stephen and Viola would behave differently to her if their father really cared about them doing so. But he doesn't.

He has his life compartmentalised. There is his business, Grazia and his children, and all three have separate compartments. If she puts a boundary up, then Bernard flattens it. Only his boundaries matter, not hers.

Grazia doesn't think she wants to live like this any more.

'Let's not fight, darling,' he adds now. 'It is not worth it. We love each other.'

Love can do a lot of things, Grazia knows, but compensate for contemptuous behaviour? No.

Grazia allows Bernard to hug her.

She has only one more trick up her sleeve.

She needs to talk to Rose, tell her the full truth about their marriage.

But Grazia knows that if she does, Bernard will never forgive her.

The September sun beats down on India and Keera as they sit beside the infinity pool and drink iced tea.

Letting the sun warm their limbs is a glorious release after the tension of the terrace. Even the cicadas and the sounds of tiny chirping birds add to the sense of a break away from the world. The heat of the sun makes every movement slow and languid.

'Do you miss not being able to drink or use drugs?' asks India, arching her body luxuriously on the sunlounger.

Keera's sitting upright on hers and, in reply, she pats India's skinny bare knee.

'Thank you for asking,' she says. 'People don't. Not many people know I've been in rehab but the ones who do don't ask about it. It's like this big Not My Problem area that people walk around and try very hard to pretend is not there.'

'Oh sweetie. That's hard. Does your mom get it?'

Keera winces at the question. Everything comes back to her mother. 'Sort of. Mom doesn't do failure and being an addict is a failure. She's all about winning and being the best.'

'Competitive?'

'Yes. She wanted me to be the absolute best, both for me and her. But she was kinda ruthless with it.'

India's fascinated by the intricacies of Keera's relationship with her mother. It's all so intense: nothing like India's relationships with her parents and stepmother.

Sonja's less of a mother than a lovely godmother who dances into India's life every now and then. Georgie's always careful not to overstep. She can't imagine either of them pushing her the way Keera has clearly been pushed to succeed.

'In what way was your mom ruthless?' India asks.

Keera shrugs. 'Where do I start? "You don't get in the charts by being ready to settle for second best": that's my mom's motto.'

Keera begins to list it all:

'Being the right shape was really important. Skinny but not worryingly skinny – not that I ever managed too skinny,' she says ruefully. 'Wearing the right clothes from the right people. Being "on" all the time. Which is exhausting, to be frank. "*It's all part of it!*" Mom used to say.'

'Gosh, that's pushing you straight into an eating disorder,' India says, sitting up. 'It must have been hard.'

'Yeah, it was. It is. My mom is one of the most driven people I know, and she can be really funny. But tough. Very tough. We lived out of a suitcase for years and she never had relationships. Not that she didn't date, but it was never about men: it was about my career.'

They both digest this.

'I used to weigh myself every morning,' Keera goes on. 'Part of Mom's rules but I stopped doing it in rehab. It was all so much about self-hatred.' She shudders.

'You're so gorgeous and lovely, you shouldn't hate yourself,' says India earnestly. 'Body-shaming is so toxic and it's everywhere. I could never do what you've done, for that reason. Everyone saying you're too thin or too fat. It's horrible. Are you going back to that world after this?'

Keera hugs her knees to her chest.

'I don't know. It's lovely here: nobody knows I'm here, nobody's trying to pap me coming out of a shop or a club. I'm not *on* all the time. That's lovely. If I'm honest, I . . .'

She pauses. Even saying it feels weird.

'I could totally retire from music and TV but we have very little money left and if I want to settle down somewhere and do something else, I'll need some more money.'

There, she's said it.

Said to another person that she wants to retire from music.

Not from writing it, she thinks, but from performing.

Saying it aloud has real power.

India seems to sense this and smiles at her new friend.

'Georgie likes to say "Courage, ma chère." Be brave, darling. So be brave, Keera!'

'Hey ladies,' says Dan appearing behind them, tall and wonderfully tanned from barely a day and a half in the sun. 'Lunch is ready.'

'I can only achieve that colour with fake tan,' says Keera jokily.

'This?' Dan holds out an arm in confusion.

'Yeah, that,' Keera replies.

Dan looks happier than he did yesterday, India thinks.

Lighter, almost.

The women leave their sunbeds and India grabs Keera's hand as they leave, squeezing it in sisterly support.

'This place is beautiful,' Dan says as they walk up to the terrace. 'If my job allowed remote working, I'd love to live here.'

'What about your girlfriend? Would she like it?' asks India guilelessly.

Dan is stumped.

'It's a bit quiet for her. She'd like a wilder island. She likes Ibiza. And she's my ex,' he adds formally, as if he feels obliged to correct this information.

Keera and India nod and say nothing, but India secretly pokes Keera in the ribs.

'He's absolutely gorgeous,' she whispers to Keera as they make their way back to their seats on the terrace.

'I thought you were here to work out why you keep dating the wrong men,' Keera hisses back.

'Am I?' asks India, and they grin at each other.

Lunch is a buffet in the dining room and there's not a lot of talking. Grazia hasn't turned up at all, while Bernard takes his plate and heads out to the bar where he orders a glass of the villa's best wine.

Adriana serves him herself.

'Is this to your liking, Sir Bernard?' she asks formally.

It gives him no option but to be polite back.

'Yes, perfectly acceptable, thank you.'

India and Keera try to get Dianne to join them at their table but she shakes her head.

'I think she was crying, don't you think?' India says to Keera when Dianne's gone.

'Looks like it,' says Keera sadly.

Dan sits with them and they eat Greek salads with freshly baked soft rolls and talk about plans for when they're not in session.

'I'd love to go on a hike,' says Dan wistfully. 'I cycle a lot at home.'

He begins to tell them about his bike and they tease him cheerfully about it.

'I like reformer Pilates and barre,' says India.

'I like strawberry shortcake ice cream,' jokes Keera.

They're still joking as they carry their plates into the kitchen.

Christos begins to tell them about tonight's barbecue.

'Do we help with the cooking?' Keera wants to know.

She actually enjoyed last night's session in the kitchen: it felt gloriously normal.

She's suddenly imagining a life where she has a small house with a yard out the back and a barbecue. She can have people over, friends like Cat and Taniqua, some of her NA people. India, definitely. India is a friend, for sure. Maybe dogs – she's always wanted a dog.

'Of course you can cook,' says Christos, who really likes this earnest girl with the blonde hair and the friendly smile.

His wife tells him she is very famous but she does not behave that way. In his hotel career, before he and Adriana came back to live in Corfu to run his family's restaurant, Christos had met many famous people.

Some had outlandish demands and didn't want any member of staff looking into their eyes.

Some were charming, polite and decent. It's clear that Keera is in the latter group, so he smiles at her.

'Let me tell you what we are making,' he says.

Rose arrives on the terrace after lunch in a haze of freshly applied lime and mandarin perfume. She scans the retreaters skilfully.

Keera, India and Dan look relaxed. They know the next session isn't going to be about them.

Rose beams at them and wishes for a moment that she had two weeks with the whole group – then she'd really get down into the weeds with them. But nobody would come to a two-week retreat, would they? Maybe.

She saves the thought to talk about with Adriana and Christos later.

'Let's go back to you, Grazia and Bernard,' Rose says. They need to unpack the tricky situation that is a second marriage, difficult adult children and resentment.

'Earlier, we were looking at the dynamics behind your blended family. How long have you been married?'

'Twenty-five years,' says Grazia.

Rose notes that Grazia is sitting bolt upright now, no more elegantly lazing in her chair.

'I was thirty-seven. Bernard, he is fifteen years older and his wife was dead a long time. I am not stupid. I knew there was a risk; I thought it would be OK. I thought that Stephen and Viola would accept me because I was not trying to be their mother, and yet they did not accept me.'

Rose is astonished to learn that Grazia is sixty-two: she looks a decade younger.

'The children did their best,' Bernard says gamely.

For the first time Rose sees Grazia's face really flare with anger as she looks at her husband.

'You still think that?' she asks frostily. 'Because they did not try as far as I can see. They never tried. Did Stephen and his wife let us take the children to the cinema or to our house on Sundays? No. Only if I was not involved. I was not a grandparent and they made that very clear from the first. And Viola . . .' Grazia snorts.

'She was the worst. I tried to help her. That stupid man she married. He was a user. He hurt her and even then, when I tried to step in and save her, she did not want my help. I knew what she was going through, but my help wasn't needed.'

Grazia looks tense, the memory obvious from her body language.

'In what way was he a user?' asks Rose mildly.

'He was only interested in her for money and contacts,'

Grazia says bitterly. 'He loved that she had a rich father, knew lots of other rich people. Then he ran up debts, got her to apply for huge loans for investments – all failed, of course.

'He was a whiner and a parasite, leeching off the family. Pretending the money was his to his useless friends. Unfortunately, I understand men like him. Bernard had to pay in the end to get rid of him.'

She looks at her husband with approval for a moment.

'It took a long time for Bernard to understand that the man was a parasite. He helped Viola. I tried to help too. Yet still she was against me.'

Grazia's sorrow is evident now. Even Botox cannot hide the utter misery in her eyes.

'After all I did to help her, Viola still believed I was like her ex-husband. Leeching off them all, fattened up with cash like a proper blood-sucker. Can you imagine how that made me feel?'

She turns to her husband and his benign, unworried face seems to enrage her.

'You knew how hurt I was and you did nothing, you let her speak to me as if I was a worthless gold-digger. That is the most painful thing.'

Rose sees that Grazia's anger is unsheathed now: white hot with the memory of how her husband's children made her feel.

'Now hold on, darling, this is not the time nor the place—' begins Bernard.

'It is exactly the time and the place,' she hisses. 'I had my own money when we married. I did not need your money. For sure, I was not a very wealthy person by your children's standards but I had my own money, my own pension, my career. They are still stupid, immature children who do not care who they hurt,' she says, turning to Rose now.

'You spoiled them, Bernard, you *know* you did,' Grazia switches her attention back. 'Their main worry was that my marriage to their father would divert some of his money away from them. Or that I'd have a child with you and destroy their inheritance.'

'It isn't like that,' says Bernard in a placating tone. 'You're misrepresenting the facts, my dear. They care for you, but you're not their mother, that's all.'

Dianne snorts loudly.

Grazia's incandescent with rage and everyone in the group can see it.

'It's nothing to do with me being their mother – it's to do with what you will allow, Bernard, and how you have let Stephen and Viola worship only privilege and money.'

Again Rose wonders how she ever thought that Grazia was expressionless because her face is alive with expression now.

She's heroic in her anger.

'Not true at all,' mutters Bernard. 'You're being overemotional, Grazia.'

India glares at Bernard but he doesn't notice anyone else. He's looking to Rose as if to confirm that his wife is having some emotional breakdown which is nothing to do with him.

Rose sees it all now.

Bernard runs his life his way, and he expects Grazia to do all the emotional labour in their relationship. If his kids are rude to her, that's none of his business.

Grazia brought her husband to Corfu because she thought she could tell him how she felt only in the presence of other people. And Rose Talisman.

Rose feels both the burden and the honour of being seen as the person who can fix this.

She will do her absolute best.

But it doesn't look good.

Grazia's prepared to spend a week in the sun ripping her inner life open in order to fix the chasms in their family unit.

But Rose can tell that Bernard simply doesn't care what his wife says here – he isn't interested in other people's opinions.

Only one opinion matters: his own. He's clearly convinced that Grazia will calm down eventually.

'Bernard, what does it feel like to hear these things?' Rose asks softly.

She sees the complete calm in his eyes.

'It is airing dirty laundry in public. I didn't want to come here,' he adds unnecessarily. 'People sometimes don't get on. I don't know what I can do to change that.'

Rose has really only one question she can ask at this point.

'Are you really sure you don't know what to do?' she asks.

'No, I have no idea how to fix this. It upsets me,' he says, looking not in the least upset.

Rose decides that the cage-rattling has to start. She has to get a real response from Bernard.

'Do you feel frightened that if you stand up for Grazia, you will lose your children?' she asks.

Before Bernard has a chance to answer, she races on: 'You still feel the guilt for their mother dying, even though you could not have prevented that. You still feel the guilt of not being there for them when they were younger because you were building your business. Possibly in their eyes, you chose work over them.

'Now that you're older and have a wife you love, you're scared of losing them by admitting this, so it's easier for you to let this current state of affairs continue.'

Grazia looks as if she's only just holding back tears and for the first time, Bernard shows some reaction to Rose's comments. His fingers are tapping a rapid tattoo on the olive-wood table but he says nothing.

Rose continues.

'You enable Stephen and Viola to treat Grazia badly. If you never stand up for her in their presence, it's tacit approval for them to treat Grazia as if she is an employee, there only to sleep beside you.'

Rose pauses to see if this has any effect.

Bernard's plaster façade is beginning to crack: a muscle in his jaw is vibrating with tension and for the first time, Rose thinks she's seeing the real Bernard.

'I love Grazia,' he says hoarsely. 'She is good to me. I am so happy with her but this is tearing us apart,' and he stops talking.

Grazia, who is normally so demonstrative with her husband, does not touch him now.

She's holding her little gold cigarette lighter, constantly clicking it, waiting for the next moment when she can smoke one of her beloved cigarettes.

'I know they have stress-relieving properties but they also cause cancer,' says Rose, looking at the cigarette lighter.

Grazia shrugs: 'My only sin,' she says. 'But Bernard's children would be delighted if I were dead.'

India winces at this.

'But if you were dead, Bernard would have nobody,' India interrupts, unable to keep quiet any longer. 'Your kids, Bernard, who are obviously older than me, would have *their* lives but you'd be lonely as hell. Single dinners at home. Nobody to watch Netflix with. Is that what they want?' India demands. 'I'm sorry but your children sound like horrible people, Bernard. It's your happiness, Bernard and Grazia, versus the adult children waiting for you to drop dead before they get their hands on the serious money. They should be ashamed of themselves.'

Bernard is reddening and, this time, Grazia is back holding his hand.

'They're good people,' he bleats desperately.

'Really?' Keera says, joining in. 'I've met lots of people in my business who glue themselves to famous people for a piece of the pie. It's gross. Blood-suckers. Some people go totally cray-cray over money. It's all they think about.'

Rose watches Bernard's face tighten with anger.

When Keera, a woman almost young enough to be his granddaughter, tells him that his adult children's actions are cruel and money-grabbing, he can't ignore that.

He might ignore Grazia or try to numb out her words, but when the whole group is looking at him with pity mixed in with faint disgust, that's another story.

'You're lucky you've had a decent marriage, Grazia.'

Dianne surprises them all by talking.

'You didn't, then?' asks Rose quickly.

'This isn't about me,' replies Dianne. 'Just that Grazia has plenty of power. Lucky her. She got her man to come here. I salute you, Grazia. Those kids sound like entitled brats. You're lucky old Bernard there didn't flip his lid when you told him you wanted to come to a Rose Talisman retreat.'

Everyone stares at Dianne.

'All I'm saying is that Bernard gets a few points for that.'

'What are you feeling now, Grazia?' Rose asks.

Grazia angles her elegant head. She's wearing different gold jewellery, beautiful museum-quality pieces today, along with another fitted outfit: slim cream trousers and a silk shirt that never sticks to her skin with sweat.

Rose, who is feeling the heat despite the sea breeze, wonders what Grazia does to avoid sweating in the sun. This isn't the time to ask.

'I feel glad I have said it, and glad you all heard,' Grazia says. 'Bernard does not like to air his private life in public. But . . .' She shrugs elegantly. 'I cannot go on the way I used to.'

Bernard is now looking at his toes in his sandals.

'That is why we are here. Isn't it, Bernard?' asks Rose.

Bernard doesn't reply.

Instead, he glares at Rose.

'No comment,' he snaps.

He shoves his chair back from the table and stumbles off.

Grazia doesn't follow him the way she usually does.

She sits in her chair, watching, fingers still playing with her cigarette lighter.

'A break till half six?' Rose suggests. 'I want everyone to write a few lines to encapsulate what we talked about today.

'Family jealousy, perhaps. Stepfamilies. What it's like to feel unheard. Then we have meditation on the beach tonight when it's cooler, and then the beach barbecue.'

Chapter Twenty-Five

'Meditation on the beach sounds fabulous,' says Keera to India when the group splits up. By unspoken agreement, the two women head for the infinity pool where the little jewelled bar will be open and they can order juices or iced tea.

India wants more than iced tea but won't ask for it when she's with Keera. Drinking wine would seem insulting to her new friend.

'Me and Dianne are the only ones who haven't talked,' she says in worried tones to Keera.

'It's not so bad,' Keera says. 'It's freeing to talk about all the crap you never talk about normally. Nobody falls over in shock, people listen and, here anyway, they don't judge.'

'Dianne does,' mutters India.

'That's just for the men,' Keera points out. 'Some guy broke her heart, for sure. She's nice to the women. She hates the men.'

'Not my problem,' says India.

'If you get it over first thing tomorrow, then you can relax and learn how to fix all the things you do wrong,' Keera says.

'In her book, Rose never says we do things wrong,' India explains. 'It's more that we learned survival techniques and we keep using them. But that's not my problem.'

Rose's flowing shirt swirls out behind her as she hurries to the private part of the hotel and finds Adriana in the small white living room with the air-con on.

Adriana's sitting at a small desk with a big notebook.

'How's it going?' she asks Rose.

Adriana looks so Greek now, Rose thinks suddenly. Adriana's hair has been a rich chocolate colour since she was a little girl, but now her pale skin is tanned to a glowing caramel. In her blue flower-print cotton dress, with the necklace made in the village from fake coral and tiny orange glass beads, Adriana looks like a beautiful Greek woman from a fashion magazine. She now speaks Greek fluently, far better than Rose, who has been learning, but then Adriana has lived here for much longer. Rose could not have dreamed up a happier life for her baby sister.

'Well,' Rose says, sitting down on one of the big couches and putting her feet up on a footstool. 'Bernard marched off at the end after glaring at me like he wished he could say "you're fired!"'

'Ouch,' says Adriana.

'Ouch indeed. Is he very wealthy?' Rose asks. She doesn't want to tell her sister the details of the therapy – the guests are owed privacy.

'Filthy rich,' Adriana replies. 'Company listed on the UK stock market.'

'His adult kids are worried about their inheritance,' Rose says carefully.

'That's going to be some inheritance.'

'How people react to money is an interesting weather vane,' Rose says, shrugging. 'I saw it all the time in LA. Some people get rich and then there simply isn't enough money in the world for them. They become obsessed, think they'll never have enough and they don't care whose lives they ruin in the pursuit of it.'

'Not our problem,' jokes Adriana.

Rose grins.

'You were always brilliant at spending money,' Rose teases. 'Lipsticks, nail varnish, that expensive thing with your hair to straighten it.'

Adriana laughs the way only a sister can laugh.

'I was dreadful, wasn't I?' she says. 'I wanted to be grown-up and glamorous like you. But I never could catch up.'

Adriana gets up and goes to sit beside her big sister on the couch.

'I think this is working brilliantly.'

'I know,' Rose agrees. 'Bar Bernard, I think the guests are enjoying it. Well . . .' She rephrases it. 'Maybe not enjoying it but appreciating it. Keera and India are happy and so, amazingly, is Dan. He seems more relaxed today. Obviously he's never talked about himself to anyone ever before.'

'I know I'm not a therapist and you can't really talk about that side of things with me,' says Adriana. 'You did with Theo, didn't you—?'

'Stop with the Theo stuff,' begs Rose. 'He's in the past. Sure, we talked about work but it's perfectly possible to run a retreat with one therapist. If this works out, we might think of having another person with me—'

Adriana interrupts her.

'I know you said yesterday that's all in the past but

you've never tried to get in touch with Theo, have you? When the show blew up, you just ran and he's had no idea where you've been for the past five years. I bet you he was looking for you, Rose, but you've changed everything – from phone number to email address. There was no way to track you down.'

'He wouldn't have wanted to find me,' Rose says firmly, 'and I'm OK with that.'

'You're so not OK with it,' Adriana chides. 'I'm your sister, I know you better than anyone. You miss him. I can tell. I just want you to be happy.'

Rose says nothing for a beat. She loves the way her sister worries about her but it's a lost cause.

'I miss being with someone who loved me the way he did, but I lied to him, Adriana, you know that.'

'A lie of omission,' her sister reminds her. 'It was entirely understandable, Rose. I lied about it myself.'

'But you didn't reinvent yourself for the television,' Rose reminds her. '*I* created a whole new person.'

'Remember what you've always told me, what you wrote in your book,' Adriana says. 'Forgive yourself for what you had to do to survive.'

'Should we have that embroidered on the bags in the gift shop?' asks Rose wryly. 'They'd be best sellers.'

The day that Rose meets Theo for the first time, she's just spent part of the afternoon taping an 'ask your therapist' segment for a morning TV show. It's the first time she's ever done anything like this.

When she's finished taping her segment, a twenty-something assistant producer tells her that the show is never live with newbies because 'Some people don't spark on film.'

'You were really good, though,' the woman says as an afterthought as Rose leaves the set.

'Thank you,' says Rose, not believing a word of it.

In the dressing room, she takes off the grey linen trouser suit she decided to wear on camera and pulls on the pale-pink silk dress she's wearing with strappy sandals to her friends' dinner party later.

'You'll message me when it's going to be on?' Rose asks the young assistant producer before she leaves.

She might as well know precisely when she's going to look dreadful on television instead of having all her friends phone her when it happens.

'Sure, sure,' says the woman.

Rose laughs to herself.

In LA, that's code for *Not a hope. You're not important.*

It takes Rose an hour to navigate the traffic to get to her friends Victor and Celeste's house.

They're landscape gardeners who love the theatre, cloud trees and entertaining.

The dinner party guests are in the garden when Rose arrives and, as usual, it's an eclectic mix of people. A Swedish director whose garden they designed, the two lovely guys who run an art gallery in Santa Fe but are in town for an exhibition, Celeste's two nieces, one of whom is trying to break into TV work and is nose to nose with the film director.

Victor's daughter from his first marriage is there, along with their neighbour Liza and her twenty-something son who does something in tech. There's also a man Rose doesn't recognise.

He's got curly dark hair with a hint of grey around his hairline, wears horn-rimmed glasses and a cream sweater that looks darned, and he's laughing at something Victor's saying.

He's got a warm, clever face and Rose finds herself wondering where his significant other is.

'Stop talking about terracing,' says Celeste impatiently, pulling Rose in his direction. 'Rose, you must meet Theo. He's new in town and he's single. He's also a therapist! We've told him all about you.'

Rose flushes. Now he'll think she's a desperate single woman who forces her friends to matchmake on every occasion.

When Victor and Celeste finally leave them alone, Rose apologises.

'I promise I didn't ask Celeste to set me up,' she says ruefully. 'I am so sorry. A new single man in this neck of the woods gets the married people excited because they think there's someone new for all their single friends. Normally, Celeste and Victor aren't matchmakers but they appear to have lost the plot tonight.'

'I don't mind,' says Theo. 'I don't mind at all. How about we make our hosts really happy by having a heart to heart?'

'You're very kind and gentlemanly,' Rose says, smiling.

Theo surprises her by leaning close and whispering in her ear: 'I am not actually being kind at all, Ms Talisman.'

Rose looks him in the eye.

He's being serious. Despite all she knows about dating in this city, she allows herself to smile at him.

They're on their first date – lunch in a nearby vineyard – when a different, more senior producer from the breakfast television show phones offering Rose a weekly slot.

Discussions will have to happen with her agent, the producer says, but they're really keen.

'I can't believe this is happening,' Rose says to Theo.

'Why not? I'd want to watch you on TV,' he says.

'Really?' she says.

'Really, truly,' Theo replies.

It's like all her dreams have come true at once: her career is in the ascendent and this handsome man who ticks every box on the 'decent men to date' list seems to be crazy about her.

But the TV people want her potted biography and Rose, who has tried so very hard to disguise her past, spins them the story she always tells people.

Theo hears it too.

She can't risk telling him that her truth is wildly different. It's hard to explain her real life story: it's messy and complex, nothing like the lovely CV she gives people.

They're only just dating, after all. What if she tells him and he leaves with all her secrets?

No, it's better this way, she thinks.

But Rose finds out that the longer a lie exists, the harder it is to come clean.

Rose doesn't think she's ever seen such beauty as Massachusetts in what Theo calls 'the Fall'.

'Ochre, honey, gold, burned sienna, acid green . . .?' she wonders as she spots a tree with stunning greens still on its leaves in the midst of the great russet explosion of autumn.

They've been dating six months and Theo is driving her to meet his parents.

'They'll love you,' says Theo.

Theo has driven from Logan airport because Rose has never been a fan of driving on the vast US roads.

It's lovely to be driven – she tries to relax and stop worrying about how she'll fit into Theo's parents' world.

Instead, she concentrates on the colours of the trees as they drive towards the small town of Falmouth on the coast.

Theo had grown up in Philadelphia and, in their retirement, his parents had moved to what Theo called 'possibly the prettiest colonial house on the eastern seaboard that you can imagine'.

His parents are a retired surgeon, his mother, and a retired psychiatrist, his father. Contrary to what Theo says, Rose has absolutely no belief that his parents will love her.

They are old-school intellectuals, he's said, and sound like charming people who represent the sort of background that is nothing like Rose's.

She doesn't say this to Theo.

She's forty-three and has never fallen in love like this before.

Theo, with his horn-rimmed glasses, his runner's body, his wise smile – she's never known anyone smile the way Theo does! – has entirely stolen her heart.

Rose feels as if nobody has ever taken care of her the way Theo does. They're on the verge of moving in together: she'll move in to his small house outside Carmel, an expensive house that overlooks the ocean.

When she stays over, he makes her coffee in the morning and, in the evenings, he cooks.

'Linguine with clams,' he'll say when she arrives over for dinner, barefoot in shorts, with a linen shirt thrown over a T-shirt, holding a spoon out for her to taste.

Or 'Tomato sauce with confit garlic,' which will taste like some angel made it.

'How did you learn to cook like this?' she once asked, after moaning with pleasure as she ate.

'Cooking is one of the great arts,' Theo said. 'Get people

around a dinner table talking and you have the perfect mix of family and friends.'

Rose loves this idea, loves the notion of them sharing this sort of life, the life that she and Adriana were denied as kids. She holds the preciousness of this deep in her heart, as if this wondrous new life with Theo is something she can see only from afar.

Most of all, she wants to tell him all about Adriana and their true story, but she keeps putting it off. *Soon*, she thinks.

If she tells him, he might leave and she can't bear to think about that.

Spending time with Theo, curled up on his couch watching old movies or just staring into the ocean, cradling a glass of wine, talking about their days, is blissful.

Theo is a homebird. He likes sea swimming in the early morning before going to his office. In the evenings, he and Rose sit with their feet up on the deck rails, solving the problems of the world.

He massages her feet when she's tired and then leads her to bed so she can sleep. Sometimes, Theo is so kind and loving that Rose thinks she doesn't deserve him: she's too flawed, reacts too quickly. None of this makes sense, she knows that, but feelings don't always make sense. Every therapist knows that.

His parents, Susan and Henry, welcome Rose into the house which is just as pretty as Theo has said, with bookcases all over the place and art on the walls.

The house is like a Norman Rockwell illustration of a home: garden flowers on the table, a fluffy cat on the windowsill and a sense of warmth engrained in every inch.

'We've heard so much about you, Rose,' Susan says warmly when they sit down to dinner, second family animal, a rescue Heinz 57 dancing around excitedly and being told, gently, to sit in his basket by Henry.

'I've heard so much about you too,' beams Rose.

'Are there going to be wedding bells, that's what I want to know,' says Henry, earning a 'Dad!' from Theo and a groan from his wife.

'Forgive my husband,' Susan begs. 'We're merely happy that you and Theo have found each other. Tell us about yourself . . .'

And Rose, smiling at lovely Theo whom she adores with all her heart, the man who has no idea what her actual real name is, does what she has to do. She lies.

Chapter Twenty-Six

Diana Ross' disco classic 'Love Hangover' is belting out of the yoga studio as India and Keera approach.

The yoga studio is underneath the pool area, a vast glass door slightly open as Diana breathily purrs along to the pumping beat.

'Love this,' says India, shaking her hips as they slip past a trellis hanging with bougainvillea.

'Hello ladies,' says a polite voice as they enter.

India and Keera nearly collide.

'Sorry—'

'Uh, hello!' says Keera.

Neither of them have met Alexei before but their eyes meet in astonishment as they settle down on the two pale-blue yoga mats laid out on the floor.

'So lovely to meet you,' says Alexei, turning off 'Love Hangover' with a click of a button. 'Adriana tells me you both do yoga regularly?'

'That's not entirely true,' admits Keera. She does not want to embarrass herself in front of this beautiful man.

Adriana or Rose should have warned us! He's a Greek god!

She has no idea why Alexei's not modelling for billboards in Times Square: his face is like a sculpture made by some Italian master and his bare bronzed chest speaks of many, many hours of yoga or something.

Keera finds herself flushing at the thought of the 'something'.

'Phew, hot in here,' she says to India, who grins.

India doesn't seem as affected by the sight of Alexei. She's doubtless seen many beautiful people with yoga/gym bodies at home and she's immune at this stage. India's always felt she's too gangly; she thinks that no self-respecting gym bunny wants a girlfriend without visible muscle.

After ascertaining what their preferences are, Alexei leads the two women in forty minutes of energising viniyoga flow.

By the end, he's not even sweating but Keera feels her legs wobbling as she gets up after five minutes of a relaxing savasana.

'I don't know if I can make it onto the beach for meditation and a barbecue,' she says as they slowly climb the stairs to their rooms.

'A cold shower and you'll be fine,' says India, still bouncy.

'How come you're not in a coma too?'

'I'm hyper flexible,' says India, folding her torso onto her legs in a perfect yoga fold to show Keera.

'Wow. I'm not even normally flexible,' says Keera in awe.

That evening, the beach is transformed.

'It looks wonderful!' Rose says to Christos, gazing at what he's done.

There are mats on the sand along with the villa's dark wooden loungers and sun parasols in deep cream. In keeping with the quiet luxury of Villa Artemis, Christos and his team have laid out soft lounger cushions and beautiful blue beach towels, as well as light throws in azure blues and sunshine yellows in case it's cold.

Small tables beside the loungers hold water, fruit and the handblown blue glasses that Rose loves.

Citronella candles glow on two low tables, while Christos has already perfumed the area with herbs on the barbecue, set up a hundred yards away from the meditation end and already full of white-hot coals.

Adriana and Beata have been arranging everything prettily, Christos explains, and Rose already knows that his cousin's teenage sons were keen to earn extra pocket money hefting all the umbrellas, sunbeds and the barbecue things onto the beach.

Rose feels a sense of pride in the Villa Artemis staff as she watches everyone arrive onto the beach.

She, Adriana and Christos have created this beautiful escape from the world and it is already a success.

'Hello!' chorus Keera and India, arriving together. They're laughing about external oblique muscles, while Dan walks a step behind them, looking both weary and wary.

Dianne, who Rose noticed sitting high up in the acropolis the previous evening, walks slowly down the sandy path with a big glass of wine. She's bright in an emerald-green tennis top this evening and looks just as wary as Dan.

Grazia follows Dianne, cigarette in a long, elegant hand, looking as if she's about to join an international cocktail party instead of a beachside meditation.

While Grazia gets herself some wine, Rose thinks it's a pity she didn't stipulate no drinks before meditation but realises that it's too late now. Christos, ever the super host, has put it out.

Bernard's the last to arrive and ostentatiously sits apart from his wife, setting himself up like a pasha on his lounger with several cushions behind him.

Dianne glares at Bernard but he pretends that he doesn't notice.

Rose feels it's time to extract Dianne's hidden story, but she knows it won't be easy.

Dianne is clearly determined to walk away with her secrets intact.

Rose recalls what Dianne's daughter, Lauren, told her: their father had died tragically a year earlier and Dianne had changed afterwards. How exactly had Dianne's husband died? Rose wonders.

For now, Dianne is on the to-be-done list; Grazia and Bernard are on the 'today' Post-it.

Despite the chatter, the group are certainly tired out.

Rose knows that deep emotional work is physically exhausting but people rarely realise it. It's the intensity of the work – and the exhalation as great monuments of walled-up pain begin to crack.

Time to do more cracking, Rose thinks, and bangs her tiny gong.

'We're going to do fifteen minutes of guided meditation but, beforehand, let's look over today. How did we all get on with the homework?' she asks. 'Your notebooks.'

Keera and India, both stretched out luxuriously on loungers, look at each other with dismay.

'It was difficult, this homework,' announces Grazia. 'I do not tell lies so there's nothing to write.'

Rose gives her a knowing look.

'Really?'

'I don't lie!' protests Grazia.

'That's commendable,' Rose goes on. 'But what I mean

really are the small lies we tell ourselves. That we are not hurt by someone else's actions, that we are strong when, actually, we feel fragile and vulnerable.'

She just throws it out there and Grazia doesn't pick it up.

Grazia tries to adopt her usual haughty expression but it no longer works on the group or Rose. They've seen behind her mask.

She's rattling around in the handbag again, searching for her cigarettes.

Hell, thinks Rose. Grazia's going to get lung cancer from trying to sort out her life.

Rose tries another tack.

'It can happen,' she says, 'that when one parent is gone and another person comes into the family to stand in the metaphorical place where the first parent has been, the natural instinct for some offspring is to see the person as an interloper. Like a virus in the family body, and they want to stamp out this virus.'

Everyone but Bernard and Grazia looks suitably appalled. Grazia is nodding.

'But when the children, grown or otherwise – and incredibly, grown children often find this harder than younger ones – succeed in pushing out the so-called interloper, then they are astonished that nothing goes back to the way it was before.'

'Exactly!' says Grazia. 'They are so stupid – they have no idea what it would mean if I left.'

'They might feel shame,' Rose goes on, 'because they made their parent pick who mattered most: their children or their new partner. They couldn't be bigger people and understand that a human can love their children *and* their new wife at the same time. Both things can be true simultaneously.'

Rose gazes meaningfully at Grazia and Bernard.

'If you were gone from Bernard's life, Grazia, his children would suddenly be called upon to be there for their father in new ways. He's older. He's more likely to die first. Sorry, Bernard,' Rose says, with a little bow to him.

'You're only telling the truth,' he says magnanimously.

'So who'd go with you to doctor's appointments, play chess with you in the evening, do all the things you do with Grazia . . .?' Rose asks.

Astonishingly, Rose realises that tears have appeared in Bernard's eyes.

Real tears? She's not sure.

Is he thinking of the enormous loss in his life if Grazia wasn't there? Or perhaps these are merely the tears of the wily old crocodile realising that he loses no matter what happens.

Grazia might make him choose: them or me.

Grazia says nothing but stares at the barbecue.

Rose moves slightly to see what she's looking at.

Stavros, Christos's nephew, is on the beach busily helping Beata and Christos ferry food for the barbecue. He's twenty-five, Rose knows, a sweet, handsome boy who possibly reminds Grazia of the children she doesn't have? Grazia has said she doesn't have children, but did she want them?

Who knows?

'Rose, I think it's important to note that I was all the children had when Maria died,' says Bernard, now speaking like he's at a board meeting and minutes are being taken. 'You know how it is, when they were older, I was the only stability.'

Grazia turns to look at him with disdain. 'They were like big kids even when they were fully adult. You got them out of scrapes all the time,' she points out. 'When Stephen's investments failed, who picked up the pieces? You did. Same with Viola. She knew Daddy would always help. They have never had to behave in the real world like adults because Daddy was always there for them.'

'Do you agree with what Grazia's saying?' Rose asks Bernard.

His eyes are misty with unshed tears and he says nothing, shaking his head as if he can't speak.

Rose wants to leave some time for him to think about what she and Grazia have just said.

'I love them and I love you,' Bernard finally says in a croaky voice. 'I am so sorry, Grazia, so sorry—'

To Rose's astonishment, given Grazia's previously steely demeanour, Grazia gets out of her chair and puts her arms around her husband.

'Would you like a moment or two?' asks Rose.

Grazia nods.

'We'll start the meditation in five minutes, OK?'

'Thank you,' says Grazia and she and Bernard walk down the beach.

'I hope they get all sorted out with his kids,' says India a bit tearfully. 'They're a sweet couple and I don't understand why children wouldn't want their dad to be happy. Doesn't everyone want the people they love to be happy?'

Rose loves India's genuine kindness.

'Sometimes the people who are our nearest and dearest don't want us to be happy. If we are, the contrast is too great. It is easier for them when everyone is unhappy. Does that shock you?'

'It doesn't shock me,' says Dianne.

'Not everyone is as lovely as you, India,' Dianne

continues. 'You need to be aware, that's all I'm saying. Be aware. Red flags!'

'What sort of red flags, Dianne?' asks Rose.

Dianne holds a hand up. 'No, you're not catching me that easily!' she says, and her face goes blank.

It's incredible how she does that, Rose thinks.

One minute, her face can be all *I'm putting your head in the blender*, and the next minute, it's a flat mask. Incredible really.

Rose moves on to Dan.

'How are you feeling, Dan?'

Dan hesitates a beat, as if scanning his body for tension or any other issues.

'I'm fine,' he says, sounding slightly surprised.

'Excellent. And you, Keera?'

Keera smiles sunnily back at Rose.

'I have pains in muscles I didn't know I had,' she says, then adds by way of explanation: 'India and I met Alexei.'

'Ah yes,' says Rose sagely. 'He's an excellent yoga teacher.'

'He is!' agrees India. 'Really top notch.'

This time, it's Rose and Keera whose eyes meet knowingly.

'Well, if everyone's heart rate has come down enough, let's meditate,' says Rose, and Keera smothers a laugh.

Truly, Rose loves running this retreat. She's really getting places with the guests.

Chapter Twenty-Seven

'It's all fine!' says Mercedes confidently on the phone. 'We were worried over nothing!'

Mercedes is happy as she talks to Rose and Adriana early on Wednesday morning.

'I have to apologise for worrying you,' Mercedes is saying.

'The weird messages are not about you at all,' she says happily. 'Haters. See: I've sent the screenshot to you, Adriana. The message is for an Alys Flint . . .'

Rose feels her legs grow weak but, somehow, she holds herself upright.

If she collapsed either physically or metaphorically, it would scare Adriana, and the thing Rose is proudest about in her whole life is how she has taken care of her baby sister.

That will not stop now.

'I see,' says Rose with infinite calm.

Adriana's eyes are huge as she stares at Rose.

'Don't send any messages or block them,' Rose tells Mercedes. 'I'm in touch with someone about identifying them.'

'But none of these crazy posts are for you,' protests Mercedes. 'We don't need to do anything—'

'This poor person clearly needs help and, given that our business revolves around emotional health, we can't ignore this,' interrupts Rose smoothly. 'Send me all the log-in details. I've got someone looking into this.'

When a clearly confused Mercedes is off the phone, Rose sits at Adriana's laptop and begins to write another email.

'Rose, is it going to be all right?' asks a scared Adriana.

Rose wants to be truthful. It's never just *one* lie, she has found.

Once you start lying, you're committed to a tangled web of mistruths.

'Yes, of course it's going to be all right, darling,' she says to Adriana, even though she doesn't know any such thing. 'Nothing's going to get in our way now. We've been through enough, darling. I'll sort it.'

'But they said Alys Flint—' protests Adriana.

'It's going to be fine, I'll sort it out,' repeats Rose.

She thinks briefly about Dan and his co-dependent relationship, about how he tries to fix all aspects of Julia's life.

Rose has protected Adriana since they were children. It's not the same thing at all.

The disco beats of 'Love Hangover' have given them a yen for disco music, so Keera's playing a speedily curated soundtrack of Earth, Wind and Fire, Chaka Khan and Nile Rodgers's music while she and India sit in India's bedroom.

India's twirling in time to 'Ain't Nobody' while holding out the skirt of the cream dress with its swirling designs in lemon and pale green.

'This one's vintage Ossie Clark,' she says. 'It was my mum's but it was torn so I fixed it. Look . . .'

India holds up the bottom tier of flounces which have been beautifully sewn on and patched with another similar fabric.

'This is amazing work,' says Keera, impressed, studying the tiny, neat stitches.

'It's not nearly well done enough,' India goes on, examining her own work. 'Some of his dresses are in the V&A, so me fixing this one up is a bit risky. Still, there were so many holes in it that I had to try to not change the design with my repairs.'

'Seriously, you're really good at this,' Keera repeats. 'You could do this professionally.'

'Sew things? No, I'm not good enough—'

'No, I mean sell vintage. Fix things up and sell them on.'

'Nah,' says India, adding a tangle of orange beads to her neck. She examines the look in the mirror with the narrowed eyes of the expert. 'It's just a hobby and a way to save money.'

Keera finds her fingers automatically playing the bass line of Stevie Wonder's 'Sir Duke' as she listens. She has her own skills, she thinks happily.

Despite the heat, everyone is drinking coffee on the terrace this morning.

'We're going to have a little break this afternoon, an hour and a half off,' Rose announces. 'We'll recommence on the beach at half three but once we break here at twelve, the spa is ready for anyone who wants a massage or a facial. Alexei is around for yoga again too. I'll be on the beach later if anyone wants to talk to me. Or if anyone wants a little walk down to Xanthe between half one and half two, I'm available.'

'OK then, India.' Rose turns in her chair and sees that India is both nervous and waiting for her turn to come.

'I know, I'm next. I'm really bad at talking in front of people, Rose,' India says nervously. 'I warn you, I'm really hopeless at it.'

Rose smiles at her warmly.

You can do this, she seems to be trying to say without words.

India feels a wild sense of love for Rose's kindness. But still, this is hard.

'I'm scared my stuff sounds silly, compared with everybody else,' she adds.

'Have you heard the phrase: comparison is the thief of joy?' Rose asks.

Rose can be intense when she prods people, India thinks, but she understands human pain.

It's just that what India has to say seems so silly compared to everyone else . . .

Keera's had to be so brave about addiction. Dan's had so much pain to wade through with poor Julia, and as for Bernard's horrible children . . .

India can't compare. She fidgets with her floaty Ossie Clark dress sleeves.

'My stuff is all first-world problems,' she says lamely. 'I didn't fully think this out. I thought it might be more spa treatments and a bit of shamanic work. I was stupid, really—'

'Please don't call yourself stupid, India,' says Rose. 'You're certainly not that. Breathe deeply and think about the first question: what trouble brought you here?'

India nods, and takes a deep inhale. She's here and she's going to be brave.

*

Jake was one of India's first boyfriends: the son of one of Georgie's clients, he was deliciously handsome.

He had olive skin, muscles from lots of time spent in the gym and perfectly tousled hair.

That he'd never worked a proper day in his life and dabbled as a part-time DJ didn't worry India.

She'd been nineteen at the time, a very young nineteen, she knows now, but then, she thought she was the last word in cool.

She'd just spent the summer in the Caribbean with her mother, Sonja, and Magnús and a retinue of beautiful people, all of whom were forty years older than India and vaguely famous.

They were a lovely group to hang out with, all athletic and yoga toned, wise beyond their years and always smoking rolled-up cigarettes on the beach.

They ribbed each other, and were very kind to India and the only other young person there, a fourteen-year-old boy called Phoenix, whose dad was a drummer in a German stadium band.

Phoenix was wildly shy and barely spoke to India, which everyone thought was cute.

'I think he likes you, honey,' Sonja had said. 'But why wouldn't he?'

It was as if the universe was telling her it was the time to find her Great Love.

Back in London, she applied for a foundation course to study interior design along with a friend.

In the evenings, they went to each other's homes to study but the studying ended when India began dating Jake.

He was twenty-one, took himself very seriously and

wanted to be a music producer. The DJ gig was just for fun, he told her.

'You're so beautiful, India,' he said the first time they slept together.

He stroked her face as he gazed into her eyes, saying she should be on the cover of the first album he produced.

India almost died with love.

She belonged to this gorgeous boy/man, they were twin souls, destined to be together for ever.

At night, India could hardly bear to leave Jake.

What if something happened to him when they were apart? What if he found another twin soul?

India couldn't bear the thought. She stopped concentrating on her foundation course and spent hours daydreaming about her life with Jake.

Where they'd live, what they'd do, where they'd go on holidays . . .

They had six glorious weeks together.

Six weeks where India didn't eat, listened to Jake talking about music and football, and pretended she had no needs of her own.

She cancelled a night out with Lizzie and Cleo, her friends since school, because Jake wanted to go to Barcelona for a night to see a football match.

Lizzie and Cleo had gone out anyway without her when she'd cancelled.

They'd had the best time, while India was stuck on a charter flight with loads of men, all getting horribly drunk.

Turns out she'd hated the football. All that shouty screaming made her nervous. Men pumped up on testosterone and football fever.

Not that she'd said that to Jake.

'I love being with you,' she'd said eagerly when he'd

asked her – the bastard had actually *asked* her if she was having fun. He must have seen that she was fibbing?

Lizzie and Cleo were hurt.

'Sisters before misters,' they reminded her sadly. India knew she could never make it up to them.

Jake broke up with her a week later.

He didn't want to be tied down, it seemed.

'Live together? Nah.'

Plus, he'd fallen for a girl he met in a club.

India had been heartbroken but recovered quickly because Jake's older brother, Nicky, had told her his little brother must be mad to have dumped her.

'You're a jewel, nobody could leave you. Little bro's a moron. I know you must have heard this before but you should be a model like your mum. I love your stepdad, Magnús, too: he's so cool.'

Nicky was twenty-four and liked Formula One.

India studied it diligently. But it transpired that she hadn't liked that sport much either. The *noise*!

Then Nicky had dumped her and she'd been heartbroken.

A furious Georgie told her that Nicky and Jake were spoiled and she ought to date outside their circle.

'Don't let men walk all over you, sweetie,' Georgie said grimly, which was in direct opposition to the sort of thing her mother said.

Sonja believed that your man was your lodestone. The yang to a woman's yin.

That a woman could only be free when she had the right lover by her side.

'You need to concentrate on college, India,' Georgie said firmly, which was as close as she ever came to criticising her predecessor.

Had Georgie seen that India was falling for the wrong guys?

In college, India kept rediscovering her love of interior design, but each time she knuckled down, she fell for another guy.

There was Freddie, who was on the course because his mother was an Italian princess and owned a palazzo by the River Arno, a stone's throw from Florence. India began learning Italian. She read Italian cookbooks and immersed herself in Florentine artists.

Turned out Italian was tricky, but India was so happy, daydreaming of her and Freddie sitting on a terrace with a vineyard beneath them, dogs dancing at their feet.

They'd lasted two months. A record, India thought, once she'd stopped sobbing over sad songs on repeat.

There was Oscar, another football fan. Leonardo, from Cornwall rather than Italy. Josef, with a thing for taller women.

None of them lasted.

By the time she was thirty-three, India had dated approximately four guys a year on a serious basis, had been engaged twice, and had not kept either of the rings because that would be unfair.

Horribly, she'd also been a bridesmaid on eight separate occasions and finally was convinced she was doing something wrong, but what?

Was she inherently unlovable?

Her father said that none of these guys were good enough for her.

Meanwhile, Georgie was still careful about stepping on Sonja's feet when it came to mothering.

She thought India shouldn't give herself over so totally to being in love when she met someone new.

'You're all heart, India, and you expect the same of other people. But you're too trusting. Too giving. You let these guys get away with murder.'

India began to see that her high-speed male turnover was a problem.

She asked her mother for help.

'I'm so glad you came to me for help, sweetie,' Sonja said delightedly.

Sonja explained that fragile unicorn-butterfly people like them – India's mother had these symbols tattooed on her slender back – can't behave like other women.

'We are different, India. We are fragile, we are as rare as unicorns, we are elemental like butterflies. We have our own way of living. It's not that complicated,' Sonja added earnestly, as if she was explaining something Einstein-y. 'When you find the right guy, it will fall into place. It's destiny. It will just happen.'

Finally, thought India: an explanation.

She just needed to follow certain rules.

Doing anything but nibbling a sliver of food in the presence of a man was very fragile unicorn-butterfly behaviour. Possibly the most important rule. Sonja was whisper-thin for this very reason.

If appearing to exist on an astral plane without food was rule one, mastering the art of cherishing your man was rule two.

'Wear make-up so that it looks like you're not wearing make-up': rule three.

'Always be a free spirit. Nobody can tame you, so they'll do anything to keep you.'

Sonja still follows the rules, even though she is in her early sixties without actually looking it – even India doesn't know her mother's true age.

Sonja is ageless in a beautiful but very modern, aesthetic way. Her wide-apart eyes are one of her most beautiful features, one which India has inherited. Her face is an oval with a wide, full mouth, which India also has inherited.

Sonja is a muse to several musicians.

This was rare, though, she explained to India.

In her past lives, she was never a muse, but now she is. It's the cosmic cycle.

Before the break-up with Chad, there was a brief moment when it occurred to India that she'd been following her mother's difficult diktats all her life, even though her mother left years ago.

Was it ever Sonja's dream to be a mother . . .?

India stops her story and finds she has almost talked herself out.

She's back on the terrace in Corfu, the scent of lavender, rosemary and bougainvillea heady in her nostrils, only the cicadas making any noise.

Everyone else is looking at her with interest, apart from Keera by her side, who has been patting India's knee in comfort.

There's no point in trying to pretend any more: India has laid herself bare so she has to get on with it.

'My friend, Lizzie – the one I left to go to the football with Jake – she got married. I was a bridesmaid, me and Cleo were, in fact. I wore a cap-sleeved pink Monique Lhuillier and Lizzie was in white with lace flowers. Lizzie's dad kept saying he should give his taxi firm to Monique Lhuillier: it would be a fairer trade.'

Dan laughs and India smiles at him. She loves making people laugh. She's good at it too, that's one crumb of happiness in the middle of this.

'Keep going, India,' prods Rose.

'So, Lizzie had a baby. Lily-Blossom. She's so exquisite . . .'
And there, India stops.

She can't describe Lily-Blossom any more. She'd never visited anyone in hospital having a baby before Lizzie, so she'd had no idea what it would be like. It was all noise and India wondered how any baby managed to sleep, and then she came upon Lizzie in bed, tired but with this, like, *glow*, and there was the baby.

'Do you want to hold her?' Lizzie had said and delicately transferred the tiny bundle of baby clothes over to India.

'I couldn't breathe the first time I held her,' India says slowly.

She suddenly no longer cares how she sounds.

What is the point of only saying what is publicly acceptable when you've so much pain inside that squashing it down destroys you?

India had held Lizzie's tiny baby and the simultaneous feelings of joy and utter grief at her own childlessness had made her heart ache.

India had never felt anything like it.

She still hasn't.

'Lily-Blossom is so precious, no – that's a silly word.'

India closes her eyes, feeling her way through.

'She's perfect, beautiful, fragile. That translucent skin is like silk and her eyes, they don't really see you, apparently, but Lily-Blossom looked up at me and I could see her beautiful little perfect soul right there.'

Beside India, Keera makes a soft noise.

India ignores it. She will say what's inside her now.

Then maybe it won't hurt so much . . .?

'Nothing else felt as if it mattered when I was holding her. She was, she *is*, perfect. Then I had to give her back.'

India almost cries now at the memory: India adores her friend, Lizzie, but she felt something primal when she held Lizzie's baby.

The sense of loss for this child she may never bear is like being ripped open and left empty. India cannot cope with the ache.

She tries to drag herself away from the London hospital and back to the group on the terrace.

They're all utterly silent.

'I understand how women kidnap babies when they're in such agony over not having their own. Wanting my own baby is such a powerful force. I know I sound obsessional maybe . . .'

'No, I'm not seeing obsessional, India,' says Rose gently. 'Wanting a child – that's evolution kicking in. Wanting a child is one of humanity's most powerful forces. Not everyone feels it but, if they do, it's usually all-encompassing.'

'OK,' says India slowly. She realises that she can't talk about having a baby right now, can't share it with the group. She pulls this pain back inside her.

Later with Rose, perhaps, but not now. It's too fragile, too newborn.

She gets up and pours herself more coffee from the pot, then returns to her seat.

'Rose,' she says, 'would you mind if we didn't touch on the baby stuff now? Talk about it later?'

Rose nods. She really wants to delve into India's past and see who abandoned her. But for now, they need a break. This retreat is a learning curve for Rose too.

'Ten-minute break and then back here?' she says.

*

India and Keera take hats and drinks up to the acropolis. There's a faint sea mist today, a little dreamy haze in the distance making all the boats in the sea look as if they're sailing into a fairy story.

'I wish I hadn't talked about that,' India says tiredly as she blindly scans the horizon. 'I just want to lie down and sleep. I feel so worn out.'

'Slicing into yourself is very hard,' Keera says with feeling, 'but it's worth it, India. I promise.'

'Can we talk about something else?' begs India. 'Clothes. Handbags. How much exercise Alexei does to keep looking like that?'

'Sure,' agrees Keera. 'What's your favourite type of handbag ever?'

'OK.' India closes her eyes. She can play this game.

'Vintage Fendi baguette or else a Vuitton travelling trunk. Which is not exactly a handbag but they're so beautiful.'

Adriana and Christos walk down to the village holding hands.

Normally, they're both too busy in the morning for this but Adriana has told Christos about the new message on Instagram.

He instantly suggested that they take time off.

'Come on,' he said. 'We need a break.'

'We don't have time,' said Adriana.

'We do,' he insisted.

They stroll hand in hand, waving to all their friends. Everyone wants to say hello and ask how the inaugural retreat is doing.

Mama Tati, who has a honey stall, presses a jar of her latest honey into Adriana's hands.

'Take it!' she commands.

Mama Tati is one of Xanthe's grandmothers, the strong women who run the village and let their husbands think that they run the village.

Adriana hugs her and she and Christos walk on.

They're offered free coffee, have to promise to come back another day to try out a new olive oil, and spend five minutes admiring the latest pots to come from the local ceramicist's kiln.

They finish up in a sun-bleached wooden café stand with turquoise-coloured chairs and tables. Small fishing boats are tied alongside them and the smell of the fruits of the sea fill their nostrils.

'Iced café,' says Christos, putting two little pottery cups on the table where his wife is sitting.

'I'm worried,' reveals Adriana. 'Rose says not to, that it's going to be all right, but how can it be? All these years we've kept this big secret and now if it comes out, it's going to look as if Rose cannot be trusted. If she lies about the past, how can anyone believe her? It'll ruin everything we've set up here, it will ruin us.'

'If Rose says it's going to be fine, then I for one believe her,' says Christos. 'She's very impressive, your sister. Like you, my beloved.'

Adriana leans into him.

'I hope you're right,' she says.

Back on the terrace, there's no escaping Rose.

The group have barely settled into their seats before Rose has India in her sights again.

'I think we need to reframe the way you look at relationships,' Rose says, 'and concentrate on what you get out of these connections, India. Do you think you put too much emphasis on finding a true love or "great love" as you call it?'

'Isn't everyone looking for love?' India replies, feeling instantly hemmed in at having to explain her choices.

Rose has a way of angling her head that signals understanding.

'People look for lots of things – emotional security, financial security, safety, acceptance,' she says gently. 'The list goes on. But there is a particular type of emotional reward some people get from love: the glow of love itself, the focusing of all of your hopes on one person you have chosen.'

India nods. She can buy this idea.

'Is this what you feel when you fall in love, India? As if this one guy alone holds the key to your life?'

India nods again. She sounds like an idiot when Rose explains it all back to her but she's still reeling from thinking about Lily-Blossom.

'We're all a by-product of our history,' Rose goes on earnestly. 'Your mother has a world view that tells you how to live – to be a lovely butterfly – what was it?'

'Fragile unicorn-butterfly,' recites India. 'It's stupid, right? Really stupid.'

'Yes and no,' says Rose thoughtfully. 'It's your mother's theory and it's worked for her but it shouldn't be yours just because she advises you to behave the same way. You don't have to be a fragile unicorn-butterfly. You're funny, India,' Rose says. 'Funny, sparky, enthusiastic. And clever.'

'I'm not clever,' India says flatly. 'I was terrible at school. That's why I took so much time off and watched your show with my friends.'

'Intelligence is not simply about how well you do at school,' Rose says. 'There are so many types. You say your stepmother is an interior designer. Where did she learn this?'

'It's a gift, she sees things totally differently. It's vision, it's—'

'It's not something she learned in school at the age of fourteen, is it?'

India laughs. 'No. She did study it but she has natural ability.'

'As do you,' says Rose. 'Look at your clothes today – everything you wear is a piece of art. Can you not see that?'

India looks down, almost bewildered. This is not how she's ever looked at how she dresses.

'You're so good with clothes,' Keera interjects. 'Look at how you mended this dress.'

'Fabulous,' says Grazia, getting up to peer at the patchworked frill Keera is holding up. 'Think of yourself like a curator of clothes.'

'Now, the relationships . . .' Rose goes on. 'We need to look at what they mean to you. The first thing in my mind is how you invest so much in a relationship. How you're vigilant for any sign of abandonment.

'But another word keeps popping in: limerence.'

She smiles to herself, while everyone else looks confused.

'Bear with me,' says Rose, holding up a hand. 'Limerence is an almost obsessive love where the most important thing is not the person but the miasma of love itself.'

India stares. What is this?

Limerence. It sounds like something you paint on your toes if you've got a toenail infection.

This cannot be her problem. And what about Lily-Blossom? She'd bared her soul there?

'Limerence means that you are totally absorbed in the

notion of this new love,' Rose is saying. 'Before you really know the person, you've already created this vision in your head of a life you're going to lead together. Is that a fair assessment of things, India?'

'... Er, yes ...' mutters India, thinking back to her first love, Jake, and how she'd imagined them living together, imagined them cooking in the evening, laughing at the table and holding each other close in bed at night.

They would be each other's perfect other.

Or at least he was going to be *her* perfect other.

'Perhaps you put the concept of love on a pedestal,' Rose is saying. 'Achieving love was the main goal. But that's not how it works for young men, in general terms. In a first relationship, they want fun, freedom, sex – not being tied in a relationship. It makes sense why they ran, India,' Rose finishes.

'Limerence sounds ridiculous,' says India, rubbing her temples.

'Is it like addictive behaviour?' Keera asks Rose. 'The looking for love or taking drugs is the byproduct of something in life. If you feel alone, you become addicted to finding partners?'

Sweet Keera, thinks India. Trying to workshop India's stupidity.

But both Rose and Keera's analyses make sense.

'If your world view is that the world is a hard place and you need a partner to navigate it, then you will do everything in your power to have a partner. That's your main aim, your attachment style, to use jargon. You romanticise the relationship early on.'

Rose pauses. 'You are afraid of being abandoned. When you are, you search for the connection again.'

'I'm such an idiot,' India says quickly. Easier to say it herself than have anyone else say it.

'No, you're not,' says Keera. 'We all fall in love and imagine it'll be for ever. I mean, who goes out on a date thinking it's going to end in a week? Nobody.'

'Exactly,' agrees Rose. 'Negative feelings about yourself are a huge part of this. Therapy can change how you feel about yourself, change the negative self-talk. We're unpacking this so you can go forward in a different way, India. Next time you fall for someone, you won't automatically envision life with them for ever. That's putting huge pressure on both you and the date.'

'How do I stop myself doing that?' says India. She still feels exhausted from talking about wanting a baby. This new theory is making her feel stupid as well as tired. She wants it all to end, now.

'You know what it is now,' says Rose kindly. 'The thing about patterns is that once you identify that there is a pattern, you can learn to avoid making that mistake again. Once you see it, you can't unsee it.'

India and Keera nod at that.

'Your future does not rely on random people, India. It lies with you.'

Rose wants to give time for all of this to sink in but they're running out of morning now.

'Did you ever talk about having children with any of the men you've been involved with?' she asks delicately.

'Of course not,' says India and, as soon as she says it, she knows it's the stupidest thing she's ever said.

The boyfriends and her desire for her own baby Lily-Blossom are separate things. Two fairy tales. The limerence one with the guys, and the wild pain of baby hunger.

Or maybe they're not so separate.

The crazy, all-encompassing love affairs allow her not to think at all about having her own child. Perhaps not at first, when she was young, but now – it all makes sense.

'Can we stop?' she asks. 'I see it now but I need a break.'

'Of course,' says Rose. 'Now we've got lunch and any spa treatments you want. As I said, I'll be on the beach or around for a walk from one thirty, OK?'

Losing the baby changed everything. It wasn't that he wanted one, but me losing it made things far worse. It was a failure. He hated failure, believing somebody needed to be responsible for any failure.

I didn't see any of this then. I was so stupid. But then, I was still trying to do the impossible: please him. I thought we were normal people in a normal marriage and that I was messing it up constantly.

Everything that went wrong was my fault. Now, I know precisely what this is – but then, I merely thought I was the most useless person on the planet.

I can see now that I was depressed.

How could I not be?

Let me tell you that feeling depressed is agonising when you're with someone who simply doesn't want to hear your pain.

The neighbourhood women attempted to be kind about the loss of the baby.

Nobody knew what to say, but they came around, bringing food, hugs, kindness. They really tried, I can see that. But what to say? There are no words.

He sucked all the air out of the room when they came around, pretending he was a good husband. He was an expert at it.

'Isn't he a pet,' the neighbour ladies would say to me when he made a pot of coffee for them all, commenting on new hairdos, pretty dresses.

He could pinpoint what people wanted to hear.

'Kev never notices when I get my hair done!' they might say. 'You're a lucky woman to have a man like him.'

And then they'd catch themselves because every one of us knew that nothing could make up for the loss of my child.

Still, a supportive husband was seen as an enormous benefit.

If only they'd been able to see what he really was . . .

We moved house soon after because he couldn't bear to live in the place where he'd thought we'd have everything. We left so quickly that we didn't have time to say goodbye to our 'friends'.

We were starting over and he hoped I wouldn't be such a 'drama queen' in the new house. It was supposed to be a new beginning.

He got a promotion, then another. I had always seen how he could be two different people, one person to me and another one entirely to other people, but his promotions showed just how good he was at this.

There were more people in our circle in the new neighbourhood. More men and women to impress which meant he had to be careful how he treated me in public.

And the more careful he was, the more punishment came my way. He watched my spending like I was Imelda Marcos. I had to ask for money. Beg him.

When I bought groceries, I'd haul them all in,

unpack and laboriously put them away as he sat unmoving in a kitchen chair, overseeing, examining the purchases forensically.

'Why did you buy apples? We have apples.'

I'd try to explain that we had eating apples and I'd bought cookers to make him dessert.

He didn't want an explanation: the apples were simply the weapon of the day.

He wanted to control, to beat me down, to show me how bad I was at everything.

When I bought anything for myself, he wanted to see me in it. He'd put his head to one side and say: 'It would really suit someone thinner.'

I was the thinnest I'd ever been but this was immaterial. I was a mess. He was ashamed of me.

Even his first wife had dressed better and had style.

I never met her, obviously, but had been taught to despise her.

How did I not see this as the reddest of all red flags?

Because I was imprisoned in the sort of prison where you don't see the bars.

Instead, I kept my head down, tried to take up as little space as possible. Tried to avoid being a mess, being overemotional or dramatic. These were my flaws and I did anything to avoid punishment.

It was almost impossible to make sense of it all. For so long, I lived in this chaotic state of high anxiety, waiting for the next attack, the next vicious comment.

I looked back over the past, recalling how much he'd loved me at first. I thought that if I could see where I'd gone wrong, where I'd made him so angry, then I could make it all better.

Initially, he'd run after me and besieged me.
Sworn his undying love.
He'd been so lovely to my mother. After he'd met and charmed her.
'I wanted her to like me, silly,' he'd said.
He said it so easily that the clarity of those words was lost entirely.
I understood it later, though.

Chapter Twenty-Eight

Bernard spends Wednesday afternoon drinking too much beside the infinity pool.

He rarely does this now because he can't cope with hangovers but he wants to escape all the noise in his head. Grazia is barely speaking to him and she says she's having a spa treatment at half one.

'Do what you want,' he says and goes back to sunbathing, his Negroni beside him. He's tried two other cocktails already, one with peach liqueur, which was a bit sickly sweet but he drank it anyway.

There's a pretty young girl at the bar today serving him cocktails, not like that supercilious bitch who glared at him as she swept out of his and Grazia's room with the laundry the other day.

He wouldn't employ anyone like that.

Bernard likes staff who treat him with respect. He insists upon it.

He broods angrily that he doesn't feel fully respected in Villa Artemis.

It's definitely Grazia's fault. Everyone is on her side.

He's sure Rose is telling the entire staff that he's not nice to his wife – well, he's going to put a stop to that.

He knows things about Rose Talisman.

Bernard has ruined other people's businesses before. He doesn't feel any guilt about that – it's survival of the fittest, he thinks. Rose had better watch out.

Grazia finds Rose at lunch.

'May I join you on a walk to the village?' she asks Rose. 'Can it be just me?'

Not for a moment does Rose betray her surprise.

'Of course,' she says. Perhaps she can get to the nub of the problem. Grazia and Bernard's issues are not just about his adult children, Rose is sure of it.

India and Keera have lunch, then sit on the beach with Dan, occasionally wading into the sea to cool down.

'It's nice this doing nothing,' says Keera.

'Lovely,' says India, who looks sleepy.

She is lying on her stomach, long legs stretched out on the sand.

Keera sees Dan sneaking a look at India but she says nothing. She feels such kinship with the two of them.

They're all a bit mixed up but they care about each other. Funny how this has happened so quickly.

Rose finishes writing up her notes from the morning and wonders how Grazia is doing.

'I am embarrassed to share this with you,' Grazia had said to Rose as they walked to the village.

'There's nothing I haven't heard,' Rose told her.

Now Rose thinks she understands Grazia and Bernard's marriage more.

Poor Grazia.

What a risk to tell the story to someone else. Bernard will be enraged when he finds out. He will probably storm out of the retreat.

Rose has prepared Grazia for that. Not every relationship can be saved.

Rose knows that Bernard is getting drunk beside the pool, but she will not worry about him.

She thinks instead of this afternoon's late session on the terrace which will focus on people's stories but also on the mind–body link.

Once, a million years ago when she was a practising therapist, a young man with an eating disorder leaped out of his chair and screamed that he was fed up talking about his body.

His body was 'my business, OK?!' he shrieked. He stormed off and hadn't paid.

At the time, Rose decided that a couch might be the way to go. It was harder for people to leap out of the prone position than out of a chair. She also looked into a contractual agreement which meant non-payers had a month to cough up, but it was too tricky to enforce.

On her TV show, the producers had never been keen on focusing on physical signs of emotional pain.

'It's kinda boring,' said the second-in-command producer, whose credentials included the fact that he once speed-read *Men Are from Mars, Women Are from Venus*. 'I like it when people cry, but not immediately. Fourteen minutes in is the perfect slot – after the first commercial break but just before the second one.'

'I'll do my best to remember that,' Rose had replied gravely.

American TV had far too many commercial breaks and she doubted if Carl Jung and Melanie Klein in a tag team with a stopwatch could make people cry on demand fourteen minutes into a session.

This afternoon, Rose starts on the physical side of pain.

On the terrace, she's astonished to see that Bernard is present. He's sitting apart from his wife at the table and has the red face of someone who's drunk too much in the sun.

Drinking in the sunshine is like drinking on aeroplanes, Rose thinks. Every drink is like a double measure.

The donkey who lives two rocky fields away is roaring hello to the donkey who lives close to the Kri Kri beach. Rose always brings fruit to the beach donkey, who's called Zeus.

In the background, there's a hum of the slow scooters that tourists rent to traverse the island. Rose worries every time she sees them blithely riding helmet-less and biker-clothes-less. The roads in Corfu are just as rock hard as the roads wherever the holidaymakers come from, and one small brush with the road can leave many scars.

But still – people make stupid choices all the time. She's done it herself.

Rose stands up. She likes to roam when she's working.

'We live in a world where we're reminded to be aware of our bodies – how we eat, if it's processed or non-processed, how much exercise we take, running or weight-lifting. But the impact of emotional stress on our bodies is covered much less frequently and that's a huge disconnect because our minds and our bodies are inextricably connected.'

She walks around the table on the terrace, forcing the retreat guests to turn in their chairs.

'Think about your body now. How does it feel after yesterday and this morning? Looser, tighter? Where do your emotions hide in your body? For some people, it's a tautness in their head and their neck. Others feel it in their shoulders or the gut.'

Shoulders and guts – she sees Keera look up when she says this.

'How do you feel physically right now?' she asks Keera. 'Your shoulders are tense. Can you let them drop? Is your jaw tight?'

Keera nods at Rose. 'I grind my teeth,' she says.

'Don't we all,' India mutters, then turns to Keera. 'Sorry, babe, interrupted you.'

'We carry emotional tension in our bodies,' Rose says. 'All the hurts and traumas show up in us physically. It's important to be aware of that. If your physical self becomes locked with certain people or in certain circumstances, that means something.'

'My mother . . .' Keera hears herself say the words without thinking. 'She . . . she makes me anxious when she's annoyed.'

Rose nods at her with that calm, kind face: you wouldn't know what Rose is thinking, Keera feels, but it's always thoughtful, gentle. She would never hurt anyone.

'Can you think of any specific times when this happened?' Rose asks.

'When an article appeared about me in February. It was in *Empress*. It's a women's magazine, movie star interviews, the perfect wardrobe for spring, and that sort of thing.'

She stops.

'My mom hated the way they wrote about me but she blamed me for it. I took a lot of medication that day. And drank. Oh yeah,' she adds, remembering, 'I smoked a joint with a complete stranger in the back yard of a cool restaurant.'

Her gaze goes curiously blank, as if she's blocking another memory.

'Did any of that help?' Rose asks.

Keera winces. 'What do you think? Sorry,' she amends. 'No. She still gets mad and it still makes me nervous.'

Rose just nods at this information.

'Let's try a group practice,' she suggests.

She takes a rounded pebble about half the size of one of the villa's morning bread rolls and puts it on the table in front of them.

'This is from our beach,' she says. 'It's a little bit of Corfu. Blasted in and out of the sea for generations. It was probably bigger once. Now it's smaller and round, burnished by the water. I'm going to leave it here and I want each of you to stare at it carefully.'

Dutifully, every eye is on the pebble.

'Now move it with your mind,' says Rose.

As one, the group looks up.

'That's ridiculous,' says Dan.

Rose nods. 'India, what do you think?'

'What is that – telekinesis?' says India. 'Not on my CV.' She laughs.

'Nobody can move it without touching it,' snarls Bernard. 'Or is it a trick question?'

'No trick,' says Rose. 'Dianne?'

'No, I can't move it, obviously—'

'You're showing us what we can't do,' says Keera suddenly. 'None of us can move the pebble without touching it.'

India jumps in suddenly: 'And none of us can move anyone else's mind or change their mind. It's what you said: you can't change anyone.'

'Excellent answers,' says Rose, beaming. 'If the pebble was a person, we couldn't make it happy or sad. The pebble would be in charge of all that. We could try, but it's a hopeless case, don't you all agree?'

The group are staring at her now.

Excellent.

Rose continues: 'It's easier to feel guilty over *not* doing the things that will make someone happy than to face the reality that we *cannot make them happy at all*. That's down to them. We are as powerless over their moods and feelings as we are over this pebble.

'If we bend ourselves into contortions to fix other people, we betray ourselves. If we pour our love into new people all the time to make up for inner pain, we also betray ourselves. We cannot move this pebble but we can move, and change, ourselves and our reactions to life.'

Nobody speaks but they all look down at the pebble itself.

Rose watches everyone processing the information.

Dan stares down at the pebble blankly as if it holds some vital scientific secret.

Dianne's gaze is slightly glazed.

Did she have wine at lunch too? Rose does not approve.

Bernard looks sceptical of the pebble parable.

He thinks he can control everything, Rose feels.

Big mistake.

Huge.

Grazia is concentrating on the pebble. Her eye make-up has been beautifully reapplied since she and Rose walked into Xanthe together after lunch.

Grazia thought that Rose would be shocked at what she'd said but Rose isn't. She's heard everything, a fact which comforts the crying Grazia.

Bernard has now closed his eyes and steepled his fingers.

He could be having a nap but has perfected the art of looking thoughtful with his steepled fingers.

'Bernard, what do you think?' Rose asks.

'Er . . .'

Bernard jerks into a more upright position.

He *was* dozing off.

Rose gives him a stern look but continues. 'Now imagine the pebble every time you think of a person you somehow try to control or placate. Keera, you first?'

Keera needs to be jerked out of her scepticism.

'Is there a person in your life who you try to keep happy? This is a type of control – controlling as much as you can with the aim of making a particular person love you or understand you.'

Keera keeps looking at the stone on the table and Rose waits.

Keera doesn't answer but she's thinking.

'I don't know . . .' she says slowly.

Oh you do, but you don't want to say it out loud yet, Rose thinks. Co-dependency.

They can move on.

There's a magic about this part of the process.

Rose loves it.

It's when people become aware that they are not able to control anything but themselves.

Rose decides the silence has gone on long enough.

'Elephants have little passengers,' she says. 'A white bird called the egret. The egret sits on the elephant or flies behind it and eats the insects that the elephant stirs up when it walks. Can the elephant exist without the egret? Yes. Can the egret make the elephant do anything it wants the elephant to do? No.'

Pausing to see how everyone is taking this fable, Rose carries on.

'Humans are not like egrets and elephants but when we try to make people feel a certain way, we are just like the egret on the elephant's back. Powerless.'

She hands out six pieces of notebook paper and six pencils.

'I want you each to write down who you try to control. It can be that you try to make them happy by doing exactly what they want. It could be that you try to adhere to their rules or control them to make your life easier. It could be that you enable their bad behaviour as a way to stop them leaving you. You don't have to share these names – just list them for your own benefit. Be ruthlessly honest.'

She goes over to pour some water from the jug of iced lemon water on the buffet table and gives the participants some time.

So far, she knows that Dan feels responsible for Julia to the extent that they're in a co-dependent relationship. He truly believes he can control whether she takes drugs, drinks or overdoses.

Keera's mother lives her life vicariously through her daughter but now Keera has broken free. Going to rehab when her mother didn't want her to was a huge first step.

Dianne needs to be prodded. Rose has an idea about Dianne's anger but she needs some confirmation. Dianne's anger is a barrier she hides behind.

'Does anyone have any questions?' Rose asks.

'Why is this all so painful?' asks Dan.

'You have to go through the pain to get to the other side,' offers Keera.

*

It's dusk when the whole group slowly makes their way down to the beach for evening meditation. A light breeze floats in from the sea but the women are still bare-armed, with Grazia carrying a light wrap.

Dan, India and Keera are walking together when Keera's phone rings and she looks at it doubtfully.

DR BOBBI flashes on the call screen. For a brief second, Keera wonders why she's never put *Mom* on the phone. Perhaps because her mother is Dr Bobbi, manager first and mother second.

'Hi,' says Keera hesitantly, holding back and gesturing to India and Dan to go on without her.

She should have left her phone in her room but having it with her is a habit. Keera's tired of breaking habits.

'Where the heck are you?' shrieks her mother as soon as Keera answers. 'I've been trying to get a hold of you for days!'

'You can't have tried very hard because this is the first time you've called me,' Keera replies, feeling the familiar sting.

'Rude!' shrieks her mother. 'I was trying to give you space. But you just vanished. So I asked Taniqua, then Luka, because you never tell me anything any more.' Her mother's outrage is plain. 'I even rang that rehab place in case you'd gone back for some reason and nobody ever answers their cell there. Goddamn idiots. When they do, nobody will tell me anything!'

Dr Bobbi's voice is getting more high pitched, a sure sign she's heading for a full-blown shouting session.

Keera can feel her body reacting of its own accord: all her muscles tense, her shoulders tighten and her stomach clenches.

'I didn't tell Taniqua where I was going,' says Keera, determined not to get her friend in trouble. 'The rehab place can't tell you because they don't know and besides they are bound by confidentiality. Remember that?'

'Confidentiality means nothing, not between you and me,' says her mom dismissively. 'Besides, I paid for that place—'

'No, you didn't!' says Keera, shocked at the outright lie. 'I paid for it.'

'With money we earned together!' shouts back her mother.

For a second, Keera stares at the path down to the beach. Everyone else has moved on.

She can see India up in front, tiptoeing across the toasty, warm sand, holding her flip-flops in her hand. Bernard and Grazia are moving at a much slower pace and Dan, lovely, gentlemanly Dan, is helping Dianne.

It's unusual to see anyone touch Dianne because she's the sort of person who doesn't like physical contact. This morning, Keera had automatically reached to hug her and had seen Dianne actually wince.

'You still there?' shrieks Keera's mom down the phone.

'Yes.'

'Where the hell are you?'

'Are you in LA?' asks Keera, not answering the question.

'No, I'm in Vegas. It's gone downhill, to hell in a handbasket,' her mother says dismissively.

If Dr Bobbi was in Vegas, it was fine for Keera to say where she really was.

'I'm in Greece.'

'Greece where? Greece the country?' Her mother sounds stunned.

'Yes, Greece the country. The island of Corfu, in fact.' Keera decides to give her mother a bit more information given that Dr Bobbi is both thousands of miles and nine hours away. Plus, their credit cards are pretty much maxed out. Some of her mother's jewellery would have to be sold speedily to pay for any more flights, not that Keera would put it past her mother. But Dr Bobbi does love her diamonds. The bigger the better.

Keera's living on the money she stashed in her own private account, one Dr Bobbi doesn't know about.

'I'm on a retreat.'

'What do you mean by retreat?' her mother asks suspiciously. 'A retreat where you rest your voice so you're able to sing?'

It always comes back to work and, through work, to money, Keera realises. Her mother hasn't asked her how she is or even *why* she felt the need to go to Greece.

She's less like a mother and more like an employer checking up on a recalcitrant member of staff.

'No,' says Keera flatly.

'Well, people are looking for you,' Dr Bobbi informs her daughter. 'You're hotter than ever since you've vanished, although I don't suppose you know that because you've apparently turned all your socials off,' she adds crossly. 'It's real easy to get forgotten in this business, Keera, and don't you forget it. One minute you're somebody and the next, you're a nobody waiting tables in a dive telling people who you used to be. I've worked too hard to let that happen, missy.'

Keera isn't sure whether Rose would approve or not but she can't let this last jibe pass her.

'*You've* worked too hard?' Keera says, disbelief colouring her words. 'What about all the work *I've* done? What about the hours I worked when I was a kid and I really should have been in school or playing with friends? What about then? The problem with you, Mom, is that you still think that I'm your creation!'

As the words fly out of her with passion, Keera realises that she's wanted to say this for a very long time.

But it seems her mother hasn't even heard her.

'Honey, we've all worked very hard to get you where you are now,' says Dr Bobbi, sighing, 'but the time for holidays, retreats and all that crap is over. Remember that producer, Santi, he's ready to work with you again. He definitely didn't like it when you were drinking too much and the whole thing with his ex-wife and her son and the coke – well, that didn't look good. It was trashy behaviour, Keera. But he's on board now. Honey, you have no idea the favours I had to wrangle to get this to happen.'

There's the pause.

The pause where Keera's supposed to reply with how fabulous her mother is, how much she appreciates all the hard work, how she can't thank her enough.

Keera's been trained to say these things like a seal in the aquarium is trained to jump for fish.

Even in interviews when she was younger, she'd known enough to say: 'Oh my mom is just the most amazing person in the world. I can't imagine what I'd do without her.'

Keera knew without ever being told that this was part of the contract, this endlessly being grateful to her mother. She was never able to say that her own talent had had a part to play in her success. That would have been heresy.

The party line was that Dr Bobbi had created Keera like a miniature Frankenstein's monster. Dr Bobbi was the person who turned on and off the electricity in the background.

Without her, Keera was nothing.

'You still there?' Bobbi says, as if she has to shout to make her voice heard in Europe.

Keera can see everyone settled on the beach now. The blankets are down and they're all sitting in a circle in the sunset.

Dan appears to be trying to light a small fire and Keera hopes he's receiving direction from Rose about this. The idea of lighting a fire in a tinder-dry country seems like a crazy one but then, they are beside the sea . . . ?

The thought makes her smile. She has started to really like this gang, actually.

She wants to get to know India more, and Dan too.

Not Dianne because nobody can get inside Dianne's head and she has a massive amount of tension surrounding her.

But possibly Grazia too.

They might all meet up some Christmas, have a dinner party and discuss the retreat and how fabulous Rose was.

Dinner parties are what normal people have.

Keera's never been to one.

She's seen them on films and in cooking shows, obviously.

But sitting with friends around a table full of food is not something there's been room for in her and her mother's lives.

India waves to her from the beach and Keera waves back.

She holds her hand up: 'Five minutes,' she mouths.

Keera suddenly imagines what will happen when the retreat is over and she flies back home.

Home to the small, rented house in San Francisco where she has to pretend she's living in a massive celeb-style house; where all interviews take place in beautiful hotels as reporters can't come to the house and see where they really live.

Nobody can see that the person in charge of the money,

Dr Bobbi, has mishandled it so badly that Keera's capital has dwindled.

Two albums made years ago.

The money from her TV shows is long gone. The residuals are tiny.

She'll have to go back on the tour bus again: touring and selling merchandise because that's the only way to keep their heads above water.

That life stretches out in front of her unless she changes something.

This week is it.

She's not ready to go back and . . . she's not ready to confront her mother, either. It's too hard.

Instead, she does the only thing she can think of.

'Mom, I can't deal with what you want right now. I have to make decisions about the rest of my life.'

Then she hangs up, turns her phone to silent and makes her way down to the beach where everyone else has settled themselves on beach towels. There are extra blankets in case it gets cooler later and, already, the group is preparing for the deep breathing in front of the Ionian Sea.

The phone continues vibrating for the next ten minutes. Her mother is not keen on being hung up on, although Keera herself has never done it before. But there's a first time for everything.

On Thursday morning, Dianne's sick.

'She was fine on the beach last night,' says Grazia, who appeared to be the person who says what everyone else is thinking and does not say. 'I do not think she is sick, pah!'

Rose doesn't think Dianne's sick, either. She's the only

person who hasn't revealed their personal story and she's ruining Rose's carefully worked out plans.

Dianne is getting a home visit in her villa bedroom this afternoon when everyone else is going to be getting some exercise and working on their notebooks. Dianne's notebook was found in the garden on Tuesday, so Rose got Beata to put it back in Dianne's room that evening. It has not been thrown out since, so far as Rose knows.

'Keera,' says Rose, once they've done their ten minutes of morning breathwork, 'I wonder how you'll feel if we come back to you, my dear?'

Keera is ready for this.

Since her mother's outraged phone call last night, Keera's mind has been full of moments when Dr Bobbi shouted at her or manipulated her.

She had told Rose about the call.

'You've never hung up on your mother before,' Rose had said. 'It would have been an insane concept, but you just did it. That's progress. You're laying down boundaries.'

Throughout the meditation on the beach, all Keera thought of was the day the interview came out. It was the first time she'd felt that everything was falling apart.

Sunshine fills the hotel suite where Empress *has come to interview singing superstar, Keera. Already one of the artists who are known by one name only, Keera joins icons like Beyoncé and Zendaya, whose career hers most closely resembles.*

Plucked from obscurity to appear in a kids' TV show, Keera's talent was immediately obvious, and a meteoric rise to teen stardom followed.

Yet it's hard to reconcile a girl who turned her kooky smile and exquisite voice into millions of dollars with the thoughtful young woman I'm interviewing today.

In the flesh, Keera is refreshingly normal. Polite.

'Do you want coffee or water?' she asks, gesturing at the juices and coffee pot laid out on a side table.

She's drinking only iced water, which I mention must be proof of what it takes to take care of the luminous Celtic skin that's rumoured to be responsible for a top-secret-for-now deal with Lancôme.

She can't talk about that, she says apologetically, neither denying nor confirming it.

But she can talk about the album she's making with a multi-award-winning producer – 'It's such a privilege to work with Santi Montavano,' she says earnestly.

She's also eager to talk about the children's charity she's donating her early TV wardrobe to for a star-studded auction.

Some of the outfits from the early days of Keera & Cat are on show already: including the red gingham pinafore Keera wore for at least half of the first series.

Her face angled towards the LA sun, the now-twenty-eight-year-old Keera's beauty is ethereal. She has 1950s screen goddess curves, what she laughingly calls 'Proof that I actually eat.'

Dressed in a norm-core pair of Levis and a vintage tee with her luxuriant dark hair shining in waves, she's an intriguing combination of honesty and normality.

The latter quality has earned her many fans but, in a luxe suite in The Contessa Hotel in Bel Air, she's as glamorous . . .

'Fuck.'

It's taken Keera one minute to scan the start of the article and realise that despite being as charming as humanly possible to the bone-thin forty-something woman who interviewed her two months ago, she's been fat-shamed.

'Screen goddess curves . . .' She can imagine her mom's reaction to that.

Knowing it was coming out today, Keera was anxious as she opened the pre-publication online *Empress* interview messaged to her by Lara LaGrand, the current publicist. Dr Bobbi believes publicists need to be kept on their toes so, no matter how tough it is, she fires them regularly.

Lara has made the cut for longer than usual because of mentions of her family's vast home on Philadelphia's old-money Main Line.

Keera knows her mom is a sucker for inherited wealth.

Lara fixed the interview and has just messaged that it's 'fabulous!', which it is. Except for one thing that's going to ruin Dr Bobbi's day. And it's not the mention of the possible Lancôme deal, which is a totally manufactured piece of news created by Dr Bobbi herself.

'Makes you sound sought-after,' she said, ignoring her daughter's look of horror.

It's after half nine in the morning and it's been a slightly foggy start to the day on Martina Street in San Francisco. February can be like that. The day starts with a mist around the house, and then suddenly it lifts, allowing the sun to glitter the bay.

Keera likes this house on the hill. She likes the utter anonymity of San Francisco and how the beach is only a walk from the house. Los Angeles is all entertainment industry, where nobody's ever an ordinary person – they're an influencer waiting for a big break or they're peering over your shoulder to see if anyone more important is coming along.

Dr Bobbi's great at that.

She's got the three-minute attention span of the relentless social climber.

This means endless lies about everything.

She's told Keera to be vague about where they live.

'Say Pacific Avenue,' she insists. 'We're renting a huge house there. With . . .' Dr Bobbi has to think of what she can add on to this mythical house – 'a housekeeper, a zen garden with a cloud tree, a sauna, gym with a barre and Pilates reformer, and an infinity pool.'

'Sure,' Keera always says.

Sure is a word that says nothing.

Now she makes her third cup of coffee of the day and walks out into the back yard where she was sitting earlier with an old furry blanket around her. She's been smoking and the aluminium ashtray has three butts in it already.

Stressed, Keera lights another, knowing this will boil her mother's blood.

Her mother smokes.

In fact, it's a mystery to Keera as to why Big Tobacco hasn't flown Dr Bobbi out to Kentucky and planted a tree in her honour.

But Keera is *not* allowed to smoke.

It's about appealing to the widest age group – both young girls and people in their twenties.

No smoking, no drinking, smile politely all the fucking time.

Her mother's rules.

Oh yeah, and be thin.

Pretend to not care about being thin but work really

hard at being thin so that she can fit into size zero pants and have the hips of a twelve-year-old.

Dr Bobbi makes the rules and insists on a weigh-in every week.

Keera has tried slimming pills but amphetamines make her wildly nervous and weight-loss injections affect her particularly badly with nausea.

Now she's smoking and, while that works in terms of flattening her appetite, she's not supposed to be smoking. She's supposed to be doing intensive training with a guy who allegedly once got Lady Gaga in shape for a tour.

She's exhausted trying to be thin. Why is this the only metric by which she's measured? Thin first. Pretty next. Only then is her actual work considered.

Keera hates the misogyny of it.

She's come to realise that women artists are never celebrated purely for their art: instead, it's all folded up with physical attractiveness and ranked depending on how the powers that be – men – define women's art.

Today, she and her mother have lunch – which means lines of coke and possibly margaritas – with Santi Montavano's ex-wife, who is an old pal of Dr Bobbi's and the one who got them the introduction to Santi himself.

They've only done one day in the studio so far. Keera feels too burned out to have sung well. It had not been a good day.

Santi's heavily booked for the next two months, so with its implications of much time to come with the fabulous producer, the article contained another half-truth, which she hates.

With her coffee and her cigarette, Keera sits and looks out at the parts of the bay where the fog is lifting.

Peace.

Blissful peace.

And then she hears her mother's roar of temper.

Dr Bobbi has clearly seen the article too.

Wearing an old Disney TV tee as a nightshirt, her hair askew and last night's make-up still mashed into her eyes, her mother does not paint a pretty picture. Her evident rage doesn't help.

'Did you see this?' she demands, waving her phone at Keera. 'Why didn't you wake me when you got it? Look at it, just look!'

'I did.'

Keera gets up but holds on to her cigarette, almost as a defence. She tenses, every muscle now locked tight.

'You didn't think it was worth waking me?'

This is a rhetorical question.

Dr Bobbi rages on. 'See this crap about you having curves! She means fat,' screeched Dr Bobbi. 'How many times have I told you?'

Again, rhetorical.

The fog is lifting.

Keera hopes the neighbours have already left for the day or they'll hear every word of the row.

Her mother is in a full-on temper now.

'I don't care if a hundred women *"with curves"* make it on the socials – they might sell a few hundred control knickers and slimming corsets but they will never be players. *Never!*'

She screams this last bit.

Keera thinks what she might say: *It's a lovely article, apart from that one bit. The journalist made me sound like a decent person* . . .

No, that would never do.

Dr Bobbi has spent years patiently explaining to Keera that stars are not normal. Stars have to be different. Special.

It was tough but, one day, Keera would appreciate all her mother's work . . .

'I thought I sounded nice in this, normal—'

That's a mistake.

'*Normal*? Stars aren't supposed to be normal,' Dr Bobbi hisses. '*Normal* writes the music for other people or stays in the background, never making it, always on the fringes. You're supposed to be a *star*, stupid girl!'

Keera steps back, as if the words are physical.

'That's what I've taught you for years and you've never understood it, have you? Were Vuitton or Dior offering you gowns for the last Grammys?' Dr Bobbi is in her stride now. 'Any of the big fashion houses? No! You get offered cheap tramp clothes or dresses from people who want to revitalise their careers after being cancelled.'

Keera winces.

Her mother is so into social media and watches the guillotine of cancellation closely. Women who pop their head up get brutally eviscerated.

That's why women like Keera can't be trendsetters, Bobbi often says. They have to follow the crowd.

'And why is that? Why do you not get offered vintage Balenciaga or JW Anderson? Because of your weight! I work so hard and fixed up this interview and you blow it by not being able to stick to any fucking diet or exercise plan. I have given up my whole life to take care of you, to be your manager, and this is how you treat that sacrifice.'

In the distance, someone slams a screen door and it brings Dr Bobbi back to realising she's not in a sound-proofed room.

'Look what you made me do. I hate shouting at you,' she says in lower tones.

The shift from anger to recrimination is sudden.

Dr Bobbi's eyes suddenly glisten with tears and Keera knows the worst of it is over.

Relief means that Keera's body unlocks.

But coming back into herself means she can now *feel* everything. Her heart thudding in anxiety. Her body slowly creeping out of its taut rictus.

She drops her cigarette in the ashtray and pulls the blanket around her.

Her mother loses it sometimes but this feels like another level.

'I told you to get a handle on your weight, didn't I?'

Dr Bobbi is calmer now.

But the ache of rejection means that Keera suddenly wants something to take away the pain of not being enough.

A few Xanax, maybe with a tequila shot or six. Tequila works wonderfully fast. She wants that bone-melting sense of not being able to feel.

Her neck aches. Tension, she knows.

A massage will not touch this, nor even one of her mother's chiropractic sessions.

No, only the soft release of Xanax to soften her edges and a meltingly fabulous amount of alcohol. Then some coke to make her happy and she'll want to dance, whirling in an energetic haze and she won't have to feel anything.

'Did you take something to calm yourself?' asks Rose.

The sunny terrace in Villa Artemis comes into view again.

'Yeah,' says Keera. 'I took a lot of stuff.'

'What's it like reliving that moment?'

The group are silent.

'Scary,' says Keera finally. 'Shocking. I didn't see how

negative it was until I told you all. It was a huge interview to get, the interviewer was positive about me and that one thing made Mom go off at the deep end. I was fat and I was disappointing her, ruining all her work by that one thing.'

She pauses.

It's a tough moment, Rose knows: speaking about her relationship with her mother makes Keera see it through other people's eyes.

She also feels that Keera doesn't entirely trust her own version of events. There's no other child to ask how such a situation looked. No sibling.

There's only Keera with her memories.

'How does it make you feel physically?' Rose asks.

The body doesn't lie.

'Fat, ugly, like a whale-sized piece of blubber . . .' Keera's voice breaks a little.

'You're not,' shrieks India and suddenly she's on her knees beside Keera's chair, holding her. 'You're so beautiful. How dare anyone tell you otherwise. That's a fucking lie!'

They stay like that for several minutes, Keera sobbing and India sobbing too, holding on to her.

Dan finds a pack of tissues and hands them gently to both women.

Finally, Keera stops crying and she's wiping away the tears with the tissue Dan handed her.

Rose can feel that he wants to say something but he's not sure if he can speak. 'Dan, do you want to say something to Keera?'

'Actually, yes,' he says in his soft deep voice. 'In your story, you talk about being famous from when you were nine. I lecture students in my university and when they come in first, at eighteen, nineteen, they're very vulnerable. I know what I was like then: scared, unsure of myself. I found friends in uni, and I had met Julia at school . . .'

He pauses. Nobody says anything.

'But you've never had these experiences. Never had a normal chance to grow up. You were almost an adult from when you were nine? What age were you when you started in TV?'

'Nine,' confirms Keera.

'I can understand that your mother wanted you to use your talent, but there's nothing there about taking care of you as a child. She treats you like a commodity and that's a betrayal . . . Sorry,' he adds, 'that's a harsh word.'

Keera is nodding now, tears drying on her face, which is blotchy.

'It is the right word,' agrees Grazia fiercely. 'Your mother is a terrible person. When you tell your story, I can see that she bullies you. Why does *she* not make the money? Why always you? I do not like your mother.'

Grazia crosses her arms and Rose hopes that Dr Bobbi does not ever encounter her. Grazia may have perfectly manicured nails and wear expensive clothes but there is something of the street fighter in her.

Interesting.

'Thank you all,' sniffs Keera. 'I feel sick now – like I'm bitching about Mom and I love her and everything but it's just . . .'

'It's all a bit much,' finishes Rose. 'Keera, you've touched on so much here – the world-wide body shaming of women primarily, the pressure to be thin in your particular career. Then your mother is not on your side in this battle. That's a lot to handle. Can you see how powerful you are to have decided to go to rehab? Nobody booked you in: you chose it. That's very powerful, that's taking control over your life.'

Keera nods.

'I know but I know it intellectually. I can't feel it.'

'You will,' says Rose. 'The fact that your mother is the person who is angry with you over the sort of body she thinks you need to have: do you have any insight into why she is that person? I'm not looking for blanket forgiveness, but an understanding of where she came from.'

'She wanted to be famous,' says Keera shrugging. 'But it didn't work out.'

Rose nods. 'You can see the misguided love there,' she says. 'Your mother has done everything she can to give you the gift she wanted most in the world: fame. Now you know it's her dream, not yours. You have decisions to make. Let's take a break.'

Christos is in his chef whites and he's looking at a message on Adriana's phone.

'Don't show Rose,' says Christos to his wife.

'We need to!' says Adriana. 'She's been emailing this person in Los Angeles about what to do. We have to tell her.'

I know what you did, Alys, and I will tell the world if you don't shut down your so-called retreat, the message says.

This time, it's come in to the villa's website email from a very anonymous-sounding address.

Christos shakes his head.

'This time it's different,' he says thoughtfully. 'I will ask Marco for help.'

'Marco? This is just about us, it's hardly Europol business,' says Adriana.

'Someone is blackmailing our business,' Christos replies. 'I think that's very much Europol business.'

'Rose says she can handle it,' protests Adriana.

'She has handled so much, my darling,' says Christos. 'Let me take over now. Please.'

Dan wants to join India and Keera at the acropolis, where they've gone with some iced lemonade and sun cream. But he thinks Rose is going to be onto him again for not doing his homework, so he goes back to his room, finds his blasted notebook and picks up a pen.

He still loves Julia but she's mercurial, if he's honest. Her moods change in the blink of an eye and what she wants changes all the time.

He wanted to marry her and she said she didn't want to be tied down. It had nearly killed him. He'd felt wounded, rejected.

Dan had spent a very long time thinking about the right sort of ring. In the end, he decided upon an antique one he spent ages tracking down. Julia loves emeralds, and it was a 1930s ring: one long emerald baguette with tiny diamonds lined up each side of it.

Julia had said that she loved the ring, thank you very much, but not the engagement thing.

'It's a bit old school for me, sweetie,' she'd said, admiring the ring she'd put on her right hand, the wrong hand.

His sister had been enraged at the time.

'She takes you for granted, uses you,' Vicky said. 'You mop up her messes and give her undying devotion without asking for anything in return. I understand her far better than you, big bro. She needs you and you need to be needed.'

For a long time, Dan has denied Vicky's claims.

But despite himself, he can see that she's right.

Co-dependency is the word, according to Rose. Dan hates this word, hates that his and Julia's beautiful love can be described with this tawdry word.

When he and Julia met, she saved him from his insecurities and his introversion. But now, he saves her from herself.

He spends lots of money on her because she's never had a career as such.

'I'm a professional party girl!' she likes to say, when she's off to Glastonbury with the expensive wellington boots she acquired mysteriously, long tanned legs and a coolly torn green Barbour, also mysteriously acquired.

People in big houses often lost things when Julia came to stay but nobody said anything: it might be seen as rude.

Sometimes she wears a cowboy hat, sequinned shorts and a vintage tee that says it's from a Jimi Hendrix gig, which seems unlikely.

She always has a beaten-up Dior tote bag for her belongings. Dan bought her that from Vestiaire, so he knows it's not stolen. Her tangled necklaces are half junk and her hair is always tangled, bleached blonde and falling over eyes with pupils enlarged due to the post-festival joint she's smoking.

Dan had only been to Glastonbury with her once. He hated it: the early drug-taking and the fact that most of their crew are out of their minds by four p.m. He hates camping too. It's only a reasonable proposition when the campers are totally stoned. He never is.

'You're no fun!' Julia said teasingly, but soon everyone was saying it.

He loves music and tried to get in the mood by drinking beer but it was impossible to catch up with the true partygoers who were in another sphere entirely.

Dan didn't judge them: he's known many of Julia's friends for years and he's fond of some of them, but he doesn't adore them. Neither does he adore the new friends who keep enlarging the circle. New partygoers when the old ones fall prey to getting married, having kids, having to make money with actual jobs.

Julia works to live rather than lives to work.

As for Dan's career in science, she never asks about it.

She's everything he's not: extrovert, thrill-seeking, careless with money.

They are as different as two people can possibly be.

Dan closes his notebook.

He's not sure what he feels right now.

Happy that he understands things at last or sad that his main relationship in life has been held up to the light and found wanting? Has he wasted his life?

Back on the terrace, Rose finishes her coffee. She's suddenly exhausted. She'd forgotten how much this kind of work takes out of you. She has to find Dianne, who's not in her room, and discuss why Dianne has skipped out of the morning's sessions.

The retreat is going so well but they're not there yet.

'Dan, going back to you, do you feel you are in control of your life?' Rose asks him.

Dan considers this, his intelligent thin face instantly taken away into cerebral reasoning.

'Yes,' he says firmly, 'yes I do.'

Rose wonders if this is the lie he tells himself most frequently but it's not her place to name that lie.

'That's interesting,' she says, which is her way of saying, *I don't believe this for one second, honey*. 'So what's the lie you tell yourself most frequently?'

Now Dan begins to flounder.

Rose can see the battle behind his eyes.

'My sister says I need to be needed,' he says stiffly now.

Rose nods. Now they're getting somewhere.

'Vicky thinks I should forget about Julia and get on with my life,' Dan says.

He has just been thinking this and yet he can't say it in public yet – it feels like a betrayal. Guilt for everything he's already said overwhelms him. He loves Julia, for heaven's sake! Isn't that enough?

Nobody's saying anything on the terrace at Villa Artemis.

If anything, it's hotter than yesterday. Dan can feel India fanning herself with her notebook beside him.

Without asking if he's thirsty, Keera puts a glass of iced water in front of him.

She knows he doesn't like juice, which is so kind.

Briefly, he wonders if Julia knows that he doesn't like juice.

He knows how she likes her coffee, black, that she prefers dirty martinis and champagne to any other drink, that her favourite meal is blue loin tuna seared for a few moments in a pan, and that she thinks getting up before eleven on a weekend is for people who don't know how to enjoy parties.

Julia wants Dan but he's suddenly aware that she really wants a different sort of Dan: a Dan who's free to party all the time and doesn't have a career. He needs to have no other responsibilities except her and then she'll know he's absolutely committed to her.

'Perhaps you can work more on the lies we tell ourselves and what we really want later this afternoon, Dan,' Rose suggests.

He nods absently.

'To link back to you, India, let's talk about the things you both haven't said to partners. Dan: I think you said that you and Julia have never had a conversation about children. Why not?'

Dan flails a bit.

'Don't know,' he says, uncomfortably. 'I sensed Julia didn't want them.'

Rose lets the word *sensed* sit with him for a moment.

'And India, you've hidden the fact that you want to be a mother, which is a very valid desire for a woman. Sure, not all women want children but you do, so why hide it?'

'Because the men I see would not be interested in having a baby,' India says cautiously. She isn't ready to talk about this yet. 'It was a nonsensical idea anyway.'

'Don't betray yourself like this,' says Rose briskly. 'You want what most people want – love, a family, a child. What's wrong with wanting those things?'

'Nothing,' says India cautiously.

'The question is whether you choose these men because they won't be interested in children – or whether you're stuck repeating old twenty-something patterns now that you're more mature and have mature wants and needs?'

The words crowd India's head: attachment theory, longing for motherhood, limerence, her mother's crazy unicorn-butterfly stuff, the line of men: Andrey, Felippe . . . she could probably do it alphabetically and hit every letter of the alphabet. A for Andrey, B for Boris, C for Chad . . . 'I want to be loved and needed,' India says quietly. 'I want to have my person. My mother has Magnús, Dad has Georgie. Everyone has someone—'

'You want someone for the right reasons, the right someone,' Rose says.

India nods gloomily.

Rose moves on.

'Keera, going back to you: do you think your relationship with your mother was one where you protected her from how you were really feeling? Because she reacted so badly when your needs were different to hers?'

Keera nods cautiously.

'I don't want you to get the wrong impression: Mom protected me too,' Keera says softly. 'She'd had to be tough and she wanted me to be tough.'

'But that type of protection doesn't work for you any more. It was fine when you were using drugs and drinking, then you allowed her behaviour to continue. She didn't call you out on your cocaine use and you didn't call her out on treating you like a hopeless employee.'

Keera nods. It all makes so much sense when Rose explains it.

Like putting lots of keys in a door and none of them fit no matter how much you wiggle them in the lock. Then suddenly, someone hands you the right key, it fits and the door opens. Simple.

'I was so angry with her, especially over Cat, my friend. We did the TV show together and once she was ill – she got lupus – I did the show on my own. I was fourteen, I think. The ratings went up.'

Keera smiles sadly.

'It's cheaper to pay one kid in a TV show than pay two, plus it was easier to launch one singing star. It's all about the numbers.'

'Did your mother really dislike Cat?' asks Rose curiously.

'I'm not sure. I think she didn't mind me being friends with Taniqua or Luka because they were part of the team. Mom liked them but we paid them as professionals, therefore they weren't a threat. Cat *was* a threat.

'At any point, audience screenings could have shown she was more popular than me. The business is ruthless. I'd have been gone. Therefore, Cat was an opponent. She could have taken away my stardom if she became the more famous one.'

Rose gets up and fills a glass with ice and some orange juice from Christos' little fridge in the side table.

'Drink this,' she says. 'You've got to keep your blood sugar up when you're examining painful truths. As you say, once you've seen this you can't unsee it. You said you haven't met up with Cat in a long time: it sounds as though you have complex feelings about that?'

Keera flushes.

'Cat didn't really care about being famous. It was fun to her. So when she got canned from the show, I was OK with that. She didn't care. Me and Mom, we would have killed to keep that show on the road.'

She looks up suddenly. 'Does that make me a horrible person, Rose?'

'You were fourteen,' Rose says. 'Think about how vulnerable you are when you're fourteen. The atmosphere you live in is one where you must succeed to make your mother happy. Dr Bobbi is the primary person in your life. She comes first.'

'I feel like such a terrible friend,' Keera says. 'I haven't seen Cat in years. She must think I'm such a bitch. We used to sleep in each other's beds when we were little. She braided my hair, I did her eye make-up. I painted her toes every week with a different colour for each toe.'

'Have you been going over other incidents in your mind with you and your mother where you don't like what you see?'

'Yeah,' says Keera wearily. She drinks her juice. 'When I got out of rehab, Mom expected me to start work all over again. I was too fragile. Mom thought rehab was self-indulgent. She didn't come on family day.'

The terrace is silent.

'When I got out, she said all that rehab stuff was in the past. I was a superstar and I had work to do.'

Keera bursts into tears. 'I know we're messed up but I love her. I guess I grew up and she didn't want me to.'

It takes Rose a while to calm Keera down.

'You can love your mother and want to change things, Keera: both of these statements can be true at the same time.'

'But I'm betraying her—'

'If you don't stand up for what you feel, then the person you're betraying is yourself,' says Rose firmly.

She can tell that the group are all on edge, so she shifts her focus.

'India,' Rose says, 'tell us about your outfit today?'

India looks astonished.

'Me? This was dirt cheap,' she says holding up the linen skating skirt she's wearing with tennis shoes and a floppy cerise polka-dot blouse. 'I got it in the Oxfam shop. This,' she waves her arms around and the small sleeves of her blouse wave, 'was expensive. It's Chloé. Twenty-five quid at a car boot sale.'

'That is not expensive,' says Grazia, 'but it is lovely.'

'Twenty-five's a lot at a car boot,' India explains. 'I put ribbons in the tennis shoes for fun.'

She holds up one long leg with the shoe at the end decorated with neon-green ribbon laces.

'Who says you're not clever?' Rose remarks and India laughs.

'I told you: you're an artist.'

Rose ends the session by standing up.

'You're all free from now till six this evening when we meet to discuss any insights from your notebooks. Yours too, Bernard,' she says.

Bernard glares at her.

Once she's walked away, Dan stands up and stretches his long arms over his head.

'I'm going to do a hike,' he says to India and Keera. 'You two want to come?'

Keera shakes her head.

'Didn't sleep well last night,' she says.

Her sleep was full of rehab-style nightmares where she's been drinking and lying about it. She needs to phone her closest NA friend, Yolande. Ask what it means when you haven't had a drink or used, but think you have.

'I'll go with you,' says India suddenly. 'I think a march will be good for me!'

'I didn't say a march,' says Dan. 'We can't be out too long – you heard what Rose said, it's too hot and we can only carry a certain amount of water with us.'

'Fine,' says India. 'Where are we starting from?'

'The beach,' says Dan.

'See you there in half an hour, then,' India says and skips off.

Rose gets a cup of coffee from the kitchen, then goes into the air-conditioned cool of her room and sits down at her desk, pulling her notepad towards her.

Rose thinks again about how Keera thought she was an empath.

Rose is fed up of the word – to her, it just means people who were raised on a knife-edge and who've learned to anticipate the inevitable explosions.

If you learned as a kid how to predict the anger/rage/whatever of your supposed adult carer, you knew how to hide or get out of the way.

Rose learned that early on.

Being raised in care didn't actually mean care. There weren't enough caring people to go around.

But there were plenty of supposed empaths.

Rose's own gift at seeing people's pain was the result of it. She'd always thought it was half magic, but she finally realised that life had taught her to thin-slice people expertly.

It was a technique whereby one noted every facial and emotional tic, every word, every syllable, every roll of the eyes, every sliver of contempt until you could tell exactly what sort of person was in front of you.

Most people had to train to do this but, after her childhood, Rose is an expert.

After that, it's about how you help other people to heal.

She was lucky, she knows. She'd been in care all her young life and she'd had some lovely foster parents. Some mediocre ones.

None of them ever lasted.

Now Rose knows it's a hellish job to do and that foster parents burn out.

Rose has been Rose Talisman for so long that she can barely recall being Alys Rosemarie Flint.

Flint is a harsh name and names have meaning.

Rose has always understood this. Little Alys Flint had been raised without so much.

Without real parents and, for a very long time, without much in the way of love or kindness.

Sometimes, when she'd been on the TV show and people came to her with families so broken and damaged that they seemed unfixable, Rose would wish she could hold their hands and tell them that she really understood.

You can escape, she'd have said. *I did.*

But she'd said nothing. Not to them, not to her beloved Theo. Nobody knew. Holding on to her secret was insurance against the past emerging.

Rose understood trauma because she'd grown up in it.

There was nothing to beat the lived experience to understand pain.

Her way out of that trauma came from her vast ability to learn.

She learned that education could help her clamber out of the world of foster parents and damaged foster siblings.

When she hit eighteen, she'd changed her name and magicked up a French mother and a background in the Auvergne, a rural part of France.

Nobody searching for Rosemary Talisman would ever find the remnants of little Alys Flint who'd been in fourteen foster homes before the age of ten.

Nor would they find her little adopted sister. After everything they'd gone through together, Rose would keep Adriana safe no matter what.

Dan sits on the sand waiting for India and stares into the sea. There's the lightest of breezes down here on the beach, and the beach goat has already come up to say hello, bumped Dan in the ribs, and then wandered off when it was obvious that Dan had nothing for him to eat.

Now Dan's trying to sit cross-legged on the sand, a position he finds hard to hold but Julia makes him do it because it's 'good for your hips, babes'.

She's hyper flexible so she can do anything bendy, but Dan's a cycling man and the sort of muscles that help him power up hills mean his muscles are taut rather than lean and stretchy like Julia's.

It always comes back to Julia, doesn't it? Always.

His mind goes to one of their last big rows. He's in the faculty meeting; they're discussing the car parking. The faculty is always discussing car parking.

Dan is not interested because he does not drive into college. His daily routine involves cycling four miles from his two-bedroom redbrick, hauling the Boardman SLR 8.9 Disc up the stairs to his office and hanging it on the wall.

It cost so much, there is no way he's leaving it chained in the bike shed. Bikes mysteriously disappear. Especially items of beauty like the Boardi.

'It's art,' he shrugs whenever people mutter about having a large custom-painted racing bike dangling from the wall.

There are twenty people at the meeting, and Dan has tuned out.

He's looking down at the hardback notebook he uses for all his non-research notes, and is thinking of a lecture he has to give on optogenetics, when his phone starts to vibrate.

It's on silent but he absentmindedly placed it on the desk in front of him and when Julia's picture flashes up, it feels as if the vibrations are somehow louder.

She picked the picture herself – one of her at a party looking spectacular in a silvery sequinned dress that appears to be a very small, slightly elongated vest to Dan. He never understands women's clothes. Julia's are all ridiculously flimsy, barely covering her long limbs and the appropriate bits in a way that makes many men long to see what's underneath.

Dan is used to men lusting over Julia. Has been since they were first going out, when they were both seventeen and *different*.

He can still recall the wonder he felt that someone as beautiful as Julia would want to talk to him, never mind kiss him. He was tall, awkward, knew he was clever but worried that his cleverness made him stand out in the wrong way. He hadn't worked out then that cleverness sometimes needed to be hidden because nobody liked a know-it-all.

Julia was someone who seemed to shimmer like a star. That she should say she didn't fit in either, that she liked him *and* his cleverness, still astonishes him on many levels.

In her currently pulsating phone picture, Julia's beautiful face is thrown back as if she's laughing at something and her deliciously sexy mouth is open, displaying perfect teeth and that soft pink tongue.

The phone continues pulsing.

With anyone else, Dan could click on the 'can I call you later' option. But not his on-off girlfriend of twenty years. Julia will keep phoning and phoning until he gives up and answers.

'Sorry, sorry, got to take this,' he murmurs at the faculty, bowing his head in apology as he unwinds his long legs out of the steel chair.

Outside the meeting room, Dan leans against the only wall without college notices taped on it and answers.

'Bunny Wabbit!' shrieks Julia. 'I thought you were avoiding me?'

'Never,' says Dan in comforting tones but he feels a certain wariness.

He is only Bunny Wabbit at certain times. Times when Julia has done something she feels guilty about.

Guilt means confession which, it turns out, has never been helpful to Dan's soul.

'Where are you?' he asks.

'That's a very loaded question, babes,' says Julia, the bunny wabbitiness suddenly all gone. Her accent is harsher now, more London than the neutral accent she adopts most of the time.

'Just asking,' he says brightly, feeling a tremor of anxiety.

Dan has learned to be careful when he talks to Julia. She's very sensitive and feels things that other people don't.

'Oh, good. Thought you were getting grizzly with me,' she says in happier tones. 'Whatcha doing?'

'At work,' says Dan, which is where he always is, actually. He tried one of those work/life-balance questionnaires in the science block staffroom one day and it turned out he has the private life of someone who thinks introverts take too many social risks.

Except when he's with Julia.

'Work!' says Julia crossly. 'It's so boring. Can't you come out?' she wheedles. 'Me and some of the gang had this fabulous idea. Xavier's aged parents are away, he went to agricultural college, remember? Has to run the family farm. Pigs. How impossibly boring!'

She sounds like one of the posh girlfriends she pals around with. Livia, Dan thinks. Livia comes from money and says things like 'Gosh' and 'Impossibly boring'.

Julia's still talking.

'He's got the run of the house. Outside Cirencester – remember it from his sister's wedding? Acres of land, horses, that huge house with mossy portraits on the wall, and it's perfect for Billy's band to play. We're having a mini-festival indoors this afternoon in the ballroom, but we need to bring our own duvets. Or at least a hot water bottle! It'll be a right laugh.'

Dan can remember the wedding in the vast manor house outside Cirencester quite well. Somebody had overdosed by accident at the after party, an ambulance had whisked them off after Narcanning them.

People who got Narcanned to save their lives were surprisingly aggressive when they came to, all the fun of the drug sucked out of them by their life-saving treatment, it turned out.

Dan had watched it all anxiously. He'd been the one who'd called the ambulance because he was the only one who wasn't out of his mind on drugs or a lethal absinthe cocktail called Spiced Green Devils.

Astonishingly, after the ambulance had departed, everyone – well, Julia's pals – had continued drinking, partying and taking Class As.

Dan had gone to bed alone and yes, it had been Baltic. The overdosed person had survived, but Dan hadn't heard mention of them lately. Maybe they'd left the scene.

'I can't,' he says gently. 'I've got tutorials this afternoon. I still haven't finished that paper I'm writing, either.'

'Please,' begs Julia.

He's tempted. But he can't. He has to work.

Julia does not have a career.

'Careers are for boring people,' she likes to say.

'Except for you, darling,' she'll add if they are out with friends.

Dan has two sets of friends, actually. The ones he has himself, which is a very small bunch, mainly college friends who all have careers, ordinary homes, small children if they're lucky, and who can happily spend an evening discussing a paper in the *Journal of Neuroscience* or *Trends in Biochemical Sciences* over a couple of bottles of red in their favourite restaurant.

Julia's friends are a wilder bunch, many with precarious ways of earning money, some with trust funds and great-aunts with a Lowry or a Dante Gabriel Rossetti just waiting to be inherited. Others with jobs they barely cling on to who live in shared houses and spend every penny on fun.

'Darling girl,' he says now.

Julia loves being called a girl. She's nearly forty now too but doesn't like to be reminded of it.

'Darling girl, I can't come. I wish I could but I've got to work now. I could come over tonight,' he adds, thinking that if he got up early the next morning, he could get a head start on the papers he needs to read for his team of second years.

'When?' she asks.

Dan feels his heart lift: it's going to be OK.

'Perhaps seven,' he says, mentally calculating finishing up here, working on his paper for a few hours and then prepping for the lecture.

'Seven! We're going now,' she says in her special voice, the one that sounds as if she's so disappointed in him. 'It's an afternoon thing. You can't have a festival at night.'

'I know but I have to work,' says Dan.

'You always choose your work over me,' says Julia faintly. It's as if she's so sad, she can barely speak. 'I don't know why I stay with you at all.'

She hangs up abruptly and Dan is left in the corridor

outside the faculty meeting, from where he can still hear the gentle droning of conversation.

He leans against the wall, catching his breath and feeling the ache in his heart that he so often feels after arguments with Julia.

He loves her so much. They have this shared history that he can't escape, doesn't want to escape.

Julia is the light in his life, a dizzying star in a dull firmament. Her mind is not like other people's minds, full of mortgages and grocery shopping, work tasks and duty visits to aged grandparents. She's different.

As if a galaxy of suns, planets and stars was contained in that beautiful head, a head crammed full of joy, love, art, ideas, visions that nobody else dared to have. Julia can recite poetry, declaim whole scenes of Shakespeare, dance to any sort of music, literally anything. It's as if there is so much energy and brilliance in her that she can't live in the ordinary world.

A long time ago, she chose him.

She loves him, too, he knows that. It's just that she wants a different version of him: the one who is the smartest guy in every room, but who can party at the drop of a hat, who can magic up bottles of vodka or cases of wine whenever she wants it, who has a Lowry in his attic.

But he's not those things. Never will be.

When she's mad at him, like now, he gets scared she'll leave his life – or try to leave life completely. He is never sure which is more terrifying. Life without Julia is unimaginable and yet life—

Dan finds that he's instinctively breathing deeply to calm himself.

Life *with* Julia is very, very hard.

A hike will burn this energy off.

Chapter Twenty-Nine

The midday heat has simmered off as Dan and India climb the rocky hills high beyond the sea. India has brought the rucksack Keera lent her and she's filled it with two bottles of water, her journal, sunblock, a vial of perfume and a little bag of nuts for sustenance. She did toy with the idea of bringing a couple of squares of very dark chocolate from the tiny minibar but realised it would melt.

Dan has a dark, sporty-looking rucksack and she has no idea what's in it but it seems quite empty.

He's faster than her at clambering over rocks and dusty scree.

After forty-five minutes of climbing like the ever-present mountain goats, India is panting as if she's on a run. Yoga-fit is not the same as mountain-climbing fit.

'Slow down, Dan,' she says. 'I can't go as fast as you.'

'Sorry.' He stops instantly.

India reaches him, bends over to catch her breath and says 'Can we take a breather?'

She's taking one either way. Pulling off her hat, she wipes

her sweaty forehead and thinks, automatically, that it's a pity Dan is seeing her looking hot and sweaty.

No! she tells herself quickly. *You are not here to hook up with Dan. You can't fall in love with him.*

Anxious attachment style. And limerence, remember limerence.

This time yesterday, she didn't know what the damn word meant and now it haunts her.

She is addicted to limerence! Who knew?

Her addiction is to the joyous feeling of being loved by men she barely knows and it's Not Real.

It's like being addicted to handbags or gambling. India's got two girlfriends who are *totally* addicted to handbags but they're both children of wealthy people, so that's OK. They can afford it.

She pokes inside her bag for some water and then decides that there's nothing for it but to sit down on a rock for a rest.

Perching on the only vaguely flat rock in sight, she stretches out her legs and drinks deeply from the first of her two water bottles.

Dan has also found a rock to sit on, some way away from her, and she stares through the woods and tries to catch sight of the sea.

Rose's session with India in the dock had hurt.

No matter what spin Rose tried to put on it, India wasn't a perfectly normal person who might want a baby and liked dating lovely men.

No. She was obsessed with the feelings of being happily involved with any stupid guy who came along.

Well, paint her pink and mail her to Guam – everything in India's life comes down to limerence.

India hates it. Hates herself for being addicted to something so stupid.

Does everyone else know? Her family? Dad? Georgie?

An insect skims close to her eyes and lands on her forehead, so she swats it away ineffectively.

'Bloody flies,' she mutters. 'It's too hot for a walk,' she says to Dan, fanning herself with her baseball hat, aware that she must look dreadful with her hair all sweaty and gross.

She catches the thought and winces. She's done it again!

Dan is most definitely *not* a romantic interest. He is another person on Rose's course who wants to be healed. He is out of bounds, specifically for her.

She needs to go cold turkey on men. Especially ones who have to have life explained back to them like they're aliens.

Dan, for all his cleverness and PhD, is clueless about people. Worse, he didn't realise he was clueless.

But she can't help but look at Dan, his long muscular legs stretched out. He must do marathons or something. Did he mention cycling?

India had not been paying attention then but now she is.

The retreat is a very female zone, now that she thinks about it. There are no other guests apart from Rose's people. Rose must have chosen the male staff to make sure they were too old for her and Keera, India thinks. Apart from the delicious Alexei, of course.

Therefore, apart from Dan and Alexei, who is clearly obsessed with himself, the only gorgeous man around is Christos, who is married to Adriana.

India concedes that Dan *is* pretty hot.

One of those clever, distracted men who never really look at India because she doesn't have a power job or know clever stuff.

But still – Dan falling in love with her would be

incredibly special. He'd come home at night and talk about how science was fun but really, all day, he's been thinking of her and couldn't wait to hold her tenderly in his arms . . . Shit!

She's doing it again! What is wrong with her? If Keera can give up drugs, she can give up men!

India crossly opens her bag of nuts, scoops out a handful and shoves the bag in Dan's direction.

'Do you have anything sugary?' she asks, determined to sabotage any hope of anything romantic.

Eating in the presence of a man is a no-no in India's mind. Her mother installed that information years ago.

She kicks the ground savagely and a few beetles scatter frantically.

'I have some boiled sweets,' Dan says, pulling something from the depths of his rucksack.

'Gimme.'

India holds her hand out.

She wants sugar. Lots of it.

Ice cream. She'd kill for ice cream.

No, *cheesecake*.

It's been years since she had cheesecake. *Years*.

What else has she given up so she can appear like a bloody unicorn to a litany of stupid men who don't deserve her?

She thinks Rose said that, didn't she?

'These guys are creatures you have burnished to make them seem better,' Rose had said. 'They're half real, half invented. You're falling in love with the invented parts of them, the *promise* of what life would be like if you were together.'

Dan watches India unwrap two sweets at once and stuff them in her mouth.

She moans as she tastes both a hard-boiled lemon and a hard-boiled orange sweet at the same time.

Bliss.

She wants more sugar.

'You don't have a Coke?' she asks, mouth full.

Dan shakes his head.

'I thought you were a vegetarian and didn't eat processed foods?' he says, looking adorably confused.

India feels the automatic pull deep inside her. He *listened*.

'I can't date you,' she says fiercely.

'I . . . I . . . don't want you to,' he says, entirely taken aback.

Dan realises that India has a wild glint in her eyes and he feels a hint of nervousness.

'Are you feeling OK?' he asks. 'Do you want to go back?'

'No, I want to keep walking. Can we go via a shop? I think a Coke will help.'

India decides that exercising this stupid feeling will – ha! – exorcise it.

She will walk all over this damned island twice if she can stop thinking about how stupid she's been.

She plans to tell her mother off for all the unicorn claptrap.

But then, India is thirty-four. Old enough to know better.

The unicorn thing must be something India loved, an idea that played into her own hopes and desires.

'I like the Sanskrit idea that one is given lessons, and that they will be repeated until we have learned them,' Rose had said the previous evening on the beach.

'I'm a bit woolly about Sanskrit,' India had said carefully to Dianne, sitting beside her, perched high on a lumbar-support cushion.

'It's a very ancient language in India. It's Hindu, I think.'

'The answers lie inside you,' Rose had gone on.

India now thinks that she's spent far too long worrying about her outside and clearly not enough time on the inside. *That's all about to change*, she thinks grimly.

They set off again in a slightly different direction after Dan has consulted his small map.

'Do you want to see?' he asks, holding it out to her.

'Nope,' says India, voice firm.

Rule five: always be interested in your man.

'OK,' he says.

Yes, definitely something up but he is not asking what.

Asking women what's wrong with them never, ever works out well.

'Do you want me to go first,' Dan asks brightly, 'or do you want to lead so we'll go at your pace?'

'I'll lead,' India says, striding off. 'You tell me left or right.'

She stomps along, feeling crosser all the time as her past unravels in front of her.

She trips on a piece of gorse and only manages to stop falling because Dan reaches out and grabs her elbow.

'You OK?' he asks.

With his new-found awareness of sensitive people, he doesn't want to screw up.

'Yes!' shrieks India, pulling her arm out of his grasp.

Dan backs off.

That's pretty conclusive: she's OK and she doesn't want to be touched.

Fine. He can do that.

They continue heading in the direction of Paleokastritsa where Dan thinks, from looking on Google Maps earlier, that there's a small cluster of shops on the way into the village. He doesn't have his phone because he likes the challenge of finding his way without a smartphone app helping him.

That may have been a mistake.

It takes another hour of walking down through tangles of gorse and dense forest and loud insects that make India shriek, until they reach a road. It's dusty, very narrow and is definitely not the main road from Xanthe into Paleokastritsa.

Dan decides he won't say this because India is displaying definite on-the-edge signs that he's unhappily familiar with.

She's drunk nearly all her water and he's been eking out his last bottle. Dan is beginning to think that heat stroke is next on the agenda and he's wondering if he'd be able to carry India to safety.

She's skinny but taller than Julia, he thinks. A tall dead weight will be hard to carry but he won't *say* this. Even he knows that implying a woman is overweight is a fatal mistake to make.

'Are we nearly there yet?' demands India, who is now red-faced from the heat and holding her second water bottle which she has nearly drained.

'Think so,' Dan says, which is a total lie. They are completely lost but it's easier to worry in his own head. They'll make it to civilisation soon.

At ten to six, Rose and the team set up the small beach for the pre-dinner beach meditation.

Christos and Stavros, who manages the grounds, have carried down the mats, tiny bolster cushions, sunloungers and sunshades the group will need to meditate that evening.

'Is it going to be too warm?' worries Rose.

Bernard worries her in particular because of his age.

But then, when he's not in sessions or eating, he's down at the cliff-face infinity pool baking himself the colour of mahogany. So perhaps she shouldn't worry about him.

'This is not hot,' says Stavros, Corfu born and bred. 'This is nothing.'

Christos laughs.

'True,' he agrees. 'It was cool last night. I have to wear my sweater in the evenings.'

'We're used to it,' sighs Rose, who feels at home in the heat after five years in Corfu. Here the blindingly hot summer sun has swirling sea winds to take the sting out but in LA, where she lived for years, it was hot desert sun that baked the land and Rose's skin like old leather.

Now she uses organic face oils from the Sia sisters who run the spa and is never out without a hat. Her skin has improved no end.

'The guests all like the heat,' points out Christos.

'I suppose,' says Rose but she has the oddest feeling that something is wrong. It's a fleeting sensation that skips across her brain and then vanishes.

Today's sessions were excellent. Everything is going so well . . .

Rose tells herself to stop worrying and admires her handiwork on the beach.

It's tough to move everything up and down every day but the beach does not belong to Villa Artemis, so they cannot leave valuable things out overnight.

As usual, Rose has put out towels, bottled water on a small table, as well as some throws should anyone feel cool. She has her teeny gong to use at the start and end of meditation. Everything is perfect.

'Rose!'

Rose, Stavros and Christos all look up to see Keera,

blonde hair bouncing in a plait behind her, running down the wooden path from the hotel.

Rose's anxiety ratchets up instantly.

'Have you seen India? Or Dan?' asks Keera breathlessly, coming to a halt beside them and panting in the late afternoon heat.

'No,' Rose says.

'India went out with Dan for a hike, that's more than three hours ago,' pants Keera, 'and they're still not back! No way they planned to be out that long. India was going to come into Xanthe with me later. She's not answering her phone.'

Rose feels her heart lurch. This is serious. Three hours! They are clearly lost.

'Search party?' she says, turning to the two Greek men. Christos and Stavros exchange worried glances.

Christos does not need to say anything. People have died on the islands in the past years. The hills can be treacherous to anyone not used to walking here. There are rocks, jagged ravines – all places where the unwary can fall and break limbs. And more than anything, the heat can kill.

Rose stands perfectly still, thinking, her eyes focused in the distance. Nothing betrays the way her heart is racing with panic.

'They're young,' says Christos. 'That matters.'

'We did warn them about going off without enough liquids, with maps, didn't we?' Rose asks.

Christos nods. 'Dan is clever,' he says. 'Plus, there are two of them,' he says.

But he takes out his mobile phone.

'I'll ring the police.'

*

India is sitting on a rock under the shade of a large cypress tree, draining the last of her water and glaring at Dan.

'That was a brilliant plan, wasn't it?' she snarls at Dan, who is holding India's phone high above his head trying to get coverage.

Phone detox much?

He had used an eSIM so he could easily connect to the local phone companies but India had not.

'You have no signal,' he says lamely, wondering where the hell they are. 'If there were stars, we could navigate our way back—' he begins.

'Stars! I don't want to be here at night!' she shrieks.

'We won't,' says Dan firmly. 'I promise.'

'But how do you know? You don't, do you? Nobody knows anything.'

India feels the exhaustion rise up in her and meet the fear head-on. They're stuck somewhere in Corfu, which is almost six hundred square kilometres, as Dan has told her.

His vast knowledge is absolutely useless right now.

Anything could happen. Anything!

Are there mad wild animals here? Wolves?

India has no clue. She only concentrated on the nice part of Greece, not any scary bits.

They have no food, nothing left to drink, her phone isn't working.

India starts to scream.

'Help! Help!' she yells into the still air, doing nothing but stopping the insect life from making noise for a brief, startled moment.

Dan stares at her in alarm.

'Shout too!' she says. 'They could be looking for us!'

Privately, Dan doesn't think anyone is looking for two youngish fit people who went off for a hike.

No point saying that.

'Let's head downhill,' he says. 'We've come too far up and that's a mistake. We might be going around in circles. Let's go down, straight down, OK?'

He holds out a hand to India who stares at it for a moment, before taking it.

Fifteen minutes later, they come to a gap in the forest and spy a glitter of sea.

'The sea!!! There must be a road nearby,' says India.

She starts to run and Dan keeps up with her.

'Be careful,' he says. 'Don't fall.'

But India's too hyped up at the thought of safety now. She skips lightly over rocks and pebbles, dances over small plants.

And then Dan sees it, just as India shrieks, 'Omigod, it's a road!' She stops running, backing into Dan in relief.

He catches her, supports her, both of them laughing manically with relief.

'It's a road,' he agrees delightedly.

Chapter Thirty

When Dan and India walk tiredly into the foyer of Villa Artemis, dusty, sunburned, exhausted, it is filling up with people, all, it turns out, assembling ready to search for them.

'India!' screams Keera. 'We thought you were lost!'

'We were,' says India, half grinning, half crying now because they're safe and she feels shaky after the adventure of it all.

'It's my fault,' says Dan, going straight up to Christos and a man in a police uniform. 'I didn't take my phone with me and India's had no coverage and then ran out of juice.'

'You're here now!' says Christos, vastly relieved as Rose hurries over to hug India. Grazia has to sit down on one of the cream couches as she's overcome with an adrenaline rush.

'I don't think I can meditate tonight, Rose,' India says, and Rose laughs with relief.

'I don't think any of us can,' Rose says fervently. 'We need tonight off after what's happened.'

In the dining room later, Adriana insists that Dan and

India have her special fish pie followed by bougatsa, the filling Greek custard pie that India has refused to eat up to now on the basis that it's a fat-filled pleasure that girls should avoid.

After one forkful of bougatsa, India moans with pleasure and keeps eating.

She doesn't know why Dan keeps glancing at her as she eats, but she laughs when she catches his eye.

Guilt, probably. He was the one who was supposed to know where they were going, idiot man. Nonetheless she blushes. The hike had been a funny kind of bonding experience.

'You need food and to sleep,' fusses Adriana, allowing them only a small glass of wine each.

Christos hovers with his special brandy but Adriana shoos him away.

'Spirits will stop them sleeping, agapitós,' she says.

'What's "agapitós"?' asks India, now in a lovely happy haze of being physically exhausted, safe and satiated.

'Beloved,' says Christos, putting an arm around his wife.

Dan gazes at them soppily.

India decides that the heat has addled his brain. Keera and the others have gone off to the terrace for a mini slow-breathing session without them, so India has nobody to laugh with over Dan.

Adriana goes back to reception and, as soon as she's out of the room, Christos whisks over with some brandy and three crystal glasses.

'It's my best brandy,' he whispers. 'Just a small sip to celebrate your return. Metaxa Private Reserve. It's too strong for most people but a sip won't hurt you. Quick!'

He pours them each a giant measure, then holds up his own glass to clink against theirs.

'To your safe return, oi fíloi mou – my friends.'

They all cheer and India takes a sip.

She's no brandy aficionado but it tastes hot, somewhat spicy and definitely celebratory.

'Gorgeous!' India raises her glass again.

Definitely time to celebrate – this week, she's learned she's addicted to men, has got lost in the Corfu countryside and escaped back to her luxury hotel, all in the same day! Cheers!

By the time Adriana is back in the dining room, Christos has magicked the glasses away and belted back into the kitchen.

'I could sleep for a week,' says India, yawning.

'Come on.' Dan holds out his hand. 'I'll walk you to your room. It's the least I can do after nearly losing us both in the mountains.'

'It's not totally your fault—' begins India and then adds: 'Actually, it is! You were doing the map stuff. But – I could have done the map stuff.'

Being the cute, fragile unicorn-butterfly woman is simple – women don't read maps. But why not?

Programming, that's why. She gives a little shiver as Dan takes her hand to pull her up.

India pretends they're going the wrong way as they head upstairs.

'Ooh, let's take this door, it might lead to my room,' she teases, passing a door marked *Staff only*. 'Oh no, we're lost!'

'I'm sorry,' mutters Dan.

'It's a joke, you muppet,' she says easily as they reach her room. 'There was nothing to stop me finding my way. You weren't in charge. I'm a grown-up.

'Eos,' she says to him when they reach her door, pointing to the name carved beautifully on a piece of wood. 'Goddess of the dawn, which is funny because I'm not good first thing in the morning. What are you?'

'Phoebe, bright intellect,' he says grudgingly. 'No sign of bright intellect today.'

'Give yourself a break, Professor,' India says, poking him in the chest with her left index finger. 'We all screw up.'

'But we could have died . . .' Dan says.

'Come down off the cross,' India says, parroting something she heard Dianne say. 'Somebody needs the wood. Nobody died, OK? Do you want another brandy? There's definitely some more Metaxa in the minibar, but probably not amazing stuff like Christos's.'

She's walking ahead of him into her room, which is still slightly dishevelled since she got back earlier and dropped her clothes on the floor before showering.

'No.' He's still in the doorway, looking hesitant.

'Why not?' she demands. 'You afraid I'm going to climb onto your lap and fall in love with you?'

'No,' he says, looking mildly insulted. 'One drink,' he says and shuts the door. 'You're impossible.'

'That's what they say.'

India's examining the contents of the minibar.

'It's a mistake to invite strange men into your room,' Dan goes on.

'You're not strange – well, *not that* strange. Definitely got some spectrum stuff going on there, but you're OK, Professor Dan,' India's saying idly as she examines the alcohol.

Spectrum stuff? thinks Dan, knowing he should be insulted by this but, somehow, he's not.

India talked today about the limerence concept. She's not shy about it. She accepts it.

''Kay, so we've got brandy, vodka, smoky rum, whatever that is, and special gin made with . . .' India peers at the little bottle, 'orange and pomegranate?'

'Brandy. Just one, no ice, thank you.'

Dan has opened the terrace door and sits on one of the curved rattan chairs outside.

Night has arrived and the sky is lit with sprinkled stars, jewels shining down on the islands where wise people mapped them and gave them their names.

'I'm glad we didn't have to wait for the stars to guide us home,' India says, following his gaze as she puts two glasses, a bowl of ice and a tiny tin of tonic on the table. She's gone for the orange gin, which smells lovely.

'Although now that I'm in touch with my inner limerence, I wouldn't have let you live if we were still in the woods at night: I'd have killed you for making me get lost.'

Dan laughs and India remembers that she likes making him laugh.

Why has she never bothered with this before? Being funny is way more fun than being a girlie girl and falling in love with every third man who smiles at her.

She's been waiting to be picked all her life.

No more – now *she* does the picking, girlfriend!

'You think the retreat is helping you?' she asks.

Dan grimaces. 'Yes and no. It's no fun.'

'It's not supposed to be fun,' India says, with a shrug. 'I thought it would be at first but seeing Keera open up, and then having Grazia get so emotional over Bernard's children . . . well, it's hard, isn't it? I can understand why people don't want to look inside themselves but . . .' she stares into the sky pensively. 'Once you do, you can't go back, can you?'

Dan laughs dryly. 'I can easily understand never sampling the inside of my head ever again.'

'That's the cowardly way out,' India points out. 'You're not really a coward, so you don't mean that.'

They drink their drinks and look out at the view, Xanthe glittering below them with tavernas decorated with trails of prettily strung lights, the lights around the tiny harbour where the fishermen come in. There's a main street in Xanthe where all the local shops sell their wares interspersed with a couple of high-end boutiques where tourists can stock up on Missoni, Melissa Odabash and Zeus+Dione.

India was going to meander down there with Keera this afternoon but they've missed their chance. Tomorrow evening, perhaps?

India knows that buying stuff is another aching-personal-abyss-filling activity but she still likes it.

'I'd never even heard of limerence until yesterday,' she says dreamily. She likes the way the word rolls off her tongue. 'Should I get a tattoo? "Limerence Lady"?'

'Julia has an "om" symbol on her ankle,' says Dan. 'She said it was very painful getting it done as it's not a fatty area.'

'My mother has a peace symbol on her right wrist, and a butterfly and a unicorn with flowers around them on the lower curve of her back. My mother is probably very into limerence, now that I know what it is,' India sighs.

'I guess Rose would say we're products of both our past experiences and our inability to see patterns.' Dan seems sanguine. The brandy helps.

India goes into her en suite to pee and, afterwards, stares at herself in the mirror as she washes her hands. She's mildly sunburned after the afternoon on the mountains.

She looks, she is startled to realise, beautiful.

There's no artifice to her look. Her eyeliner has melted off, she has no lip gloss on, no careful sculpting of her face or tweaking of her cascading copper hair.

Without trying at all, she looks healthy and very, very alive.

She *feels* alive as if jolts of electricity are zapping through her.

Into her groin.

Is it the near-death-ish experience?

Grabbing her toothbrush, India speedily brushes her teeth. She knows what that means and doesn't care.

This is not a good idea, she tells herself, but she takes the hotel's mouthwash and swills it around in her mouth anyway.

Not a good idea at all for a recovering romantic.

She adds some perfume – a blast of Byredo's Gypsy Water – and puts cherry lip balm on her wide, full mouth.

Also bad.

India can't help it.

Outside, Dan's on his feet, smiling a polite smile.

'I should go,' he says. 'Rose said we've an nine a.m. start, but thank you for the drink. See you in the morning.'

In reply, India stands in front of him, reaches up to put both hands on his face and kisses him.

His mouth instantly opens to hers and his hands snake around her body to hold her to him.

India lets out a little moan as she leans in to his body, letting her fingers get tangled in his dark hair, smelling whatever cologne he put on after his shower earlier.

It's gingery mixed with vanilla, and perhaps patchouli? India knows and loves men's fragrances. She's bought enough of it for boyfriends.

'This is . . .' he mutters.

'A bad idea,' India replies.

'The worst.' Dan keeps kissing her, his mouth roaming over her jawline, into the curve of her ears, his hands holding her as if she's a bit of precious china.

'Not limerence, I promise,' India says.

Instantly, Dan pulls back. 'No,' he says. 'I can't do this to you. We can't do this, you're a vulnerable person, India—'

'I'm not in love with you,' she says firmly. 'Not. In. Love.'

And she isn't, she's sure of that. He's seen her at her most real and she doesn't mind, doesn't mind that he isn't looking at the fake, fragile unicorn-butterfly India.

To show him how important this is, she kisses him three times.

'Not limerence, not full-on romantic fantasy where I have a wedding dress in mind. I am thinking with my body not my mind. This is sex.'

Their mouths are entwined.

'This is a mistake.' He's still holding her, kissing her.

'Why is it a mistake?' India arches her back as Dan leans in to her. She feels molten everywhere.

'Rose will kill us,' Dan murmurs.

'We don't have to tell her.' India makes a growling noise as one of Dan's hands finds her right breast, nipple erect under her silky T-shirt.

'She'll know.'

'I don't see why? I'm not going to tell her.'

'She'll just know. She knows stuff.' Dan can't seem to stop himself even as he protests Rose will be furious.

Somehow, he manages to extract himself from the embrace and stands, breathing heavily, a few feet away from India.

'This is wrong,' he says. 'You're vulnerable, I mean, and . . .'

'I'm not!' protests India. 'Would you stay if I tell you I want this and I don't care what Rose thinks? This is not me doing the limerence thing – this is . . .' She thinks for a moment. 'Because I want to have sex with you.'

She doesn't call it making love on purpose.
Confusing love and sex has got her precisely nowhere.
'Truly?'
'Truly,' she replies and holds out her hand.
Dan waits a beat then takes it.
She leads him to her bed and pulls him down onto it.
And in the tangle of limbs and pulling off of T-shirts, there's no more thinking. Just bodies, skin against warm, sunburned skin, melting mouths and their bodies arching together.
India wakes up early to the sunrise because they never shut the curtains.
She's deliciously naked, spooned against Dan and she wriggles closer, loving the feeling of his hard body against hers. He's taller than her, which she likes. Guys get so stressed if a woman is taller than them. Which is a sign, definitely.
She is going to be on the lookout for signs of the wrong sort of guy from now on.
Upset because she's taller than them – red flag.
No job – a red flag.
Taking her to sporting events she would have no interest in – a very big red flag.
Rich parents and therefore no job – a huge bloody red flag.
She yawns and wonders if she might get up and grab a juice from the minibar. She doesn't want to wake Dan because it's nice having him here.
Which is a good sign.
She's not wearing make-up, probably looks a bit shattered and never did her night-time face routine, so her skin will be rank. But weirdly, India doesn't care.
She pauses to test if she really isn't bothered.
She gets out of bed and opens up a bottle of juice from the minibar, then goes into the en suite to pee.

Miraculously, her face looks good. She brushes her teeth, cleanses her face and rubs some after-sun face cream on.

Her hair is a tangle but she looks happy. India beams at herself. She likes this new her, the one who can say what she thinks, who doesn't self-edit to please a guy.

Dan is half awake when she returns to bed.

He enfolds her in his arms and India wonders if they can skip the morning session to snooze, but then Dan begins kissing her again.

'If Rose is going to kill us,' he says, his mouth moving over the curve of her collarbone, 'then we might as well do it again.'

How do you catch a big fish? You reel it in very slowly and gently.

At the start, he seemed to understand everything about me. He loved me for who I was. This had never happened before, not with my parents.

I was the grown-up in that house, took care of my mother, fixed things, made her cheer up when she fell into the hole of depression. It was my duty. Since I'd been able to toddle and bring a tissue to a crying woman.

Now, staring into my own daughter's little smiling face, I realised that my mother had raised me to meet her own needs.

So that when he came around, I thought he loved me. My experience of love was so very flawed.

I saw none of the red flags.

Others had never understood him.

Marta, his first wife, was a bitch.

That should have been the first red flag.

I sailed past all the flags until it was too late.

Now, when it was terrifying, I wondered how I was going to get out of it alive.

Forgive yourself for not knowing what you didn't know.

Nobody would believe me.

Nobody. It was the simplest crime. None of the people who thought they were our friends would believe it for a second.

Because he was a shape-shifter. Not the nice kind, the kind that shifted from one type of decency to another.

No, he was the dangerous kind. Society never noticed them. They were predators and they could kill.

They certainly knew how to destroy women, that was for sure.

Chapter Thirty-One

Keera sees Rose gives India and Dan a knowing look as they walk onto the terrace.

'Told you,' she hears Dan mutter.

But India, grinning broadly, doesn't care.

So what's happened there then? Keera knows Rose won't mind. It's not rehab. If India and Dan were here for sex addiction that might be different, but they're not.

India beams at Keera, who grins back, and raises a hand.

'Rose, I need . . .' she pauses. It's hard to say this out loud.

She's been told that nobody needs to know she's a member of Narcotics Anonymous or Alcoholics Anonymous but, here, she has to say something. These people have heard some of her deepest secrets.

'I need an NA or AA meeting,' she says. 'I've done some online ones but I need an in-person one.'

Yolande had told her that it would be grounding for her to meet people in person.

'There's a meeting in Corfu Town, an English-speaking

one, but it's six fifteen tonight and I know we have evening meditation.'

Rose springs into action.

'Of course, Keera, we want to support you in working on staying clean and sober. Now, someone should go with you. We'll book a taxi and someone will stay with you until you go into your meeting and meet you then afterwards—'

'I don't need that,' says Keera immediately. 'I can go to Corfu Town on my own.'

'Nonsense,' says Rose, smiling calmly.

She's running this group and the person who looked most shocked at this very human sign of real life is Bernard. Without noticing he was doing it, he wrinkled up his old nose.

Bernard still feels superior to everyone. She's really going to have to figure out a breakthrough. Or is that an impossible task?

'Bernard,' Rose says in a voice that brooks no dissent, 'in place of the meditation, you're offering service to the group. You're accompanying Keera tonight. Christos will give you a light snack at five, you'll get the taxi at five twenty, and then when you find the place, you can have a wander around the Old Town while Keera does her stuff.'

Bernard looks outraged and Rose is sorry that she's dumping a grizzly Bernard onto Keera. But she knows that Keera understands the theory behind rehab whereby people are made to do things they don't want to do.

'There's often coffee afterwards,' says Keera apologetically to him. 'So it goes on a bit longer than the standard hour.'

'I don't see why—'

Rose cuts Bernard off with a steely gaze that says she is not finished with him yet but that he won't like it when she is.

'Even better. Bernard will be fine. We'll keep your dinner for you.'

Rose has a stare that can cut sheet metal. Under it, even Bernard begins to quail.

He subsides. 'Yes,' he grumbles. 'I'll be fine.'

'I can go too,' says Grazia eagerly but Rose holds up a hand.

'No you won't,' she says softly. 'I'm postponing evening meditation. You and I will have a walk on the beach before dinner. Marvellous,' Rose finishes.

This is all working out extremely well.

'This morning, we're going to talk to Dianne.'

'No, you're not,' says Dianne quickly. 'My life is boring,' she adds. 'I'm not sure what I'm doing here, really . . .'

'Indulge us,' says Rose.

Dianne glares at her. 'No,' she says.

'Will you speak to me alone?'

Dianne looks out past Rose's shoulder to the trees covering the hills.

The silence seems unending.

'Yes,' says Dianne finally.

Rose waits a beat.

'Bernard and Grazia,' she says, 'how are you doing?'

'Fine, fine,' says Bernard. He waves a hand in the air. 'We can get through anything,' he adds. 'Young people today don't realise what people of our vintage . . .' here, he gestures to Grazia and Dianne, who are both younger than him, 'are capable of. Resilience, that's the key.'

Just before Rose screams at someone for the first time in her therapeutic practice, Dianne speaks.

'Bernard, you're a total arse and you don't deserve Grazia,' she says unexpectedly. 'He's convinced himself that he can do what he wants. You're better on your own, Grazia.'

'I object strenuously,' roars Bernard, getting up from his seat.

'Please, Bernard,' says Rose gently.

He sits down grumpily, which doesn't surprise Rose. He doesn't want his real secret coming out. That's why he's so compliant.

Or is it something else?

For once, Grazia isn't looking at her husband with anything close to fondness.

This might be the time to launch the Bernard-shaped grenade, Rose decides.

'Bernard, I feel there's more you aren't telling us,' she begins.

She can see the group shifting in their chairs.

'We've talked and we're good now,' he says, smiling.

The old liar.

Rose knows there are two ways this can go – he might storm out or he might stay. But she has to risk it.

This was what Grazia wanted to talk about most.

'You've sorted out the club issue with Grazia, then? You've agreed with Grazia not to visit the S&M clubs any more to have sex with strange girls?'

There's a synchronised mouth-falling-open thing going on with everyone except Grazia, who's gazing at one of her manicured hands.

Bernard is half out of his chair. 'How dare you . . .' he begins and Rose knows the mask is off now. 'How fucking dare you . . .'

His eyes are blazing with sheer rage. 'You are going to regret this!' he hisses.

'Sit down, Bernard,' says Rose and she's aware that

when she's at her most fierce, she could be wielding a leather paddle and whip and wearing thigh-high PVC. That's never been her thing.

'Sit!' she commands again, more dog trainer now.

Grazia turns her head to look at her husband and only then does he lower himself slowly back onto his chair.

They exchange a look. Bernard reaches out to touch her hand and she lets him, but she doesn't take his fingers in return.

Instead, she looks at Rose, and Bernard slumps back in his seat, mouth like a steel trap.

'There's no judgement here on your sex life, Bernard,' says Rose as matter-of-factly as she can manage. 'But you need to share with the group. Can you do that?'

Bernard sneers at her.

'You're going to be very sorry for this,' he says.

'Bernard, I'm not here to hurt you,' says Rose, 'but you came here to fix your marriage, didn't you?'

Rose waits.

Everybody waits.

The cicadas sing.

Bernard's still staring at Rose.

So she turns to his wife.

'Grazia, are you frightened of Bernard's reaction because you've told me a second huge barrier to your marriage's survival?'

'Yes, I am frightened,' says Grazia unexpectedly, staring at Rose, her gaze not even taking in her agitated husband. 'I am not frightened normally but on this subject, he gets so angry. As if I have no right to question him when he has sex with these women. It is not my business, he says. How dare he!'

Bernard snorts again, more loudly.

It's like family day in rehab, Keera thinks. Carnage.

India looks as if she's afraid to breathe, while Dan looks mildly confused. He's remarkably willing to work on himself, but thinks people can only have one issue. Not the smorgasbord that people generally have.

Dianne is on the edge of her chair. Her face is set in rage: not her usual irritation but in a fierce, unleashed anger.

'I don't care how you get your sexual kicks – whips, high heels, it doesn't matter,' Rose goes on. 'It's about thinking you can pretend this doesn't affect your marriage. You're hiding behind the mask of saying you need this.'

'You sick bastard,' hisses Dianne.

Bernard actually winces.

'Sick, sick bastard. You don't deserve her.'

'You don't understand—'

'Damn straight we don't.' Dianne is in her stride now. 'Screwing around on your wife and pretending it's OK. Letting your kids treat her like shit! How dare you!'

'Dianne,' says Rose, using her dog-trainer voice. 'Stop.'

Dianne stops.

'We're here to learn about relationships,' Rose goes on. 'Relationships are incredibly complex and, yet, understanding them is simple. What's our first lesson on relationships, Keera?'

'Becoming aware of other people's needs and emotions,' says Keera.

'Gold star.' Rose beams. 'What do you do with that information, Keera?'

'Personally?'

Rose nods.

'OK, I do everything I can to make the other person happy. In my mom's case, I jump on command if she's not happy. But not any more.'

'Excellent,' Rose says and beams again. 'Some people overdo this one. Like Keera, possibly India—'

'Yeah,' India nods and the silk flower in her hair – today it's white – bobs. 'Totes me. Want everyone to like me. My bad.'

Rose nods. 'Some people are so attuned to others that they ignore their own emotions and thoughts, and focus totally on the other people. Which is not good. Others can't see that other people have different emotions.'

Dan shifts in his seat. 'You mean me?'

Rose considers it. 'Well – you assume that your thinking is the right thinking all the time, specifically with certain people. You need to face that emotion and understand it, tolerate it. You can't control other people. Sometimes you have to walk away from relationships when it becomes obvious that they are toxic to both you and the other person.'

'What's that got to do with pervy Bernard, then?' snaps Dianne.

'No judgement, Dianne,' says Rose and skewers Dianne with a look. 'Do you want to be judged?'

Dianne considers this and then shakes her head slowly.

'So in this situation we are tolerant to our partner's viewpoints, we try to understand them and respond with empathy. But,' Rose pauses, 'there are some situations which are too hurtful. We need reassurance. We don't need conflict and situations being ignored. That's why you're here, Grazia, isn't it?'

Grazia nods.

She doesn't look at any of the rest of the group, just at Bernard, who looks calm apart from the faint shaking of his hands which are clasped on the table in front of him.

'We didn't have to do this in public, Grazia,' he says.

'I can't believe you wanted to discuss this here, now. You betrayed me and our family in the worst way. Taking out our dirty laundry in public and making me look like the bad guy.'

Rose sees Grazia's jaw quiver. She can't back out now.

'Bernard, has Grazia ever discussed this with you before? In the privacy of your own home?'

'I can't say, possibly: I don't really remember,' he blusters.

'Really?'

She adjusts her position so she's sitting as upright as possible in her throne chair.

She's about to break all the rules but it's the right thing to do, she's sure of it.

'You're lying, Bernard,' she says quietly. 'Lying. Grazia has asked you repeatedly not to visit S&M clubs. You've told her that it's, and I quote . . .' She looks at her notes. '*Not the sort of thing that can affect your marriage when you're paying for it.* Which is an interesting view.'

Bernard's turning red.

Rose hopes he's had his blood pressure tablets this morning.

'How can you say it's not affecting your marriage? It's fundamentally a betrayal of your relationship as man and wife and of the expectations you both brought with you. Grazia never agreed to this. You know that.'

Bernard scowls.

'You made a unilateral decision about it. So does it work both ways? Is Grazia allowed the same latitude in your marriage? If you can have sex with young women wearing latex, then is Grazia allowed to have sex with other men?'

Rose can see Bernard is truly ready to blow now.

'I'm sure there are many much younger men who would adore to make love to Grazia. She's younger than you, she's very beautiful, is clever, cultured. She's prepared to walk away because you don't respect her boundaries. This is the last-chance saloon for you, Bernard.'

'I'm not listening to this any more,' says Bernard. 'I am shocked that you would bring this up, Grazia,' he turns on his wife, shaking with rage and humiliation. 'It is my business, not yours. And you, charlatan . . .' He glares at Rose. 'You will regret this so badly.' Standing jerkily, he walks off.

'You're accompanying Keera to Corfu this evening, Bernard, don't forget,' calls Rose, but she's wary of pushing further.

'I'd rather he didn't,' says Keera.

'He'll have calmed down by then,' says Grazia.

'Still don't want to go with him,' says Keera. 'Why do you stay, Grazia?' she asks.

'Love,' says Grazia with a shrug of slim shoulders. 'The heart wants . . .' she begins, but India interrupts her.

'Grazia, *What the heart wants* is not a helpful phrase,' India explains quickly. 'Think in business terms the way Bernard would. You love Bernard and you're holding out for ninety-five per cent love, OK?'

Grazia is gazing at her in amazement.

'I'm only figuring this stuff out myself, Grazia,' says India. 'It's how I'm going to look at all my relationships from now on. It's like the red flag thing but with percentages.

'So Bernard's only willing to love you unconditionally say, fifty per cent, right? He won't give up what he wants. That's a dealbreaker for him. He'll do a deal for fifty per cent, fine. Know what you're getting, Grazia and then you can decide on whether he's worth you being upset and getting only fifty per cent of Bernard.'

'Go girl!' says Keera.

'Excellent analysis,' says Rose. 'How about a break?' she adds. 'I think we all need it.'

As soon as everyone begins to collect their stuff and move off the terrace, Rose notices that she's shaking. Delayed shock. There was something vicious in the way Bernard threatened her. Something unexpected.

She finds her sister in the huge bed-linen cupboard with Beata. They're discussing white towels versus cream ones for longevity.

'Can I talk to you?' Rose says urgently.

There's nobody in the villa's entrance hall.

Rose wanted the entrance hall to look like somebody's grand house with a cosy feel that involves armchairs, a stone fireplace and wildflower bouquets.

They could easily talk in private in one of the two vast window seats but Rose wants absolute privacy. She leads Adriana to the big oak-wood desk that serves as reception and then swerves to the right to the double doors that lead to the private quarters and the compact office where the villa's administration work is done.

Rose sinks into a chair and holds her head in her hands.

'Sorry,' she mutters, as Adriana kneels in front of her. 'I'm really sorry. I needed a moment. I think I've screwed up. There's something about Bernard that's scaring me. I'm not sure if he's going to go crazy or do what he says and try to ruin us all. I'm afraid I've made a terrible mistake. What with the Instagram thing and now Bernard. I've messed up.

'Again.'

Rose is remembering being in the TV building where her show was filmed. It's the day everything went wrong. The last day.

A sunny Tuesday in early September, the show is back after a very successful last season.

She's talking with her hairdresser – discussing new hair products. Of all things!

'Protein products, Rose: that's what your hair needs. I'll bring some in for you,' Denise, the hairdresser, is saying.

Rose gets lots of free stuff. She can have any hair product she wants by just getting her team to phone the right PR people.

But she doesn't care about hair products now. She's operating on automatic. Talking about hair and make-up, smiling at the right moments.

'Thank you, Denise,' she says, smiling.

She's operating on automatic because her beloved Theo is gone. He left two weeks ago and Rose has been heartbroken but doing her best not to show it ever since.

They'd argued at dinner. They never argued.

It was one of their strengths – they discussed everything and came to compromises but, this time, they'd gone to bed without resolving it.

'Love you,' Rose had mumbled as she slid into bed beside him, and Theo had turned and said, 'Love you, too.'

He'd then turned a bare tanned shoulder to her and lain down, sleeping so quickly that Rose felt hurt.

She'd lain there awake, running over the argument in her head, watching him sleeping deeply and wishing he'd just agree with her.

Theo had said that she should renegotiate her contract when the last series ended.

'I am not trying to tell you what to do,' he'd said. 'But I think *The Talisman Effect* is so popular that the producers are going to push for more and more drama. You need to protect your reputation, darling. They will push you to the limit.'

Rose's agent hadn't wanted her to renegotiate if it meant putting the brakes on her career.

'It's a stratospheric show!' Maylene had shouted down the phone. Maylene didn't really need the phone: she could probably communicate just by yelling. 'The only way we'll renegotiate is upwards when we push the show further!'

So Rose had done nothing, changed nothing, had not asked for the show to be more mindful of guests and their issues.

She'd thought about it but had decided it would ruin everything.

During the evening, she'd told Theo this.

'Is this really what you want, Rose?' he'd asked quietly.

Theo never got angry – he was the most even-tempered man she'd ever met.

But she could see something worse in his eyes that evening. Sadness.

And an awareness that they were standing on different sides of a fault line.

He worried for her reputation, meanwhile she was aligned with the reputation-be-damned producers and her agent.

'You're so good at what you do but not this way,' Theo had said. 'It frightens me because it's changing you too. Rose,' he'd pleaded. 'You'd never have countenanced this sort of high-speed therapy when we first met. The show has moved on so much since you started it and it's become unsustainable. It's not you, please be careful before it all goes up in flames,' he'd begged.

'I can't leave, not yet,' Rose had insisted. 'I know the buzz is addictive but I *am* helping people—'

'It will implode,' he'd interrupted wearily. 'I don't know how it hasn't already, Rosie, honey. This is changing you.

You're becoming someone for whom it's all about the ratings. That's not you.'

She'd chosen not to listen to him. She loved the buzz of television, couldn't explain that, for a kid who'd come from nothing, this success was the ultimate validation. But then, Theo didn't know where she'd really come from.

All he knew was what she told everyone: childhood in the Auvergne with parents who'd travelled a lot and were now dead. A terrible house fire had burned all her childhood photos. The perfect cover story in these privacy-less times.

She'd chosen France because the French privacy laws were much stricter and harsher than UK ones. Rose had been interviewed about her so-called peripatetic childhood.

'We moved so much, I think that has helped me understand other people's problems: that's why I can be devil's advocate on the show.'

She was rarely on social media and was never photographed in anything other than her work outfits with her beautifully styled chestnut hair.

Amazingly, it had worked. Except that Theo also believed it. There was almost no way Rose could tell him the truth now.

'It's my fault for thinking you agreed with me,' he said.

'I do and I don't,' Rose replied, torn. 'You don't understand, Theo—'

'No.' He held a hand up. 'I understand, it's your career and you get to make the decisions surrounding it. I would never stand in your way, Rose. I worry, but I won't any more. It's fine, you do what you think is right.'

For most people, it would hardly have registered as an argument.

For them, it was like the Cold War.

Rose has gone over that night endlessly in her head.

If only she'd reacted differently. If only she'd stopped for a moment and asked herself if she was protected in case of a disaster. If only Theo knew about her childhood, he might understand her desperate need for acceptance.

But she hadn't told him about her past, she'd let her anger and ego take over.

He was trying to control her, she'd decided furiously.

In the morning, Rose had barely spoken.

They were both off, had planned to swim later in the day.

But there was no swimming. Instead, Theo had stood looking at Rose, in his threadbare jeans and old striped collarless shirt, bare feet from being out on the deck of their Carmel home high above the Pacific.

His dark eyes had shone with worry through his horn-rimmed glasses and, for once, the man whose face was always wreathed with a smile when he looked at Rose was grave.

'Do you still feel the same way?' he asked cautiously.

'It's my show, I can do good, Theo, you know I can,' Rose had said.

If she could just convince Theo that *The Talisman Effect* wasn't going the way of all TV shows, to hell in a handbasket.

The following morning, he was gone.

Pride stopped Rose from contacting him.

He was right; she knew it.

'Can we do a segment called "Fix It in Fifteen"?' one of the producers had asked only the other day. 'I can see it: a mini part of the show in between the actual family you're working with. Show them, discuss their problems, then cut to fix-it-in-fifteen, then back to the original family. You think?'

'I don't think,' Rose had said, shocked.

What was wrong with these people? Couldn't they see that the guests were becoming increasingly unstable, that this was the type of person the show was now attracting?

Suddenly she felt very alone, out on her own with nobody at her back.

Theo had been the first person who'd ever been stronger than she was and who was totally behind her.

She'd been the strong one for Adriana.

Theo had been the strong one for her.

After a series of altercations outside the studio, the number of security guards on the door was doubled on the show.

'It's fine, it's all safe,' the executive producer had said. 'We're taking this very seriously.'

Rose took this with a pinch of salt.

The studio only cared about ratings.

So that final day when Rose is talking about hair products with Denise, she is only half-listening to the stylist, and half-listening to the noise from the studio, metres away.

Theo had predicted something would go wrong. She knows he's right. She thrums with low-level anxiety.

The gunshots were unmistakable.

A suspended moment of *Is that what I think it is?*

Denise throws herself on the ground but Rose is frozen in her seat.

'It's all her fault,' a man is screaming so loudly that he's heard above all the noise.

Rose knows exactly who he's talking about.

It's her.

Theo was right: she's about to lose everything.

Her ego, her hubris have brought her here.

It's a miracle only the shooter himself is hurt. Another

miracle that he isn't actually killed, merely receiving a shoulder wound.

So many miracles that Rose knows her time is up: she has to get out of there.

When Rose walks back onto the terrace, only Dianne is sitting there. She looks tired and old.

Rose finds it hard to pull herself out of her own worries to run the retreat, but she has to.

'Talk to me, Dianne,' says Rose encouragingly, as Dan collapses into a chair nearby, Keera and India trailing behind him, hot and tired.

'I can't,' says Dianne. 'I would love to but I really, really can't. Not here . . .'

She stares Rose in the face for a full minute.

Rose gets it.

'I know this is a group but I think perhaps Dianne and I need to speak alone—' she says.

'But no—' interrupts Dan, who obviously wants to hear all. He's exposed his pain and everyone else should too.

'Read the room, Dan,' says Keera crossly.

Dan slumps. India leans over and kisses him on the cheek.

'Baby steps, Dan,' she says. 'Baby steps.'

Rose gets to her feet and leads Dianne away.

Where can they go, Rose wonders wearily. Not her bedroom but then not Dianne's either.

They walk inside, Dianne following meekly, and Rose catches sight of Adriana striding down the corridor.

'Adriana!' she calls and explains the situation.

Adriana's lovely face is creased with worry for her sister.

'The third therapy room in the spa is free. It has a couch too. Are you OK to do this?' she adds in a whisper.

Rose nods. 'It's going to be fine,' she says and then realises she's lying to her sister again.

She knows Dianne's secrets since she found the notebook again. Dianne couldn't help writing in it and then, in an act of self-sabotage, she threw it out the window again.

Adriana brings them homemade lemonade and a pot of Magic Tea which is Rose's favourite from the tea shop in Xanthe.

Dianne sits on the couch with her glass of lemonade but doesn't drink.

'That tea smells vile,' she says.

'Yeah, but it works,' Rose says. She pours a little out to see if it's brewed yet. 'I found your notebook, by the way,' she adds.

Dianne nods.

'I hoped you would. I didn't know if I could tell you it all – I thought it might break me, to be honest.'

'It won't break you,' Rose says calmly. 'We have all the time in the world to talk, Dianne.'

Chapter Thirty-Two

Dianne is not wearing one of her tennis shirts today: instead, she wears a white singlet that emphasises how small-boned she is, how delicate her wrists are, the fine line of a scar on her right shoulder.

Her silvery hair is not bouncy today, her pale-grey eyes are unlined with the 1980s liner she favours, instead she's presenting a naked face to the world.

'I should have known what was happening from the very start,' she says slowly. 'It's totally my fault. I put the children through it all.'

'They don't know it all, though, do they? Even now. You shielded them,' Rose says.

Dianne half-nods. 'I shielded them as much as I could but it wasn't enough, Rose. That kills me. I hate myself for that and I still can't see where they're damaged but they must be, right?'

'Children just need one good parent,' Rose reminds her.

Dianne nods. For the first time on the retreat, she seems to lose her aura of control. It slips out almost physically.

Rose can see Dianne's shoulders drop, her hands loosen.

'I wrote it down because I didn't think anyone could understand truly if they haven't gone through this.'

'Try me,' says Rose evenly. 'Say what is inside, tell me.'

Dianne fiddles with her watch.

She doesn't wear jewellery, Rose realised from day one. No wedding ring, no bracelet, no golden spoils of a long marriage.

'I don't like talking about it,' Dianne says.

'Nobody does at first,' Rose says, her voice soft.

Dianne does some more watch-fiddling. Then she gets up abruptly and Rose is sure she's going to leave but, instead, Dianne goes to the drinks station and pours herself a glass of Adriana's mint-and-lemon-flavoured sparkling water.

She sits down slowly, drinks her water and then slumps back into her chair.

'I don't want anybody to feel sorry for me,' Dianne says. 'I'm not a victim.'

'The word "victim" gets overused,' Rose comments gently. 'People can be badly hurt by their life experiences or by another person's behaviour. The idea of victimhood is that someone wallows in the pain caused by these things and, in that context, it's both an unfair and unhelpful label.

'To reframe it, we can be victims of circumstances and we are allowed to both feel that pain and express it without people assuming we like being victims.'

Dianne nods.

She exhales slowly.

Rose sees her make the decision to speak.

The island retreat has worked its magic.

'I'm trying to figure it out,' she says, still hesitant. 'I've talked to myself about this for a long time but I've never said it out loud. To other people. In my head, yes. But my kids don't know it.'

'They were worried about your behaviour; that's why you're here,' Rose said.

'I never wanted them to grow up the way I did,' Dianne says softly and, for the first time, Rose feels as if this gently spoken woman is the real Dianne Wilkins.

The hard and angry person is merely a protective wall.

'How did you grow up?' she asks.

Dianne takes a deep breath.

'I thought we were normal,' she begins. 'We were my mum, my dad, my younger brother, Kev, and me. Both my grandmothers lived with us. It was a lot for my mother to take on. It made her bitter . . .'

Dianne's eyes begin to lose focus on Rose.

She's in the past.

Her mother had adored Geoff.

'He's nice, isn't he?' she'd said to Dianne approvingly when Geoff had gone to the loo.

For a millisecond, Dianne had felt that she'd done something right, which was not a feeling she was familiar with.

'Yes,' she'd breathed. 'He is.'

'Don't screw it up the way you normally do,' her mother had gone on, reaching out for her cigarettes. She smoked Winfields, two packs a day when she was in good form, three packs on bad days. She and Dianne looked a lot alike but Dianne was small and neat, a bundle of nervous energy, while her mother was taller, thin like a bicycle frame, her face caved in from bitterness and inhaling.

'Tina.' Geoff had walked into the room exuding masculinity and good humour. 'I love the way you've decorated the place. There's a sense of heritage here, you know?'

Dianne has often replayed this in her head because only the most fantastical of liars could say such a thing and be believed. Her family home was a four-bed brick house with a tacked-on wooden verandah around half of the house where her mother liked to sit, smoke, read her magazines and watch what the neighbours were up to. In place of an actual hobby, she had judgy watching of everyone else.

She'd learned it from Ida and Antoinette, the two women who'd ruled the house for so long. Now they were dead, Tina could judge all by herself.

Dianne had watched her mother preen in front of Geoff.

'I do my best, Geoff, love,' her mother had said, waving the skeletal hand with the cigarette in it, not noticing ash landing on the wooden verandah floor. The floor was used to it.

'You've certainly done your best with your darling daughter, who, I can now say, has agreed to be my wife.'

Dianne had beamed, taken Geoff's hand and watched him take her mother's free one.

She should have run.

But she didn't.

She couldn't forgive herself for not knowing better. Because how could anybody have been that stupid?

Losing the baby made everything worse. Geoff blamed her for it and she, already broken, began to blame herself too.

When she finally gave birth to Lauren, she suffered from what she knows now was post-natal depression. But it was a long time ago and no cavalry came to help her.

The garden and verandah of Geoff and Dianne's house is thronged with the couple's friends and family.

There is Geoff's sister, Sal, from Perth, who's flown over with her three kids, now tearing around the garden playing loud games of tag with the other small children brought to the Wilkins' house. Sal is nose to nose with Dianne's mother, Tina, who is wearing her Sunday best in honour of the church service.

This means a white hat with a violet feather, her pale-purple skirt suit and high-heeled shoes that are now plugged into the hopeless lawn at the back of the house. The outfit is accessorised with two packets of ciggies, and a swipe of Revlon's Foxy Brown lipstick that Tina reapplies after every smoke.

Dianne can relax because both her mother and husband are happy. Geoff has given up his position in front of the barbie to his best friend, Ralph, and is now leaning against the pale-green verandah that Dianne had slowly painted while she was pregnant. He has a beer in one hand and beneath him is a plastic container filled with ice and bottles of beer.

Dianne is pleased that everyone is there to help them celebrate but she is so tired. The first six weeks of a baby are supposed to be the hardest but Lauren is four months now, and she still sleeps only in two-hour segments, leaving Dianne exhausted and on the verge of insanity. She still dreams of the other baby, the one who died. The one with the perfect little face who never breathed a breath.

'You're coddling that baby,' her mother says. 'Babies need to know who's in charge.'

Dianne isn't sure how babies find out they are not in charge. The only option would be to leave Lauren to cry herself sick.

'Here she is, the best baby in the world!' Geoff holds out

his arms to Dianne to take Lauren, clad in her fluffy white christening robe.

Dianne smiles weakly as she hands the baby over. Lauren is the best baby in the world but she hates being passed from person to person. Her little face is red and Dianne knows she is ready to roar. But she can do nothing.

Geoff wants the world to look at his new child, proof that he is fertile, very male, after the tragedy of the first one, the one he never speaks about.

Tina comes over, ciggie still in the corner of her mouth.

'Come to your nana,' Tina says.

Geoff hands her over, Lauren stiffens, arches her back and begins to scream.

Her child's scream is like a dog whistle for Dianne, one only she is programmed to react to. It hits her ears, goes straight into her central nervous system, and her adrenaline spikes.

'Little pet needs her daddy,' says Geoff, all charm and smiles for the audience.

In his arms, Lauren screams even more.

Someone laughs. 'Give her a beer, Geoff, then she'll be happy!'

'Shut up, Mac,' hisses a woman. 'She's a baby.'

Dianne moves closer to her husband, mask fully on.

'I think she's hungry, darling,' she says loudly. 'You know what they're like when they're hungry.'

Geoff's eyes are like flint as he hands the baby over.

'He made me suffer for that,' she says flatly to Rose. 'The baby had shown him up in public. I had shown him up. I got no grocery money for a week afterwards. I had to use cloth nappies and, I can tell you, those things are a bitch to clean. He complained about the smell, too.'

'But he'd made you use them,' said Rose.

'Yeah,' agrees Dianne, 'but I'd upset him and I had to pay.'

'Tell me how you met.'

'I met Geoff when I was a kid. Eighteen. I had no idea what I wanted in life, no idea that people were supposed to treat me with kindness or respect. My mother loved Geoff. Do you know why?' Dianne asks.

'Because he treated you with no respect in front of her and she liked it,' says Rose gently.

'Got it in one,' Dianne says bitterly. 'My mother loved him, couldn't wait for the wedding, the kids. Geoff was a golden boy.'

'From your diary it sounds as if your mother had some narcissistic tendencies, so she might have felt envious of you, jealous even . . .?'

Dianne nods again.

'You're on the money, Rose. I learned how to walk on eggshells as a kid in case anything I did upset my mother. She wasn't interested in anybody's problems – just her own. She hated her own mother, hated my father's mother too.

'If you're scared of upsetting your parents when you're a kid, then that's what you consider is normal.'

Dianne looks at Rose square in the face.

'I wasn't trained to care about myself or have standards about how other people treated me. That's the problem. So when some guy turns out to treat you like absolute crap, you think that's normal. That it's actually your fault. Your fault they're upset, your fault they don't have what they want.'

Dianne's face is stony.

'But it's familiar. You leave an abusive home and go right into abusive relationships. It was like I had a beacon on me that shone for people like Geoff: someone who wanted a person to treat like absolute crap and who would accept it.'

'What was he like with the children?' asks Rose.

'He was a tough father. Made a big deal out of everyone doing their best, yadda yadda. Was rarely angry with them, though. He had different rules with different people. He liked the girls – Lauren was so clever, so he adored that. His clever daughter. Ellie was very pretty and brilliant at sports, so that was all inherited from him too.'

'They never witnessed his cruelty to you?' Rose asks.

'They certainly did as they got older but I made it all seem OK. "Daddy and Mummy were having words," or "Mummy did something silly" . . .

'I protected them as well as I could from him. I never thought of leaving because I thought I was stupid, I thought I was all the useless things he told me I was. I made us a part of the community. We were always having cake sales, the kids played all sorts of sports, Lauren played clarinet for years. The hours I spent in the car driving them around. I got us into a car pool. Other women were coming into our house picking the kids up. We always had someone else's child in for dinner.'

'You hid in the herd,' says Rose softly.

'Yeah. Geoff didn't realise what I was doing. He liked it because I told my friends he was the perfect man. I said we would have lovely special dinners at home when the kids were in bed. I said I was so lucky to be with the love of my life.'

Dianne stares up at Rose.

'People really believed that shit,' she growls. 'Nobody ever looked any further. I mean, a fucking idiot with half a brain cell could see that I was exhausted, never had any money for myself although my husband had a decent job. I froze when he came into a room, jumped if I heard a loud noise – I was a walking, talking case of domestic abuse and nobody noticed.

'I was so thin, my mind raced and my heart raced, I was always behind. Behind with the laundry, running low on housekeeping, trying to keep up with all the school stuff and parents' groups, doing the kids' homework with them. He never did anything. Came home from work and sat on the verandah with a beer,' Dianne went on. 'At night, he'd expect the kids to be in bed, the place tidy and me to be waiting for him in our bed. I always said yes.'

Her face looks haunted but she keeps going, as if she has to get it all out in one go.

'He'd lie on top of me, bang and bang into me and I'd cry, silent crying, but still crying. I'd have tears on my face. He'd see me wiping them away and he never said *anything*. I was his, he could do what he liked to me.'

'I am so sorry you had to go through this—' began Rose but Dianne waves her concern away.

'Just let me get to the end. But you can't tell anyone, OK? Promise?'

'I promise but you can't blame yourself, Dianne.'

'I do. *I* married the bastard. I chose him. It's like my daughter Ellie's married to Tate and I don't trust him. He seems fine but then every man can seem fine from the outside. I'm not sure if I'm any judge. Because how can I be? I lived with abuse for so long, all my life, to be honest, and I never knew. I thought it was normal.'

'You explain your family of origin pretty well,' Rose says. 'A life of never confronting anything, of emotional cruelty, the silent treatment. How could you have known that was wrong when Geoff began doing the same thing to you?'

Dianne drinks some of her sparkling water.

'Perhaps you didn't choose him, either, Dianne. Perhaps he chose you. Abusers are very good at finding the sort of people who'll . . .' Rose reaches blindly for the words.

'Who'll be stupid enough to put up with them?' finishes Dianne harshly.

'No, not that. People who are gentle, people who are used to being treated badly within their families: there are a lot of people like that in the world. They're not victims, Dianne, they're simply people who did not see the red flags. If you've been raised to think that anger and cruelty are acceptable from the people who are supposed to love you, then you assume that you are loved by people who do that later in life.'

'When Geoff died the girls were so upset and I didn't know how to comfort them. After the numbness wore off, I had to pretend to be sad, pretend to keep the whole thing going. Otherwise, I'd be saying that their whole happy childhood is a myth. I can't do that, can I?'

'Perhaps you can?' asks Rose. 'Tell me, how did Geoff die?'

Dianne closes her eyes as if she cannot possibly look at another person while she recounts this part of her story.

'We were home together, he was up on some steps trying to change a lightbulb. The back of the house has an extension and there's a high ceiling with the skylight.

'I had to wait around always whenever he did any stuff around the house, like his slave. And then one moment, his face changed. I could see it happening, it looked as if he was in pain and he dropped the bulb and he grabbed his arm. I knew he was having a heart attack.'

'Go on,' says Rose gently, but Dianne doesn't open her eyes.

'He fell onto the floor and he lay there still moving, calling out for me to call an ambulance. If he'd been able to cry out loudly, some of the neighbours might have heard him but his voice was so faint. So weak . . .'

Dianne finally opens her eyes.

'I sat on a kitchen chair and I watched him,' she says quietly. 'I watched him die, Rose. It didn't take long: five minutes, a hundred minutes, I don't know.'

'You didn't kill him, Dianne, you know that,' says Rose, wondering if this is what upsets Dianne.

'I know I didn't,' says Dianne, 'but I had so much guilt about it, for not calling the ambulance. I could have saved him.' She shrugs. 'I could have performed CPR. But I didn't. For about a week after the funeral, I was numb. The girls were worried about me. Ellie said I needed to see the doctor and I thought of all the times I'd go to the doctor for nerves and he'd tell me I was lucky I had a good man – ha!'

Rose feels overwhelmed with compassion for Dianne but the only thing she can do right now is hear her confession.

'Then one day I woke up and I realised he was gone.'

Dianne is whispering now.

'I was free. There was nobody to tell me that I was stupid, nobody to shout at me. I didn't have to jump through hoops any more for Geoff. Do you know what I felt then, Rose?' Dianne asks, not waiting for an answer. 'Bloody rage. Rage that I hadn't known how to escape, rage that he'd won in the end. He was dead and he'd destroyed my life. The rage won't go. It's there all the time—'

'You've lived on an emotional tightrope for years,' says Rose, 'living in virtual battlefield conditions for years. That takes its toll on every part of the body. I think in time, and you'll need to discuss this with a future therapist, but you've got to think of telling your family what it was really like. They're going to want to know where the rage came from, what made you so upset,' Rose adds.

'That's ruining the memory of their perfect childhood,' says Dianne sadly.

'Do you think it's possible that they already know the truth?' Rose asks carefully. 'They might never have put words on what they grew up with but they'll know somewhere deep inside that their father treated you badly. Just because he didn't hit you does not make it OK. It's still domestic abuse. Emotional abuse.'

'If a man hits you, you have a bruise, wounds. What Geoff did to me – the wounds were on the inside. I still can't cry about him, though. I didn't cry at the funeral. Everyone thought I was too numb with grief,' she laughs loudly. 'It wasn't grief, it was numbness . . .'

'It might take a long time to cry,' Rose says. 'Please realise that your anger makes total sense. All your life, you haven't been able to be angry in case it upset someone. That anger goes somewhere – inside you. Now that it's safe, the anger is coming out.'

They sit there in silence. Rose drinks some water. Minutes pass. Twenty minutes.

Rose knows that sometimes walking alongside someone in pain, being silent with them, is enough.

Finally, she notices that Dianne has started to cry. Not heaving sobs the way children cry. But a stream of silent tears.

Dianne doesn't move to wipe them away: instead she lets them flood out.

Rose picks up the box of tissues from the shelves and puts it beside Dianne. Then she sits back in her chair, silently. She has nowhere else more important to be.

Chapter Thirty-Three

India, Keera and Dan sit together on the beach and feel the sea breeze gently caress their skin.

India has come down in her bikini so she can swim. She stretches out on her towel, her body long and lean in the cherry-patterned bikini. Her skin is lightly golden and Dan tries not to look.

Keera lies back on her beach towel and closes her eyes against the sun's rays.

'I don't want to go into Corfu with Bernard,' she says morosely. 'He's appalling.'

'I think it's supposed to be good for him,' says India.

'What about me?' demands Keera.

'I'll come instead,' India says.

'We can both come,' Dan suggests.

He knows it's the right thing to do but he's mentally sidetracked by India's long bare legs beside him.

All he can think about all day is the night before and this morning. What it was like being loved by India: her laughter, the sense that making love could be fun.

She's a bolt of wonder, truly sparkling. And she's not asking anything of him.

'That was lovely,' she'd said this morning before he left and she'd kissed him lightly on the lips, leaving a faint taste of strawberries.

There had been no sulking over some perceived slight the way there always was after lovemaking with Julia.

Being with India and enjoying the way she liked her body has clarified things for Dan.

He has always known that if he doesn't tell Julia how thin she is when they make love, she'll freeze him out. She's wonderful but there are so many complexes buried deep within her. He's spent his life managing them all, handling Julia like a piece of fine pottery in case he breaks her.

But India – she's a breath of fresh air.

'No thanks,' says Keera sighing. 'I'll go with Bernard – if he comes. He's a good example of what happens when people refuse to see how their behaviour affects other people. Very Al Anon.'

When Keera heads off back to the hotel, India turns and smiles at Dan.

'Don't,' he says but he doesn't mean it.

'I'm not in love with you, Dan,' says India firmly. 'But it's fun being with someone when you aren't planning the rest of your life, working out where you'll both live and how many children you'll have. Who knew that sex could be fun?' she adds and, at that, Dan groans.

He no longer cares that they're on the beach and that while it's deserted now, anyone could appear. He stands up and reaches out for India's hand.

'Behind the rocks,' he suggests, looking to the only hidden part of the cove.

'You're on,' laughs India.

The tiny cove behind the rocks boasts one huge slab of rock that's set at thirty degrees to the beach. The sun is burnishing it to a glorious, glittering warmth.

They sit on it and begin kissing, Dan's fingers tangled in India's hair, holding her tenderly, while her hands roam his body, loving the muscled arms, the flat plane of his stomach, the strength of his cyclist's thighs.

'You taste of strawberries,' Dan says, letting his hands lazily skim her shoulders as he slips the skinny bikini strap off.

'Do you like strawberries?' says India playfully.

'Never thought much about it,' he groans as he nuzzles the erect nub of her nipple. He tries biting it gently and India arches beneath him.

'Keep doing that,' she instructs.

'Then what?' he asks jokily. 'Is there a ten-point plan?'

'Yes,' says India, reaching for the button on his shorts. 'But whatever it is you're doing, keep doing it.'

'Do you want the whole hundred per cent or just fifty, like Bernard?'

'Ugh,' says India, shuddering. 'No Bernard remarks. But one hundred per cent? I do like that.'

Then there was no more talking, only the smooth noises of skin on skin and the sound of cicadas and tiny birds, and then, soft moans of pleasure.

Rose is determined to see Keera to her taxi.

'Take as long as you like, Keera,' Rose instructs her as they walk out of the hotel.

Keera shoots an anxious gaze at Bernard, who's emerging from the hotel ostentatiously carrying a slim leather folio which looks as if it has an iPad inside, and with the British *Times* newspaper folded neatly beside it.

'I think Bernard might be a bit grizzly, so you sit in the front with Marceline.'

Bernard shoots her a look so hostile that Rose feels dizzy. What is he planning?

She quickly stuffs all her fears deep inside her and opens the taxi passenger door.

'Hello Marceline,' she says brightly to the taxi driver. 'How is your mother's leg?'

Marceline, a cheerful woman in her fifties with a mane of blonde hair with black roots, smiles out at Rose and waves a hand heavily braceleted with silver bangles of varying sizes.

'Much better. She can manage the crutches so well now. Did I tell you she met a lovely man in the hospital and they've arranged to meet when she's better?'

'Single man?' asks Rose, delighted at this news.

'Widowed, many children – all of whom worry he's lonely. He has a small hotel in Benitses.'

'Sounds lovely. Listen, Marceline, will you take care of my friend, Keera?' Rose lowers her voice to a whisper. 'She has to travel with this grumpy man tonight and she needs a little kindness. She will be in town for two hours, perhaps, and then back here?'

Marceline examines Bernard who's clambering into the back.

She pats the passenger seat beside her, which has a pink-and-white crocheted seat cover.

'Sit here, pet. I will visit my friend in the town and then drive you home. Grandpapa can sit in the back.'

*

Rose takes Grazia down to the beach. On the way there, they encounter India and Dan, both with a flushed look on their faces.

Rose smiles at them both but feels anxious at what these encounters will do to Dan.

India is free but Dan doesn't feel he is.

Will he be able to cope?

Not something she can deal with tonight.

'Were you a model in a previous life?' she asks Grazia as they walk slowly along the beach, moving from the curve of the sand onto the pebbly part. The sun is still meltingly hot even though it's now after six.

'No,' says Grazia, adjusting her hat so that the sun does not touch her face. She never sunbathes like her husband, Rose has noticed.

'Everyone thinks this. Years ago, a man in Georgia wanted me to be a model when I was very young but I knew it was not safe. Myself and my friends were at the Tbilisi rock festival in 1980 and this man was very keen to take pictures of me. But he was connected to many party people and I was scared.' Grazia shrugs. 'It was not like the West.'

Rose has researched Georgia but has many questions about what it was like when Grazia was young, before the country was liberated from Soviet rule in 1991.

'This was before Georgia became free of the Soviet Union?'

'Yes. I love my country very much but I do not want to live there any more.'

'What do you want?'

'I want your advice,' says Grazia firmly.

'Fire ahead,' says Rose.

'This behaviour with Bernard and these clubs, this is not normal, no?' asks Grazia.

'Normal is a very elastic concept,' says Rose slowly. 'As is sexual desire. I'm sorry to use this phrase again but it's a spectrum. Where you are on the spectrum and where Bernard is are two different places. Perhaps the only way Bernard can get sexual release is from no longer being in charge.'

'That is not the case,' says Grazia. 'He does not need a girl with a whip.'

'Well then that makes things a little different. Was he doing this when you met and married?'

Grazia nods. 'I didn't find out for years. After the children, it was another straw that has broken the camel's back. I want to ask you, Rose, should I stay with him or divorce him? I am not with Bernard for money but he knows that if I divorce him, I will become a rich woman in my own right.'

'Only you can answer that question, Grazia. If Bernard is not willing to give up seeing other women outside your marriage then the question is whether that's a dealbreaker for you or not.'

Rose risks a final question: 'Forgive me for asking this, Grazia, but Bernard says he will make me sorry for helping you. Do you think he's serious?'

Grazia is silent. 'Very serious. I am sorry I have brought this trouble to you.'

'Well,' Rose sighs, 'I've brought a certain amount of trouble on myself. My past is not what everyone thinks it is.'

Grazia laughs. 'That's all?' she says. 'You are a strong woman to come out of that fire and forge a new life. If life is a book, we all have chapters we keep to ourselves. It's our business. Who has a right to know?'

Rose is listening in fascination.

'In my previous career, people wanted to know where I came from and what shaped me,' Rose remarks.

'Who says you have to tell them?' demands Grazia. 'I have parts of my life nobody can know. That is my business. Who we become in spite of everything: *that* is who we are. The rest of our past is just gossip.'

Chapter Thirty-Four

Keera sits in the front of the taxi with Marceline on the way home and listens to the music: Fleetwood Mac are harmonising along to 'Dreams'.

'I love Fleetwood Mac,' explains Marceline. 'When I was younger, my friends all said I looked like Stevie Nicks,' she adds happily, navigating the roads out of Corfu Town and speeding into the darkness on the way to Xanthe. 'My hair was blonde and I loved a long, tiered skirt for sure – but I can't sing a note!' She laughs throatily at her own joke.

The sea glitters to the right of the car and Keera stares out into the silky darkness as Marceline drives towards Dassia and Ipsos. She likes to come into Xanthe from the mountains, she says because she was born in the village of Lafki so loves to be close to the island's mountain ranges.

Bernard hasn't spoken a single word, which no longer worries Keera.

If he wants to be a horrible person, then that's his prerogative. He's clearly spent his life doing just that.

It's late and they're her last drive of the evening, so Marceline is happy to listen to music now and not talk.

Keera sits quietly and listens to the guitars and drums soaring into the opening verse of 'Dreams'. When Stevie's exquisite contralto with its hints of vibrato starts, Keera feels an overwhelming sense of shame that she achieved so little in her music career.

She had so many chances and she blew them.

Tonight's meeting has also made her think back to rehab.

Talking about the worst stuff she'd done while drinking and using. The sheer shame of that too.

She's proud of what she's achieved, kicking the drugs and booze. But it's hard to look back at what might have been . . .

'So singer girl, whaddya think? Everyone's busy. Nobody will notice if we shut the door and make out . . .'

The tanned, fabulously ripped man in a white singlet and very low-hanging sweatpants gestures to the long bench covered with cushions.

'We'd just about fit if you were on top. You up for it?' he says. 'The doors don't lock, but we can be quick!'

Oliver (sex addiction) and Keera are cleaning the dining room after dinner.

She glares at him.

'Fuck off, Oliver,' she says, scraping the remains of food off a plate.

'Or – fuck Oliver?' he says, sidling up close to her, not touching but being way too close.

Oliver is the perfect person to practise boundaries with.

He's good-humoured and surprisingly unthreatening, so Keera finds it easy to say no to him.

Keera's sure she's partnered with Oliver for chores so she can learn how to say no.

She feels as if she's several steps ahead of him in her rehab – Oliver's addiction is still pulsing through him relentlessly.

'No,' Keera tells him again, even more firmly.

'I'd make it lovely for you . . .' he wheedles.

Oliver's West-Coast gorgeous, which is why he wears singlets day and night irrespective of temperature, to display his muscles.

He has the face of a movie icon with wavy black hair and eyes that can suck a woman's soul out.

This is just his outside look, though.

Inside, Keera knows he's a lonely, desperate man who has the emotional bandwidth of a lettuce.

Group therapy has revealed that Oliver can only feel *anything* when he's with a woman sexually.

Otherwise, he's a black hole of self-hatred.

Now, he trails one hand along Keera's arm hopefully.

She elbows him hard in the ribs.

'I said fuck off, Oliver,' she says as he bends over in pain. 'Boundaries, remember them? You get thrown out if you step inside anyone's boundaries.'

'I didn't,' he says now, sulkily, and arranges his beautiful body onto a chair, instantly looking like a male model awaiting a fashion photographer.

'You did.'

'Don't tell,' he pleads.

'Get up and help, then,' she orders. 'I'm not doing your share of the cleaning-up work too.'

'You talked about one-night stands,' Oliver says crossly as he slams plates upon plates. 'I overheard you talking to one of the other women. It wouldn't matter to you, just five minutes is all I'm asking.'

'What part of the privacy don't you get?' Keera rages.

'I was having a private conversation with another person sharing painful past stories and you're treating that overheard discussion like I'm a menu card showing what's available.'

'Sorry.'

Finally Oliver looks repentant.

'I'm really sorry,' he repeats. 'I want to block things out and sex does that for me.'

'We *all* want to block things out, Oliver. That's why we're here,' Keera says with irritation. 'But the numbing never lasts long. It's a temporary fix. Like drugs, alcohol, food, gambling. It never lasts!'

'Yeah, I know.' He shuffles off to the kitchen with a pile of plates, still beautiful but forlorn now. 'You won't tell on me, will you?'

'No but if it happens again, I will.'

''Kay.'

Keera follows him into the kitchen with a tray loaded up with cups and glasses. She sees how woebegone he is but knows that hugging Oliver would be a rookie mistake so, when she puts her tray down, she fist-bumps him instead.

'Another learning experience in rehab,' she says cheerily.

Look at you all functional and helping another addict, she thinks with a sliver-thin slice of pride. *That's got to be something.*

'Join me outside for a cigarette after we clean up?' he asks.

Keera thinks about it.

Nicotine is the only addictive substance available to the people in the rehab centre but she realises that she only liked to smoke when she was drinking. Without alcohol, she doesn't actually like nicotine. It was merely a bad girl accessory.

'Nah. I've enough addictions going on right now,' she says.

The next day in group is Keera's fourteenth day in Little Rock.

Today's group leader is Sasha, the scariest of all the counsellors. Sasha makes people cry every time she runs group.

'Sasha's an excavator. She digs the pain out of you,' explains Lexi, Keera's favourite counsellor.

'What if I don't want anything dug out? Can't she use an anaesthetic?' Keera sobs to Lexi.

'Funny,' says Lexi. 'Anaesthetic, right!'

Now the group are assembling, all eighteen of them, all trying to sit in nice chairs but also position themselves so they aren't in Sasha's direct eye-line. Oliver, Kat and Jordy (eating disorder and cocaine) sit quite close to Sasha so she'll have to turn her majestic head to see them.

Last into the room is the most recent newcomer, Tyrone. He's an imposing man. Basketball-player tall, he towers over Keera but he's a gentle giant at heart. Talks about his four small children and nightly bemoans the fact that they're not allowed their mobile phones in rehab so he can't look at their photos.

He's been in for two days and Keera has no idea what addiction he's in for.

'I am a good man,' he says to everyone who tries to winkle it out of him.

'Drugs?' asks Oliver, who likes to sit beside Keera.

'Don't think so,' says Keera.

'I think sex addict,' whispers Jordy.

'No,' says Oliver. 'I can tell. He's too . . . pure-looking.'

'Not meth or crack, for sure,' Jordy says.

They all avoid looking at Sketch who is wraith-thin with a frightening rictus of a smile because of having so many decayed teeth. Sketch has been in the group a week now, after two weeks in the detox unit of the facility. He speaks to no one and Keera feels both sorry for him and scared of him.

'Welcome,' says Sasha cheerily. 'How are you today, Tyrone?'

Keera, Jordy and Oliver sink lower into their chairs.

Tyrone's on the rack and they don't want to get involved.

'Good,' beams Tyrone. 'Still dunno why I'm here but I'll go along.'

Keera winces.

Sasha will murder him. But Sasha makes no more comments to Tyrone. Instead she turns to Keera.

'Keera, do you know what day today is?'

Keera shakes her head.

'Your rock-bottom story.'

Keera's heart feels like a solid lump of ice has been dropped on it. She feels rather than sees Oliver and Jordy pulling their chairs away from her.

'Fourteenth day's the killer,' mutters Oliver.

Keera glares at him. He could have told her.

She pulls her feet up from the floor and curls them under her.

'Stop cocooning, Keera,' says Sasha. 'We need the story. You've been here fourteen days and you're playing along nicely, but we haven't got all of your story yet.'

'Yeah, we haven't,' says Hank, angry and young: alcohol, steroids and drugs.

'I drink,' says Keera in desperation. 'I drink when I'm sad and when I'm happy and no matter what, it can always be celebrated with a drink. I do drugs too. Mainly prescription but sometimes coke if it's around.'

Sasha looks unimpressed. 'Why do you drink and do drugs?'

'Numbing, I suppose.'

'What's it been like being here and not having any substance to take you away from yourself?'

Without thinking about it, Keera exhales long and deeply. 'Strange,' she says. 'I have nothing to make things feel better. I can't sleep at night because my mind won't stop . . .'

'Ah,' says Sasha. 'What goes round and round in your mind at night? Your rock bottom?'

And Keera tells them. The day of the interview appearing in *Empress*, drinks and lunch with one of her mother's friends.

Keera had sneaked off to a nearby bar and ordered tequila shots when the friend was paying the bill. Dr Bobbi arrived as the taxi pulled up to drive them all to a drinks party.

'My mother was angry with me,' she says. 'I felt so low. She'd said I should have stuck to a diet.'

'What happened at the party?' asks Sasha.

Keera has talked about so much in rehab: she's told drinking stories, drugs stories and about that time she was so hungover she licked the inside of her cosmetics purse to get at any cocaine remnants left there in order to go onstage.

She feels that she has already been laid bare – yet she's always kept something back.

It shames her so much that she can feel the sweat on her back at the thought of saying this out loud.

She doesn't want to be judged.

Yet, in here, people are more judgy when inmates lie.

Not facing the truth is the big sin in rehab.

'It's horrible to think about it now because I'm clean and sober – really sober,' Keera says, wincing.

Most of the group grin.

'Feeling your feelings is horrible. I can't believe I can never drink again or never use anything.'

'You *can*,' says Sasha with a shrug. 'But it'll kill you. Addiction is a progressive disease.'

'I know.'

Keera looks at the floor and then forces herself to lift her head and look at everyone in the room, apart from Sketch.

She has no idea how Sketch particularly will stay clean when he leaves.

He's been in rehab four times already, Oliver had told her.

Keera does not want to come back here if she can help it.

'I had sex in a back hallway with the son of my mother's friend, someone I'd only met in passing a few times before. We were both wasted. I am not sure how we were able to remain vertical.'

She can almost feel as if she's back there. It had been the day that *Empress* magazine had published her interview. Bobbi had been so angry with her for things that Keera felt were not her fault!

So Keera had done what she always did to avoid her mother's anger. She'd started drinking. By evening, when she and Bobbi arrived at Bobbi's friend's house in a convoy of taxis after leaving the restaurant, everyone was buzzing after a successful lunch.

The party was whisked through to the garden room which was jammed with orchids and jungle foliage.

There was music, more drinks, laughter and gossip.

Keera hadn't been buzzing, though.

She'd been nursing her bruised heart and was so drunk that she almost couldn't remember why she'd been so sad.

All she knew was that she needed more.

The skinny shy guy with the bad shag haircut would never have been on Keera's 'must-date' list but, same as the last time they'd met, he had drugs. Cocaine and a lot of some downer he called 'La La Land' which they were saving for afters.

'I wasn't thinking at all,' Keera says now. 'The thinking part of me went out the window when I was drinking and with coke, I became this horrible person. I thought I was funny and clever, yeah, sexy too.'

Beside her, Jordy nods.

'Nothing else mattered but getting more stuff, more not-thinking juice. I kept taking it and taking it and I was jammed up against this guy when his mother found us. She screamed and he ran. She called my mother, who turned up and I was giggling because I'd taken my boots off and couldn't get them back on—'

She feels the familiar wave of self-disgust at this story, at the thought of herself standing with her jeans lying on the floor along with skinny Bad-Haircut's tee and his yellow Gucci slides.

Today, for the first time, the wave isn't as intense.

Nobody's pushing chairs back and saying they can't be in the same room as her.

An older woman with grey curls and a broken arm in a sling is nodding in sympathy with Keera, tears flowing down her face.

'Been there,' she mutters, to Keera's astonishment.

Jordy speaks up: 'Me too,' she says sadly.

'Bet you were hot, though,' mumbles Sketch, instantly ruining the feeling of shared experience.

This time, revulsion sweeps over Keera.

'Not helpful, Sketch,' says Sasha icily. 'We need to talk about how you left your twelve-year-old daughter having chemo because you needed a hit.'

Everyone gapes and, for the first time, Sketch's gaunt face looks human.

Human and bleak with shame.

Keera stares at him.

'That was a shitty thing to say,' she says calmly. 'I'm owning my mistakes.'

'Sorry,' he mumbles, not meeting her gaze.

Keera lets the wave of triumph flood her. She's told them her worst stuff, nobody shrank from it. She's still here and she's able to speak out for the first time ever.

She realises that Sasha's smiling at her.

'I haven't cried yet today,' Keera says.

'There's an urban myth that I make everyone cry,' Sasha says, 'but that only happens when people refuse to do the work. You do the work, Keera. It's entirely true what they say, breaking ourselves open is truly the way the light gets in.'

Marceline's taxi rolls up to Villa Artemis in a haze of smoky oud perfume and Billie Holiday singing about a man she loves.

Keera pays her and waits until Bernard has marched off to his room, anger seeping out of every pore.

'Thank you,' Keera says to Marceline. 'It's been lovely to go to town with you. You do look like Stevie Nicks and thank you for the great soundtrack to the drive. It's been so helpful, thank you.'

'I liked your "Firebird" song,' says Marceline to Keera's complete astonishment. She's been so sure that nobody on Corfu has recognised her. 'You've a beautiful voice, don't stop singing because life got hard. The rest of us need your music.'

'Thank you,' stammers Keera.

Marceline waves and drives off.

Keera knows it's time for bed because they've another early start, but she feels too wound up to go to her room.

Why had that memory of rehab come into her head?

She absolutely knows that a drink would be the wrong thing, but she ends up going out to the terrace so she can go to the bar.

The feel-good memories of drinking are in her head.

She can remember what happens to her when she drinks, feel that mellow buzz deep in her belly—

She stops as she realises that Dan's standing on the terrace.

She's about to say 'Hi' offhandedly but then she realises that he's on the phone leaving a message.

'Julia, I am so sorry. I felt I had to tell you. I am so sorry, so sorry. I know we're on a break and that you wanted to be able to . . .'

Dan pauses and Keera hides in the shadows, really wishing she wasn't hearing this, hoping Dan doesn't see her.

She's afraid to move in case he does.

'I know you're free to see other people, date other men. But I never wanted that, Julia. I didn't want us to split up.'

He sounds both wound up and totally confused.

'I'm terrified I've hurt you. It's – this is all so strange. Talking about yourself, it's not me, darling. Call me when you get this message. You're beautiful, Julia, you're the only one I love . . .'

Keera cringes at the desperation in his voice. Who precisely is he trying to convince?

'You do understand that it wasn't about beauty, nobody's as beautiful as you,' he pauses, helplessly. 'Everything is different here, that's all I can say.'

Shit. Keera feels the desire for alcohol soar right over her. That was a near miss.

But poor Dan.

And poor India.

Chapter Thirty-Five

There's a yacht far out to sea, drifting lazily in the glittering ocean as Rose stands on the beach ready for the morning meditation.

Xanthe's gentle morning breeze lifts tendrils of her hair. She feels the breeze skate over her face, bringing the scent of the sea: salt, seaweed and some Greek magic.

The only fly in the ointment today is the threatening Instagram messager and the fact her friend in LA has finally replied.

Not in this business any more, Rose. But I've got a name for you. Contact these people and they use open source intelligence and linguistic profiling to find out if the account's fake and to see who they are. It'll cost you, though. These people are good but not cheap. And not always fast. Greece looks amazing in the pictures. Go you!

The group are beginning to arrive on the beach and Rose firmly closes the mental door on the Instagram menace. What is the point in helping people to be happy and calm if you yourself are not happy and calm?

Rose always believes that you can't teach what you haven't got.

'Good morning!' she smiles at the group, who are beginning to look tired under the pressure of work and long, therapeutic days.

India's the only one who still looks bouncy and happy, today dressed in a yellow crochet mini-skirt and a white-flowered halter top that's straight out of Twiggy's 1960s wardrobe.

She's a tall, lithe ray of sunshine and Rose is incredibly fond of her.

India has a sunny personality and is genuinely lovely to everyone in the hotel.

Bernard – Rose looks around to see if her smiling alligator is here – is the opposite. He's settling down in a sunlounger on the edge of the group, beside Grazia.

Despite the whole no-phone-during-sessions diktat, Bernard is poking the screen of his phone while there's another one beside him on a small table.

In the you-can't-make-me stakes, Bernard is being spectacularly rude, which is hardly news given how the staff described him early on.

'Grazia's embarrassed by his rudeness,' Adriana had said. 'You can see her face whenever he does something horrid. She goes white around the mouth. But she never says anything to him. Why not?'

'Why not indeed,' Rose had replied. Now she can see how uncomfortable Bernard's behaviour makes Grazia. Initially, she couldn't read the other woman at all.

'I'm sorry we let him in,' Adriana had said.

The stakes had been so high and Rose had stupidly thought she could handle this incredibly rich man.

Big mistake. She'd forgotten the lessons from the

sprinkling of narcissists she'd met when she was on *The Talisman Effect*. They would stop at nothing to destroy people who questioned them.

Bernard has not become rich from behaving with decency. Rose can just about cope with the Instagram menace if it's a person from the past, she might be able to confront them.

Bernard is too rich and powerful to confront. He can destroy Rose and the Villa Artemis.

Exactly how stupid has she been?

She manages a smile for the group.

Everyone is there except Dan.

Rose cannot fault him for trying to work on himself. He may still think it's all woo-woo, but he's working the woo-woo for all he's worth.

She doesn't have time to deal with latecomers.

'We'll start without Dan,' she announces.

Everything is going to be fine. What rousing thought has she got for keeping her spirits up when a toxic troll is trying to destroy her life?

Oh yes: being a peaceful woman does not mean she is unskilled in the art of war.

Bernard might think he knows who Rose really is, but he doesn't understand her.

The person on Instagram might think they can threaten her. But Rose has had to fight a lot of battles to keep Adriana safe and she's not going to stop now.

On the gently curving drive up to Villa Artemis, Christos is tending the small pond where he's been valiantly trying to grow water lilies.

They don't seem to be thriving. His dream is to have

koi in the pond swimming happily under lily pads but he's definitely doing something wrong.

He thinks fish will be calming, and God knows, they need calm right now.

Christos is worried.

He's heard nothing from Marco, his old friend who now works for Europol and who he hopes can rein in this Instagram threat, although Marco has said nothing will be fast.

Adriana says that Rose briefly mentioned that Bernard also threatened to smear the villa's reputation. Christos can't bear the thought of their beloved business failing.

It's not just about the money – although that's nothing to be sniffed at. They'll have to claim bankruptcy and will lose everything. The saddest thought is the sense of their dream failing: that's what makes him feel sad. It had been such a lovely dream, too, the reason for the back-breaking hard work.

How can one Instagram troll and one dismal, short rich man destroy their dreams? It's not right.

Christos pulls up a few weeds gloomily. He needs to let these fears go. He has to be strong for his beloved Adriana and for Rose.

He will never forget what Rose did for his wife. Never.

The hotel's fluffy white cat, Hecate, pads down the drive and Christos reflects that if he *had* koi, Hecate would scoop them out with a fat paw and eat them before they had a chance to swell and become big, flashy, happy fish.

Maybe Adriana's right: he should stick to a fish tank.

He looks up from inspecting the pond to see India and Keera.

'How are you, ladies?' he asks cheerfully.

'Great. Relaxed. I can't believe it's the end of the week already,' says India. 'Time has flown.'

'You've enjoyed it?'

'Loved it,' says Keera. 'See you later, Christos.'

Keera's phone has been silently buzzing all morning. She should have left it in her room as Rose expects.

As she and India walk back up from the beach after the morning session, having lingered to look for shells, she feels the vibration of the phone once again in her cotton trouser pocket.

She is not going to look at it. It's probably her mother leaving more outraged voice notes about life, the universe and everything.

She is not dealing with her mother right now. There is no need.

As they wait to cross over to the villa's gardens, a taxi whizzes past her and India.

'I thought . . .?' Keera squints through her sunglasses. 'I must be imagining things,' she says. 'I thought – I thought I saw my mother in the back of that cab.'

'Hardly,' says India cheerfully. 'What are the chances, right?'

'Yeah.'

Keera and India walk on.

The beautiful path to Villa Artemis is steep at first, then flattens out.

Keera decides to ask India about Dan; last night's phone call is on her mind.

She doesn't want to rain on India's parade but she feels she ought to tell her friend what she overheard. Dan beseeching Julia to forgive him would be deeply upsetting if India really is crazy about him.

'Do you think you're falling for Dan?' she asks.

'No and yes,' says India quickly. She *has* thought about this. 'He's utterly lovely and kind . . .'

Keera's nodding.

'And . . .' India pauses. 'I'm not a fan of leaping into bed with people straight off because I love the idea of being romanced by someone . . .' She sighs. Limerence, that's what it sounds like.

She tries to explain that she and Dan aren't like that: the connection between them has been truthful and intense.

'But I said to him it was no-strings. And he was fabulous,' finishes India.

'Sweet,' says Keera, who hasn't slept with anyone since before rehab and frankly can't imagine having the desire to do so for a long time.

She smiles at India, who grins back.

'Was that too much information?' asks India. 'Yes, probably. But I'm not falling in love with him,' she adds. 'He's totally confused about what he wants and he's a very straight-up sort of man; I know he'll worry he was unfaithful to Julia by sleeping with me.'

Keera nods. Perhaps Dan has confessed to India already?

'I thought they weren't a thing any more?' she asks delicately. 'That was the whole point of his being here?'

'Yes, except his having sex with another person on the retreat isn't what she was hoping for either, I guess.'

'True,' says Keera. 'But you're not responsible for Dan's actions.'

'I did kiss him first,' India admits.

Keera laughs loudly. 'Go, India!' she says.

A second taxi speeds past them as they round the curve to reach the front of the hotel.

'Normally it's so quiet here,' Christos says behind them, coming up the drive with a handful of weeds.

The first taxi has clearly disgorged its passenger and is doing a laborious turn in front of the hotel.

The inhabitant of the second taxi emerges and slams the car door shut loudly. The passenger is tall, pale-skinned and has long blonde hair. She's wearing a pale-blue fringed top with spaghetti straps, tiny white shorts and silver cowboy boots, none of which are the sort of things many people around here would wear.

With a mother as free-spirited as Sonja, India is the last person to censure any woman for wearing what she wants: there's no age limit on clothes. Any other idea is pure misogyny.

But if India's wearing a mini, she combines it with something contrastingly flowy. The blonde at the villa door has gone for a tight top which shows off her enviable breasts, but the skinny shorts don't quite work, India thinks—

She stops, and gives herself an inwards shake.

It can't be – surely not?

'Is that . . . does that person look like Julia?' she says to Keera.

Keera squints again.

They've seen Julia on Dan's phone lock screen. Glossy, sexy, alluring and yet doing that blinky thing that India's mother does when she talks about being a unicorn person.

That version of Julia doesn't match this version. The phone Julia looks young and unlined, while this one is a woman of Dan's age.

'I mean, it's unlikely, isn't it . . .?'
'Very,' says India.
'I mean, no way, right?'
'He describes this fairy person, all tiny elegance,' says India. 'This woman is, well, normal.'
'Can't be her, then,' says Keera. 'Julia sounds like a supermodel.'

Chapter Thirty-Six

'Come here! We've got a slight problem!'

Rose meets India and Keera at the French doors to the left of the villa's huge wooden front door.

For once, she is not the picture of calm serenity.

Her silvery hair is tousled as if she's been putting her sunglasses on and off her head, and there's a hint of panic in her voice.

'Follow me,' she commands and takes them around the rear of the reception area and into an area marked *Private*.

She leads the way past an office and into what's clearly the family part of Villa Artemis. It's decorated in the same pale colours as the rest of the hotel, but it's different, with bookshelves and lovely paintings on the walls, with green fronds from many plants spilling from macramé hanging baskets.

'You are not going to believe what's happened,' Rose says.

India begins to mouth the words but Keera says them first.

'That's Julia out there, isn't it?' she says.

'Yes,' says Rose. 'It is. We have ourselves a bit of a situation here and we have to be careful – I honestly have no idea why she came.'

India bites her lip.

She's not sorry that she slept with Dan.

But Julia is now here and it is going to get very awkward. Just when India thought she was going to have a lovely, romantic fling with Dan.

No, she chides herself. Not romantic. Just the opportunity for lots of delicious sex with a handsome, very talented man who is the first man ever that she doesn't want a relationship with.

'She doesn't have to know anything, does she?' asks India, feeling more than a little bit sad. But they have to be kind to Dan's former girlfriend. She needs kindness and understanding.

'Er—' begins Keera but Rose interrupts her.

'The problem is not so much that Julia is here,' says Rose and she sinks down onto a big squashy cream couch. 'The problem is that Dan *isn't* here.'

'Again?' says Keera in exasperation. 'What's wrong with him? He hasn't got lost in the mountains again, has he?'

'Where is he?' says India sharply.

'I hoped you might know,' says Rose.

India and Keera just stare at her.

'We know nothing,' says Keera.

'Absolutely nothing,' agrees India.

Rose sighs. 'According to Julia, who must clearly have booked the first flight from London this morning, he phoned her last night and begged her to come, and he left her a message telling her he was "upset". Her word. She just told all this to Adriana who is saying that she can't give out details of the other guests. Which is true but also to buy time.'

'Shit,' Keera says. 'I honestly didn't hear him telling her to come to Corfu.'

It's Rose and India's turn to stare.

'I heard Dan on the terrace last night leaving the message,' Keera admits. 'I walked onto the terrace when I got back from Corfu Town and he was there, he didn't know I was there and I overheard a lot of it.'

'I'm so sorry, India,' she wails. 'I didn't know how to tell you, I knew it would be hurtful. He was apologising to Julia for being with another woman – he didn't name you, which is handy! And I sort of understood where he was coming from. But running off? What sort of an idiot is he?'

India's mouth trembles and Keera puts an arm around her friend.

'Shit,' says Rose in the most un-therapist way possible. 'We can only assume that this is the reason he's gone. Lydia went to clean his room this morning and he was leaving it with his rucksack – but without his suitcase. She didn't think anything of it but nobody's seen him since.'

'What an idiot!' says India. 'Running away from your problems never works. Wherever you land, there you still are with all your damn problems.'

'Excellently put,' Rose says.

India leans back against the wall.

'Is it my fault?'

'No, it's not your fault, India,' says Rose briskly, sounding more like her old self. 'Dan is an adult and if he wants to sleep with you, then that's his business. Nobody died, right?'

Keera grins.

'Well, there's that,' she says. 'I like that as a therapy quote. We could have wall hangings with it on: *At least nobody died.*'

Rose smiles.

'The problem is that we don't know where he is and he's not answering his phone. Now Julia's here and, unless Dan has been lying through his teeth, she has some mental health issues, which is what worries me. She's clearly vulnerable and I am assuming she has a mental health team. But who knows what'll happen when she finds out that he's left.'

'Or when she finds out who he has a thing going with,' says Keera and then claps her hand over her mouth. 'Sorry,' she says. 'I'm nervous. My mouth just says stuff.'

'What if she does find out? What if she . . .' India's voice tails off.

'You are not responsible for what Julia does or doesn't do,' says Rose sternly. 'The same as with Dan. Julia is an adult. But she won't find out because we'll make sure she doesn't,' adds Rose.

'I only heard some of the message but he didn't use your name, India.'

'It's my fault for sleeping with him,' India says mournfully.

'It's not,' Rose and Keera say at the same time.

'This is not rehab,' says Rose. 'It's not ideal to have people having relationships on the retreat, but I can't stop people being people. I need to talk to Julia but I wanted to see you both and find out if you knew anything.'

She gets to her feet.

'Rose, stop,' says a voice.

It's Adriana, with Christos following her. 'Please, hold on. Another problem. I am so sorry, Rose.'

'What is it?'

Adriana turns to Keera. 'Your mother is here too.'

Keera feels the world turn. 'I wasn't imagining it! I thought I saw her in the taxi.'

She and India peep out of the door.

Dr Bobbi has opened a huge suitcase on the reception floor and is rummaging through its contents looking for something. Finally, she triumphs and holds up a small electric fan. She gets to her feet and comes up against a tall blonde.

'You!' says Bobbi, looking Julia up and down as if she's something unsavoury Bobbi has found stuck to her shoe.

'Oh no,' breathes Keera to India, who is doing her best to hide behind her much shorter friend. 'Mom can go extra when she's mad. I mean, totally extra. I don't want to be here—'

'You can't go!' hisses India, not watching Keera's mother but staring at Julia, who is every bit as glamorous as Dan had implied. She's less fairy child than Dan described and while not beautiful, she's *something*, India thinks.

Julia's quirky with those very long legs shown off in small white shorts like she's in a tampon commercial and just needs to get her roller-skates on.

She looks like the woman everyone wants to party with: wild, fun and ready for absolutely anything. No wonder Dan's been in love with her for ever. India feels jealousy stab her with its green, poisoned dagger.

'You!' says Dr Bobbi to Julia again, more loudly this time.

'You!' snarls Julia. 'You stole my taxi at the airport.'

'You stole my seat on the plane,' hisses Bobbi.

Keera looks at India with horror.

The women have met before? Help!

At least they're not on to rude words yet, Keera thinks. Her mother has a vocabulary that can raze paint off a door.

'They only give people seat numbers so they know who you are if you crash,' snaps Julia dismissively. 'Who cares about the damn seats?'

'I care,' says Bobbi, fingers jabbing in Julia's direction.

'Is that why you're here, then? Coming to get fixed because you worry about aeroplane seats!' Julia is scathing.

Her accent is a weird combo of a cut-glass accent with hints of *something* a bit off, India thinks.

'I don't need to be fixed, lady,' growls Bobbi.

Keera winces. When her mother says *lady*, which sounds polite, she's actually only one step away from *Look here, you dumb bitch, have you got any idea who you're talking to!*

'You Americans are very wearing. Always taking things so seriously . . .' Julia's saying.

'She's not the emotionally fragile person I was expecting,' India mutters to Keera.

'I think Dan has an idealised vision of her from years ago,' Keera says thoughtfully. 'You know: when he met her, she was the perfect fantasy woman and that's what she still is to him. Even if the real Julia has changed.

'I've seen my mother in arguments before: she gets very angry, very quickly,' whispers Keera.

'You can't deal with your mother if she goes postal,' says India. 'I won't let you. She pushes all your buttons.'

'I won't let you deal with Julia,' promises Keera. 'I'd say she could push buttons very easily too.'

Still in the private part of the hotel, Adriana has stopped her sister from rushing into the reception.

'Hold on,' she says.

Adriana opens the door and listens.

Definitely a fight brewing. What is *wrong* with people?

Holding on to her sister's arm, Rose knows it's all her fault.

'I can't believe I tried to do this again, Adriana. I must

have been mad. Everything's going to explode. Julia's unstable; we are not insured to deal with someone who's been through so much! We have to get her under psychiatric care in case she needs help. Keera's mother is obviously a total nightmare. Dan's AWOL! It's all falling apart.'

Adriana and Christos look at each other instead of concentrating on the catastrophe Rose is demanding they pay attention to.

'Rose,' says Christos gently, putting one huge arm around his sister-in-law. 'I promise you it will be all right. We will come through this.'

'How?' demands Rose. 'The last time I tried to help people for work, a man came to the studio with a gun and was shot by the police. It was a miracle he wasn't killed. That was my fault! Now a patient has gone missing and it's my fault again, not to mention the two interlopers. I can hear them shrieking at each other! It's chaos!'

'We worked on safeguarding everyone,' Adriana interrupts. 'Insurance-wise, we told everyone we could not be responsible for their safety if they wandered off from the villa. Christos told every single guest that people have died going off by themselves on Greek islands. There have been terrible tragedies so we were careful. Nobody could know that Dan would just leave . . .'

'I should have realised he'd go into crisis mode!' Rose can't let herself off the hook. 'I thought it was OK because he was allowing himself to be an ordinary human, not a co-dependent person focused on a troubled long-term girlfriend. I was sure there would be guilt but not this! Not this random running away. He's not the type!'

Adriana is shorter than Rose. The tip of Adriana's head nearly reaches Christos's shoulder. With Rose, she is up to Rose's chin.

They have been through so much together.

Adriana had helped her sister come out of the hellhole that was life post-shooting on *The Talisman Effect*. She isn't going to let bloody Dan ruin this. They will track the stupid man down if it's the last thing she does.

Plus, there are two tired and emotional women in reception and someone has to deal with them before they start hitting each other.

'Rose, how about you let me rescue you for once,' says Adriana.

'No,' says Rose automatically. 'It's my circus, they're my monkeys.'

'You need to be calm for the rest of the retreat. We have the rest of today and tomorrow to go. We are going to finish this. Go and make yourself some tea. Leave this to us.'

For a moment, Rose is going to object and then she stops. Adriana wants to take care of this. Rose needs to let her.

Adriana begins to issue instructions to her husband:

'Get Alexei to go out and charm those crazy women out there. Tell him that everything we said to him about not flirting with guests is now off. He can flirt like mad. *But only with those two*. Whichever one bites, he takes her. Get Stavros too. He's weeding at the entrance. He can mop up whoever Alexei leaves behind.'

Christos nods.

Alexei is only twenty-eight but he has been engaged to be married five times. Once to a woman with a yacht. Adriana says it's because Alexei is more than just an Adonis: he's got some magic ingredient that's catnip to all women.

Christos thinks that his cousin being a six-foot-two part-time fireman helps.

No woman can resist a fireman.

'Tell Alexei to take the women to the bar, get them cocktails.' Adriana is on fire giving instructions. Christos loves her when she's being fierce. Most people never see that side of her but his little Adriana is a tiger when it comes to taking care of family. He's pleased that Rose is letting her take control.

'Play that love song album that Alexei knows all the words to,' Adriana continues. 'When Stavros is there and they're settled, you can brief Pavel and Marceline. Tell them to alert all the taxi drivers, round up everyone they can. The taxi men and women know everything that happens on the island.'

Christos nods.

'We cannot phone the police about Dan for a second time. But we are going to find him. He is not leaving Greece.' Adriana is grim. 'Tell them it's the hotel's future at stake. And Rose's,' she adds softly.

Christos nods and takes out his phone.

India and Keera are still hiding in reception.

Keera's watching her mother and Julia.

Julia is taller than Bobbi and, as such, it looks as if she'll win the battle of the interlopers.

But Keera, watching, knows that her mom has a few years on Julia. Dr Bobbi was razing egos to the ground when Julia was still in knee socks.

The argument about stealing taxis and plane seats has become dirty.

Bobbi mutters something about 'trampy outfit' while staring at Julia's tiny white shorts.

'I wear what I want,' snarls Julia, losing the cut-glass accent a bit as she gets angry.

'Really?' demands Bobbi. 'I work in show business,

baby, and at a certain point, classy women know to put it away!'

'Oh yeah! The fashion police are coming for you, sister,' Julia shrieks. 'What are you wearing? A pink gingham dress made for someone much younger!'

India winces. 'So much for women enabling other women to get along in the world,' she whispers to Keera.

'They've both been drinking,' says Keera suddenly. '*That's* the magic ingredient.'

'Not drugs?' asks India.

'Nah. They'd never have got them on the plane. Wine or vodka, something for the flight.'

'That makes sense. No wonder they're riled up.'

Suddenly, Christos appears. He's not dressed in his usual chef's whites and, instead, looks like a very handsome bear in an aqua linen shirt and chinos.

'Ladies, we don't often get such beauties here,' he says in a soft purring voice and steps between Julia and Bobbi.

He has clearly switched on some hitherto unseen charm button, because the smiling chef and adoring husband of Adriana is gone and in his place is a veritable Valentino of Villa Artemis.

'I am Christos, one of the owners of this fine hotel, and I am so delighted to welcome you both, such elegant ladies, here to Greece. The birthplace of goddesses bows before such beauty.'

Keera winces. Overkill?

But both her mother and Julia seem to be buying it.

'Hey, you cannot keep the good ones to yourself,' says a chocolatey deep voice, heralding the appearance of Alexei.

He's panting slightly and again wearing his yoga outfit of tiny grey yoga top and spray-on Lycra shorts that leaves nothing to the imagination.

Keera's sure that Alexei is kept away from the hotel's female guests on purpose and, now, she can see why.

He's changed from bendy, calm yoga man into a sensual flesh and blood Greek statue who's left his fig leaf at home.

He is clearly on a mission to seduce – or to pretend to seduce.

He reaches her mother first, takes one hand in both of his and kisses her on each cheek, continental style.

From their vantage point, Keera and India can smell his aftershave. He must have sprayed the whole bottle on himself before he left the studio.

Another man appears behind Alexei, younger and nearly as handsome, wearing no shirt to cover his muscular bronzed chest, just shorts and flip-flops, and with leaves bewilderingly in his hair.

'Stavros,' says Christos joyously, expertly diverting Stavros over to Julia. 'We need your help in the bar. These ladies deserve a long, slow, comfortable cocktail to help them recover from their journeys. Where did you say you came from?' he purrs to Bobbi, putting an arm around her.

'Most recently Nevada,' says Bobbi, unable to move from Alexei's side because his big arm is encircling her cosily.

'I bet you need a little rest. You don't look as if you've come all that way,' he adds admiringly. 'You're fresh as a daisy.'

From her hiding place, Keera sees her mother bloom under Christos and Alexei's attention. It's award-winning stuff.

'I'm actually here to see my fiancé,' insists Julia.

'She's *not* his fiancé,' says India, shocked.

'I think they are on a retreat today in the mountains,' lies Christos. 'You ladies need a retreat beside our infinity pool.'

'Retreat is boring,' says Stavros, staring deeply into Julia's eyes and running a hand up and down her arm, from her shoulder to her wrist.

He's not as good as Alexei, Keera thinks, but he's going to be, very soon.

'We could have champagne,' suggests Alexei, leading the way, swaying slightly as he walks, taut buttocks displayed in his tight yoga gear.

'Is it bad to use men's sexuality for our own gain just because it's convenient?' asks Keera of India.

'If those boys can calm Julia and your mother down for even half an hour, I think it's a win-win situation,' says India. 'Now we've got to find Dan.'

Chapter Thirty-Seven

'A tall man, big shoulders, too thin, probably a cyclist, great leg muscles?' Agnes at the embroidered goods shop is listening earnestly as Pavel, another one of Christos's cousins, describes the missing tourist from Villa Artemis.

Agnes no longer reveals her age to anyone, and wears bottle-top glasses but can spot both a shoplifter and a good-looking man from at least a hundred yards away.

'Yes, that's the one,' says Pavel.

He and Marceline have already contacted as many of the island's taxi drivers as they can on their vast WhatsApp group. They're all determined to track Dan down. If Dan is on Corfu, they insist they will find him.

Without the police, Pavel has been at pains to explain.

Looking for the same man twice would annoy any policeman.

'He's trying to get away from it all,' Adriana told Pavel and Marceline. 'I can't see him leaving the island. He hasn't taken his suitcase. He panicked, I think. That's all.'

Agnes has good news for Pavel.

'This Dan, he came into the village this morning. Looked

sad,' says Agnes thoughtfully. 'I hate to see a beautiful man sad. I came out of the shop to see if he wanted to talk but he walked on, never saw me.'

Agnes sighs.

She's been experimenting with tigerish orange and black streaks in her grey hair but nobody has noticed so far, which is disheartening.

'What direction did he walk in?' asks Pavel.

'Past the Sia girls' shop and the beach shop, in the direction of La Taverna which obviously wasn't opened then.'

'Thank you,' says Pavel, kissing her hand.

He must ask his mother if Agnes's eyesight is going. Her hair is currently full of mad colours, like an explosion in a hair dye place.

Agnes smiles happily as she turns back into her shop.

Pavel kissed her hand.

Well, now.

Seventy-eight years old and she still hasn't lost it.

'They've cancelled everything for today,' says Bernard loudly as he stomps to a sunbed. 'I told you this retreat was a shoddy affair.'

'Oh shut up, Bernard,' says Keera crossly. 'You're being nasty. There's lunch laid out inside for anyone who wants it.'

He ignores her and snorts loudly, irritation leaking from every pore.

Keera knows that Grazia has gone into Xanthe to shop.

Rose has told them all that the timetable is paused until Dan is located and the unwanted visitors are dealt with.

Keera would like a few words with Dan.

But first, she needs to speak to her mother. Bobbi's at the bar, carousing with Alexei, Stavros and Julia.

Keera leans against the terrace wall and listens to the laughing and giggling. Just half an hour ago, her mother and Julia were on the verge of hitting each other but now it seems that booze and admiring men have taken the edge off.

A very cheesy French album is playing loudly and, as Keera walks up to the bar, she can hear her mother singing along to it.

Julia is looking very undone, with her bare feet up on a barstool, the strap of her tiny blue camisole falling off her shoulder revealing a sexy curved shoulder and the swell of one breast. She has one arm around Stavros, holding a giant glass of wine, and Keera feels a violent urge for a drink.

Just one sip—

'Look what the cat dragged in!' shrieks her mother.

Bobbi clambers off her barstool and hugs Keera.

The alcohol fumes hit Keera and suddenly the idea of being drunk feels like the most appalling thing in the world.

'What are you doing here, Mom?' asks Keera, leading her mother away from the bar and up to the terrace, which is mercifully empty.

Bobbi has brought her glass and plonks it on the table.

'I came to see you, honey bun,' says Bobbi, grabbing her daughter and kissing her on both cheeks now that her hands are free. 'What have you done with your hair, hon?'

Bobbi fluffs Keera's wig a little with a disapproving moue. 'It's a bit drastic. You look like Barbie. Norm-core Barbie. That's never been our brand.'

Then she stands back and looks at Keera critically.

'It's a wig, isn't it?' she says suddenly. 'Why the fuck are you wearing a wig? What have you done?'

Keera sighs and pulls off the wig, revealing her freshly shaved head.

India had done it for her the night before and had then applied some Voya lime and mandarin lotion onto Keera's skull, all the while telling her that she had a beautifully shaped head.

'You're bald!' shrieks Dr Bobbi, sinking onto one of the seats on the terrace and taking a huge gulp of her drink.

'Yeah, Mom, I shaved it off,' says Keera with irritation. 'Nobody's died, OK?'

'What about your career? Bald or Barbie, either one will kill that off. What the fuck have you done?'

'Mom, we try not to use swear words on the retreat,' Keera feels obliged to point out.

'Like I fucking care!' Bobbi's up to full shriek now.

Keera wonders if everyone in Xanthe can hear her. Their view of tourists will be broken beyond belief. But then, last season, according to Adriana, the village hosted a week-long hen night and the place was awash with pink fluffy handcuffs, cowboy hats with glitter on them and parties into the night.

Bobbi is still shouting.

'You're crazy, crazy!'

The sound grates in Keera's head.

She wants to do this away from everyone else.

'Follow me,' she says, ignoring Bobbi's shouting.

There are stone steps and a wooden handrail behind the terrace. Keera and India climbed up here before to a hidden high point overlooking the hotel, the village and the sea.

'Up here,' Keera says and starts climbing up to the acropolis without waiting for her mother to reply.

'Come down—' begins Bobbi but Keera keeps climbing the smooth stone steps. She is not talking to her mother in the bar or anywhere else with proximity to alcohol because then Bobbi will have more to drink, and drinking changes her mother into something else.

Like mother like daughter, Keera thinks ruefully as she climbs.

'OK,' she hears her mother shout and she knows Bobbi is coming up behind her, gold platform sandals clopping with each step.

De Havilland sandals, Keera knows. Nobody can ever say that Bobbi doesn't give every outfit the full rock-chick look.

At the top, Rose and Adriana have planted aromatic peachy-pink oleander bushes that smell of floral talcum powder. They're blooming, clusters of flowers with vibrant green leaves. There's a long wooden bench installed by Christos close to the edge of the tiny terrace and Keera sits on it now, taking in the sight of the sea. In the distance she can see boats – large luxury yachts with vast masts and sheeny white flanks, alongside colourful small fishing boats.

Keera closes her eyes and lets the sun warm her face. She loves it here.

If only she could stay, but she can't. She has to go back to the real world and face it.

But the retreat and Rose have opened a door for Keera. A door that allows her to realise that she has to make her own choices.

'I don't know why we have to clamber up here,' pants Bobbi as she arrives and sinks on the bench, slipping off her golden platforms.

Keera stays silent. Once Bobbi has her breath back, she starts afresh.

'I'm angry, Keera, and I have a right to be angry! You disappear, telling me damn all about where you're going, with fuck all money left in our accounts – and don't pretend you don't know this, madam – and then, when I need you to come home to record songs with Santi, you don't answer your phone any more. You're just – *pouf.*' Bobbi mimes blowing a bubble. 'Gone. What have you got to say for yourself?'

The idyllic calm of Xanthe has allowed Keera's mind to step off the cortisol merry-go-round. She sees her mother almost frothing at the mouth and yet, in her head, she hears Rose speaking to her.

You can't control other people or what they feel. You can only control your own feelings, thoughts and actions. You are not responsible for other people or their happiness.

This is what she came to the retreat for. This clarity.

She's also mindful of Rose's dictum about approaching difficult conversations with love.

'Mom, I love you,' she starts.

Bobbi makes a 'hmfff' noise.

'Funny way of showing it. I had to hawk myself around Vegas trying to get work!'

Keera feels her scalp itch with irritation and anxiety.

This is hard. She has never spoken to her mother honestly – not about important stuff.

Bobbi's the one who makes the decisions and Keera has to follow those decisions.

But then she thinks about all the work she's done here on herself: how she knows she tries to keep her mother happy and how, as Rose explains it, we can't fix other people.

'Mom, I'm sorry we don't have much money left but let's live in the real world now. I'm not making any money right now. Why didn't you look for a normal job if you couldn't get singing work?'

Bobbi explodes.

'Normal job!' she shrieks. 'I don't do normal jobs. I'm a performer! I'm in the entertainment business!'

It's now or never, Keera thinks. In her head, she sees the whirling dreams of her mother – from a small Donegal town to the dizzying heights of backstage at Madison Square Gardens where her daughter had once, just once, played two opening numbers before a teenage country-music star had headlined.

Keera had been so excited at the time but it was nothing compared to her mother. Bobbi had been on a high for weeks.

Her mother had needed that buzz more than Keera had.

'Mom, we both need normal jobs from now on,' says Keera. 'I can't go back to touring and making records: not in the same way, anyway. It's bad for me. I'm clean and sober and I won't be for long if I stay in the industry.'

'Don't be ridiculous. It's what we do,' says her mother dismissively.

'I don't want to do it any more,' Keera says. 'We've got to find other ways to make money, Mom. We've lots of contacts, we could get personal assistant jobs or stuff like that—'

'Personal assistants! I'm not going to be some wage slave,' Bobbi hisses. 'How can you even say that? We're artists: people would kill to have even a tenth of our talent.'

'Yeah, but look where it brought me,' says Keera. 'I can't be in a music job and stay sober. Not now anyway.'

'You could if you wanted to,' her mother says, wheedling.

She's very drunk, Keera realises belatedly. Once, she'd have been matching her mother drink for drink, so she knew if Bobbi had had too much. But now, her awareness of drunk people is awry.

Unless they actually fall off stools, she can't see how advanced it is.

Bobbi must be drunk if she's using her wheedling voice.

'Mom, this dream is over,' says Keera. 'Really over and you have to accept that. I'm out of the music business. You need to get a job.'

'What? You really mean that?' Bobbi has shades of the girl from *The Exorcist* in her voice now. 'I can't believe how ungrateful you are! After all I've done for you—'

Keera hates to be even sharing the bench with this version of her mother.

'You didn't do it for me, Mom, you did it for yourself,' she says bluntly. 'It was fabulous but it was your dream. Always your dream.'

'You liar!' shrieks Bobbi. 'Who wanted that role in the Disney show? *Watch me practise one more time, Mommy . . .*'

'*I was eleven years old!* Eleven-year-olds don't really know what they want. Of course I wanted it: *you* wanted it and I wanted to make you happy! That's what kids do.'

'Liar,' shouts her mother again.

Keera stands up, the glittering view behind her, and faces her mother.

'I'm not your slave, Mom. I'm your daughter and my career – or *our career*, as you call it – nearly broke me. I became an addict. Not saying that's your fault – nobody made me do it, but drugs and alcohol nearly destroyed me.'

Keera feels tearful as she says this but it's all true. She's heard people talk about recovery in terms of how many recoveries they have in them. Most people say they get one recovery and don't want to risk going back to drinking or using.

She'd hoped her mom would understand that but she doesn't: it was a silly hope, really.

'I'll talk to you when you're sober,' Keera says and speeds down the stone steps, knowing her mother's sandals are off and that she'll never be able to follow as quickly.

Perhaps she was mad to think there might be a resolution with her mother. Just because Keera's changed, doesn't mean anyone else has.

Chapter Thirty-Eight

India's tried to meditate back down on the beach but she simply can't.

Her mind is buzzing, so she's put her headphones on and is listening to Lana Del Rey singing about heartbreak.

Emptying her mind is impossible. Eventually, she gets up from her seated position and begins to collect pretty stones and shells.

All the while, her inner voice is shouting at her: *You idiot, you should never have slept with Dan. He doesn't care for you, he's shown that. He rang his girlfriend to confess. He was ashamed, yes ashamed.*

She goes back to her room without checking in reception to see if Dan has shown up.

It's not her business any more.

She doesn't hate him. But she hates how he's made her feel.

In her room, she examines the notebook Rose left for them.

India hadn't written anything in it at first.

India sits, opens Rose's notebook and breathes deeply.

She doesn't want to write anything new, which is startling.

She's written down stuff for years and never took stock of any of it.

All the guys, and the plans she made for the same guys, and it transpires that she never realised what she was doing.

She was building castles in the sky without any foundation.

Crying about not having a child but then doing nothing about it. Why not? She doesn't actually need a man in order to have a child.

She could use a fertility clinic, get donor sperm.

Without thinking, she finds she's drawn a very childish version of a sperm swimming with its little wiggly tail.

She gets out her stickers and puts little stars and rainbows beside it.

Imagines herself pregnant, pregnant on her own and fully, joyfully in charge of her own life.

India stops doodling and thinks about this.

First, she'd need a proper job.

What is she good at?

Clothes. That's what.

Rose said that India's clothes are art, that she dresses with artistry.

That's what she's good at.

But how to monetise it?

How to move on with her life, without relying on a man . . .

Georgie, hello! How are you, darling? And Dad? The retreat's been interesting! I've met some amazing people and a fabulous new friend, Keera.

I'm messaging because I want your advice. Business advice.

I'd like to start a business selling vintage clothes. I know, everyone and their lawyer does it and I don't want this to be a nepo-thing where you and Dad set me up and help if I lose money. No! Definitely not! But I'm good at buying stuff and selling it on. What I was thinking of was . . .

India pauses. If she says this, it's out there. There's no turning back.

. . . going to college to do a one- or two-year business course. Is that a good plan?
Love you, see you soon!! xxx

The previous night, Rose had dreamed about *The Talisman Effect*: how it started and how everything went slowly wrong.

She finds scent incredibly redolent and, now, a trio of scents floods her senses.

The grapefruit stuff that the hair stylist used every day before filming and that lingered in her hair when she went over to Theo's house, the scent of whatever he was cooking, the rough tang of the sea when they walked on the beach after dinner.

'You can't practise proper therapy but you can teach people something,' said Theo when the TV show was first mooted after six months of Rose appearing on the breakfast show. 'Just be careful, Rose. We treat enough people in the movie and TV business: it can be a very cruel world. The producers of your show want great TV and don't care about great therapy.'

'I know,' said Rose.

But she hadn't really known.

The TV show meant she had to rapidly break out of the sort of formal therapy that Theo still practised and into the area of a quick-fix approach.

The Talisman Effect had quickly become huge and the producers wanted more excitement, more arguments on the show. Chaos, suffering, fights on live TV.

The TV sites were jammed with news about crazy people from the show – like the woman who fell for her daughter's teenage husband, which was a huge draw on the tabloid sites.

As the show grew bigger, Rose was scared that her own backstory would come out, but she found that her role as the calm therapist meant media outlets focused on her wisdom rather than trawling her background.

Inevitably, ratings overcame the requirement of actual therapy or the questions of morality about who they had on the show.

Other therapists openly dissed her for her approach, angry at how Rose had made a business out of 'people's pain'.

All of it stung Rose. She knew what was happening and yet she felt stuck on the juggernaut of a successful show.

Rose treating the weirder guests upset her beloved Theo, still steadily by her side but unhappy about the way the show had gone.

'Someone is going to get hurt, Rose, and you've got to pull back. Nobody gets the help they need in an hour-long show and it's going to backfire. The guests are getting closer to the edge where nobody's going to be able to help them.'

'I do my best!' Rose protested. 'Doesn't everyone deserve mental health help?'

'Yes, but some of the people on the show need psychiatric help before they can benefit from therapy! You know this,

Rose. Please, get off the merry-go-round. You're better than this.'

That comment had hurt most of all.

Better than a TV show that was watched by millions and did try to help troubled people?

'How can you say that?' she hurled back at him. 'Am I too low-rent for you?'

That night, he came home very late and slept in the spare bedroom.

Rose felt the arctic blast of being dismissed.

The next day, she moved out of his house and into a hotel. She thought it was just for some breathing space. But when the pops of the gun were heard two weeks later on *The Talisman Effect*, Rose was alone.

In the midst of the fear and chaos, she had no beloved Theo to hold her in the maelstrom.

TV Guru Silent on Traumatic Live-Show Shooting.

Who's Gonna Fix It Now Rose Has Fled?

What Can TV Experts Learn from The Talisman Effect's *Crash and Burn?*

New Therapist Steps into Rose's Shoes – She's Young and She's Hot!

That was the history of her show in four headlines.

The news outlets didn't know about the producers' anger at Rose for leaving, their desire for someone to carry the can, her agent's many attempts to coax Rose back to LA.

'If you go, your TV career will be over,' her agent said in a message that Rose deleted instantly.

She didn't *want* a TV career any more.

As she hadn't witnessed the on-set shooting, she didn't need to hang around once her original statement had been taken.

There was no point showing the world the emails she'd sent to the producers after she and Theo had split.

'We need to rethink the show,' she'd written. 'It is becoming dangerous to guests' psychological well-being to create so much tension on set. We are risking lives here. As a professional, I will have to step away from the show if we cannot address these issues.'

Within a few days of the shooting, Rose Talisman was in the wind, leaving the home she'd shared with Theo, and her life, behind.

Rose stops pacing and tries to fix her hair in one of Adriana's big mirrors. Her hair has come down out of its knot and she didn't wash it today, so it's flyaway, needs taming.

Standing still for a moment in front of the mirror, a coil of hair in one hand, she realises something: she can't sit in front of her laptop and phone in here and wait for news, wait for everything to come crashing down around her.

That was what happened with the show. She waited when she should have acted. She relied on others to change the format.

Villa Artemis is the beloved home she's made with Adriana and Christos, her brave venture back into running a therapy retreat. Nobody else can fix this except Rose. She has to fight back and she needs some quiet time to figure out what to do.

Five minutes in the kitchen with the coffee machine gives her a steaming, double-strength coffee. Rose grabs one of Adriana's hats, jams it on her head and slips out a side door then goes onto the terrace.

There's lots of noise coming from the bar.

Peering around the corner and hidden from sight by

vast shrubs and a curled olive tree in a pot, she sees Julia drinking with Alexei and Stavros. All previous animosity seems to have disappeared.

Rose avoids being seen by taking the rocky back steps down to the gardens and descends into the bower that is her hidden Greek garden.

Rose needs to think clearly away from the hectic energy of the others if she is to save her beloved retreat. She knows it doesn't take her long. She just needs to be able to go within.

She'd never been even vaguely interested in gardening before but, when the remains of the original stone house were being excavated, Rose decided to create a peaceful green area where guests could relax, surrounded by the scents of Corfu.

Christos had said he didn't know what would grow there, when she showed him her sketch of this garden, an oblong surrounded by terraced flowerbeds and with local sculptures dotted around.

'I know nothing about plants,' he said, shrugging, 'but this area will be dry. We won't have any money left over from landscaping the rest of the villa. We are eco-friendly with all that watering, but here?' He shrugged again. 'We can't afford to add it to the irrigation system.'

Rose had thought it was unlikely that the Ancient Greeks, who'd achieved such mathematical, philosophical and architectural brilliance, didn't have a plan for watering gardens that didn't involve linking it to the villa's clever use of grey water to keep the plants watered.

She researched and found that ollas were the key: terracotta cylinders planted in the garden, they were filled with water which slowly seeped out into the earth when the nearby shrubs were dry and needed it.

Dotted all over this now flourishing garden are countless simple, terracotta ollas which are carefully monitored by Stavros. Thanks to the watering system of the ancients, there are flourishing waves of lady's mantle which has grown like wildfire.

There's bushy catmint and lavender, both wafting fabulous scents into the air, and currently a magnet for clusters of happy bees. Low-lying sedums and leggy agapanthus grow side by side, and little clumps of sea holly and rosemary dot the raised rockery that Stavros was working on last week.

Rose finds the little stone bench at the bottom of the garden where their property is bordered by another one. The goat who lives in the next-door field has seen Rose arrive and has bustled over in the hope of something to eat.

He peers over his fence at the seated woman. His name is Elvis, according to Stavros.

'I've nothing for you, Elvis,' Rose tells him. 'Not a thing.'

If goats could pout, Rose knows Elvis is pouting. He fully expects all visitors to the garden to bring him treats.

He paws sullenly at the earth a bit, then goes back to staring out to sea.

Rose stares too.

Below her is the curving road to Xanthe and the small path to the Kri Kri beach where she's had so many successful sessions with her retreaters. A single boat is in the distance, sails high in search of a breeze which Rose feels is unlikely today.

She keeps watching it but it appears the boat is becalmed: no wind to puff her sails.

Like us, Rose thinks.

Becalmed.

She doesn't want to fail in this beautiful place. She doesn't know if she has it in her to start her life all over again.

THE ISLAND RETREAT

Corfu is magical. If Villa Artemis fails, she knows that her sister and Christos can move into his mother's house until they get back on their feet. Rose could live there too but she doesn't want to. She thinks she'd never get over the failure.

Bored, Elvis is now banging his head against his fence for attention and, as she looks at him, her eyes catch a few single shoots of clover in the soil.

The watering of her ollas has made snippets of grass grow too, so she gets up and picks the clover's fluffy purple heads as well as a few blades of grass for her companion.

'No biting,' Rose warns, holding the clover out as if feeding a horse, with her hand flat.

The goat delicately nibbles at her flat palm and Rose can't help but smile at the sensation of his soft muzzle.

She loves animals. And then she thinks in a rush of lovely Biscuit, with a warm canine heart and the most loving eyes. What happened with Biscuit was what started the whole series of lies.

Chapter Thirty-Nine

Alys Rosemarie Flint thought animals were more reliable than people when she made friends with Aunt Patsy's small, fluffy brown mongrel, Biscuit.

Biscuit was a sweet old dog and liked lying with children having his tummy petted. He was always there for children to sit with him and tell him their woes. Biscuit never told anyone of the secrets whispered to him. He asked for nothing and gave love eagerly.

Aunt Patsy's house was on the outskirts of Aberystwyth, and as well as five foster kids, she had two apricot gerbils. Biscuit watched the gerbils' cage with jaw-dropped fascination. The gerbils didn't last. Someone opened their cage and let them out for Biscuit to chase.

Teenage Alys was grown up beyond her years and had known exactly who'd done this. Biscuit didn't mean to be cruel: he was merely being a dog.

The gerbils had been a warning.

Aunt Patsy had been one of the best foster mums Alys had known. She'd been thirteen when she'd gone there and had long since given up the notion that one day her real parents would appear out of the mist and take care of her.

What Alys had long realised was that she wanted to go to college to learn how to help kids like her. To change something, anything, because she had so many skills after a childhood in care.

She was wise, as wise as if she'd lived a thousand years. She knew that the care people considered her worryingly silent. Thought that she kept all her pain inside.

But she was fixing herself slowly. One day, she would help other people.

She's been in Aunt Patsy's house for two years when Ivan, nicknamed The Terrible, arrived.

He was fifteen, skinny and had an innocent face. But Alys didn't trust that face. Ivan had been in eleven different homes at this point. A childhood in that many homes said he'd either been very unlucky – or was trouble. He let the gerbils out, And after that, Alys was on her guard.

She discovered that Ivan was watching violent porn videos late at night. Had seen him watching Adriana, the smallest of Aunt Patsy's foster children. When he didn't think anyone was looking, he sat open-mouthed and stared at her, his eyes dull with longing.

Adriana was small for her age, with dark hair and glowing dark eyes that shone in an eager little face as if she was always waiting for the sheer happiness she just knew was coming.

Alys was sure that Ivan wanted a real-life victim. There was no point, she thought, in telling her foster mother. Aunt Patsy was lovely, but she was like the other foster carers Rose had known: too worn down trying to care for an assortment of tricky, traumatised kids to give any of them the absolute love they all longed for.

'Alys, give him a chance,' Aunt Patsy would say.

Alys Flint was too young for people to believe that she understood the cruelties of life.

When she was older and had left the memory of Alys behind for a new name and a new life, Alys was determined that people would take her seriously.

She'd come up with a name for this new person she'd become: Rose Talisman.

She told nobody of her plans and watched her little sister carefully.

She knew Ivan had opened the gerbil cage so they'd be killed by poor Biscuit. Could see he bullied the other kids. Could see him watching Adriana, trying to sit beside her at meals and touching her little legs, pinching her, scaring her.

What he didn't realise was that even though Adriana and Alys weren't blood relatives, over the past two years Alys had grown to love the little girl as her sister. Adriana felt like the only family Alys had.

The two of them slept in the same room: Alys in a single bed and little Adriana in a child's bed set at a ninety-degree angle to hers. Adriana told her stories about her teddies and Alys vowed that nobody would ever hurt Adriana.

The day it had happened, Alys saw Ivan make his move through Aunt Patsy's glass doors.

He'd thought it was safe. He hadn't understood Alys's love for Adriana and her awareness of the damage that could be inflicted on small children.

Ivan didn't understand love because he loved nobody.

He'd taken her four-year-old sister by the hand and led her upstairs.

Alys made it into the bathroom just in time.

'Fucking bitch—' began Ivan and then she crashed the cistern lid down on his right hand.

He began screaming and holding his mangled hand.

'I didn't do nothing,' Ivan had roared with pain, as he lay on the ground clutching his hand.

Alys knew he was telling the truth, that he hadn't actually done anything yet.

Yet.

She'd been so quick following him.

'You're a fucking bitch, Alys Flint, and I'm going to get you!' he yelled, which was a mistake.

Alys realised that she'd just made him more dangerous.

He needed more injuries so he'd be moved away from Aberystwyth. She couldn't risk him staying near Adriana.

'No, you won't, you little prick,' she said coldly, angling the cistern a bit better this time.

The cistern lid broke after it had been bashed against Ivan's ankle a few times but it had done its work well.

With a hand and an ankle requiring medical intervention, Ivan would not be hurting small children for a while.

Alys yelled for Aunt Patsy.

'Tell her the truth about why you dragged my little sister up here or I'll break your other ankle,' she hissed to Ivan. 'You touch Adriana again, and you'll regret it.'

To the accompaniment of Ivan's squeals of pain, Alys had scooped Adriana up and brought her out of the bathroom.

'You're my little sister now,' she said to Adriana. 'I'm going to look after you. Let's tell Aunt Patsy what Ivan has done. We like nice people, not nasty ones.'

Ivan never came back to Aberystwyth. She always kept tabs on him. He was in jail now for two brutal assaults. *Best place for him*, she thought.

Ivan had been in her mind when she first met Theo's parents.

It had been talking of Wales that had done it.

Rose's cover story was that she'd travelled around a lot as a child, mainly in France, briefly in Wales (to cover any accent issues) and, of course, she mentioned her conveniently dead parents.

They died.

Such a pity.

Life moves on.

If people thought she sounded cold discussing them, they assumed she was hiding grief behind a façade.

'We love Wales,' Theo's father had said. 'We went there in the nineties to Snowdonia and we visited the Jurassic part, the Glamorgan Coast I think it is.'

'Of course,' Rose had echoed, smiling.

She thought for a millisecond about how she'd never heard of the Glamorgan Heritage Coast as a child and then how these kind people would be shocked to hear she'd crushed another foster kid's hand and ankle with a cistern lid.

She'd even managed to give Ivan a limp for good measure. It was mentioned in all his criminal trials. He was disabled, the reports said.

Rose did not feel guilty about him. He'd been in the system the same as she had. Her childhood had been about pure survival. But she had not preyed on weaker kids.

She was sure that Theo's parents, educated, thoughtful people, would have viewed her as *other* if she'd told them or her beloved Theo the truth.

They knew childhoods like hers *existed* – but they'd never seen such damage so close up.

So she made the decision.

She'd never be able to tell them.

She lied coolly to Theo about her family, about her dead parents, how she rarely spoke to any of her other relatives.

Foster kids were experts at lying. She'd seen many of them in her private practice before she got her TV show. Plenty of them afterwards too.

When Rose was eighteen, she'd tried to adopt Adriana but her application was refused.

So she stayed very close and finally, when Adriana was eleven and Aunt Patsy decided to retire, Rose took her little sister and ran.

It was easy to run with a foster kid.

So many of them slipped through the cracks of an overstretched system into trafficking or drugs.

One missing eleven-year-old girl didn't actually cause that much of a fuss.

Rose knew how to work the system, how not to leave a trail.

She wanted to escape their childhood files: abandonment, foster homes, the attempted abuse of four-year-old Adriana, Alys's defence of the small girl that ended up with a teenage sexual predator in detention.

Nobody needed to know that Rose was a foster kid, that another foster home inhabitant had tried to sexually abuse Adriana.

They'd earned their privacy.

When Rose had moved to Los Angeles, Adriana had been beginning hotel management training.

Rose never spoke of a sister in interviews because she told Adriana that if Rose's past was revealed, at least Adriana would not be connected with it.

Now, it seems that the past might be catching up with her. Someone knows that she and Alys Flint are the same person.

*

Keera's sitting on the edge of the infinity pool, dangling her feet in its glorious cool.

She can see Bernard still at the other side of the infinity pool, baking himself in the sun. His skin must be like leather, she thinks.

She's wearing a hat and a soft linen shirt that covers her body over her one-piece swimsuit.

The sun beating down relentlessly makes her slip the shirt off and slide into the pool.

The cool water surrounds her like a balm.

She thinks about what she's got to do before she leaves this haven.

She has to finish up her notebook. Journaling has helped her so much already. She wouldn't have been brave enough to enter rehab if she hadn't been journaling thanks to Rose's self-help book.

But what next? Keera can't leave without facing up to what she needs to say to her mother.

After their time on the acropolis, Bobbi stomped back to the bar.

Keera knows Bobbi can't see her from here.

Keera floats in the pool, staring up at the cloudless blue sky.

Singing and touring means there is no stability in her life, none of the things she now realises she wants.

'*A dog, pets, having close friends, sleepovers, dinner parties . . .*' She'd told Rose and the group that she'd never experienced these things.

Simple ordinary pleasures.

Her one close childhood friend was someone whom she never saw any more because she wasn't in the same industry.

The endless regime of touring meant never sleeping in the same bed more than a few days. She'd been to Europe as a teenager, had seen nothing but the greatest hits of every capital city from the back of a people carrier or bus.

Her normal was taking pills to help her wake up, pills to calm her, alcohol to give her a buzz, cocaine to get her high.

It had left her feeling hollow and ashamed, and in rehab. She will drink and drug again if she goes back into that world and now that she's clean, she truly wants to stay that way.

The peace of mind, the calmness – she can't give that up. Even for Bobbi.

Keera slides under the water to escape the feelings, letting the pool close over her head, hiding her from the world.

She pushes up through the water, feeling it streaming off her shorn head, and swims to the pool edge like a seal.

What if . . .

She suddenly has a plan.

'Rose!'

Adriana calls out when Rose comes back into their private quarters from her walk around the garden.

'We've found Dan,' she says. 'He's fine. He's in Corfu, he's been talking about taking the ferry to Igoumenitsa but he obviously doesn't mean it: he's missed all of today's sailings so far.'

Rose almost can't believe it. Relief floods through her.

'Is he coming back?'

'Yes, just not yet,' Adriana says.

'Pavel's cousin found him. Now they're in a restaurant waiting for dinner.'

Rose rolls her eyes. '*Seriously?*'

'Pavel's friend owns it and the friend's grandmother cooks there and she has insisted they cannot leave until they have had her lamb souvlaki – her special marinade recipe – and her galaktoboureko.'

'In other words, they may be hours while Yaya stuffs them with filo pastry and custard filling because they are too thin,' says Rose.

'Precisely.'

Somehow, this vision of a Greek grandmother fussing over Dan and Pavel's cousin makes Rose laugh. The stress leaches out of her.

Half the island are looking for Dan for the second time and he's dallying in a restaurant with Pavel's cousin because a Greek yaya is determined they need to taste her souvlaki. Nobody can argue with a yaya.

The sisters begin to laugh and then Adriana is sitting beside Rose on the couch and they're holding each other, convulsing with laughter.

'I hope this isn't the last retreat,' says Adriana seriously.

'It won't be,' says Rose.

India can't help herself:

She needs to look at Julia up close.

See what makes her so special.

Brushing her curls till they're glossy, she pulls her hair into an easy knot at the base of her neck. She applies a coat of mascara, a smear of cherry lip balm and a heady blast of Byredo perfume.

She's clad in very cool mannish trousers in a khaki linen, worn with a light-weave cotton halter neck in rich copper that matches her hair tones. She looks businesslike, she thinks approvingly. A woman in control.

Then she leaves the safety of her room and goes to the bar.

Keera's mother, Alexei, Stavros and Julia are all arranged around it, with bartender Jimi shaking the cocktail shaker to some Latin-sounding music.

'I love this song,' says Bobbi, hopping off her barstool and shimmying dangerously close to the infinity pool.

Julia is deep in conversation with Stacy, the evening bartender. Julia is also holding Stavros's muscular arm as if to stop him leaving.

Stacy's twenty-something, studying hotel management, loves Villa Artemis but has to go back to her college in Belgium when this placement is over. She looks a trifle bored at whatever monologue Julia is delivering.

India grins hello and slips in at the end of the bar. Alexei and Stavros both see her and nod, while Bobbi and Julia see her but make no gesture of welcome.

India asks for a cucumber martini and some iced water.

'Which one is yours?' Jimi asks quietly as he starts making the cocktail.

'None of them,' India says. 'But that one,' she gestures towards Julia, 'is Dan's ex, and me and Dan were involved and . . .'

She trails off.

Jimi appears to grapple with some vital rule of hotel management, then leans close.

'I shouldn't say this but I don't like her,' he says. 'She hasn't shut up about how she travels to all the best places, and I have friends all over the place and the "top" hotels she says she's been in don't exist! She's told me that she's getting married.'

'She and Dan are not getting married,' says India crossly. 'She "didn't want to be tied down".'

Jimi shrugs.

'We all know people like that. They don't want something

until they can't have it and then, they'll scream to get their hands on it. Dan is cute, he's a decent guy. You fight for him. I have to book a taxi for her now; Rose doesn't want them drunk in the bar any more. We're sending Julia to Casa Siren and Keera's mother is staying here.'

Bobbi's stopped dancing and is gulping back the glass of iced white wine that Alexei is keeping filled up. India's not sure about this method of keeping Bobbi and Julia calm. Seems to her that they'll only get even more upset when they've had too much to drink and can't find their significant others. She hopes the taxi comes soon for Julia and that Bobbi gets sent to her room, with an empty minibar.

'It's very hot,' says Bobbi, fanning herself with a little plastic battery-powered fan.

She catches sight of India.

'Hello, are you on this retreat?' Bobbi asks.

India shakes her head. 'Just a guest,' she fibs. 'I think the retreat people are off somewhere . . .' she adds vaguely.

'My daughter's one of the retreaters,' says Bobbi. 'Can I tell you a secret?'

She leans closer to India, who is afraid Bobbi will fall off her stool.

'I think they're brainwashing them. It's the only answer.'

For a moment, Bobbi looks lost.

'My daughter's acting crazy, that's all I'm saying.'

'Really?' says India, attempting to sound as if she's not paying that much attention. 'What about you?' she asks Julia.

Alexei gives her a heavy-lidded look that says *What are you playing at?*

India ignores him. She can't help herself.

'My fiancé's here too,' says Julia, reaching into her pocket to find a shocking pink lipstick, which she proceeds to apply without once confirming her application in the bar's mirrored surfaces.

India's face betrays nothing.

'Is there a family part of the therapy?' India asks innocently now. 'Is that why you're both here?'

Bobbi nods gloomily but Julia narrows her eyes.

'No, I don't do stupid therapy. It's all a con,' she says, assessing India.

India sips her cocktail.

'Are you here with your family?' demands Julia.

'No, no husband or boyfriend. It's a me-time holiday,' India answers, then steals her stepmother's career for her own. 'I work in interior design and needed a break after doing a big job in Hackney. How about you?' she asks slyly.

'I'm a trust-fund girl,' says Julia smugly. 'I'm terribly lucky. But I *know* how lucky I am,' she coos with a fake smile. 'That's key,' she adds.

India hides how shocked she is with all the lies.

Dan had never mentioned the fantasy-creating side of his former girlfriend. But clearly Julia has a very tenuous relationship with the truth.

Also, she must have had therapy in hospital, surely?

Is she embarrassed at what happened? India can understand that.

Making up a fantasy to cover up the pain about her suicide attempt would make sense in some ways. India wants to feel sympathy for the other woman.

Except Julia is not exactly sympathetic.

'Your fiancé . . .' India says, unable to let it go. She has to find out what sort of person Julia truly is. 'What does he look like? I may have seen him . . .'

'Tall, handsome,' says Julia airily. 'He asked me to fly out. Can't bear to be without me!'

She turns to Stacy and waggles her fingers at the bartender, signalling a request for another cocktail.

India thinks she might just explode with rage.

What a cow!

Alexei intervenes: 'I thought there was a message for you up at reception,' he says to India. His expressive eyes say that he wants her gone before it all falls apart.

With Julia and Bobbi both looking elsewhere, India sticks her tongue out at him.

'When are you getting married?' she asks Julia.

She can't help herself.

She is convinced that Dan is not lying about him and Julia being on a break, which means that Julia is the most barefaced liar India has ever met.

'And have you got a dress?' India adds.

Julia drinks at least half of her new cocktail in one fell swoop without even flinching.

'I'll probably wear one of Mummy's couture dresses,' she says, twirling some of her long blonde hair. 'October. That's when we're getting married. October. Daddy will just book somewhere lovely when the time comes. I'm feeling Venice . . .'

India is finally rendered speechless. She knows she's been working on her own wedding dress looks without having a spouse-to-be but at least she wasn't lying about it.

She glares at Alexei who's still staring at her.

'I must go and get that message,' she tells him grimly. 'Bye all,' she says and leaves the bar.

India is supercharged with temper.

Dan cannot continue to date Julia.

She's a complete stranger to the truth and is nothing like the fragile woman Dan described. She might have been once but now, all India sees is someone who is pretending to be someone she's not.

Rose will know how to sort the situation.

India stomps up to her room. Even though Dan's not hers, he doesn't deserve Julia.

Rose has made her mind up: no matter what happens, she will handle it.

If the Instagram menace tries to out her, she will make sure that Adriana is not involved.

If Bernard tries to destroy the Villa Artemis business, Rose will give interviews to everyone and their lawyer about how she was threatened by him.

She is going to fight back.

At half four, Rose puts on her big straw hat and another blast of factor 50. She has definitely had too much sun over the past few weeks. She peers into her mirror, angling her face this way and that.

She has sun spots.

Years ago in Los Angeles she had laser treatment to get rid of all blemishes. Her ancestry is Celtic via Wales and sun spots are part of the deal, along with pale skin that doesn't tan easily.

But she's a long way from her old cosmetic surgeon and the life that required such a doctor.

She picks up her white-and-blue hand-sewn tote bag with sea urchins, fish and pretty starfish embroidered upon it. If she's going to rescue the retreat, she needs to walk off her worries and plan what to do next.

She also needs some of Elena's Magic Tea. The one that's known to calm every anxiety but has the side effect of smelling like a witch's brew with frogs thrown in.

It's siesta time, but she knows there is a shady path down through the woods to the village and she can be back in time for the evening session and dinner.

She needs to take the hidden path to avoid any more questions from her retreaters.

First, Keera had come into the private part of the hotel and told Rose about her confrontation with her mother.

'I walked away,' Keera said sadly. 'I can't see her any more.'

'We can talk about it after dinner on the beach,' Rose said. 'You can see her and you can be honest with her, I promise.'

'I don't know,' says Keera. 'I showed her my shaved head and she went mad.'

Keera is still wearing her wig and Rose has an idea.

'Why don't you ditch the wig for good?' she suggests. 'Then your mother will have a very visual cue that life is going to be different.'

India had been next.

She'd been upset about Dan but also keen to share that Julia was totally the wrong person for him.

'Rose, I hate saying this about another woman, especially one who's gone through so much. I mean, I am a woman's woman, you know!'

India had been upset that what she'd been told about Julia and what Julia is now presenting vary so much.

'Dan didn't lie, did he?' India had asked.

Rose had shaken her head.

'He loves her but he loves this vision of her and that's not who she is!' India said. 'If you'd heard the things she was saying in the bar!' It was all invented.

'She could still be very emotionally fragile,' Rose explained. 'If looking at your life is too painful, people can invent a fantasy life.'

'Like I used to,' India had said wryly. 'Ones where I was the princess with my handsome prince coming along. Why do they tell us those fairy stories as girls? The ones about men rescuing women and how our lives are not fulfilled unless we have a partner. It's not realistic,' she added crossly. 'Whole rafts of clever women think some guy is going to save them and all they have to be is a unicorn woman with no needs.'

'You know better now,' said Rose firmly.

India nodded.

Rose reached into her pocket and took out her ever-present package of tissues. She handed them to India before she launched into more about Dan.

'Even if you don't like Julia, remember that she's been through a lot. We don't know her story, only Dan's perception of it, which is idealised.'

'You're very kind, Rose,' said India.

'That's me – always kind,' Rose agreed smiling. 'I have to go to the village but we'll meet on the beach at six, before dinner, OK?'

The way things were going, Rose thinks as she gathers up her belongings, there was going to be a full session with everyone on the beach. Which is OK.

Finally, she's on her way. She's wearing her light cotton tennis shoes and walks at quite a pace down the dusty track to Xanthe.

In the off-season, the shops are all closed at this time and only the tavernas and bars are open. But now in the glorious warmth of September, the shops are all open again after their mesimeri, the Greek siesta.

The village will become busy fast, Rose knows.

People from the various rental villas and little apartments are wandering through the town, along with the stragglers from day trips to Xanthe who are heading to the coaches to drive back to their holiday apartments and hotels.

They're trailing bags with souvenirs in them: the iconic little Greek horses with the patina of green on the brass manes, pieces of pottery with pretty flowers painted on.

Rose likes the village best in the early mornings when only the locals are there, drinking strong coffee, setting up for the day, breathing in the sea air.

But it's beautiful anytime: sloped streets heading to the harbour, bright flowers in window boxes, elegant little houses side by side with older whitewashed ones, Greek history and architecture everywhere.

She speeds past people dawdling outside the straw hat and handbag shop and makes it to La Bella Graca, a little gem on Ermou Street, its stonework walls and richly ornate wooden door opening up to a bright, scented shop.

Herbs hang from the ceiling and Rose inhales as she walks in, identifying the scent of apples, strawberry leaf and luscious liquorice root.

'Hello Rose,' sings out Elena, in the work area behind the counter, mixing up blends of herbs. 'How did you find the Shepherd's Tea? Did it help with your cold?'

'Yes, it was marvellous,' says Rose, 'but I need something stronger today. I need a calming tea to help me finish the retreat properly.'

'Of course.' Elena nods thoughtfully. 'I see everyone has been looking for one of your guests.'

'We found him,' Rose says. 'Well, we located him. I won't feel right until I have him back in Villa Artemis.'

'Guests are often tricky,' Elena agrees. 'So – you are looking for my Magic Tea, perhaps?'

Rose nods.

'Can you wait ten minutes? I have a small quantity ready but need to package it.'

'Of course.'

'No new medications I should know about?'

The Magic Tea is the strongest herbal tea Rose has ever had. Its exact ingredients are a secret known only to Elena and her elderly mother, which is why Elena only sells it to people who divulge all of their medications to her.

'Herbs are powerful and some herbs cannot be taken with some medicine,' Elena has always said.

'No new medications,' Rose answers.

'Good. Have some of today's blend while you wait.' Elena gestures to the teapot warming on a little flame. 'It's raspberry and pomegranate.'

Rose takes a cup and sits to wait.

She needs to plan her next moves.

Chapter Forty

When Rose makes it back to the hotel, focused on her final evening session, Adriana is waiting for her with an anxious look on her face.

'What's up?' asks Rose, bracing herself for more bad news.

'It's Keera's mother,' Adriana whispers with a backwards glance towards the office.

'Is she in there?' Rose whispers back.

Adriana nods.

'Was it Alexei and the champagne? Please tell me Alexei didn't behave inappropriately with her?'

Adriana shakes her head and hisses 'No!'

'Phew,' mutters Rose in relief.

Rose, Adriana and Christos had warned him to keep the Alexei power sheathed around the hotel and their guests.

'He knows you'd murder him in his sleep,' Adriana says. 'Plus, he is a good man. So, early on in the afternoon, Bobbi went with Keera up to the acropolis. I have no idea what happened but Keera vanished and Bobbi stormed down and went straight back to the bar. Stacy and Jimi were on duty and she ordered a lot of cocktails. We tried to settle her in a room but she's restless and is looking for you.'

'She needs to give me a piece of her mind, I daresay,' says Rose.

She hands the Magic Tea to her sister. 'Can I have a cup of this while I deal with her?'

'You can have two cups if you get her out of the office,' says Adriana brightly. 'You don't have much time – you've got the beach before dinner.'

'Where's Julia?'

'Christos put her in a taxi to Casa Siren, the Airbnb we booked for her.'

'That's something,' says Rose.

'Christos says Dan will be back in the morning to do the last session and check out. He's staying in Corfu Town tonight.'

'I should have promised I'd murder *him* in his bed if he went missing again,' Rose says ruefully.

'No one ever thinks you can be so scary,' says Adriana fondly. 'You look so serene. But I know better.'

They hug.

'When you're happy, I'm happy,' says Rose.

The hotel office is just about big enough for three people sitting at desks and answering phones but there's nobody there now.

Bobbi is sitting on the most industrial-looking of the office chairs, the one Christos uses.

When she arrived at Villa Artemis, Bobbi looked glamorously made-up in a pink-gingham linen shift dress that highlighted long, tanned bare legs finished off with spectacular gold sandals.

Now she's barefoot, her wedge sandals are splayed on the floor, and she's playing with a pack of cigarettes. Her mascara has moved south and the chunky gold bangles she wore on her elegant wrists are on the desk beside her.

Rose thinks that Bobbi's probably younger than her, somewhere in her late forties at most, but now, she looks worn down.

Rose's need to help people reasserts itself.

Theo used to say she was a hopeless case for a therapist.

'You have to stop helping people we meet at dinner parties,' he said one night when they came home after Rose had spent an hour telling a sobbing guest that there was help available for her disordered eating.

'But that's what we do, isn't it?' Rose had said, and he'd laughed and kissed her, said he adored her.

Just not enough, Rose thinks candidly.

'Hello Bobbi,' she says now.

'I want to know what she says about me,' mutters Bobbi.

She has a glass of clear liquid with a couple of lemon slices in it beside her.

Rose does not approve. It could be water or it could be neat vodka.

'Can I get you water?' Rose asks politely for information purposes. She moves a box of printer paper off a chair and sits down.

The room is blissfully cool thanks to the air-con. Rose had wanted the office to have a zen-like calm, even if it did have to include computers and files.

'Water? Might be nice,' Bobbi says owlishly, picking up her glass and holding it close as if someone might take it away.

Definitely not water, then.

Adriana arrives with Rose's tea, which adds a powerful valerian aroma to the room. Bobbi wrinkles her nose.

'Could we get some water, please,' asks Rose.

Adriana's back in a moment with two glasses and some Greek island spring water.

'Just drink this first,' says Bobbi, holding her glass up.

Adriana and Rose look at each other, then, as one, reach towards the glass.

'Bobbi, I can't have you getting dangerously drunk on our premises,' Rose says, forcefully taking the glass away from Bobbi.

'That's nasty,' says Bobbi crossly. 'The second nasty thing you've done to me. No, not nasty – cruel!!! You don't care who you hurt, do you? You've messed with Keera's head. What have you done to her?'

'Nothing,' says Rose calmly, knowing that her very calmness is going to enrage Bobbi even more.

People like Bobbi like operating in fight mode: it's what they know. Whoever shouts loudest gets what they want.

But Rose, who knows exactly what growing up in a shout-fest is like, had long ago vowed that her life would be about mature grown-up conversations where there was no bullying or screaming.

'You've done *something*!' Bobbi hadn't got the no-shouting memo and is pointing a finger at Rose. 'She wants to leave music behind. Do something else. Not tour!'

Bobbi stops with her mouth open, as if this concept is so wrong, she can barely continue to talk. But she regroups.

'It's your fault, Rose bloody Talisman. She wasn't like that when she came out of rehab, so it's your fault. After all I've done for her . . .'

Rose smiles. The old 'After all I've done for them' trope.

Rose didn't plan on working with clients' families but they're here now so she must.

'Did you strike a bargain with Keera when she was born?' asks Rose gently. 'Did you tell her in the hospital that you would look after her but that she had to pay a price for this care? Your bargain was that you wanted to be in the music business and Keera's job was to get you there?'

Bobbi's face scrunches up in confusion. 'No, don't be ridiculous,' she says.

'So, no bargain whereby you gave motherhood in exchange for something?'

'No!' shrieks Bobbi.

'Discussing the bargain you made when she was a baby is what *After all I've done for her* really means,' Rose says. 'You took care of Keera for a reason. It was not unconditional love—'

'How dare you?' shrieks Bobbi but Rose holds up a hand.

The power rushing through Rose is not from the Magic Tea.

She is Rose Talisman, a woman who's survived a childhood in foster care, the collapse of her relationship and the decimation of her career in the full glare of the public eye.

Bobbi doesn't stand a chance.

'I'm not doubting that you love Keera,' she enunciates, 'but, as the years went by, that love came with conditions and those conditions were that Keera allowed you back into the world from which her birth excluded you. *After all I've done for you* says there was a bargain and you expect to be paid. Is that a fair thing to do to a child?'

'It's not like that,' says Bobbi and she leans back in her chair. 'Keera loved performing, dancing, singing.'

'Lots of children do,' says Rose gently. 'But very few of them take it any further. Keera did her first audition for a commercial at the age of, what – nine? That isn't something a child can arrange.'

'She loved it,' says Bobbi. 'Everyone said she was a natural.'

'What did she miss by working for a living so young? It sounds like a difficult life where it was hard to put down roots.'

'We both made sacrifices,' says Bobbi weakly.

'You were an adult when you made those sacrifices,' Rose continues. 'Keera was only a child who wanted to please you. When you pushed her so hard, you weren't mothering her, were you? You were giving both of you a career.'

'It wasn't like that,' says Bobbi.

'Tell me what it was like.'

Bobbi falters. 'I left Ireland a long time ago and I was doing well in LA and then I got pregnant. I thought I could get back into the business after I had the baby, but I couldn't. I had Keera to look after and my body had changed and—'

Bobbi pauses.

'I was doing third-rate shows, barely scraping by and we had nothing, nothing. If I had a straight job, who'd look after Keera? So I sang and kept her with me and then—' She pauses in her story. 'One night, she started to sing one of my songs. She had this grown-up voice. She had the talent, I could see it.

'I made a life for us,' Bobbi adds defiantly.

'You looked after her the only way you knew how,'

says Rose gently, 'but there's been a price to pay for Keera. She didn't choose this life. You did. Nobody's forcing Keera to become anything. She has made her own choice.'

There's silence in the office.

'So it's my fault?' says Bobbi.

'It's nobody's fault,' explains Rose patiently. 'You did what you thought was right; you were surviving. Keera is choosing to survive a different way. That's her right. Self-determination.'

She drinks her tea slowly.

Time to let Bobbi do some thinking on her own.

Chapter Forty-One

The retreaters are at the beach before Rose.

The sun is lower in the sky, and Christos has yet again managed to arrange the wooden sunloungers beautifully, cream beach umbrellas and the blue-and-yellow throws for anyone who gets cool in the evening.

Dianne is sitting quietly on a sunlounger and looks remarkably at peace.

Rose knows the rest of the group want to know what Dianne's story is, but she thinks that sharing it is up to Dianne herself.

Each person's personal story is their own. The group concept is superseded by each person's requirements.

Grazia is sitting upright on a chair, beautifully dressed in white linen. There is no sign of Bernard.

With Dan in Corfu Town, there are only four out of the six present but that's OK.

Rose smiles hello to them all.

'Love the no-wig,' she says to Keera.

'Isn't it fabulous?' asks India.

'Thank goodness you're here, Rose,' blurts out Keera.

'I'm terrified my mother will charge down here and interrupt us all.'

'She's in the dining room,' says Rose, who had personally accompanied Bobbi there.

Keera groans. 'I simply can't face her.'

'But you did face her,' says Rose.

Keera nods slowly. 'I did.'

'Go you!' says India to her friend.

'I wanted to say more but I didn't think she'd get it.' Keera looks lost and Rose interrupts.

'I just talked to your mother, Keera. Don't give up hope yet.'

A surprised smile spreads over Keera's face.

'I can't believe it's nearly over,' says India. 'Feels like only yesterday we were all strangers and now look at us!'

Rose smiles.

'Now look at you indeed.'

'Can we talk about Julia?' India adds. 'I'm afraid she'll rock up here too.'

'She's in an Airbnb,' Rose explains.

'Phew.' India sits back cross-legged on her lounger. 'I felt sorry for Julia when Dan talked about her but she's not what I expected.'

She fills Grazia and Dianne in. 'She's saying she's engaged to Dan. She said they're getting married in October, that her father's a millionaire, her mother has a wardrobe full of couture and that she's a trust-fund person. It's all made up!'

'Julia sounds like totally the wrong person for him,' Keera adds. 'Can we tell him that?'

She and India look eagerly at Rose.

'You can but it's not up to you what Dan does in the future.'

'I know,' groans India. 'We can't control other people but . . .' She stops. 'I care about him.'

'I know,' says Rose. 'How are you, Dianne?'

'Not bad. Tired,' Dianne says thoughtfully. 'It's nice without the men. No offence but I'm nervous of men. It's easier to tell the truth now that it's only women.'

Everyone waits quietly.

'I was in an abusive marriage – can I call it that?' she asks Rose.

Rose nods fervently. 'Absolutely.'

Dianne nods. 'I need to work on accepting that. So it was a bad marriage for a very long time. A lifetime of abuse. All behind closed doors. My husband had a heart attack over two years ago. He died in front of me,' she says to the group. 'I let him die, didn't call an ambulance.'

There's silence.

'How does it feel to say that to other people?' asks Rose.

'What do you think?'

Dianne sounds almost amused. Like a chat-show host asking a question.

She looks around at the group.

'Relieved?' asks Keera anxiously.

'Happy, I hope,' says India. 'Horrible, horrible man. I am so sorry, Dianne, I thought you weren't empathetic and—'

'It's fine, India,' Dianne interrupts and she sounds like a different person now. 'You couldn't know what I was feeling because I didn't know myself. I was filled with huge rage and had nowhere to put it.'

'Because nobody knew what you had been through,' says Grazia sadly.

'You weren't able to feel anger because you couldn't get angry in real life. You suppressed it, squashed it down,' says Rose. 'Afterwards, your anger is telling the world that nobody should try to hurt you again.'

Dianne nods at this.

Grazia gets up and sits beside her. She doesn't touch Dianne, just sits: being there.

There's silence for a while and then Dianne takes them back over her life.

'I feel stupid,' Dianne says when she's finished the story. 'Why couldn't I see it?'

'The things up close to us are often very hard to focus on,' Rose says. 'And when that sort of abusive relationship is all you know, then it's familiar. You know nothing else.'

Again, silence reigns.

'I want to tell you all,' says Keera, grinning.

She looks so vibrant, Rose thinks. Sitting there with her exquisite shaved head, her beautiful little face glowing.

'I'm going to go back to San Francisco, see if I can get a job songwriting. I've got contacts, I think I can do it. The singing is too hard for me, too exposing. Some people are good at that world but I'm not ready for it again, might never be ready. There's no point being thin, beautifully made-up and dressed up, all the outside stuff, when I'm ignoring the inside.'

She beams at them all.

'I am anxious about facing my mother again because it'll be a hard conversation – and she'll go insane when she sees that I'm not wearing my wig, but I'm ready for it. The retreat's taught me that trying to please people all the time is a mistake. I have to unlearn people-pleasing.'

'Which is hard,' says Rose.

Keera nods. 'At least I can identify when I'm doing it and ask myself why I'm doing it,' she says. 'I'll know if I'm trying to make someone like me or if I'm trying to avoid difficult conversations or whatever. That's life-changing. Thank you, Rose.'

Everyone claps.

'India?' asks Rose.

'Let's talk about limerence,' says India and Keera giggles. 'I've never looked at why I do certain things – like why I thought I needed a man in my life, or why I thought I couldn't possibly have a child without a partner – I gave away all my power.'

She smiles at Rose. 'My plans for a unicorn tattoo are now off.'

Rose grins.

'In practical terms, I was going to do a business course and set up my own vintage shop. That was my grand plan. But my stepmother rang earlier and suggested I spend six months working with the person who manages the business side of her company, which is going to be nicer and I'll learn so much. I can start when I get home and see what I think.'

'That sounds wonderful,' says Rose. 'You'd like to do that? You're not being pushed into it?'

'Georgie's brilliant about boundaries,' says India. 'She's been an amazing stepmother with a very light touch. Same as you'd be if you have the chance,' she says kindly to Grazia.

'It is lovely to hear you say this,' says Grazia. 'I know that people look at me and think I am cold, removed, but I am not. It's a protection. I have got so much from this week, Rose.'

Rose feels a blast of pleasure. She's forgotten how wonderful it is when people tell her she's helped them.

'I would never have got where I feel I am now without you all. I am sorry that Bernard is not here, everyone, but we can't expect him to change. I am only sorry it has taken me this long to realise that. And Rose,' she adds, 'I am worried that Bernard will strike back at you.'

'What – what do you mean?' Rose asks.

'So he has started to hit back,' Grazia says sadly. 'I am disappointed in my husband but I know his ways.'

'What sort of ways are they?' asks Rose evenly.

Grazia takes a tiny pair of gold-rimmed glasses out of her little handbag.

'I don't like to wear these, I think they make me look old,' she says.

'What's wrong with old?' asks Dianne. 'Old is better than dead.'

India laughs out loud.

Glasses on, Grazia finds her phone and begins to look through it. Rose does not remonstrate over this.

She sits, waiting.

'He uses people to, how do I say it, blackmail sometimes. It's a last resort, I think. You must understand that Bernard had a difficult childhood. Nothing was easy. He thinks he is entitled to abuse his power now.'

'What form does the blackmail take?' asks Rose.

'I will show you an example,' Grazia announces. 'Then we can decide what we do next.'

Chapter Forty-Two

On the final morning, there's a sense of excitement in Villa Artemis.

The staff are discreetly busy preparing for departure, quietly delighted with how well the retreat has gone, despite the two uninvited guests.

Breakfast on the beach is the plan for the very last few hours.

Rose walks down to the beach with Adriana, both of them carrying rolls and fruit, laughing and talking about the retreat, how Dan arrived earlier with a huge basket of honeyed pastries from the restaurant in Corfu.

'I don't think I will give you a job yet, Dan,' says Christos, following with Dan who is clearly a bit tired from his night in Corfu and has nearly dropped the basket of pastries.

'Certainly not after a night with an elderly woman trying to make me eat more baklava and drink more Metaxa,' says Dan. 'How's India?' he asks Rose quietly, once Adriana has relieved him of his burden.

Rose considers what she can tell him. She's not a messenger. More of an interpreter.

'You heard that Julia arrived,' she says.

'I heard,' Dan replies. 'Did India meet her?'

'India will be here in five minutes,' she says, 'so you can ask her yourself.'

Grazia and Dianne arrive together, thick as thieves, Rose thinks.

Then India and Keera. India looks like a goddess in a flowing turquoise-and-white dress with strings of cool rainbow-coloured crystal beads around her neck. She deliberately doesn't look at Dan, and Rose can see him deflate a little at this.

Rose gets everyone to sit, then they do their final group deep-breathing session.

'Thank you, everyone,' Rose says. 'When I left LA, I never thought I'd work with people again. I thought my years as a therapist were over, so I want to say thank you to all of you for trusting me.'

'Thank you!' says everyone.

'Rose, you've changed my life,' says India.

'Mine too,' says Dianne.

Keera's elegant head bows. 'I can never thank you enough,' she says. 'When I'm back on social media, I'm going to tell everyone how wonderful Villa Artemis is, and that includes all the gorgeous staff and you, Rose.'

'You told me what I needed to hear,' says Grazia formally.

'Me too,' says Dan. 'I understand a lot of things now.'

Rose doesn't dare look at India.

'There's just one more thing before you leave,' Rose announces. 'I want you all to pick up a pebble from the beach. Or a rock or a shell. Small is better so you can carry it on board your planes.'

Everyone instantly seizes upon this activity with great

delight. Grazia takes off her slip-on designer sandals and is soon squelching her toes in the wet sand.

'Sea glass!' says Keera delighted, holding up a piece of pale-blue glass.

'You can get a hole drilled in that and wear it as a necklace,' says India knowledgeably.

When everyone has their pebble or shell, Rose invites them all to join in a circle.

'I want to say thank you to you all for this week: for your participation and your being here in the first place.'

'Will you do more retreats?' asks India.

Rose smiles. 'I hope so but I don't know. Now, these pebbles are to remind you of what you've learned here. Everyone takes a different lesson but if life is hard, hold on to your pebble and remember that you're strong, that you have all come through so much and that there is always help out there for you.

'I will talk to all of you next week to schedule follow-up therapy online. I am here if you need me but I am so proud of all of you and what you've come through.'

And then the group is crowding around her, hugging her and telling her she's done so much for them.

Rose finally allows herself to cry happy tears.

She's still helping people, the way she planned to all those years ago when she was a teenager.

She's always known the value of helping people.

At half ten, Adriana, Rose and Christos gather at the front door as an enormous limo rolls onto the forecourt outside Villa Artemis.

Bernard marches out of the dining room after his breakfast, holding on to his small leather folio and his two phones.

He walks with irritation, as if he's been greatly inconvenienced by every single person in the villa.

'You're leaving? You missed our closing session on the beach,' Rose reminds him, taking her own coffee out into the sunshine to talk to him.

Bernard waves his fingers at the driver, signalling that there are bags and they should be transferred into the limo by said driver.

Only then does he look at Rose. 'We're going now,' he says grandly.

She nods pleasantly at him.

'Where is Grazia?' Bernard becomes aware that his wife has not followed him, and he doesn't get into the limo, staring into the foyer of the hotel as if strength of determination alone can magic her beside him.

India and Keera appear along with Dianne, who is holding on to her phone checking messages.

Bernard appears uncomfortable in this small crowd.

'Goodbye to you all,' he says stiffly, surprised to see them all assembled. 'I trust we won't meet again.'

'That's very rude,' says Keera.

She is standing beside Dan, and Rose watches her pat him on the arm.

'You looked a bit ropey on the beach, Dan,' says Keera. 'How are you now?'

India is clearly still ignoring him.

Rose had noticed that India didn't so much as look once at Dan when they were on the beach.

He hurt India; there's no doubt about it.

Rose watches Dan leave his place beside Keera, walk over to India and take her hand.

India begins to pull it away and then stops.

She might let him speak.

'I have to apologise, India,' he says so quietly that Rose has to move closer to hear. 'I behaved badly. I am really sorry . . .' he stops.

The group are all pretending not to listen.

'I feel bad about running off on you,' he says finally.

India says nothing for a beat.

'It was very hurtful,' she says.

'Chauvinistic,' says Keera loudly.

'I know,' says Dan, 'but I didn't mean to hurt you.'

Finally, India pulls her hand from his.

She can do without this complicated *I'm-just-not-into-you* conversation.

Just then, Grazia appears and everyone turns.

She's dressed in a golden swimsuit with an expensive silk cover-up floating around her body. She's not holding her usual little handbag, although she has her cigarettes and lighter in one hand. She looks beautiful and is smiling as if she's just been given a huge prize.

'Where are your things, Grazia?' demands Bernard. 'Why aren't you ready?'

'Because I'm not going yet,' she says, moving closer to him, a waft of silk slithering behind her.

'Why not?' he asks.

'You know why,' Grazia says flatly. Her gaze burns all over him.

Rose finds Adriana's hand and holds it tightly.

'You never gave our marriage a fair chance. You won't change anything, you want to keep cheating on me, so I am finished. I want a divorce.'

Bernard's tan appears to fade as the blood leaves his face.

'You can't,' he says, still imperious despite his pallor. 'Not in front of these people,' he adds.

Grazia ignores this.

'I could have possibly coped with your cheating, your determination to ignore how much it upset me. But given how helpful everyone here has been to me, I can't forgive you for what you tried to do to Rose.'

Adriana squeezes Rose's hand

'What? I did nothing,' blusters Bernard.

'But you did,' his wife goes on. 'You have been trying to shut down the retreat from the start because you were scared of what secrets would emerge.'

'I only came here for you!' growls Bernard.

'You didn't give it a chance,' Grazia says. 'You used your old trick with businesses you wanted to buy at a low price, I know all your little games. Your fixer agreed to put up messages on social media, promising to tell secrets unless the retreat was stopped.'

Rose can hear Christos inhaling deeply behind her.

'Of course, you should be more careful of your phones, Bernard,' Grazia adds icily. 'I saw a message on one of your phones and I knew who'd sent it. I had to read it, obviously. For a clever man you can be surprisingly stupid. Getting a stooge to send a blackmailing message on Instagram is a mistake because it's easier to trace. Easy for, say, an organisation like Europol to find out who it is. Did you know that Christos has a pal in Europol?'

Christos waves menacingly at Bernard, whose face is almost totally white now.

'What have you done?' he hisses at Grazia.

'What have *I* done?' she asks with hauteur. 'Your behaviour disgusts me.'

Everyone is staring at Bernard and even the chauffeur seems to find it all riveting.

'You can't prove anything,' says Bernard wildly, looking at Rose then back to Grazia.

'We can,' says Christos grimly, waving a piece of paper. 'We have screenshots of the Instagram messages, we have an email your stooge sent us, and Europol are indeed looking into this.'

'You won't tell anyone about me,' pleads Bernard.

Grazia looks down her nose at him.

'This is why we need a divorce, Bernard,' she says crisply. 'You are more upset at the thought of me telling people about your bondage women or that you're a common blackmailer than you are at the idea of a divorce. I see where I stand in your life now.'

'I'm sorry!' Bernard moves towards her but Grazia holds up a palm.

'I want a fair and decent divorce,' she says. 'I would like your word in front of these people.'

'Nobody's filming it, are they?' cries Bernard.

The group laugh.

'I definitely am,' says Keera, a small grin threatening to emerge. She waggles her phone at him.

'Me too,' says Christos. 'It's insurance.'

Rose wants to speak.

'I try not to judge,' says Rose. 'I have met many people in my life and I try to understand what drives them, what they have gone through. You found out about my past and used it to terrify me and my family. I do not know what drives you to behave like that and I no longer care. We will be watching you, Bernard.'

'Sorry,' stammers Bernard.

'I think Europol will be in touch,' Christos says, leaning in the doorway, his presence forcing Bernard to cower.

They see Bernard's eyes widen in fear and then Christos slams the door.

'Well done,' says Dianne to Grazia as the car starts to move down the drive with an expensive hum.

Grazia has tears in her eyes but her face is strong.

'It had to end,' she says. 'There are so many things a marriage can manage but not contempt.'

'And not such lies,' Rose adds.

'Keera,' calls a voice. 'I've been looking for you! Where's your wig?' Bobbi shrieks.

'I'm up,' says Keera to India.

'You can do it,' says India. 'The rest of your life, right?'

When Keera has gone, everyone else vanishes until it's just Rose, Adriana and Christos at the front of Villa Artemis.

'I thought it was all over for us,' says Rose, her eyes misty as she looks around at the scene of all their hard work.

The pool Christos loves near the end of the drive, the wild ranks of lavender massed around olive trees.

'I knew we would come through it,' says Adriana. 'No matter what. We have each other, that's all that matters. If we lost this, we could start again.'

Chapter Forty-Three

Keera's brought a pot of coffee, some water and fruit, and they sit at the big olive table.

After some water and a little sip of coffee, Bobbi looks better, as if she's waiting for a mere moment before she launches into telling Keera just what she's doing wrong.

That's probably her mother's plan, Keera thinks.

What was that little saying Rose had about looking for help in the wrong places?

Keera's the one who has to change.

She leans closer to her mother and says 'I love you, Mom,' which surprises Bobbi.

'What?'

'Love you, Mom, I know you've been there for me for a long time but I can't have this argument with you.' The words race out of Keera and she tells herself to slow down. 'I'm not going back into the music business as a singer. Maybe as a songwriter, yes, but I can't do the touring or the performing. If I do, I'll be using meds again or drinking again. I can't do that.'

'You're a singer – that's what you do!' her mother says heatedly. 'That's the only way to get the money back.'

Keera remains calm.

'Mom, can you tell me why we're so broke?' she asks evenly. 'How much money have I earned over the years? Where's it gone?'

It's like lighting touchpaper.

'I looked after everything for you,' screeches Bobbi. 'You have no idea what I've done, what I went without in the early days . . .'

Keera stops listening to the tirade.

Keera knows her mother hasn't heard her.

Maybe she never will.

The pebble she chose from the beach is suddenly heavy in her shorts pocket.

She takes it out of her pocket and holds it on the table in front of her.

'Let's not fight,' she says. 'We only have each other, Mom. But I have to do what I want to do.'

'But—' Bobbi interrupts.

'No, Mom, let me speak. You left your home a long time ago and did what you wanted to do. Did your mother want you to move to LA? Nope, and yet what happened? You did what you wanted to do. I've got to do that now, Mom, so you're either with me or against me.'

Bobbi glares at her.

'No singing?' she says tremulously.

Keera shakes her head.

Bobbi finds something very interesting to look at far out to sea. Keera thinks she might be crying. She's not sure her mother has ever cried. Except possibly that time she met Garth Brooks.

'*You* can sing if you want to,' Keera adds.

'Who wants me?' says Bobbi.

'I do,' says her daughter and grabs Bobbi's hand.

'But how will we survive?'

'We'll survive. We're both talented and we have lots of things we can do, they're simply different things. It'll be an adjustment, Mom, but we can do it.'

'What if I can't?' asks Bobbi. She sounds like a lost child.

'We're all having lunch on the beach, Mom, I want you to come. You need a pebble.'

Everyone's in the hall sorting out bills and luggage before they go down to the beach for a speedy lunch. Rose has a schedule of online therapy slots and she's trying to organise one for everyone for a follow-up.

She's interrupted by a loud shriek: 'Dan, darling!'

Julia has just erupted from a taxi, wearing almost the same clothes she was wearing yesterday, India is sure. Although Julia might have had a bra on yesterday and, today, she's clearly not wearing one. Her blue fringed vest top slips dangerously low on one side.

'Dan!' Julia and her breasts are pressed up against Dan and she's French kissing him as if they aren't in a public place.

'Puhlease,' mutters India. 'I'm going to the beach.'

'No, India,' says Dan, unhooking Julia and grabbing India's hand to stop her leaving.

'What are you doing, DanDan?' Julia asks with a dangerous glint.

DanDan? thinks Keera.

Rank.

Dan ignores his ex-girlfriend.

'I don't want it to end like this, India.'

'You don't want what to end?' demands Julia.

'What I have with India,' says Dan firmly.

Keera holds her breath as he faces Julia.

'Do you want to sit in the garden and talk about it?'

'No! I want to do it here with that beatch!' shrieks Julia. 'What do you have with India?'

'Julia—' begins Dan, and Keera and India watch Julia's face fall.

'You slept with her, didn't you. She's the one.'

'That's private,' says Dan politely. 'We are not together any more. You ended it, remember?'

'But I didn't mean you to find someone else,' wails Julia.

'What did you mean?'

'I wanted to have fun, to feel like we used to when we were kids, partying and . . .'

Julia trails off and Keera suddenly feels sorry for her.

Facing the real world is not always easy.

'I've understood something since I've been here, Julia,' Dan is saying. 'We're no good for each other. You want something else in your life and so do I. Time has simply made us stick with each other.'

'I don't want something else!' squeals Julia. 'I want you.'

She glares at India as she says it.

'You only want me because I told you I'd been with another woman,' Dan says wearily. 'You told me you didn't want to see me again two weeks ago.'

Julia looks outraged that this information is out there in the open.

'Is that her?' she asks, pointing at India. 'She's a slut!'

India glares back. 'A woman does not call another woman a slut!' she says firmly.

'Julia,' says Keera suddenly. 'You can have anything you want in life. You don't really want Dan, do you?'

'He understands me,' protests Julia.

'What you mean is that he's safe,' says Keera. 'You split because you're bored and you don't want to hurt him, but you're not in love with Dan any more, are you?'

Rose is wondering if she should intervene here but Dan surprises her.

'Keera's right. You don't love me,' he says to Julia. 'I don't love you. We're stuck together by time and experiences, and because we've grown used to being glued together. But we're not good for each other. You need to stop taking drugs and get some sort of normal life. I can't believe I've never told you that before.'

'That lifestyle doesn't age well,' Grazia adds, rejoining the group to everyone's surprise. 'Party girl in festival outfit is not so beautiful when you get older. Our bodies change, we can't take it any more. I must give these up,' she adds, holding up her cigarette packet. 'I spend a fortune on injections to hide the lines.'

'You look wonderful,' says Julia.

India beams. 'She does, doesn't she? Yes, it was me: I slept with Dan. It was glorious fun but I'm not tying him down.'

Julia eyeballs India.

'He loves me. He'll be back,' she says carelessly. 'I've had other men and Dan comes back to me.'

Dan waits for the ache in his heart but it doesn't come.

'True,' he says thoughtfully. 'I have done in the past but not any more, Julia. You can sleep with whoever you want.'

Julia bites her lip and finally, Keera sees behind the façade to the fragile woman underneath.

'Julia, why don't we go inside and have some calming tea? Rose has some Magic Tea that will help with everything. Even hangovers.'

'I do have a bit of a headache,' Julia admits.

She stares at Dan.

'You'll still be my friend,' she says.

Dan hugs her.

'We've known each other since we were seventeen,' he says.

'He was such a nerd,' Julia says, laughing.

'I think he still is,' says Keera.

India and Dan stand at the water's edge on the Kri Kri beach feeling the sea lap luxuriously around their ankles. India's still holding Dan's hand.

If he lets go, it's a sign.

If he stays holding her hand, that's another sign.

'I'm sorry I abandoned you,' says Dan. 'Can you forgive me?'

India looks at him. 'That depends,' she says. 'I'm a different person from the woman who came here at first,' she adds.

'I fancied that woman,' says Dan.

'No you didn't!'

'I did.'

'You were in pain talking about Julia,' says India.

'Didn't mean I was dead,' Dan says.

'Why did you run?' she asks.

'I realised I'd fallen for you. It felt a huge deal given that I'd been so upset about Julia. It seemed hypocritical. I thought if I got away from Xanthe . . .'

'Never hurt me like that again,' commands India.

'Promise,' he says. 'I also promise I'll never bring you to a sporting event or make you miss a date with your girlfriends,' he vows.

'I'll never hold you to ransom,' vows India.

'Guess we're sorted then,' he says and kisses her as the water rises and laps higher and higher.

He lets her hand go but only because he's wrapping his arms around her.

The remaining group eat a barbecue lunch on the beach, one last time. Taxis are coming soon to take people to the airport and everyone wants to spend more time in Rose's calm company.

When Christos has finished cooking, he lies on the cushions under the beach umbrellas and pretends to go to sleep.

'He's joking,' says Adriana, poking him with a bare foot.

'I'm not,' says Christos, eyes still closed. 'It was a hard week.'

'Made harder by my husband,' says Grazia, apologetically. 'I apologise again.'

Rose thinks of the sheer worry about her and Adriana's past coming out, and just smiles gratefully.

She hasn't been able to fully process it yet. But she will. She's going to contact her former therapist, Vida, again.

Everybody needs help, after all.

Bobbi is on the beach too, eagerly eating the dips that Christos brought with his famous barbecue bread and drinking vast glasses of water, all the while staring at her daughter.

Keera looks different: stronger, more vital, Rose thinks. As if she's totally in charge of her new life.

Keera is telling her mother about India's new shop idea. Bobbi is full of ideas for it.

'The sandals I had on yesterday – now they're true

vintage. De Havilland. I have four pairs. I could sell them to you . . .'

The women are laughing, and Dianne is explaining that she has a few vintage bits and bobs herself.

'My daughters tell me most of my clothes are very old fogey,' she's saying to Grazia.

'Pah, you never had a chance to buy lovely clothes,' Grazia interrupts her. 'We should stay in touch, yes?'

'Yes,' says Dianne, pleased. 'You could come and stay with me?'

'And you come to stay with me. Wake up your family to see you have a life.'

'I wasn't fair on them,' Dianne says. 'I should have told them where the anger came from, but then I felt I'd be ruining their vision of a happy childhood.'

'How's the anger now?' Rose is curious. Dianne is the person she's arranged the first Zoom therapy sessions with. But everyone will have them. The retreat was never just about one week.

Dianne thinks about it.

'Sometimes, I am full of rage. It takes me over but it's not about here or any of you: it's about the past. I get so angry when I think about my husband but I understand that now. The rage was because I wanted to make sure nobody ever treated me like that again. In truth, I am not entirely in control of it but I will learn how to be.'

She looks sad but, this time, Adriana takes her hand.

'Never apologise for how you had to behave to survive,' she says.

'Do you think we should come back next year?' asks India. 'For a top-up?'

'Yes!' says Keera. 'Mom, you could come too!'

Bobbi rolls her eyes. 'Like, no way,' she says.

'I would do it,' says Dianne.

'Me also,' says Dan, gazing at India.

'I can book you in,' says Christos from his position on the sand.

'Let's see how we all get on with our Zoom therapy sessions,' Rose says.

Later, Keera, India, Bobbi and Dan are all about to head off in the same taxi.

Marceline, who drove Keera to her meeting in Corfu Town, is chatting away merrily to the music of Fleetwood Mac.

Phone diaries are being consulted.

India can't wait to get some business management skills under her belt.

'Not a normal belt,' she tells Rose. 'A vintage . . .' she looks up for inspiration, 'rope belt from a Breton fisherman that will look fabulous over a floaty 1970s midi dress!'

'I expect nothing less,' Rose says happily.

Dan, who is sitting in the front, beams.

Keera is planning to travel to Donegal to see her grandmother. She's going alone.

'On a budget,' Keera says. 'I need a job so bad.'

Bobbi is not going because Keera says they need time apart.

'That's a good idea,' Bobbi says, trying to make the best of it. 'My mother'll kill me stone dead because I haven't been back in so long.'

Keera is also planning to work on songwriting.

'I'm good at it and it's a job where you get to sleep in your own bed at night,' she says. 'I don't want to go back to LA and hang around the scene any more. I need peace.'

Dan has a lot of work to do, he says, but he's delaying it so he can stay in London to spend time with India.

'We're not a thing – yet,' India advises him. 'We're seeing if we're compatible.'

Dan nods.

'Good plan,' he says. 'We need to take it slowly . . .'

'Make sure we're compatible and not in a co-dependent relationship,' adds India. 'You need to meet my dad and Georgie.'

'You could meet my sister,' says Dan.

'That's a lot of family meetings for two people who aren't a thing yet,' teases Keera.

Dan beams again and reaches back into the taxi to grab India's hand.

'Byeee Rose, Adriana, Christos, Alexei, Lydia, Beata . . .'

They're down the sweep of the drive still calling out names and then the taxi disappears.

Ten minutes later, Grazia and Dianne's taxi rolls up.

They're flying to Athens together, then splitting up.

Grazia flew in with Bernard on a private jet but she doesn't want to go home that way.

To her complete astonishment, she's received a message from her stepdaughter, Viola, saying Bernard has telephoned her about Grazia and is distraught.

'I can't handle him,' Viola said in her message. 'Grazia, you can't be serious about a divorce. Daddy needs you.'

'These people?' Grazia says, hands held up in appeal.

'You're not going back to him?' asks Dianne, horrified.

Grazia shakes her head. 'We were good together once, but not any more. I have more life left to live and if my stepchildren want to be part of that, then I would like it. Bernard, he is what you call toast.'

'Will you explain any of this to your children?' asks Rose as Christos puts their suitcases in the car's boot.

'Possibly,' says Dianne. 'Not yet, though. I have a lot to process.'

'We have quite a while of therapy ahead of us,' Rose agrees, looking forward to their first conversation. 'You've both been very brave,' she says to Dianne and Grazia.

'So have you,' says Grazia. 'Same time next year?'

Rose breaks protocol and hugs them both.

She waves and waves until the taxi is gone and allows herself a mental pat on the back.

She's done it: run a successful island retreat.

Dan, India, Keera, Grazia and Dianne can all change their lives from things they learned in Villa Artemis. Even Bobbi has a new world view.

Bernard, not so much.

Rose thinks she'll take a walk in her little Greek garden before she goes into the villa to do some housekeeping.

Epilogue

'Did we really get through this many towels?'

Rose has sent Adriana and Christos out for a walk, while she and Beata are left in the villa tackling the mound of housekeeping left behind after the week.

'How come towels weigh so much?' asks Rose, hefting another folded pile into the big laundry hampers they send out to be washed.

She's taken the sheets off all the guests' beds, removed the towels from the bathrooms, and is counting it all off Beata's housekeeping master list.

'It's these white towels – they sing to people. "Use me!"' says Beata. 'Also, women's work is never done,' she jokes, walking past with the trolley of fresh laundry.

'True,' mutters Rose.

She's counted it all out perfectly: two hampers, one for towels and one for sheets, duvet covers and pillowcases.

Normally, she and Adriana would have worked together on this last day of their first retreat. But Adriana needs a rest.

'You do too,' her little sister had protested. 'You've been working with the guests all week.'

But Rose had insisted. 'That's all emotional stuff,' Rose says, 'mental work. Ripping sheets off beds is physical and it'll be a welcome change.'

She's done three bedrooms and has just gone into the private part of the house to get some water when she hears the villa phone buzzing and races to intercept it.

'Hello, Villa Artemis,' Rose says, aware that she's out of breath.

'I'm enquiring about the retreat,' says a woman's voice. 'I'd totally missed the posts on socials about it. I love Ms Talisman. Do you think there's going to be another one?'

Rose blinks. Wonderful but awkward. Not so cool if guests think she's there always and answers the phone herself.

It's much more niche for them to imagine that Rose Talisman drifts in for special weeks but that she never answers the phone.

Or pulls sheets from beds.

'There might be,' says Rose, hurriedly trying to channel Grazia's accent. 'Can you leaf me your contact details and we vill be back to you.'

After a few minutes, she races up to Beata.

'Tentative booking!' she says. 'Another retreat! I said we have another retreat this month but it was full. Total lie.'

Beata laughs.

'The woman said if there was another one, she and her mother would be thrilled. They'll pay anything.'

'Fantastic!' says Beata.

'We can't overcharge,' says Rose instantly. 'It would be wrong but still. Isn't that great? I can't wait to tell Adriana and Christos.'

THE ISLAND RETREAT

'You're planning another retreat,' says a man's voice. 'I would like to register interest.'

Rose catches her breath.

That voice – it can't be.

She doesn't want to appear in front of him.

He last saw her five years ago, when she was younger and looked younger too. Now she's got silver hair and all the stuff she teaches people about accepting yourself seems feeble when the man she loved is standing just feet away—

'Are you hiding?'

He's just outside the housekeeping cupboard which is stuffed with spare pillows, toilet paper and towels.

'Yes. No,' she says, leaning against the cupboard wall. 'I'm not sure I can take you on,' she says.

She hears him approach and yells, 'You can't come in here!'

She's got a lip balm in her pocket. Which is not ideal but it's better than nothing. Rose smooths her hair and then applies lip balm. She wishes there was a mirror in here but such a thing is not required in a housekeeping cupboard.

'Why can't I come in?' asks the voice.

'This is a private office.'

Where the hell is Beata? She needs help to get rid of him now and then she can appear when she's got lipstick on, a better dress, with her hair fixed . . .

But why?

If he has come all this way, then it's because of her. He will have to accept who she is now.

Biting her lip, Rose takes up the housekeeping master list and holds it as a shield. Then she stands tall and makes her way majestically out of the housekeeping cupboard.

In front of her is Theo, slightly older but still beautiful.

'Oh Rose,' he says softly and he reaches out for her.

Rose clutches the list to her chest and retreats.

'I'm working,' she says.

He nods. 'I totally understand if you want me to go,' he says earnestly. 'But I regretted that night so much – I should never have said those things. I pushed you away.'

Rose says nothing.

All week she's talked about how people need to know their truth and say what is important to them. Now Theo is here, she has so many things she needs to get off her chest and she is saying nothing.

'When the show went, I looked for you,' he says. 'I pestered your agent but she said she knew nothing. I didn't know how you could just disappear but you did and then . . .' His face looks animated. 'Three days ago, someone mentioned this retreat. That you were back. I got here as fast as I could.'

'I need a kingsize duvet—' begins Beata, rounding the corner. 'Or maybe I don't.' She looks at Rose. 'Do you know this guy?'

'Yes,' says Rose.

'I messed it up,' says Theo sadly. 'Am I too late, Rose? If I could just stay for a few days and we could talk? I met Adriana and Christos in the village,' he's saying.

Rose is clutching the housekeeping master list close to her chest.

'They're lovely people. They were both pleased that I wanted to register my interest. Adriana says I could probably partner with you on the retreat but "Only if she lets you," as your sister says.'

Beata is looking from Rose to Theo.

'OK,' she says finally. 'I get it. I'm vamoosing,' and she leaves, snatching the housekeeping list out of Rose's grasp.

Rose pulls herself together.

She's Rose Talisman.

Self-made woman. A healer.

'Your interest in what?' she says, drawing herself up majestically so that she looks as beautiful as she knows how to be.

'You,' says Theo softly.

'You don't really know me at all,' says Rose sadly.

But this time, Theo smiles. 'I went to Wales,' he says. 'It took a lot of digging but I found you and Adriana. You've been so brave. You deserved so much more than I gave you.'

Rose's breath stills.

'I'm an idiot, Rose. I hurt you. Your agent told me about the email you sent to the producers before the shooting. I understand so much more now . . .'

Rose's eyes are taking in all the little details about him. The changes that age have brought. He's still Theo but he's older and certainly wiser.

'I'm not sure I believe in second chances,' she says now. 'So much time has elapsed.'

'Can I stay for a few days?' Theo asks.

Rose tests the feelings inside. Her instincts are finely honed. Earned from a life not without difficulty.

She feels calm. In Theo's presence, standing in the corridor outside the housekeeping cupboard, she still feels like herself.

The true version of herself who's about to give herself another chance with Theo.

'We start on Monday on the beach,' she says. 'You will need to collect a pebble.'

'I'll collect a whole beachful,' he says eagerly.

'Now I'm making beds. We all work in the villa,' Rose adds.

'Tell me what to do,' says Theo obediently.

'You really mean it,' she says in wonderment.

Theo nods and then slowly, very slowly, he moves forward until he's beside her and his lips meet hers.

'You have no idea how much I've missed you, Rose,' he says.